Where We Belong

Books by Lynn Austin

All She Ever Wanted
All Things New
Eve's Daughters
Hidden Places
Pilgrimage
A Proper Pursuit
Though Waters Roar
Until We Reach Home
While We're Far Apart
Waves of Mercy
Where We Belong
Wings of Refuge
A Woman's Place
Wonderland Creek

REFINER'S FIRE
Candle in the Darkness
Fire by Night
A Light to My Path

CHRONICLES OF THE KINGS
Gods & Kings
Song of Redemption
The Strength of His Hand
Faith of My Fathers
Among the Gods

THE RESTORATION CHRONICLES
Return to Me
Keepers of the Covenant
On This Foundation

Where We Belong

LYNN AUSTIN

BETHANYHOUSE
a division of Baker Publishing Group
Minneapolis, Minnesota

© 2017 by Lynn Austin

Published by Bethany House Publishers
11400 Hampshire Avenue South
Bloomington, Minnesota 55438
www.bethanyhouse.com

Bethany House Publishers is a division of
Baker Publishing Group, Grand Rapids, Michigan

Printed in the United States of America

Library of Congress Control Number: 2017945354

ISBN 978-0-7642-3000-4 (cloth)
ISBN 978-0-7642-1762-3 (trade paper)

Scripture quotations are from the King James Version of the Bible.

Cover design by Dan Thornberg, Design Source Creative

17 18 19 20 21 22 23   7 6 5 4 3 2 1

To my family:
Ken, Joshua, Vanessa, Benjamin,
Maya, Snir, and Lyla Rose
With love and gratitude

Part I
Rebecca

Chapter 1

The Sinai Desert
1890

Rebecca Hawes lay awake in her tent, convinced that the howling wind was about to lift her entire camp into the air and hurl it to the far side of the desert. The desolate wasteland of the Sinai Peninsula lay beyond her tent door, thousands of miles and a world away from her home in Chicago. Sand pummeled the canvas; the thick material heaved and flapped as if trying to take flight. Rebecca gazed around in the darkness, her eyes open wide. She saw nothing. The sandstorm obliterated every ray of starlight and moonlight, making the darkness seem biblical, like one of the plagues God used to punish Egypt—a darkness that could be felt. She had thought, at age forty-five, that she would live at least another twenty years or so, but this storm just might be the end of her. Pity. There was so much more she hoped to accomplish.

She remembered the luxurious hotel room she had left behind in Cairo two days ago and understood why the Israelites had longed to return to Egypt after camping in this wilderness, even if it meant slavery. Moses had been leading them to Mount Sinai to worship God, and she was on her way to the Monastery of Saint Catherine, built on the same site. The centuries of history invested in that mystic place fascinated her. Imagine—Emperor Justinian built the basilica at Saint Catherine's in AD 557! She hoped she lived through the night to see it.

An odd pounding noise caught Rebecca's attention, a staccato beat that joined the shrieking wind and drumming canvas. She struggled to sit up on the sagging camp cot to listen. The sound, when she identified it, was a reassuring one—the Bedouin caravan drivers were securing the tent stakes shaken loose by the gale. Perhaps she wouldn't blow away after all. How the men could see anything at all in such profound darkness was a mystery to her. She heard them speaking to their camels, the animals hissing and growling in response. Nasty beasts!

Then a new thought occurred to her: What if the sand piled up into a mound around her tent, burying her, the equipment, the drivers, and even the camels?

She swatted away the thought with a wave of her hand. There were much worse ways to die.

"Becky? Are you awake?" her younger sister, Flora, whispered. She lay on a camp cot not two feet away, yet invisible in the gloom.

"Yes, I'm here." Rebecca groped toward the sound of Flora's voice and found her arm, giving it a reassuring pat.

"Well, this is certainly turning out to be an adventure, isn't it?" Flora asked.

Rebecca heard the suppressed laughter in Flora's voice and grinned. "Yes, I believe this is the very definition of an adventure!" She started to laugh out loud, then buried her face in her blanket to muffle the sound. She could hear Flora doing the same. They might have been schoolgirls again, whispering after lights-out, instead of two middle-aged sisters.

"If our society friends could see us now . . ." Flora sputtered.

"They would have us committed to an asylum!"

"I think Thomas Cook should add tours of the Sinai with a Bedouin camel caravan to his posh itineraries," Flora said. "Don't you?"

Rebecca laughed out loud at the idea, then quickly covered her mouth again.

"Shh . . . we'll wake up Kate," Flora whispered.

"I'm already awake, Miss Flora." Kate sounded peeved.

"Oh, I'm so sorry, dear. It's just that when I think of where we are and the absurdity of this storm—"

"Yes, shouldn't we be making social calls or raising funds for one of your charities?" Rebecca asked in her grandest voice. She and Flora laughed all over again. "We'd better control ourselves," Rebecca finally said, "or Petersen will be sticking his somber head through the tent flap, wondering if we've become unbalanced."

"The boy has been our butler for two years, Becky. He knows full well how unbalanced we are. Remember the first time he saw us doing calisthenics in our backyard in our bloomers?"

Her words brought more laughter, and Rebecca wiped tears from her eyes. She felt a fine layer of grit and tasted it on her lips. The wind pounded sand through every crack and seam and opening. She hoped it wouldn't damage her photographic equipment. "Forgive us, Katie dear. We'll settle down now, I promise. Go back to sleep."

"How can I sleep when I'm about to be blown away?" Kate grumbled. Rebecca couldn't see their so-called lady's maid in the darkness, but she could imagine the churlish frown on her face, her stiff posture and crossed arms. It had been Flora's idea to try to transform the thieving, eighteen-year-old street urchin into their lady's maid. Rebecca was beginning to believe it might be easier to spin straw into gold.

"You don't suppose we could be buried alive by morning, do

you?" Flora asked. "Remember how Nimrud's Palace was so completely engulfed by sand that the local Arabs didn't even realize it was there until Henry Layard dug it out?"

Rebecca smiled. "I had the very same thought. Perhaps some future archaeologist will find us a thousand years from now and wonder what on earth those crazy sisters were up to."

"Um . . . remind me again why we're doing this," Flora said.

Rebecca heard the smile in her sister's voice and was glad they were together. They had enjoyed exotic travel since they were schoolgirls—exploring Paris' maze-like streets, traveling up the Nile in a *dahabeeah* to see the pyramids, perusing the *souks* and dark alleyways of places like Cairo and Jerusalem.

"I believe we came here because we longed for an adventure, remember?" Rebecca replied. But that wasn't the only reason. Midway through her life, Rebecca had fallen in love. Professor Timothy Dyk was brilliant, scholarly, warm, companionable— and in love with her, too. They were so well-suited that Rebecca might have been formed from the rib plucked from his side. But she couldn't accept Timothy's marriage proposal—not yet, anyway. Perhaps never. This quest at Saint Catherine's was her last resort, and if it failed, she had no other recourse but to remain a spinster. Rebecca would endure sandstorms and desert perils and much, much more if she thought it would finally topple the wall between them.

And then there was their young maid, Kate Rafferty. Who knew what effect this journey would have on her stony heart? Or on their cheerless, nineteen-year-old butler, Petersen, whom Flora had rescued from the orphan's home? Someone had to try to reach these young people before they were lost forever. Why not Rebecca and Flora?

One of the camels began braying loudly outside their tent. "Oh, those poor animals," Flora said. "They have no shelter from the storm."

"You're not going to invite them into our tent, are you?" Kate asked. "I know how softhearted you are, Miss Flora."

"Not unless they have a bath, first," she replied, laughing. "They smell atrocious!"

"Besides, they're used to desert conditions," Rebecca said. "God created them to endure sandstorms." She didn't believe for a moment that they had *evolved* through the process of natural selection as that heathen Charles Darwin proposed. His outrageous theories were in all the newspapers these days and many of the scientists she knew seemed to be embracing them. Rebecca could not, would not.

"We should try to sleep now," she said. "It's certain to be a long day tomorrow." They had traveled seven hours across the rocky desert yesterday, then risen before sunrise and traveled eight hours today before the sandstorm had forced them to hunker down. The storm had seemed both beautiful and terrifying as it rolled toward them, darkening the sky and filling the horizon like an eerie yellow thundercloud. Tomorrow's journey would be at least as long as today's, providing the storm blew itself out as the Bedouin sheikh assured her it would. The pace was exhausting, but Rebecca had hired the camel caravan for only forty days, including traveling time to Mount Sinai and back. She wanted to spend as many of those days as she could doing research at the monastery.

"How much longer until we get there?" Kate asked.

"It should take us another week to reach Saint Catherine's."

"And are we going to have sandstorms like this every night? If so, I think we should turn around right now and go home. Besides, I don't trust those camel drivers. Their leader keeps staring at me."

"It takes more than a sandstorm to make Flora and me turn back," Rebecca said. "And I don't think the sheikh will do you any harm. He's probably staring because he thinks you're pretty. Your red hair is very unusual."

Kate's exasperated sigh was loud. The servant's cot creaked and rustled as she thrashed in the dark, rolling over.

"I was thinking about the Israelites when we were riding today," Flora said. "It must have been so hard to trust God and keep walking through such desolate land. We know how their story ends and that they finally reached the Promised Land, but they had no idea what would happen next. They simply had to trust God and keep going."

Rebecca didn't know how her journey through the Sinai would end either—whether her errand would lead to success and a breakthrough with Timothy or spell the end of their romance. She bid the other women good-night again and settled down on her cot, trying to get comfortable. She thought about how far they already had come—the cross-country train ride from Chicago to New York; the steamship voyage to France; another steamer through the Mediterranean and down to Cairo where they were delayed several days while arranging to meet with the Archbishop of Sinai to get permission to visit the monastery. Her ability to converse with him in Greek had impressed him greatly, and he not only granted permission but even took time to pray for their protection from the hot, desert winds that blew in from the Sahara. He had been kind—but his prayers obviously hadn't changed God's mind about sending the wind.

While in Cairo, they had also hired the services of an agent, Mr. Farouk, to accompany them on their journey. He had purchased all their equipment, hired a cook, arranged for a camel caravan, and stockpiled enough food and drinking water for their entire forty-day expedition. Rebecca and Flora and their entourage then crossed the Gulf of Suez and met the Bedouin drivers and their animals. The shaggy, sun-browned men might have stepped right out of the pages of *The Arabian Nights*, covered from head to toe in white robes, with turbans wound around their heads and swords at their sides. After strapping dozens of crates of live chickens and turkeys to the camels, they were on their way.

Rebecca knew it was outrageous for two unmarried women and their lady's maid to travel alone through such rugged terrain with only their young butler—the somber yet faithful Petersen— as an escort. Who knew what sort of man this Mr. Farouk would turn out to be? Not to mention the twelve Bedouin camel drivers and their sheikh, who had insisted on joining them, carrying an ancient, rusting rifle that he waved in the air dangerously from time to time. Rebecca, however, had learned not to care what people thought. As for her safety, God already knew when the end of her days would be. She had no reason to fear.

She did feel sorry for Petersen, though. He'd grown up on the streets of Chicago and had never ridden a horse, let alone a camel. He'd had a particularly difficult time staying comfortably seated these past two days, and she'd seen him rubbing his bottom whenever he dismounted. Neither sister had wished to subject Petersen to such discomfort, but he had insisted on coming along, sounding very biblical with his declaration that "wherever you go, I will go." Knowing how much Petersen distrusted Kate, Rebecca suspected he'd come along to protect them from her, rather than from pagan foreigners.

The wind howled on; the canvas thrummed. Rebecca pulled the blanket tightly around herself, seeking comfort more than warmth. What would it be like to have the man she loved sleeping beside her, curled together like spoons in a drawer, listening to the familiar rhythm of his breathing, feeling his heartbeat? She may never know. But whether Timothy was part of her future or not, Rebecca hoped that the discoveries she unearthed at Mount Sinai would make this long, perilous journey worthwhile in the end.

She fidgeted on the narrow cot, unable to get comfortable. Trying to sleep was hopeless, the shrieking wind and pelting sand too unnerving. In spite of all her carefully made plans, Rebecca was, in this moment, helpless. Yet hadn't she been in danger before on some of her other travels? Perhaps nothing as deadly as this sandstorm, but frightening, nonetheless. She decided to travel back through her memories to the very beginning, when it was just Father, Flora, and her—and the elderly servants who'd cared for them, of course. If Rebecca truly was about to die, at least her final thoughts would be of the people she loved.

For as long as Rebecca could recall, Flora had been by her side—sister, best friend, confidante, and partner in adventures, great and small. . . .

CHAPTER 2

CHICAGO
1860
THIRTY YEARS AGO

Rebecca daydreamed of a more exciting life as her carriage bounced along the drab, familiar streets of Chicago. The spring day seemed to burst with promise, yet all she had to look forward to was a long, tedious day of classes at the private school she and her sister, Flora, attended. At age fifteen, Rebecca had devoured every exciting adventure story she could lay her hands on—books like *The Adventures of Robinson Crusoe*, *The Last of the Mohicans*, *Ivanhoe*, and *The Arabian Nights*. Father had a wonderful classical library in his study at home, so she had already read Homer's *Iliad* and *Odyssey*, too. Twice, in fact. She had traveled with those heroes and heroines in her imagination, exploring exotic places. Her armchair exploits satisfied her for a time, but in the end, they were never enough. "When is it going to be my turn?" she grumbled aloud.

"Your turn for what?" her sister asked.

17

"To have an adventure. To do something different and fun and exciting. I'm so bored in school, aren't you?"

"Yes," Flora said, heaving a dramatic sigh. She was fourteen, and lately seemed to cast herself as the heroine in a tragic melodrama, falling into the annoying habits of sighing heavily and staring dreamily. "It does seem like we could learn so much more on our own. They rarely teach us anything interesting in school."

"We need to travel abroad. I'm sure we're old enough now. We could see the ruins of Pompeii for ourselves instead of reading about it in a dusty, old book."

"I would love to see France—the Palace of Versailles, the Cathedral of Notre Dame . . ." Flora gazed into the distance as if seeing visions of French palaces in the clouds.

"Then it's settled." Rebecca thumped the carriage seat with her fist, causing a puff of dust and horsehair to dance in the sunlight. "Tonight we'll ask Father to take us to France."

"The timing will be perfect, too. School will be out for the summer in a few more months."

"Yes. Perfect!" The sound of the horses' clomping hooves changed as the carriage crossed the Rush Street Bridge, then changed back again when they reached the other side. The Chicago River joined Lake Michigan a few blocks to the east, and when Rebecca gazed at the forest of masts huddled in the distance, she could barely contain her longing to sail away to distant lands. "If only it didn't take Father so long to plan everything. Before we know it, it will be September again, and we won't have gone anywhere."

"You're right," Flora said with another outrageous sigh. "He's always so busy."

Rebecca slapped the seat again. "You know what? Let's start making plans ourselves. We'll research all the transportation schedules, and find out what it costs to sail to France, and then we'll present everything to Father in a report. He won't need to do a thing—except pay for it, of course." There was little doubt in Rebecca's mind that he could afford it. Besides his modest law practice, Father had made a great deal of money by investing in railroads.

"How will we research all those things?" Flora asked.

"It can't be hard. The Great Central Depot is right back there on the other side of the Chicago River, near the lake. They'll have information about train tickets to New York—and maybe they can tell us about steamships, too. People book passages to Europe all the time."

"Which people?"

"You know . . . interesting people." Rebecca gave a vague shrug, knowing that Flora accepted everything she said as the gospel truth. They had always been close, though they didn't look at all like sisters. Rebecca resembled their father with his sturdy, robust build and dark hair—at least his hair and beard used to be dark before fading to silver. Flora had inherited their mother's fair complexion and pixie-like proportions. But heredity had played a trick on them and given Rebecca their mother's pale blue eyes to go with her dark hair, while Flora got Father's dark brown eyes to contrast with her blond hair.

Rebecca's mind spun with plans for their European trip as their carriage approached the school and slowed to a halt. She flung the door open and jumped down instead of waiting for Rufus, their carriage driver, to help. Realizing her mistake, she quickly glanced at the school doors, hoping no one had noticed. The headmistress had marched Rebecca into her office to scold her about this twice before: "Young ladies do not tumble out of carriages on their own. They wait for assistance."

"But why?" Rebecca had asked. "I don't need assistance."

"That isn't the point, Miss Hawes. Ladylike behavior must be developed early in a young woman's life. She must learn composure, equanimity, and self-control. Girls your age should be as demure and dainty as rosebuds. . . ." There had been more, but Rebecca had stopped listening. The other girls in her elite private school came from well-to-do homes like hers, but they had probably learned to be demure and ladylike by watching their mothers. Rebecca didn't have a mother to teach her such things, and in a way she was glad. Being dainty was boring. Climbing trees in the parkway near their home and skipping stones on Lake Michigan was much more fun.

Rebecca's mother had slipped away to heaven the day after Flora was born and Rebecca a mere thirteen months old. Since neither sister remembered their mother, they'd never felt particularly sad about losing her. If Father had grieved, he'd kept it to himself, never mentioning his wife who was known to Rebecca only by a small oil portrait in his study. He didn't seem the least bit inclined to marry again and provide them with a stepmother—which was a good thing, considering how stepmothers in fairy tales usually turned out. Father had moved to Chicago to open his own law firm in 1837, the year the town was incorporated. He'd married Rebecca's mother, who was twenty years younger than him, when he was forty-four. Three years later he was a widower with two small children.

Flora waited dutifully for their driver's assistance before stepping out of their carriage. Rebecca worried that her sister was succumbing to the school's attempts to make her dainty. How could she and Flora be partners in great escapades if Flora was too frail to alight from a carriage on her own? They stood together and watched as the carriage merged into the thick stream of traffic and disappeared. Groups of girls in their crisp, gray uniforms fluttered around the school's tiny courtyard, chattering like sparrows, but Rebecca felt no urge to join them. She knew she wasn't like the others, and that they giggled about her behind her back. Well, if studying hard and devouring books made her different, then so be it. At least she had Flora for her best friend.

The morning was so beautiful that Rebecca spread her arms and twirled in the warm spring sunshine. The thought of going inside and studying faded maps and dog-eared geography books made her groan. She longed to travel and explore the real world. She turned to Flora and took her hands in hers. "Let's go right now."

"To France?"

"No, silly, to the train depot. I don't want to waste any more time. Once we get the information we need, Father can book our passage and—"

"But school is going to start any minute."

"Let's skip school."

Flora stared at her in horror, as if Rebecca had suggested they remove their clothes and dance naked in the street. "We can't skip school!"

"Why not? We're the top student in each of our classes. You know we're way ahead of the other girls." In fact, Rebecca had finished reading all of her textbooks with two months remaining until the school term ended. "Come on, Flora. What will it hurt?"

"Won't we get into trouble?"

"Maybe," she said with a little grin. "But we can't have an adventure without expecting some sort of trouble. That's an integral part of it. Besides, what can the headmistress do to us—put us in jail?"

"She could expel us." Flora's voice hushed dramatically as if the very mention of expulsion might bring it to pass.

"Good, I hope she does. I'm bored to death at school. If she expels us, Father will have to hire a private tutor, which will be much more interesting." Rebecca was still holding Flora's hands in hers, and she gave them a little shake. "Come on—aren't we always wishing for a little excitement?"

A school monitor emerged through the double doors to stand on the top step and ring the bell. The other girls swarmed toward her like ducklings. Flora was trying to inch in that direction, too, but Rebecca held her firmly in place. "I'm not going inside, Flora. It's a beautiful spring day with a wonderful breeze from the lake—why sit in a stuffy classroom where the teacher won't even open a window for fear the air will be too bracing for young ladies and cause us to wilt? Come to the railroad depot with me, please?"

"By ourselves? Won't we get lost?"

"We can't get lost. Chicago's streets are laid out in a grid. If Lake Michigan is on our right, then we know we're facing north." She linked her arm through her sister's and began hurrying away from school, giving Flora no time to think. The school yard grew quiet behind them as the obedient girls disappeared inside.

"All we have to do is walk back across the river and turn toward the lake. The railroad depot will be right there. It's too big to miss."

"Are you sure about this, Becky?" Flora's dragging steps and frightened brown eyes betrayed her uncertainty. She was more timid than Rebecca and much closer to the dreaded goal of becoming ladylike. Rebecca wanted to rescue her from that fate before it was too late.

"Of course I'm sure. Don't you want to be brave and strong like the women in the Bible? Sarah walked right beside Abraham when he left home and followed God. And Deborah led an entire army into battle when all the men were afraid. Queen Esther—"

"Yes, yes, you've made your point. I'm coming with you, aren't I?" They looked at each other and grinned.

At first they followed the same route they took to and from school each day, backtracking until they crossed the Chicago River on the Rush Street Bridge. It took them nearly an hour because it was farther than Rebecca had thought—and because they stopped to watch the boats sailing on the river. Traffic was so snarled in places that they had to wait to wade through the cross streets or risk being trampled by the rushing carriages. They talked and dreamed of travel the entire time.

"Which place would you most like to visit?" Flora asked her.

"The Holy Land. I feel like I know so much about it from maps and Bible stories, but I would love to see it in person— Bethlehem, Jerusalem, the Sea of Galilee . . ." The pastor of their church spiced his Sunday sermons with stories from the Old Testament, so the Holy Land already had the dimensions of a real place in Rebecca's imagination. "If I could walk in the same places where Moses and Abraham and Jesus walked . . . that would be a dream come true."

"Could we visit the palace of Nimrud, too?" Flora asked.

"Yes! Why not? Father would love that." He had a layman's fascination with the archaeological discoveries in the ancient Bible lands, which were part of the Ottoman Empire, and he regularly pointed out newspaper articles for Rebecca and Flora to read. They knew all about the discovery of Nimrud's palace and how Henry Layard dug it out of the sand where it lay buried for millennia.

"Everyone believed the Bible was composed of fairy tales," Father had told them, a flush of excitement on his somber face. "Skeptics thought there was no such place as Assyria or a king named Sennacherib until Layard proved that the Scriptures were indeed accurate. How marvelous to make a discovery like that!"

Rebecca had wanted to point out to Father that if he truly longed to make such a discovery he would need to leave Chicago, but she hadn't wanted to spoil his good mood.

"Where would you like to go, Flora, besides France?"

"I would love to visit Egypt and see the pyramids. And the Sphinx."

"Me too." Rebecca pulled off her bonnet so she could feel the warm sunshine on her face and hair.

"But since that probably isn't possible this summer," Flora said, "I'll settle for seeing the Egyptian artifacts in the Louvre in Paris."

"We'll see the pyramids someday, Flora. I promise you." Rebecca's feet were starting to ache in her thin-soled shoes. "We'll need studier shoes when we go on our real travels," she told Flora. "Something much less ladylike."

"And we won't have to wear itchy petticoats, will we?"

"Certainly not!"

At last the arched roof of the railroad depot came into view. "There it is," Rebecca said, pointing. "See? That was easy, wasn't it?"

The moment they stepped into the enormous depot, Rebecca's heart began to race with excitement. She was born for this! The vast, rumbling space shook with the force of the locomotives thundering in and out; the air smelled of coal and steam and hot iron rails. The soaring ceiling arched high above them, magnifying the shrieking train whistles until they echoed all around her. Everywhere she looked there were knots of travelers, piles of trunks and suitcases, and porters pushing overflowing carts. Signs announced destinations like New York, Cincinnati, Philadelphia, and St. Louis.

"Doesn't this make you want to climb aboard and go somewhere, Flora?"

"It truly does." She gave a stage-worthy sigh and asked, "So, now what, Becky? Where do we start?"

Rebecca had been wondering the same thing until she spotted a kiosk marked *Information*. They waited in line while the clerk helped two other customers, then stepped forward at their turn. He frowned when he saw them—or at least frowned at their heads, which were probably all that was visible from his perch behind a window grill. "Yes, girls? May I help you?"

"I hope so." Rebecca stood on tiptoes to make herself as

tall as possible "We're interested in traveling by train to New York City, then booking passage overseas to Calais, France—escorted by our father, of course," she added when the clerk's frown deepened. "Where might we find information on train schedules and rates?"

The man twisted the ends of his pointy mustache, making him look sinister. He studied Rebecca for what seemed like a very long time, but she held her chin high and didn't break his gaze, even though her toes ached from standing on them. "You can purchase tickets to New York at window number three, over there," he finally said. "The agent can tell you the times and rates. As for the ocean voyage, you need to visit the offices of one of the steamship lines such as Cunard or the White Star Line."

"Do either of them have offices near here, by any chance?"

He looked over Rebecca's head at the growing line behind her and didn't seem inclined to answer. Rebecca elbowed Flora's ribs, hoping she would soften him up with her pleading brown eyes and sweet smile. Instead, Flora yelped, "Ow!"

"Cunard's is on Michigan Avenue," he finally said. "Who's next?"

"Thank you very much for your help," Rebecca said. No point in being rude simply because he was. She took Flora's arm, and they marched across the tiled floor to stand in line at window number three.

"Why did you poke me?" Flora asked, rubbing her rib cage.

"I wanted you to smile at him and be charming. Maybe these clerks will be more helpful if we sweeten them up. And you're much prettier than I am." They waited in line, and once again Rebecca stood on her toes to tell the ticket agent what they wanted. This time Flora beamed at him like a gas lamp. He didn't appear to notice as he studied the pages of a thick train schedule.

"A train leaves daily to New York," he told them, and he

quoted the rates for two minors and one adult. He was crisp and businesslike as he pulled out blank ticket forms and official-looking rubber stamps—then he learned that Rebecca wasn't going to purchase the tickets and became irritated. He shoved everything aside and growled, "Step aside, girls. Who's next?"

She thanked him and started to leave, then turned back to ask, "You wouldn't know where the office for the Cunard Shipping Line on Michigan Avenue is, would you?"

"Somewhere around Washington. Or maybe Madison. One of those presidents. Next, please?"

"Do you know where those streets are?" Flora asked as they walked away from the window. "Are they very far from here?"

"I don't think so. Let's see . . . which door did we come in?"

"Could we sit and rest a minute? My feet feel as though we've walked for *miles*." She stretched the last word out dramatically. Rebecca hoped she wasn't going to sigh again.

"There's an empty bench over there." They crossed the vast station and sank down on a stiff wooden seat that hadn't been designed for comfort or lingering. Rebecca looked up at the huge clock on the wall and realized that school had started nearly two hours ago. "We'll need to start a regimen of calisthenics right away to get into shape for our trip, Flora. Explorers need to be tough, you know. But isn't it exciting to be part of all this bustle and purpose? Just think, all these people are about to visit new places and see new things."

"Or maybe they've already been somewhere wonderful, and they're on their way home after a long trip. Maybe they've been out west to see the Indian lands and the buffalo." Flora seemed to be perking up after their brief rest.

"You have to admit this is fun. Today marks the very beginning of our trip! Someday we'll look back on this day and remember how it all began."

Flora giggled and said, "Or else we'll remember this as the day they expelled us from school."

"Would you be mortified if we were expelled? Because if you would be, then I'm truly sorry for making you come along. I'll tell the headmistress that it was all my fault and that I forced you to come—"

"No, we're in this together, no matter what. We're like the Three Musketeers! . . . Except there are only two of us. I do hope Father won't be too angry, though."

"He won't be. He'll be proud of us for showing initiative and independence." It was true. Father had treated them like little adults from an early age and seemed pleased that they didn't cling to him like helpless children. "But no matter what, we need to explain to him how bored we are with that school. I want to learn exciting things, not how to be ladylike. I wish they would teach us Latin. Or maybe Greek. Then we could read Homer in Greek. Father said *The Odyssey* is better in the original language."

"Let's make him promise to hire a Greek tutor for us," Flora said.

"That's the spirit! Ready to walk again?" They stood and Rebecca led the way through the door. They walked away from the lake, heading west until they reached Michigan Avenue, then turned south. "You look for the shipping company on this side of the street," Rebecca said as they walked, "and I'll look for it on the other side."

Three long city blocks later, Flora spotted it. Cunard's office had the same air of excitement as the railroad depot, even though it was small and cramped, with cluttered desks piled high with papers and thick ledgers. Rebecca decided that the excitement was mostly due to the colorful lithographs lining the walls, featuring sailing ships and schooners and steamships moored in exotic, palm-tree-lined ports. They stopped at the first desk they came to. The man behind it didn't look any friendlier than the two railroad clerks had, so since she and Flora were wearing their school uniforms, Rebecca decided to try a different approach.

"Good morning. I wonder if you would mind helping my sister and me with a project for school. We need to know what the fares would be on one of your ships to Calais, France—and also to Dover," she added, spotting a poster advertising that destination.

"That depends on which class of accommodations you'd prefer. And what time of year you plan to go."

"First class, please. During the upcoming summer months." Father wasn't one to fuss about fancy accommodations, but if she could tell him the high end of the fares, he could economize as much as he wanted to from there. She waited while the man flipped through a thick catalogue. He didn't seem to notice Flora's blond head tilted prettily or her sweet, coy smile as she tried her best to charm him. At last he quoted prices to both destinations. The fares didn't seem outrageous at all. "Would you mind writing down all the information for us, please? And we'll need to get an idea of the traveling schedules to those places."

He dug through his desk drawer and handed them a newsprint brochure, tightly packed with columns of numbers. "Here's a schedule. It lists the rates, too." They thanked him and went outside to Michigan Avenue.

"Now what?" Flora asked. "Should we walk back to school?"

Rebecca made a face. "There doesn't seem much point in going back now, does there? They'll probably send us straight to the headmistress' office, where she'll make us sit and wait until she thinks we're properly frightened. Then she'll give us a long, stern lecture, threatening doom and ruin if we don't mend our wild ways, and—"

Flora began to giggle. "You're right. Let's save the lecture for tomorrow. It's beautiful outside. I say we keep walking."

"I agree. Lake Park can't be far. By the time we get there it'll be lunchtime, and we can buy some roasted peanuts from one of the vendors. Do you have any money?"

"A little." Flora always carried loose change in her pockets in case she saw a street beggar. The youngest urchins tugged especially hard at her heart.

Rebecca and her sister continued down Michigan Avenue, arm in arm, passing gracious homes on one side of the avenue, and rows of spindly trees on the other. Beyond the trees was a narrow lagoon, separated from Lake Michigan by a spit of land where the locomotives entered and exited the Great Central Depot. Even from this distance Rebecca could hear the steam whistles hooting and see smoke pluming into the clear, blue sky. Sailing ships of all sizes and shapes dotted the distant lake. Freedom and excitement beckoned her.

An hour later they reached Lake Park and sat on a bench eating peanuts and watching squirrels chase through the trees. They composed a mental list of all the places they hoped to see and the European cities and countries they planned to visit. Rebecca thoroughly enjoyed dreaming of exotic places but soon realized it was time to walk home. They needed to arrive before Rufus left to pick them up from school.

They reached their large, wood-frame house weary and overheated, their faces flushed. Father had built the house the year he'd married, probably imagining the many parties and dinners he and his wife would hold in the spacious parlor and dining room, the dozens of children who would fill the upstairs bedrooms. But the rooms remained empty, mostly unused all these years.

The moment Rebecca and Flora walked into the foyer, their housekeeper, Mrs. Griffin, flew at them like an enraged hen.

"Here you are!" she shouted. Rebecca wasn't sure if she was about to box their ears or embrace them. Their other servants also came at a run. Their cook, Maria Elena, made the sign of the cross, then used her apron to mop tears from her eyes. She burst into such a torrent of babble in her native Italian that Rebecca couldn't tell if she was scolding them or rejoicing at their return. Rufus, their driver, leaned against the wall in relief when he saw them, wiping sweat from his forehead with his sleeve. He'd been a slave in New Orleans before purchasing his freedom and had worked as Father's faithful driver for as long as Rebecca could remember. "Thank heaven you're safe," he said.

"Of course we're safe. Why wouldn't we be?" Rebecca asked.

The housekeeper's face turned a vivid red, her features scrunched with emotion. Their butler, Griffin, laid his hand on his wife's shoulder, his face stern. "We received a note from the headmistress of your school saying you'd gone missing."

Flora gave a stage-worthy gasp. "You thought we were missing?"

"The headmistress was alarmed because several schoolgirls saw your carriage arrive, but then you vanished. We didn't know what to tell her. Rufus insisted that he'd delivered you to school on time—"

"I did! I know I did!" Rufus said, still braced against the wall. "That school bell ain't even ringing yet. All them girls still outside."

"I hope you didn't involve Father," Rebecca said.

"No. Rufus went out searching for you and returned empty-handed," Griffin explained. "We were just deciding what we should do next."

The cook finished wiping her eyes. "You are giving us a terrible scare!"

Rebecca didn't understand what all the fuss was about, but Flora's dark eyes swam with tears at the sight of their trustworthy servants' distress. "I'm so sorry we frightened you," she said. "We never dreamed you'd be worried about us. I feel terrible!" The cook offered Flora a corner of her apron to dry her tears.

"I'm sorry, too," Rebecca said. "I should have thought it through more carefully. But the day was just too beautiful to stay inside. We didn't think anyone would miss us. . . . Rufus, please don't say anything about this when you fetch Father from work. I'll explain everything to him once he's home, I promise."

"Yes, Miss Rebecca."

With the tension defused, Rebecca and Flora went upstairs to their room. They could have each had a room or two to themselves on the spacious second floor, but they preferred to share the same one, as they had since their days in the nursery. "That was awful," Rebecca said, closing the door behind her. "We'll have to make it up to them, but we can't let it derail our plans."

They spent the rest of the afternoon preparing a report for Father as carefully as they would complete a school project, neatly detailing the costs of traveling by rail to New York, then by steamship abroad. Deciphering the information from Cunard's enigmatic brochure proved nearly as difficult as translating hieroglyphics, but Rebecca eventually cracked the code and printed out the necessary details in her own hand. Father valued a well-researched proposal. In fact, he often gave them a topic to study, then listened as they presented their conclusions, reasoning and debating the issue with them over dinner. It probably never occurred to him that most girls their age didn't interact with their fathers this way. Or that in most homes, meals weren't conducted like board meetings. Rebecca knew that outsiders might view her father as cold and distant, but she adored him.

Dinner seemed hastily prepared that evening, probably due to the afternoon's upheaval. When Father finished his last bite of food and leaned back in his chair, Rebecca seized the moment.

"Father, Flora and I have prepared a proposal we would like you to consider." She handed him the first page. "Since our school is limited in what it's able to teach, we believe we could learn a great deal more if we took a trip abroad. As you can see from our list, there are several places we would like to visit, along with many interesting things we would like to see and do in each place, such as viewing the Egyptian collections in the Louvre in Paris."

Father stroked his silvery beard as he studied the page. "This looks quite thorough. . . . I suppose it might be time to broaden your education."

"In that case, we've prepared another list of projected travel expenses," she said, handing it to him. "And this third page details some of the possible railroad and steamship schedules. We thought the summer months might be a good time to go, after school is out."

"This summer?"

"Yes, Father," they said in unison.

"Please?" Flora added, gazing up at him with her melting brown eyes.

Father took a moment to think. He was a great believer in the Bible's warning to "let every man be swift to hear, slow to speak, slow to wrath," and Rebecca was counting on this to work in her favor. At last he tapped the pages into a neat pile and laid them on the table. "You've done a good job. But first you'll need to learn French. Once you're able to read and converse with some fluency, I'll take you to Paris. The same holds true for any other language you master. As I've often told you, we were put on this earth to do something productive with our lives. Rich or poor, we each have a God-given calling to fulfil. It's simply a question of finding out what that might be. Perhaps a trip abroad will help you girls with that search."

Rebecca felt like dancing. "We couldn't agree more, Father."

She and Flora exchanged excited grins. Father probably believed he was buying time by making them learn French, but he had no idea how determined Rebecca was. "Will you hire a French tutor for us?" she asked.

"Right away?" Flora added.

Again he thought for a moment. "Yes. I'll ask your headmistress to recommend someone."

Rebecca's glowing excitement dimmed. She winced as she searched for a way to introduce the next subject. "Father . . . I'm sorry, but I'm afraid the headmistress isn't too pleased with me at the moment. You see, I coaxed Flora into skipping school today so we could research those travel times and expenses for you. We never imagined that anyone would miss us or worry about us, but it seems that the headmistress did."

"You went off alone? Without Rufus?"

"Yes, Father," they said in unison. Rebecca was counting on him to remember the second half of that Bible verse: "For the wrath of man worketh not the righteousness of God."

"As you can see," she said, "we easily found our way around Chicago and home again without becoming lost. And we accomplished our goal, which you have right in front of you. We wanted to demonstrate that we're old enough and mature enough to travel."

"But of course we'll still need you to come with us to Europe," Flora added.

Rebecca waited. Father didn't seem angry; he rarely lost his temper, and when he did, it was usually over something he read in the newspaper about the political wrangling in Washington. When Rebecca could no longer endure the suspense, she said, "I don't suppose the headmistress will be pleased about our absence, but perhaps it would ease things with her if you wrote a note of explanation for us to take to school tomorrow. If you could please ask her to excuse our truancy—"

"And recommend a French tutor," Flora added.

"—we would be very grateful."

Father gave a curt nod after a moment and pushed back his chair. "Very well." He might as easily have said, "meeting adjourned." He got as far as the door before adding, "The next time you have a change in plans, I advise you to tell someone where you're going."

"Yes, Father," they said together.

When he was gone, Rebecca and Flora slid off their chairs and hugged each other. "We're going on our very first adventure!" Flora said with a squeal.

"No, it will be our second one, Flora. Today counts as our first."

CHAPTER 3

Father suffered from seasickness for the entire voyage across the Atlantic. He managed to drag himself off his bed and out of his cabin to dine with Rebecca and Flora every evening but never ate much. Rebecca, on the other hand, took to the waves like a seasoned sailor. She and Flora spoke only French with each other and practiced conversing with any other French-speaking passengers willing to talk with them. Father had seemed very surprised that they had mastered the language so quickly, but he was pleased—even though it meant honoring his word and taking them to France after school let out for the summer.

"Your daughters have a natural gift for languages," their French tutor had told him. "I recommend you employ a Greek tutor when you return from Europe. The young misses have expressed an interest in learning that language, too, and I believe they would learn it very quickly." Rebecca had made a wager with the tutor in order to get him to recommend Greek lessons, betting him that she and Flora could get perfect scores on their

French grammar test. When they had, he had honored the bet. Then he'd nearly ruined everything by adding, "Although it's quite unusual for young girls to study Greek. Quite pointless, too, no doubt."

Once their French studies had been well underway, Rebecca and Flora spent every spare minute with their cook, Maria Elena, learning a rudimentary knowledge of Italian. They couldn't read it very well, lacking a proper book to study— though Rebecca wasn't entirely sure that Maria Elena could read her native language, either. But they learned Italian well enough to converse with hotel clerks and restaurant waiters and to ask for directions to the Colosseum or Saint Peter's Basilica. Most importantly, they learned it well enough to impress Father and convince him to add Italy to their itinerary.

They landed in the port of Dover in Great Britain and boarded a train to London, spending two glorious weeks exploring that wonderful city with its pomp and pageantry and palaces. "London makes Chicago and even New York City seem brand-new," Flora commented. Father had a chance to recover from his seasickness during that time, but it came roaring back on the short but tempestuous voyage across the English Channel to Calais. After a journey south through France by train, they arrived in Paris—glorious Paris! But by the time they checked into their hotel on the *Rue de Capucines*, Father felt so dizzy that he stumbled up the stairs and into their suite like a drunken man.

"We'll see everything tomorrow, girls. I promise," he told them. He lay flat and perfectly still on his bed, eyes closed. "Tomorrow."

"Tomorrow is Sunday," Rebecca pointed out. "*Dimanche*," she added in French.

"Monday, then. . . . The Louvre, the Palace of Versailles, whatever you'd like. Just let me rest now."

"What about dinner?"

He groaned like a dying man. "Order room service."

That proved to be great fun for Rebecca, trying new foods and testing her command of French as she ordered *coq au vin* and *escargots* from the menu, then conversing with the waiter who delivered it.

Sunday turned out to be a gorgeous summer day. They were in Paris! And Father still couldn't move his head, much less rise from his bed without being overcome by waves of nausea. His face looked as pale as his silvery hair and beard.

"Should we be worried about you?" Rebecca asked him.

"Not at all. I'll be fine tomorrow. Prepare an itinerary for us. Then check with the concierge about hiring transportation and a guide for the week." He probably figured the assignment would fill the rest of their day, but Rebecca and Flora arranged a full week's worth of sightseeing before noon.

They sat by the open window in their room, the curtains fluttering in the breeze, as they nibbled from their room-service cheese and fruit plate and stared with longing at the tree-lined avenue below, jammed with people and carriages. Sunday in Paris in the summertime appeared to be the day that the entire population of the city poured from their *maisons* and *appartements*, determined to enjoy themselves. Laughing, chattering Parisians filled every boulevard and avenue as far as Rebecca could see. And many of these gaily dressed people were streaming right past her hotel. Where were they all going?

"It's going to be a very long, boring day," Flora said with a sigh. She lifted the delicate teacup with her pinky finger extended, the way they'd been taught in school.

Rebecca leapt to her feet. "It doesn't have to be boring. We can find something fun to do on our own."

"Without Father? . . . I mean, *sans Papa*?"

"Why not? What would it hurt if we took a stroll around the block? Or maybe two blocks? Or maybe we could walk to

La Seine and watch the boats? I don't think it's very far. . . . Please, Flora?"

"Won't we get lost?"

"Of course not. We didn't get lost when we explored Chicago on our own, did we?"

"Well, no. I suppose a short walk wouldn't hurt . . . if you're sure you know the way."

They set out from their room in great spirits, leaving a note for Father saying they intended to circle the block and come right back. "*Excusez-moi* . . ." Rebecca said as the uniformed doorman swept open the door for them. "But where is everyone going?" she asked in French.

He lifted his shoulders in an exaggerated shrug as if the answer should be obvious to anyone. "It's Sunday, *mademoiselle*."

"They're all going to church?"

He gave a dismissive snort, erasing the idea with a toss of his head and a wave of his white-gloved hand. "I think not, mademoiselle."

"But . . . is there a parade today? Is this a special . . . ?" She couldn't think of the word for occasion.

"Parade? There is no parade, mademoiselle." He seemed irritated that she would even ask such a ridiculous question. "There is the *Jardin des Tuileries*, the *Rue de Rivoli*, the *Champs-Elysees*!" His gestures grew more exaggerated with each place he named.

"*Merci beaucoup*," Flora said. She tugged Rebecca's arm to move away from him. "Did you understand him?" she asked. "Why did he seem so angry?"

"I don't know. It's one thing to learn a language and another thing to understand the people who speak it. Come on." She merged into the stream of pedestrians, pulling Flora along with her.

"Where are we going?"

"The same place everyone else is."

"But . . . how do we know where that is? I thought you said we were only going to circle the block and come right back."

"Listen, do you really want to sit inside our hotel room on such a beautiful day? Let's have an adventure, Flora. You want to see Paris, don't you?"

"Yes, of course, but shouldn't we wait for Father?"

"If we do, we'll never get past the front door of our hotel. He's proving to be a great disappointment as a traveling companion. We'll need to leave him behind if we want to see the world."

"But . . . but we're just schoolgirls, Becky! All alone . . . in a foreign country!"

Rebecca released her sister's arm. "You can turn around and go back if you want to, but I'm going for a walk."

Flora looked unsure for a moment as she stared at Rebecca, but she finally smiled and linked her arm through hers again. "You're fearless, aren't you?"

"I refuse to live my life like a timid, simpering damsel, waiting for a knight in shining armor to rescue me. It isn't fearlessness that propels me, it's curiosity. Why learn about the world through books when we can visit exciting places, see new things, and experience life firsthand? Besides, the Lord knows when the end of our days will be. We don't need to fear."

They merged into the crowd and continued down the street until they reached an intersection. Everyone seemed to be turning to the right, so Rebecca and Flora joined them. Rebecca searched for a street name so she could find her way back but didn't see one. She looked for a landmark instead, but the lovely, palatial stone buildings that lined the avenues all looked the same to her. Nevertheless, she knew their hotel was on *Rue des Capucines* and was confident she could retrace their steps. They passed numerous outdoor cafés, where people dined at tiny tables in the open air, and it looked like such fun she wished she could join them.

"Why on earth have we been taking our meals in our room, Flora, when we could be eating out here?"

"Because Father told us to order room service and—"

"Wouldn't it be much more fun to sit in the fresh air along the sidewalk and watch the people go by?"

"Yes, but . . . do we dare dine in Paris all alone? Our head-mistress says that young ladies should always be accompanied by a chaperone—"

"I'll bet our headmistress has never had a day of fun in her life." They passed through a small plaza and saw trees in the distance. "Look, Flora. That must be the famous *Jardin des Tuileries* up ahead." Excitement quickened their pace.

"Oh, but this is beautiful!" Flora gushed after they'd crossed *Rue de Rivoli* and entered the grounds. Acres and acres of green grass filled the huge garden, intersected by walkways and dotted with fountains and statues and reflecting ponds. People of all ages—some well-dressed and some in simple clothes—strolled the grounds or picnicked on the grass, all of them enjoying the glorious afternoon. Rebecca and Flora happily blended in with the Parisians as they walked the width of the park to the *Quai des Tuileries* on the Seine, then sat on a bench enjoying the view and the boats drifting by. After resting they walked a little farther, and Rebecca thought she spotted the famous monolith from Egypt poking above the trees.

"Look, Flora! I think that's Cleopatra's Needle from the Temple of Rameses II in Thebes. We read all about it, remember?" They followed the pathway along the length of the park until they came to the seventy-five-foot obelisk, covered with hieroglyphs. Flora circled it twice, gazing up in awe.

"I can't even comprehend how old this is!" Crowds jammed the broad *Champs-Elysees* ahead of them. It resembled a fairground, with so much to see and do that Rebecca didn't know where to look first. The hours flew past as they watched jugglers, a puppet show featuring Punch and Judy, and listened to musicians giving impromptu street concerts. They joined circles of curious onlookers to watch games of chance and see tricksters relieve the unlucky of their money. Rebecca didn't want the day to end. Rather than satisfying her hunger for adventure, it created an insatiable appetite for more.

"How long do you think we've been gone?" Flora asked when they reached the far end of the park. She resembled a flower that was starting to wilt, her fair skin turning pink from the sun.

"I don't know . . . an hour or two?" Much longer than Rebecca had ever intended to be gone.

"I think we should go back to the hotel now," Flora said. "I would hate for Father to worry."

Rebecca believed that retracing their steps would be easy, but she soon learned that the streets of Paris weren't laid out in a neat grid like Chicago's streets, nor were they well-marked. When they passed a doorman standing outside one of the many identical apartment buildings, she asked him for directions to *Rue des Capucines*, where their hotel was located. After walking an interminable distance, she discovered he had mistakenly directed them to *Boulevard des Capucines* instead. The afternoon sun had disappeared behind lowering clouds, and crowds no longer filled the streets. Rebecca's fear increased when she noticed three young men following them, laughing and making rude gestures and calling out to them. Rebecca grabbed her sister's arm and marched faster as a light rain began to fall.

"What are those men saying?" Flora asked.

"I'm not sure. I don't think our French teacher taught us those phrases." But she knew enough about the world to guess what their intentions were. Rebecca knew she was plain-looking, with a broad, square face like Father's. But Flora was innocent and attractive with fair hair and a slender figure—and Rebecca was responsible for her safety. She glanced around for a policeman but didn't spot one. Adding to everything else, the sky suddenly opened up and poured rain. She wanted to stop and take shelter beneath an awning, but if she did, the young men would surely catch up with them.

Rebecca didn't want Flora to know how worried and lost she really was, or her sister would never trust her on an expedition again. Yes, she'd been foolish to march away from the hotel on her own, but now it was up to her to lead them both out of it. *Think, Rebecca! Think!* The only weapons she had were her wits and common sense. And prayer. She whispered an apology and a quick prayer for help, and it seemed to be answered just as quickly when she spotted a small café on a side street.

"Do you have any money, Flora? Let's get out of this rain."

The café was very crowded, filled with the happy babble of French, the sound of clinking china, and the aroma of coffee and cigarette smoke. After waiting several minutes, they managed to find a tiny table for two near the front window and ordered pastries and steaming cups of *café au lait*. As Rebecca sipped the hot coffee, she drew an imaginary map in her mind of all the places they'd walked and soon realized her mistake. They had hiked too far away from the garden. She recalled crossing only two side streets between the hotel and the *Rue de Rivoli*. They needed to backtrack, toward the *Tuileries*.

"We're lost, aren't we?" Flora said.

Rebecca couldn't meet her gaze. "Yes, and I'm very, very sorry. But it's only temporary. I know where I made my mistake, and as soon as the rain lets up, I'll ask for better directions, and we'll find our way back. Will you forgive me for getting us into this?" She looked up at Flora again, waiting.

"Yes, of course," she said, reaching for her hand.

Rebecca would get them out of this predicament. She would!

As she gazed out at the streaming rain and darkening sky, she glimpsed her reflection in the window and began to laugh. No wonder the men had followed them. She and Flora resembled scruffy urchins, not respectable young ladies from a distinguished family. Their hair was dripping and plastered to their heads, their coiled braids falling from their pins. Their soaked shirtwaists stuck to their skin, and their skirts were so drenched they could have wrung a bowlful of water out of them. She hoped their shoes weren't ruined. "What's so funny?" Flora asked.

Rebecca gestured to their reflection. "Look at us!" Flora began to laugh, too.

After asking the waiter for directions, Rebecca paid the tab and set out with Flora once again. Thankfully, the rain had slackened to a drizzle. The three strangers had tired of their pursuit and disappeared. And after only a few minutes of walking, Rebecca found the right street and spotted the awning of their hotel ahead.

"That was fun, wasn't it?" she asked Flora.

"Until we got lost. And those men started following us. And we got soaked." Her usually good-natured sister sounded peeved.

"But it was an adventure, Flora. And remember, we can't have an adventure without expecting some sort of trouble. Besides, we proved once again that we can get around fine on our own, didn't we?"

"Are you going to tell Father we got lost? And that those men followed us?"

"Why would I do that? It might upset him, and he needs to stay calm and get well. Besides, they didn't do us any harm. Let me do all the talking when we see him."

When the doorman spotted them, he launched into such a furious scolding in French that Rebecca couldn't possibly follow it all. "*Pardonnez-moi, monsieur?*" she asked, baffled as he gestured at them dramatically. He huffed and pointed his white-gloved hand toward the hotel lobby where their father was standing. He was out of bed at last, but he was gripping the back of a chair to steady himself as if still sailing the high seas. He looked very pale, but whether from vertigo or anxiety, Rebecca couldn't tell. His shoulders slumped visibly with relief when he spotted them, and he sank into the chair he'd been leaning against.

Flora ran to his side and hugged him, leaving a wet patch on his shirtfront. "I'm so sorry if we worried you," she said.

"We got caught in the rain," Rebecca said, lifting her soggy skirt from her thighs.

"So I see."

"We had to take shelter in a café for a while. I'm very sorry, too, Father."

"The doorman told me you left the hotel some time ago, but he hadn't seen you return. I was growing concerned."

"The afternoon seemed too nice to spend indoors—at least at first," Rebecca said. "And we didn't think you'd want to go for a walk with us. Are you feeling well enough to do some sight-seeing tomorrow? Flora and I have the day all planned."

"Well, yes . . . I'm somewhat better. I'm glad you're back."

As Rebecca had hoped, Father chose to view them as little adults who didn't need babysitters and chaperones instead of as foolish young girls who never should have wandered the streets of Paris alone. Now she needed to make amends with Flora before she ruined everything by spilling all the worrisome details of their afternoon. "Let's go upstairs," she said, taking Father's arm and helping him from his chair. "Flora and I could use a warm bath. Do you want to go first, Flora?" she asked as she pulled the few remaining pins from her dripping hair.

"A bath sounds wonderful."

Flora shared their father's forgiving nature. All would be well once Rebecca earned back her sister's trust. She sighed with relief as she climbed the stairs to their suite. Her next adventure already beckoned.

CHAPTER 4

Rebecca held one of her father's arms and Flora the other as he stumbled along the passageway aboard their steamship home to America. Just outside their suite, an elegantly dressed woman was struggling with the lock to her cabin next door. Rebecca was eager to get Father to his bed and bucket. But ever the gracious gentleman, Father paused to ask, "Would you like some help with that?"

"Oh, that would be very kind of you," the woman replied. "I can't seem to get this key to work." Father was able to open it on the first try. The woman's thanks were so profuse he might have unlocked the door to King Solomon's treasures. When she finished gushing with praise, she extended her gloved hand to him. "I'm Priscilla Worthington."

"How do you do? Edward Hawes, and my daughters, Rebecca and Flora."

"Pleased to meet you," Flora said, while Rebecca simply nodded, eager to get her father to his bed.

"Traveling can be such a challenge, Mr. Hawes, don't you

46

agree?" Mrs. Worthington asked. "Especially when one is all alone, as I am. You see, my husband, George Worthington, passed away a little more than a year ago."

"My condolences," Father said.

She smiled up at him and touched his arm. "Thank you. I went to Europe for a change of scenery after my year of mourning ended, and I've been touring with my brother and sister-in-law for the past six weeks. They decided to stay behind in France for another month, leaving me on my own—with this wretched lock!"

"Your courage is commendable, Mrs. Worthington. I didn't have much interest in travel after my wife died."

"Oh, I'm so sorry." The widow touched his arm again, managing to inch closer through the brief physical contact. She was younger than him by about ten years and must have spilled an entire bottle of French perfume all over herself because she reeked of it. Rebecca had to pinch her nose to avoid sneezing.

"My daughters wanted to see the world," Father continued, "so I decided the time was right."

"Where do you call home, Mr. Hawes?"

"We live in Chicago, Illinois."

"Why, what a coincidence! I'm also on my way home to Chicago. I won't keep you any longer, but I do hope we'll have a chance to speak again on this trip. Perhaps we have a few acquaintances in common. I'll look forward to chatting with you, possibly at dinner one evening?"

"Father can't eat dinner," Rebecca said. "He suffers from seasickness. He can barely move from his bed while we're at sea, let alone eat dinner." She hoped to end this conversation and discourage the widow from bothering them further by pointing out Father's weaknesses. But rather than being repelled, the widow's eyes brightened.

"I used to suffer from seasickness, as well. You wait right here, Mr. Hawes. I have something that I'm certain will help you." She returned with a supply of mysterious powders, insisting that he try them mixed with water, along with a little tin of what appeared to be candy. "It's crystalized ginger," she explained. "It does wonders to settle the stomach when one chews on it." Father promised to escort her to dinner that very evening if her remedy worked.

Her cure turned out to be nothing short of miraculous, and Rebecca was grateful to the widow at first. If Father was cured, he would be able to travel anywhere in the world. It seemed only fair that Mrs. Worthington join them for dinner since Father was finally able to eat, thanks to her. But like a stray dog that keeps coming back once you feed it, the widow clung to their wealthy, distinguished father like mortar to bricks.

What followed in the succeeding days was a masterpiece of seduction on the widow's part. She wasn't classically beautiful, but she made the most of her assets—including an ample bosom—in ways that made her seem attractive, especially to the opposite sex. The way her fair skin contrasted with her dark hair, the endearing tendrils that dangled on her blushing cheeks, the way she tilted her head as she gazed up at Father in adoration—it all gave her that helpless, feminine appeal that otherwise-sensible men seemed to fall for. One week into their ocean voyage, the widow and Father were conversing as if they had known each other all their lives, calling each other Priscilla and Edward. Rebecca battled jealousy, unaccustomed to having a rival for her father's attention. Would they have to put up with her all the way to Chicago?

"Just our luck!" Rebecca grumbled as she and Flora sat in the sunshine on the passenger deck. They were reading books and watching people stroll past—including Father and the widow, who had her hand comfortably locked in the crook of his arm.

"Why did her stateroom have to be right next to ours? I wish she'd leave Father alone."

Flora barely looked up from her novel. "Just be glad he's no longer below deck with his head in a bucket." She was reading *Uncle Tom's Cabin* and seemed mesmerized by it. Rebecca had brought the novel along to read on the journey over to France, and now Flora couldn't seem to stop reading it on the way back.

"I wonder what's in those magical powders of hers. She has him completely under her spell."

Flora made a vague acknowledgment and turned the page, continuing to read. Rebecca watched as some of the other first-class passengers paraded past. There was the dour Scotsman with the straight posture who took tiny, huffing steps when he walked. And the elegant French woman who was as tall and languid as a greyhound and seemed to glide on the deck as if skating on ice. A woman from Germany with braided gray hair marched around and around the deck all day, frowning as if she were required to hike all the way to New York. Why couldn't Father have struck up a friendship with one of them?

"I once read a fascinating article about female spiders," Rebecca said. "The webs they spin are nearly invisible so they can trap unsuspecting insects and eat them as prey. One species, ironically called the black widow, eats the male spider after they've mated."

"You need to stop reading such strange things. It plays on your imagination."

"Well, I don't like Widow Worthington. I don't like the effect she's having on our father."

Flora looked over at her in surprise. "You'd rather he was lying ill belowdecks?"

"No, of course not. But why does she have to spend every spare minute with him? And she's always clutching his arm like it's a life preserver and she's about to drown."

"I'm happy for him," Flora said. "He's been a widower much too long."

"If he wants to remarry, he should wait until we're gone."

"Gone? Where are we going?"

"I don't know about you, Flora, but I plan on traveling around the world after we finish school. Maybe live in some exotic place. I was hoping Father would take us on more trips now that he's cured, but I certainly don't want her tagging along—medicine or no medicine."

"We won't graduate for a few more years, Becky. A lot can happen in that time. You're worried about nothing." Flora returned to her book.

Rebecca watched several married couples parade past. None of the pairs looked particularly happy. "Speaking of what can happen, Flora, have you ever noticed that all of the sighing and hand-holding and gazing into each other's eyes vanishes after a few years of marriage? It's not the way love is portrayed in a romantic novel."

"I never paid much attention. . . ." Flora mumbled without looking up.

"You don't think Father will be foolish enough to marry the widow, do you?"

"Of course not. They only met a week ago."

"But what if he does?"

"So what? Doesn't he deserve a little happiness?"

Rebecca put her hand over the page of her sister's book to get her attention. "We don't know anything about her, Flora. What if she's after his money? Widows do that, you know. Imagine how horrible our lives would be with a stepmother. We're too old to be mothered, don't you think?"

"I think you're worried about nothing. Father is a very sensible man. And the widow doesn't look as though she needs anyone's money, judging by her clothing and the fact that she's been touring Europe." She pushed Rebecca's hand out of her way. "Now, stop bothering me. I'm reading a very exciting part."

Rebecca tried to return to her own book but couldn't concentrate. She kept recalling the way the widow rested her slender fingers on Father's arm whenever she wanted to command his attention and how she laughed at everything he said, no matter how trivial. Her leg seemed to conveniently press against his when they sat together. And worst of all, Father seemed to enjoy the attention. He had rarely seemed so animated. Thanks to Widow Worthington, the color had seeped back in his cheeks again, in spite of the sometimes turbulent ocean voyage. Yes, the Black Widow had trapped him in her sticky web.

"I like our life the way it is," Rebecca said as she opened her book. Father had purchased it in a wonderful little bookshop they'd found in London. The owner had recommended the volume, saying it was creating a big stir in intellectual circles and newspaper editorials ever since its publication last year. Curious, Father bought it to see what all the fuss was about. *On the Origin of the Species by Means of Natural Selection*, written by an English naturalist and geologist named Charles Darwin, was subtitled *or the Preservation of Favoured Races in the Struggle for Life*. Father usually enjoyed reading scientific works, but he had strongly disliked this one.

"The author is a godless fool," he'd said. "His so-called scientific conclusions are an outrageous affront to the truth of the Bible—and to everything we hold dear. I understand why people are incensed with the book, although I don't imagine that sensible, God-fearing people will give it any credence." He was going to leave the book behind, but Rebecca asked to read it. So far, she'd been unable to concentrate on it, worried more about Father and the widow. She closed the volume again and tried to lighten her mood by reminiscing about their trip.

They had visited the Louvre the day after she and Flora had

gotten lost, studying the fascinating collections of Egyptian artifacts for hours—mummies and cartouches and monumental statues. "There's so much more to the world and to history than they ever teach us in class," she had told their father. "Please promise you'll hire a decent tutor for us when we get home instead of sending us back to that dreadful school."

"I'm surprised you girls find all of this interesting."

"Of course we find it interesting, Father. Don't you?"

"Well, yes, of course, but—"

"We do, too!"

When they finished sightseeing in France, they headed to Italy. It would have been easier to take a steamship from Marseilles to Rome, but since the mere sight of water made Father turn pale, they took a train across France, then over the Alps and into Italy. "I'm sorry, but we're going to have to skip Venice," Father told them. "It seems they have canals instead of streets and one can scarcely get anywhere in the city without a boat."

"You'll have to travel by ship in order to get home," Rebecca had pointed out. "Unless you plan on settling down here in Europe."

"Don't tempt me . . ." he grumbled.

Rebecca brightened. "I think living abroad for a few years is a wonderful idea!"

They spent two weeks in Italy, and once again, Rebecca and her sister planned all of the excursions and booked all the guides and transportation. She was disappointed that she didn't have another opportunity to venture out alone in Rome as she had in Paris, longing to prove to herself and her sister that she could navigate that city without getting lost. They made the return trip by train from Italy to France and the port of Calais.

One morning over breakfast, Father had asked Rebecca and Flora to report on their observations and any conclusions they'd drawn about what they'd seen during their journey. "I would be interested to hear your impressions and analyses after two months of travel abroad."

Rebecca spoke first, as she always did at these mealtime board meetings. "It was a wonderful trip, Father, but not nearly long enough. It was like tasting one tiny bite of a marvelous banquet before having it snatched away. I'm still hungry for more."

"That's exactly how I feel," Flora said.

"This summer has flown past," Rebecca continued. "And now I want to learn even more, study even more, and visit as many interesting places as I possibly can. I'm wondering if my desire to explore the world and learn new things means that God has something for me to do in the future that involves these passions and interests."

"Hmm . . ." Father combed his silvery beard with his fingers. "And what do you think that might be? Becoming a teacher, perhaps?"

"I hope not. I can think of nothing more frustrating than trying to teach a subject as fascinating as history to students who don't have the least bit of interest in it. If only there were a few more choices open to women than teaching. But since there aren't . . . maybe I'll travel the world and write guidebooks for other travelers to read."

"What about you, Flora?"

"I think I'm too young to figure out what my future might be. But I know I can't wait to go on another trip next summer. May we, Father? Please?"

He seemed to pale at the thought. "We'll see," he replied. They had boarded the steamship for New York the next day with Father dreading the voyage home—and then the widow came into their lives. Rebecca knew she should be grateful, but she stifled a groan at the mere thought of Mrs. Worthington's delicate, tinkling voice, as fragile as porcelain, plying Father with her phony questions and feigned interest. *"That's so fascinating, Edward! You must tell me more!"*

Rebecca opened her book again and was attempting to concentrate when one of the deck-walkers halted alongside her. She knew by the choking cloud of French perfume that it was the widow.

"May I join you?" she asked.

"Of course," Flora said. "Why don't you sit between us?" She politely closed her novel and slid into a vacant chair so the widow could sit in the middle.

"Where's our father?" Rebecca asked. She imagining him stunned and bound and dangling from a web in the corner of Widow Worthington's stateroom.

"He's in the smoking lounge with the other gentlemen."

"We can't thank you enough for sharing your cure for seasickness with him," Flora said. "He's a changed man."

"I'm so glad. It would be tragic if your father couldn't enjoy the voyage. He is such a charming traveling companion."

Rebecca barely stopped herself from snorting in disdain. No one who knew her father had ever defined him as charming. He was blunt and opinionated, with little patience for anyone who wasn't his intellectual equal. And no one who'd spent an evening with the widow would ever accuse her of being his intellectual equal. The woman's chief talent seemed to be filling out low-cut dresses and providing an attentive audience as Father lectured.

"I noticed you girls spend a lot of time reading," she began.

"Oh, yes, Mrs. Worthington," Flora said, all smiles and sunshine. "A good book can transport you to an entirely different time and place."

"That may be true," she replied, "but you're missing out on all of the wonderful social activities aboard this ship. There are several young ladies your age here. Perhaps you would find them interesting once you got to know them."

Rebecca thought she knew what the widow was up to from the hints she had dropped at the dinner table. She wanted Rebecca and Flora to make new friends so she and Father could dine alone. Rebecca had tried making conversation with other young ladies but had ended up feeling awkward and left out. The other girls were so different from her—just like the girls at school. One of them had bragged that she had never read a book in her life. Another said she hated traveling, hated visiting strange European cities and eating foreign food. They all seemed eager to get home and order new gowns for the fall season. "I have very little in common with them," Rebecca finally said. "And they don't seem to like me."

"Maybe we just need to try harder," Flora said. "They would love you, once they got to know you, Becky. You're smart and witty and you have such a unique way of looking at the world."

Rebecca knew that Flora had felt awkward, too, but she was too good-hearted to say anything negative about other people. "What bothered me most about those girls," Rebecca continued, "was that they didn't seem interested in discovering their purpose in life. In fact, they laughed when I brought up the subject. Father believes—and Flora and I agree—that no matter how rich or poor we are, how intelligent or ordinary, God has a task for each of us to do while we're here on earth. Reading books and traveling abroad and learning new things are wonderful opportunities to figure out what that task might be."

"God made you a woman, Rebecca. A woman's role is to marry and have children."

Rebecca nearly shouted in outrage. She waited until she was calm and said, "Our mother had two children and promptly died. Was that her sole purpose?"

"I really couldn't say. . . ."

"I hope to marry someday and have children," Rebecca said, "but I don't believe that's all God has for me."

"We still have plenty of time to discover our purpose," Flora said, sweet and conciliatory, as usual. "We haven't even finished school. In the meantime, there's no harm in making new friends."

"Have you discovered what your God-given task might be, Mrs. Worthington?" Rebecca asked.

The widow's cheeks brightened beneath her rouge. Her face quivered with the effort to keep her smile in place. "That's a very personal question, Rebecca dear. One must learn not to put others on the spot in such a direct way."

It was on the tip of Rebecca's tongue to say, *"You have no idea what your purpose is, do you?"* But she stopped herself in time, releasing her annoyance with a huge sigh. "I never was very good at what our headmistress calls polite conversation. Flora is much better at it. Why don't you two talk without me for a while?" She gestured for her sister to continue and then returned to Charles Darwin's book.

Flora cleared her throat. "I'm so glad the weather has been pleasant. And the sea has been comparatively calm, hasn't it?" Rebecca didn't look up again until Mrs. Worthington took her leave a few minutes later. "You were very rude, Becky," Flora said when the widow was out of earshot. "I think you may have insulted her."

"Maybe she'll stop bothering Father if she decides his daughter is obnoxious."

"Are you jealous of her, Becky?"

"Maybe." It pained her to admit it. "Most of all, I'm tired of her."

Ten minutes later, the widow strolled by on Father's arm, smiling up at him as if he had just hung the moon in place. He seemed to glow in her adoration.

Flora gave Rebecca a nudge. "Look at him, Becky . . . does he seem to be bothered by her?"

"No. And that's what worries me."

Chapter 5

Rebecca's two-month journey abroad ended on a hot, humid afternoon in August when their train came to a halt in the Great Central Depot in Chicago. Since her grand tour had begun in this very station last spring when she and Flora skipped school, it was a satisfying conclusion to her trip—except for the fact that the widow was right beside them as they stepped off the train, chattering away in her tinkling voice. She had glued herself to Father like feathers to hot tar for the entire train trip from New York to Chicago, just as she had on their ocean voyage.

Rufus was all smiles as he welcomed them home and helped collect their luggage from the baggage car. And when a driver arrived to collect Mrs. Worthington and her steamer trunks, Rebecca hoped they would finally be rid of her. But they barely had time to unpack back home before a formal invitation arrived from the widow, asking the three of them to a dinner party.

"Surely Father will come to his senses now that he's back into his old routine, won't he?" Rebecca asked as she and Flora stared at the fine, engraved stationery. "He never used to bother with nonsense like dinner parties. Hasn't he had his fill of her? I know I have."

"I think he may surprise you," Flora replied.

And he did. Father's somber face managed a faint smile as he read the invitation. "Priscilla told me she wanted us to meet her family," he said.

"Father! You can't possibly consider going!"

He looked at Rebecca in surprise. "Of course we're going. Why wouldn't we?"

She didn't know where to begin.

When the Hawes family arrived at the stately mansion on the appointed evening, Widow Worthington greeted them in the foyer in a glittering gown and sumptuous décolletage. She quickly introduced the elegant young people waiting in the foyer with her as her two nieces and three nephews, but their names slid right past Rebecca, who felt so out of place she wished she could turn around and run home. What was she doing in this ornate mansion with these fashionable people? She was certain she had nothing in common with them, including the fact that they were elegantly dressed and she was not.

"My maid will escort you to the ladies' withdrawing room," the widow said as she herded Rebecca and Flora toward the winding staircase. "You can leave your wraps there and freshen up a bit after your journey here." She nodded to the waiting maid, then turned her attention to Father.

"Freshen up?" Rebecca whispered to Flora as they climbed the steps. "This is as fresh as I'm ever going to be. And as for the 'journey,' we easily could have walked here."

The maid opened the door to a beautifully decorated sitting room. The flowered wallpaper complemented the fabric on the divan, which matched the luxurious drapes covering the windows. It felt suffocating. On the dresser below a gilded mirror lay an array of toiletries for their use. "May I help you with anything?" the maid asked.

"No, thank you," Rebecca replied, then quickly stopped the girl again. Servants were often a great source of gossip and secret information—especially disgruntled ones. Rebecca was determined to uncover the truth about the widow. "Wait . . . what's your name?"

"It's Mary, miss."

"And how long have you worked for Mrs. Worthington, Mary?"

The girl stared down at her feet, as if expecting them to detach from her legs. "I don't work for her, miss. I work for Mr. and Mrs. Charles Worthington."

"Did they loan you to her for the evening?"

She looked up in confusion. "No . . . this home belongs to them—to Mr. and Mrs. Worthington, I mean. They're still in France."

"But I thought Priscilla Worthington lives here. This is her dinner party, isn't it?"

"Mrs. Worthington had to move here after her husband died. Mr. Worthington is her brother-in-law." The maid edged toward the door. "If there's nothing else, miss, I should go." She fled, closing the door behind her.

"See? Just as I suspected!" Rebecca tossed her shawl on the chair where the other ladies had placed theirs. "The widow is destitute, and she's trying to marry Father for his money. We need to warn him—" She stopped when she turned to Flora, surprised to see she was in tears. "Flora, what's wrong?"

"I'm so mortified! Father looks distinguished in his formal attire, but I feel like a weed among roses in this dress." She lifted a pleat of fabric from her well-worn traveling dress and let it drop again. She and Flora didn't own any fancy silk gowns, just simple cottons and gabardines that traveled well. They always wore uniforms to school.

"Listen, you look very nice. But did you hear what the maid said about the widow?"

"I don't look nice! Didn't you see the gowns those other girls are wearing?"

Rebecca shook her head. "I didn't notice. I was distracted by the neckline on Widow Worthington's dress and by the way she latched onto Father like a poison-ivy vine. He seems much too eager to become her trellis. Now that we know she's poor, we need to warn him—"

"We look horribly out of place here, Becky. The other girls are all dressed in the latest styles with petticoats and hoop skirts—and look at us!"

"Who needs clumsy old hoops? Those girls can barely squeeze through a doorway wearing those stupid things, much less sit down comfortably. If they fell over they would never get up again."

"We look so drab and plain in comparison."

"They probably have lady's maids to lace them into their corsets and button them into their clothes and arrange their hair. And they have—" She started to say, *mothers to guide and advise them and take them shopping*, but she stopped herself in time. Besides, Flora wasn't listening.

"And look at my hair! It's so plain! All I ever do is yank it straight back, braid it, and pin the braid on my head. I look like that starchy old German woman who used to march around the deck of the ship every day."

Rebecca stifled a giggle. It was true, the woman had worn her hair the same way they did. "Never mind," she said, wrapping her arm around her sister's shoulders. "I'm quite sure that you're smarter than both of those hoop-skirted girls put together."

"But I don't want to be smart," she wailed. "Just once in my life I would like to be pretty!"

"You are pretty, Flora. Here, look in the mirror." She spun her around to face it. "See? You're slender and dainty and you have a lovely face with captivating eyes. They're dark and mysterious, like a Spaniard's. Mine are washed-out blue."

"You're pretty, too—" Flora started to say, but Rebecca interrupted her.

"Nonsense. The mirror tells me otherwise. Now, listen. If those people downstairs are going to judge us by our hair and our clothing, then they aren't worth our time. You and I are interesting young ladies, and if they can't see that, it's their loss."

"I suppose you're right . . . but I still feel embarrassed."

Rebecca studied her sister's fair hair, pulled back tightly from her face. "Why don't you use the comb to pull a few of those dangly, tendril things loose like the widow always does?"

"Won't that make my hair look messy?"

"In my opinion, yes. But what do I know? All the other girls seem to have them hanging around their eyes." Flora took the comb and loosened a few strands, making her face look even softer and prettier than before. Rebecca felt a stab of jealousy.

"Want me to loosen yours?" Flora said when she was finished.

"No, thanks. It would drive me crazy to have wisps of hair hanging in my eyes all evening. Are you ready?" Flora nodded. Rebecca opened the door then halted in the hallway. "Listen, I could pretend to be sick so Father will have to take us home. Then we can warn him—"

"No, don't do that. It would be rude after all the trouble the widow went through to plan this dinner for us." Flora straightened her spine, brushed imaginary wrinkles from her dress, and put on her prettiest smile. The fact that Flora wasn't concerned about the widow's trickery and didn't want to leave seemed like very bad omens to Rebecca. Flora was becoming entrapped in the widow's sticky web along with their father. This couldn't end well.

"If you change your mind, I can always vomit on cue,"

Rebecca whispered when they reached the bottom of the stairs. Flora shook her head, her newly released tendrils fluttering prettily.

Rebecca couldn't recall a more excruciating evening. She milled around the drawing room with her sister, sipping from a tiny cup of punch, and met the widow's uninteresting relatives, including a cousin and his wife and a collection of nieces and nephews who were conveniently close in age to Rebecca and Flora. The widow, it seemed, had never had any children of her own. The spacious parlor felt suffocating to Rebecca, crammed with furniture and knickknacks and bronze statues, and swathed in heavy draperies like a funeral home. Even the artwork was drab and boring—just like the conversation. No one talked about anything relevant such as the upcoming presidential election, the fight over the abolition of slavery, or the simmering political unrest between the northern and southern states. Father had seemed very concerned about all of those things when reading the newspaper at home, but none of the other guests were. Desperate for a stimulating topic of conversation, Rebecca brought up the novel *Uncle Tom's Cabin*, hoping to discuss it with the other girls her age. But they were much more interested in discussing fashions.

"I heard you recently returned from France," one of the girls said. "You must tell us what the women in Paris are wearing. Are bustles still in fashion over there? And hoop skirts?"

"I really didn't notice. I was captivated by the wonderful artwork we saw in the Louvre, painted by all the great masters."

"And the Egyptian collection, too," Flora added. "We saw an ancient obelisk covered with hieroglyphics and learned how the museum's curator, Monsieur Champollion, used the Rosetta Stone to decipher them." Rebecca saw their blank stares and knew her sister may as well have been speaking Egyptian. Rebecca was considering her earlier plan to escape by vomiting or perhaps fainting when one of the widow's nephews appeared at her side. What was his name again?

"The dinner gong has chimed," he said. "Aunt Priscilla asked me to escort you to the table." He gestured to the dining room door a dozen steps away.

"Thanks, but tell her I can find it myself. After all, I've just been traveling all over Europe." She meant it as a joke, but his unsmiling face wore a pained expression as he offered his arm—as if she were too frail to walk without support. When they reached the table, he held out her chair for her to be seated, then took a seat beside her. Rebecca wondered if he was going to cut up her meat for her, too. She hoped her sister would sit on her other side so she wouldn't feel so out-of-place, but another of the widow's nephews sat down on her left. Flora, who'd been escorted by a third nephew, was sitting too far away for Rebecca to talk to without leaning forward and raising her voice, which she knew was impolite. She wracked her brain for her escort's name and remembered it was Frederick.

"So tell me, Freddy. What else do you do when you aren't escorting damsels in distress to the dinner table?"

He made no attempt to smile, even politely. "I'll be returning to my studies at Yale University this fall."

Rebecca felt a pang of jealousy. Why did men get to study at wonderful universities like Yale while women didn't? She nearly asked that question out loud but was interrupted as the footman placed her fish course in front of her. There was enough silverware surrounding her plate for a week's worth of meals. Where to begin? She waited to see which utensil Freddy used. "What do you plan to do after you graduate?" she asked, imitating his silverware choice.

"Practice law, I think. I understand that's what your father does. I had a very interesting conversation with him before dinner."

"My pre-dinner conversation was about whether or not hoop skirts were in fashion in Paris."

He didn't blink an eye, continuing as if she hadn't spoken. "I understand your father is a brilliant investor. I would love to learn more about it from him."

"So you can make piles of money? Is that your life's goal?" Freddy chose not to respond, so Rebecca dutifully ate her fish and waited for the next course to be served. It was oysters, which evidently required a different utensil. She decided to break the silence after watching Freddy choose the proper fork to attack his oysters. "Father, Flora, and I saw the Rosetta Stone in the British Museum in London, where they also had some of the amazing artifacts that Henry Layard discovered in the Middle East. The Louvre has some Assyrian finds, too, but of course the Egyptian collection from the Valley of the Kings was the *piece de resistance*." She wasn't trying to baffle him or even impress him. She simply longed to find someone to talk with who was as fascinated by these ancient archaeological discoveries as she was. Instead, his unresponsiveness told her he wasn't interested.

Rebecca leaned forward, not caring if it was impolite, to see how her sister was faring. Maybe it was time to start choking on a piece of roast beef. But Flora was doing splendidly from the looks of things, talking animatedly with the two young men on either side of her. Judging by her delighted laughter, she had found something of common interest to talk about.

Rebecca's jaw ached from stifling her yawns long before the dessert course was served. After dinner she endured a painful piano recital by the widow's two nieces, neither of whom had a sense of rhythm. More socializing followed. It was impossible to get Father alone so she could tell him the truth about the widow. But when Rebecca heard her father laughing—laughing!—she truly did feel nauseous. It was the longest evening of her life.

The moment they settled into their carriage for the ride home,

Rebecca turned to her father. "Did you know that Mrs. Worthington doesn't own that house? It's her brother-in-law's. She had to move there after her husband died, and that means—"

"Yes, I know. She told me."

His words stopped Rebecca short. "She did?"

"Of course. But I don't see how it's any of our business."

His words were a rebuke. Rebecca didn't dare say another word until they'd returned home and she and Flora had retired to their bedroom for the night. "What a dreadful evening," she said, collapsing onto her bed. "That scheming widow has bewitched our father. The conversation was boring, the music ghastly, and I came this close to fainting just to escape from dreary Frederick." She held her thumb and forefinger an inch apart. "We need to have a meeting with Father as soon as possible. There are a few things we need to discuss with him."

"I agree," Flora replied. "We need to tell him we want new dresses. And a maid who can arrange our hair properly."

"Our *hair*? What has gotten into you, Flora? Have you been swallowing the widow's powders, too?"

"What do you mean? Isn't that what you want to talk to Father about?"

"Hardly! I want to warn him that the widow is after his money. I want to beg him to let us change schools this fall and find one that teaches us fabulous things like ancient history and Greek. Don't you?"

"I suppose so. . . ."

Rebecca tried to raise the subject of the widow's financial circumstances the following evening after dinner, but her father cut her off again. "It's none of your business, Rebecca. Let it go." Frustrated, she changed the subject to her disappointment with her school. Flora chimed in about needing a new gown. "Give me a week to look into it," Father replied. "I still have a lot of work to catch up with after being away for two months."

The meeting he convened a week later had the widow's sticky fingerprints all over it. This time he ushered them into his library, and they sat in the leather chairs facing his desk like two disgruntled employees while he puffed his cigar. The tobacco's sweet aroma hung in the air between them. "I'm sorry that you've never had a mother to advise you all these years," he began, "but I've spoken with Mrs. Worthington, and she has very kindly agreed to provide you with the guidance that has been lacking."

"What are we lacking?" Rebecca blurted. "We're both at the top of our classes at school, we're independent and mature for our age—"

"She feels you need help with manners and grooming and feminine deportment. I've heard similar concerns from your head-mistress over the years, so perhaps it's time we address them." He took a puff from his cigar and added, "Mrs. Worthington is also going to help you make the social connections you'll need in the coming years."

Rebecca felt like the library walls were collapsing on top of her, burying her beneath her father's volumes of classical literature. "I promise I'll read any book on manners that the widow recommends. In fact, I'll read a dozen books. But what I want most of all is to change to a better school."

"Mrs. Worthington assures me that the school you currently attend is one of the finest in Chicago for preparing young ladies."

"Preparing them for what? Not for using their brains, certainly."

"She feels that you may have trouble finding proper husbands in the future if you're what society calls 'bluestockings'—women who have been overeducated."

Rebecca was struck dumb. She slumped back in her chair as if the wind had been knocked out of her. In the silence that followed, Flora asked, "Is Mrs. Worthington going to help us choose new gowns?"

"Yes. I've invited her to call on you tomorrow afternoon while I'm at the office to begin the process."

Flora appeared thrilled. "That's wonderful, Father. Thank you."

"Traitor . . ." Rebecca mumbled.

"Hmm? What's that?" Father asked.

"Is your goal for us to marry rich husbands, settle down, and have children?"

He paused, exhaling a cloud of cigar smoke before saying, "It does seem to be what's best for you."

"But I would like to attend university after graduation. I know I'll have to find one that accepts women, and I know that professions like law and medicine are probably closed to me, but the more I learn, the more I want to study. Haven't you always told us we need to find God's purpose for our life? What if that doesn't include marriage?"

"Nevertheless, I would like the foundation for finding a good husband to be in place. Mrs. Worthington offered to help me with that." He grew pensive for a moment as he tapped ash from his cigar. Then he gazed intently from one of them to the other. Rebecca held her breath, fearing he was about to announce his engagement to the widow. "While we were overseas, an important client of mine passed away. He had no heirs, and he has made me the executor and one of the beneficiaries of his sizeable estate. His unfortunate passing has reminded me that I may not always be around for you girls. It would ease my heart to know you're well taken care of by fine husbands."

"I'll do whatever you'd like, Father," Flora said, standing and reaching across the desk to squeeze his hand. "We want you in our lives for many years to come."

And in that poignant moment, Rebecca felt she had little choice but to concede to his wishes, too.

⤜ ⤛

Widow Worthington swept into their foyer the following afternoon and gazed around at their stately home the way a starving man eyes a banquet table. The house no doubt had been lovely when Father built it sixteen years ago, but the furnishings looked shabby and out-of-date compared to the ones Rebecca had seen in the overly decorated home of the widow's brother. Mrs. Worthington had a look of glee in her eyes, as if she couldn't wait to get her hands on the house—using Father's abundant wealth, of course. "I've begun the process of hiring a lady's maid for you girls," she began after they were seated in the seldom-used drawing room. The servants had removed the furniture covers for the occasion and motes of dust still danced in the sunlight after being disturbed. "I've already arranged for several candidates to be interviewed and—"

"You mean by Flora and me?" Rebecca asked.

"No, I'll be doing the interviewing myself. . . . I have an excellent seamstress who is waiting to work on your new gowns once we take your measurements and choose the patterns. You'll need morning dresses for making and receiving calls, as well as evening dresses for parties and dinners and social events. You'll also need what we call a walking dress for shopping or traveling, something not too colorful or vulgar. We'll shop together for accessories such as gloves and bonnets and shoes for every occasion."

Rebecca closed her eyes. She felt weary and the widow was just getting started. "You must each have a scent," she continued. "A memorable one that's associated only with you. Men love perfume. Your scent will remind him of you so you'll captivate him and fill his thoughts."

68

You mean gag him so he can't breathe, Rebecca wanted to say. The servants would have to open all the windows to air out the sitting room after the widow and her memorable scent departed.

"My stationer is already printing calling cards for each of you. Once you've learned how to conduct yourselves and dress properly for social occasions, we'll plan an event here in your home, so you can learn to be gracious hostesses. You'll need to learn poise along with all of the other social graces. I'll teach you how to manage servants, run a home, and entertain your future husband's guests."

Flora appeared entranced, sitting on the edge of her seat like a lap dog waiting for her master's whistle. "They already teach us many of those things at school, and—"

"And those classes bore us to death," Rebecca interrupted. "Be honest, Flora. We've laughed at how stupid those classes are."

The widow gave Rebecca a long-suffering look, then continued as if she hadn't spoken. "I noticed that you both looked uncomfortable at times during dinner last week. But I can teach you how to be an attentive listener and to contribute demurely to the conversation."

"But I would much rather contribute intelligently to the conversation," Rebecca said.

"That isn't important right now, Rebecca."

"It is to me," she mumbled as she slouched back in her seat.

"We'll be discussing proper posture, as well," the widow added. Rebecca wanted to scream.

She managed to control herself for the rest of the long afternoon until the widow finally left, promising to return for the many future lessons they would certainly require. "Do you really want to learn all those worthless things?" Rebecca asked her sister when they were alone. "Do you want to be an exact reproduction of Widow Worthington, or would you rather become your true self?"

They had returned to their upstairs bedroom where Flora stood gazing in dismay at the dresses hanging inside their wardrobe, probably dreaming of all the new ones she soon would own. "Father does seem to have his heart set on us becoming proper ladies," she replied. "I want to please him."

"Nonsense! The widow has cast some sort of spell over him, making him think this is what's best for us. It isn't! I refuse to believe that God gave us brains and curiosity and a love for learning so we could talk demurely at dinner parties and sit with proper posture."

Flora slowly closed the wardrobe doors and turned to face her. "Maybe we can do both, Becky. Why can't we learn to be proper ladies and still continue our studies?"

"The widow will never allow it. She says we'll never find proper husbands if we're bluestockings. But I don't want a proper husband if he won't let me be myself. I want to marry someone who loves learning and travel as much as I do, don't you? Tell me the truth, Flora, and I'll never bother you again—do you honestly believe you could live the way the widow does for the rest of your life? Would you be happy with a man who doesn't respect your God-given intelligence and is only interested in a wife who is a pretty adornment on his arm?"

"I think we should at least try to learn what Mrs. Worthington is teaching us, for Father's sake. We can study all the other things we want to on our own. Besides, we have several more years to decide what our futures will be, don't we?"

In the end, Rebecca gave in. She would learn to be a lady to please her father and because Flora wanted to be one. But for every concession she made, Rebecca vowed to present a demand of her own. She held negotiations at one of Father's after-dinner meetings in his library a week later. "Mrs. Worthington believes you would benefit from dancing lessons," he began.

"I'll agree provided we can also take horseback riding lessons."

"Horseback riding? What on earth for?"

"We'll need to know how to manage a horse for some of our overseas travels. The lost city of Petra is in the middle of nowhere."

"I'll have Rufus look into lessons for you," he said. "You should know that Mrs. Worthington has also arranged a private piano tutor for you."

"Fine. As long as you hire a Greek tutor, too. Flora and I are hoping you'll take us to Greece next summer."

He sighed in resignation and tamped out his cigar. "Very well."

"And one more thing, Father. Flora and I aren't getting enough physical exercise. We need to be able to climb the pyramids and explore the more remote parts of the world. Could you arrange to install some exercise bars in our backyard?"

"I'll ask Mrs. Worthington what she thinks."

"Please don't. She's trying to turn us into dainty maidens who can't walk ten steps without feeling faint and reaching for the smelling salts. Flora and I are healthy and strong, and we want to stay that way. We're doing everything else the widow wants us to do, so please let us have this one thing. . . . Please?"

"Exercise equipment?"

"Yes! Remember the story in the Bible about Daniel and his friends? The king wanted them to eat his food, but they refused, and they ended up healthier than all of the others. Let us do a few things our way—please, Father?"

"Very well. I'll install exercise equipment in the back garden. I hope that's all."

Rebecca gave him her sweetest smile. "Yes, Father . . . for now."

Mrs. Worthington's weekly etiquette lessons in their dusty

drawing room were filled with taboos: Don't eat too quickly; never eat every morsel on your plate; avoid making large gestures at the table; don't stand with your hands on your hips or your arms folded; never read in company. She insisted that shopping was one of a woman's highest callings, and she spent hours teaching them how to do it. Rebecca endured the shopping treks, along with the dress fittings, dancing lessons, and piano lessons, but the highlights of her week were her riding lessons at a nearby equestrian stable that Rufus found for them and her Greek studies with a wild-haired scholar named Professor Vasilakis. The professor was teaching them to read classical Greek works such as Homer, but he was also teaching them modern Greek phrases and pronunciations so they could visit Greece next summer. When the city grew cold and snowy, Rebecca and Flora planned their traveling itinerary in great detail.

Then everything changed.

In November of that year, 1860, Abraham Lincoln won the presidential election and seven southern states seceded from the Union. Then, on a sunny morning in April of 1861, Rebecca awoke to the news that the Confederate States had bombarded Union troops at Fort Sumter, forcing their surrender. "What does this mean?" she asked her father, who was grimly reading the latest edition of the newspaper.

He folded it carefully and laid it on the table. "It means that war has broken out between the states. I was afraid this would happen."

"Will it be over by June? In time for us to sail to Greece?"

He shook his head. "I'm sorry, but we'll have to postpone our plans. My investments and business affairs are going to require my full attention until this is over."

"What if you hired a chaperone to accompany us?"

"I'm sorry, but it may not be safe to travel abroad with a war going on."

Rebecca didn't cry easily, but she wanted to now. "We can still travel a year from now, can't we? The war won't last that long, will it?"

"I don't imagine it will. A matter of months—a year at the most. But I could be wrong."

He was.

CHAPTER 6

THE SINAI DESERT
1890

Sometime during the night, the sandstorm blew itself out, replaced by a profound silence. The sun hadn't dawned yet when Rebecca awoke from a nightmare that included Flora and Widow Worthington. She listened to the muffled sound of activity outside the tent as the Bedouins loaded the camels and prepared to break camp to continue the journey. The aroma of kerosene and baking bread wafted inside. She dressed as quietly as possible so as not to awaken Flora and Kate, pulling on her skirt and shirtwaist over her bloomers and camisole. Sand crunched on the tent floor beneath her feet as she slipped into her sturdy boots and jacket. Rebecca untied the tent flap and ducked outside, then stumbled backward, startled. The Bedouin sheikh sat on a rocky outcropping not five feet in front of her tent, cradling his ancient rifle.

"Oh, my goodness!" she said, clutching her racing heart. "I wasn't expecting to find you on my doorstep!" The sheikh's hawklike face showed no emotion at all as he stared past her at the tent. He was a formidable-looking man, like a villain from a dime novel, and he gripped his rifle as if guarding an important dignitary. Rebecca regained her footing and walked to where their cook was baking flatbread on the camp stove.

Petersen, their young butler, was also up and dressed and preparing the folding camp table for breakfast. He hurried over when he saw Rebecca and greeted her with a bow. "Good morning, Miss Rebecca. Your tea is brewing. I hope you and Miss Flora were able to sleep through the storm."

"Yes, we slept well enough, in the end. How about you?"

He gave another bow. "Don't worry about me, Miss Rebecca." She'd told Petersen countless times that he needn't be so formal with her and Flora and that his deferential bow was completely unnecessary, especially out here in the desert. Her words had done nothing to change his behavior, however. She spread her hands near the stove to warm them while Petersen located a cup and saucer and the tea strainer. She'd also told him repeatedly that he needn't wait on her, but also to no effect. He handed her a cup of blissfully strong tea, then smoothly produced a folding camp stool for her to sit on.

Soren Petersen was as tall and thin as a birch tree, and very, very blond. It was proving to be quite a task to keep his pale skin covered during the day so the desert sun didn't turn it as red as a pomegranate. Their agent, Mr. Farouk, had purchased a flowing white robe and burnoose for Petersen to wear over his clothing, but instead of transforming him into a Bedouin, the clothing had the amusing effect of making him look like a ghost. Petersen may have been thin, but he was quite fit and strong. Rebecca had seen him doing chin-ups on the exercise bars in their backyard when he thought no one was looking. She entrusted only him to lift and move her heavy camera equipment.

"Why don't you pour yourself a cup and join me, Soren?" She deliberately used his given name from time to time, hoping to break through his icy exterior and unearth the real Soren

Petersen beneath his reserve, but her attempts at warmth only seemed to make him grumpier. She often wondered if his chilly demeanor was a remnant of his Scandinavian heritage, or if it had been formed within the cold, gray walls of the Chicago Orphan Asylum. "Please, Soren. Sit down," she said when he hesitated. "I could use some company this morning. That's an order." She added the last to ensure he would do it, though she hated to.

"Yes, Miss Rebecca." He dragged over a crate to sit on and filled a battered tin cup with tea. The steam rose from both cups in the chilly air.

"Don't you find it amazing that the fickle desert temperatures can go from frying-pan hot during the day to teeth-chattering cold during the night?" she asked.

"Yes, Miss Rebecca." Petersen didn't look or sound at all amazed.

"Have you ever experienced weather like this, with such extreme temperatures and violent sandstorms?"

"No, Miss Rebecca."

She watched Mr. Farouk scuttle around the campsite like a worker ant, yanking out stakes from the tent where he and Petersen had slept, piling their bedding and traveling supplies beside the load of goods and foodstuffs that would be strapped to the camels. Mr. Farouk reminded Rebecca of a beetle with his short, spindly legs, round body and shiny, dark hair. He and Soren were two entirely different breeds of men, as different as a wolfhound and a dachshund. She looked up at the fading stars and stark panorama slowly becoming visible in the dawning light. "After last night's storm, I think I understand why these mountains are so bleak and barren. The wind and sand must scour them clean like a bristle broom on a brick pavement."

"So it seems, Miss Rebecca."

"What do you make of the desert, so far? Do you see any beauty here at all?"

"No, Miss Rebecca." Conversing with Petersen reminded her of the tedious process of drawing water from a well she'd once encountered in the Holy Land. The water had been hundreds of feet below ground, and the only way to get to it was to descend into a deep pit on narrow stone stairs that circled around and around until they eventually reached the bottom. Once there, she had to lower a bucket and rope even deeper into the ground to reach the water. By the time she finished, she was thirstier than when she began. Talking with Petersen seemed equally tedious, and she wondered if it was worth the effort.

"Do you have any idea why the sheikh is standing guard over our tent this morning?" she asked, blowing on her tea to cool it.

"No, Miss Rebecca. He was sitting there this morning when I got up."

She watched the Bedouin drivers hurry through their chores, feeding their camels and brushing off the thick layer of sand that coated the saddles and everything else that had been left outside during the night. Rebecca hoped the sand hadn't damaged her camera or the lenses. The sheikh stood up from his vigil near her tent and studied the eastern sky as the stars gradually faded in the dawning light. At his command, all of the men, including Mr. Farouk and the cook, dropped their work and unrolled their prayer rugs to kneel down and pray. They repeated this ritual five times a day: before dawn, when they paused for lunch, when they rested mid-afternoon, before sunset, and for a final time before bedding down for the night.

"What do you make of their devotion, Petersen? Have you noticed how they pause to pray five times a day, every single day?"

Petersen took so long to reply that Rebecca wasn't at all sure he would. "I think they're wasting their time," he said at last.

"Hmm . . . Do you mean to say that all prayer is a waste of

time? Or is it a waste because they're not praying to the God of the Bible?"

Petersen stared down at the cup in his hands, slowly turning it around and around as if to keep the hot metal from burning his skin. He had long, graceful fingers—artist's hands—although he wasn't the least bit imaginative or artistic as far as Rebecca could tell. He had faithfully attended church with her and Flora ever since becoming their butler two years ago, but he'd given no indication during that time whether he believed a word of it or not. Rebecca had longed to question him—she'd grown fond of the young man and worried about his eternal soul—but Flora insisted they be patient with him. He would reveal what he thought and believed in his own time, she'd said. Even so, Rebecca had decided to take advantage of this moment to ask his opinion as they watched the Bedouin perform their morning prayers.

"I don't know," Petersen finally replied. "What do you think of their religion, Miss Rebecca?"

"Well, they are correct in believing there is only one God, not many. But after hearing the Muslims describe what their god is like and what he requires of believers, I must conclude that they don't know the same God I do."

Petersen's ice-blue eyes met hers for a moment, as if asking for an explanation.

"Look at it this way," she said. "Suppose I asked, 'Do you know John Smith?' and you said, 'Yes, I know him very well.' But then as we talked about John, and I described him as being tall and thin with red hair, and you said, 'No, you're quite wrong. John is short and fat and bald,' wouldn't it be clear that we aren't acquainted with the same John Smith?"

"It seems so, miss."

"Their god is quite different from ours. Nevertheless," she said, gesturing to the bowing men, "we Christians would do well to stop what we're doing and pray throughout the day as they do, don't you think? After all, the Apostle Paul did counsel us to pray without ceasing. But back to my question, Petersen. Do you think all prayer is a waste—?"

"Good morning, good morning!" Flora's cheery voice interrupted before Rebecca could finish. "My, just look at that sunrise. What a glorious sight!" She pointed to where the pre-dawn sun was painting the sky with wide brushstrokes of pink and mauve. "And we didn't get buried alive in the sand last night after all, so we have a lot to be thankful for this morning, don't we?"

"Yes, Miss Flora." Petersen had leaped to his feet at the sound of her voice and was hurrying to fetch a folding stool and cup of tea for her. When she was seated, he carefully lifted the camp table with the breakfast that the cook had prepared and placed it between Rebecca and Flora.

"Thank you, Petersen. This looks wonderful," Flora said. "You're welcome to sit down and eat with us, you know. No need for formality out here in the Sinai Desert."

"I must pack your things, Miss Flora." He opened the pot of date honey for her when he saw her struggling with it, then said, "Shouldn't your lady's maid be helping you?"

Flora smiled up at him. "I'm letting Kate sleep a little longer, the poor dear. The storm kept her awake last night."

"It kept all of us awake, miss. She is no exception." Petersen looked as if he would like to throw back the flap and yank the sleeping maid from her cot. Instead, he gave a little bow and silently picked up the crate he'd been sitting on, stomping off with it so Kate would have no place to sit when she did get up. Rebecca saw him rounding up all the other camp stools, too, and stacking them near the tethered camels, aware that Kate wouldn't go near the cantankerous animals by herself. He returned to the tent and carried the bulky photography equipment to the waiting caravan as well, then did the same with his neatly rolled bedding and traveling bag.

"Why do you suppose Petersen hates Kate so much?" Rebecca asked as Flora passed her the date honey. The sticky syrup tasted wonderful drizzled on the cook's freshly-baked flatbread.

"He doesn't hate her. Hate is such a strong word. But I do wonder if he might be a trifle jealous of her, don't you think?"

"You mean because he had us all to himself for more than a year before we took in Kate?"

"Yes. And because she came to us for quite different reasons than he did. He hasn't trusted Kate since the day she robbed us."

"Petersen does have a very rigid sense of what crime and punishment should entail," Rebecca replied. "I think he would have preferred that we send Kate to jail. Or to some dark, dank prison. Even to the gallows. I believe he still would prefer it."

"I don't think it's as bad as all that. Petersen is very protective of you and me, that's all. It's his nature. He can't help himself."

"Who says we need protection?" Rebecca said, frowning. "Haven't the two of us done just fine all these years? When have we ever been afraid to travel by ourselves?"

Flora smiled. "You're right, Becky. We're quite fearless, aren't we? We don't need Petersen, and we really don't need Kate, either. No one needs a lady's maid or a butler in the Sinai Desert." She laughed and leaned closer to add, "The truth is, Kate and Soren need *us*. Isn't that why we brought them along?"

Rebecca took another bite of bread. "Yes, but those poor dears had no idea what they'd volunteered for, did they?" She and Flora were still laughing when Kate crawled out of the tent looking cross and bedraggled, her red hair tangled from sleeping.

"What's so funny?" she asked, folding her arms across her chest. She packed enough fire and grit to fill a girl three times her size. Rebecca thought of the lessons in grooming and ladylike deportment that Mrs. Worthington had once tried to drum into her, and she smiled at the irony of their erstwhile lady's maid needing a lady's maid herself.

"We're simply enjoying the morning," Flora said. "And this wonderful date honey. Come and have some with us."

"I'm not hungry."

"Oh, but you will be later on. We have another long journey ahead of us today."

Kate huffed and rolled her eyes. "How do those stupid camel drivers even know where they're going?"

"Now, you mustn't call people stupid, Katie, dear," Flora said, wagging her finger.

"Look at this place!" she continued, undeterred. "There's nothing but rocks and more rocks! No roads or signs to mark the way, just miles and miles of nothing! What if we've been lost all along, and they don't want to admit it? How do we even know we're going in the right direction? Who knows where they're taking us?"

"You're right, we don't know any of those things," Rebecca said. "We simply have to trust them and Mr. Farouk."

Kate threw her arms in the air. "Well, that's just great! We could all die out here, and nobody would even know or care!"

She would be pretty, Rebecca thought, *if she weren't as bristly as a wire brush.* "Have some tea, dear. There must be another cup around here someplace." She heard a whooshing sound and turned to see that Petersen had pulled down the center pole of his tent, causing it to collapse with a rush of air. He emerged from beneath the canvas with the pole in his hand, looking as though he would like to beat Kate over the head with it.

"There you are," he growled. "It's about time. Is everything packed inside your tent? We need to start moving before the sun gets too hot."

She glared at him, her chin raised in defiance. "Pack it yourself if you're in such a hurry."

"That's your job, Kate. One they pay you very well to do, remember?"

She huffed in disgust. "I'd rather work in the shirtwaist factory again than with you!" She whirled around and stalked back to the tent.

"That factory probably fired you!" Petersen called after her. "Probably for good reason!" Kate disappeared inside, hurling the tent flap closed as if slamming a door. A shower of sand cascaded from the sloping roof. "I know it may not be my place to say this," Petersen said as he watched her go, "but she shouldn't be so disrespectful."

"You're absolutely right," Rebecca said with a smile. "Perhaps we should send her home immediately. All by herself. Across the desert."

"It would serve her right, Miss Rebecca."

"Actually, I think she would prefer to go home," Flora added with a laugh.

Rebecca heard men shouting and stood to see what was going on. The Bedouin had finished their prayers, and the sheikh and Mr. Farouk were embroiled in an argument. The sheikh gestured wildly as if he was about to knock the little man over like a bowling pin. But what worried Rebecca was that he kept pointing to her tent and waving his rifle. She hurried toward them, but the sheikh stalked away before she reached him. "What's going on, Mr. Farouk?" she asked the little agent.

"Is nothing, miss. Not to worry."

"I clearly heard you arguing. And why was the sheikh sitting outside my tent this morning with his rifle?"

"Not to worry. I take care over him." He bowed repeatedly as he backed away, hurrying off to help the drivers finish loading the caravan. In their haste, the men tied one of the crates of chickens upside down, and there was a furious squawking and flapping of feathers as the birds righted themselves. One of the drivers helped Rebecca climb aboard the crouching camel, and it swayed to its feet, pitching her backward momentarily as it straightened its front legs, then leveling out again as it rose on its rear legs. This was nothing at all like riding a horse. For one thing, Rebecca sat perched ridiculously high above the ground. And camels were much grumpier than horses. No one could possibly make friends with one, she suspected, even their own drivers. The swaying motion as they walked reminded her of sailing on a very stormy sea. Poor Father would undoubtedly become seasick riding one. And camels smelled much worse than horses, too. Even so, she and Flora were accustomed to riding them, having done so on their travels in the past. Petersen and Kate were having a much harder time, especially since they didn't have a goal to accomplish at the end of their journey as she did. The anticipation of discovery, the joy of uncovering a long-hidden mystery, didn't beckon to them the way it did Rebecca.

They traveled for about an hour before Rebecca found Kate riding alongside her and she decided to chat with the girl. "May I ask you something, Kate? You mentioned this morning that you wished you still worked in the shirtwaist factory instead of for Flora and me. I know firsthand how horrific the working conditions are in those places, so I wondered, are you truly that unhappy with us? Because if so, I want to apologize for dragging you along. Flora and I tried to prepare you for what you might face out here, and I thought we made it very clear that you were free to stay home in Chicago, if you wished. We wanted it to be your choice whether or not you came with us."

"I know, I know. It's my own fault for saying yes," she grudgingly replied.

"May I ask what made you decide to come?"

"I figured it couldn't be any worse than staying in the city, living on the streets." She gave a short laugh. "Shows how wrong I was! I didn't guess it would be like this." She gestured to the endless hills, barren and brown and as wrinkled as an old potato.

"I'm sorry, Kate. I'm sure you've already been through a great deal in your life. Flora and I never intended to add more hardship to it."

"I got no complaints with you and Miss Flora. . . . I can't say the same about Petersen, though."

"He's just doing his job."

She gave a sigh, as enormous as the cloudless sky. "It's just that . . . I don't know. . . . Never mind . . ."

"Talk to me, Kate. You can tell me anything you want. We have all day."

It took the girl a long time to reply, and when she did, her voice sounded tiny and subdued, not at all like the brash Kate Rafferty that Rebecca knew. "I feel so lost out here. And every step of the way, as we get farther and farther from home, I feel even more lost. Everything's so . . . different! I can take care of myself just fine back in Chicago. I don't need nobody else. But out here I feel . . . small."

"We do need each other out here, don't we? We especially need Mr. Farouk and the Bedouin."

"Well, I don't like it. I don't like depending on nobody but myself. How do we know we can trust them? And the sheikh keeps staring at me."

Rebecca couldn't imagine what Kate had suffered in her short life to so thoroughly destroy her trust in people, making her unwilling to depend on anyone but herself. "Mr. Farouk was recommended to us by the Archbishop of Cairo," Rebecca replied. "He comes with the highest credentials. But you're right, we really don't know if we can trust any of these men. Yet we serve a God who is completely trustworthy, and Flora and I believe He is leading us on this expedition. We're His servants, just as you and Petersen are ours. We're obeying orders, just like you do."

Kate didn't reply. Rebecca glanced over and saw her hunched on the swaying animal with her chin lowered. Her straw hat was swathed in gauzy linen to protect her from the sun, so Rebecca couldn't see her face. She wondered if Kate was crying. For as long as Rebecca had known her, Kate Rafferty had never cried. The poor child was as out of place here as the swarthy Bedouin would be on the streets of Chicago. "Are you okay?" Rebecca asked.

"Yeah," she sniffed. "I just don't like feeling small."

"I understand. . . . But just think what you would have missed if you had stayed behind. You never would have seen the vastness of the ocean, or tasted the salty air, or experienced the mighty power of the waves. You wouldn't have met people from other countries and cultures, sampled their food, and discovered how wonderfully different we all are. You never would have seen mountains or palm trees or crocodiles on the Nile River . . . or ridden on a camel. You can bring all of those memories home with you and keep them for as long as you live. You might lose all your possessions, as Flora and I once did, but no one can ever take your memories away from you."

"That goes for the bad ones, too, though."

Her response jolted Rebecca. Such a negative outlook for someone so young. "Maybe by the time we return home," she said gently, "all your bad memories will have been buried beneath a pile of new ones."

"If we ever do make it home again," Kate mumbled.

Rebecca started to reply, then let it go. Flora had advised her not to try to change Kate or Petersen but to let the Almighty do His work. With a long day ahead of her, Rebecca decided to dig deep into her storehouse of memories again, traveling backward through time as she had during the night, to relive some of her many experiences—the good ones and the bad.

CHAPTER 7

The War Between the States raged on with no end in sight as Rebecca turned seventeen. She and her sister were now firmly entrapped in Mrs. Worthington's webs of etiquette and propriety and social obligation. They attended dinner parties and dances with young men and women who looked at Rebecca strangely whenever she tried to talk about topics that interested her. The world she was being stuffed inside of felt much too small.

Everything around her was changing. The widow also hired decorators who turned their peaceful home from a place of quiet study and rest into a house of bedlam with workmen renovating rooms, moving furniture, and installing draperies. Even the servants had been forced to learn how to bow and curtsy and greet guests properly. Griffin, their butler, looked uncomfortable answering the door in formalwear. Mrs. Griffin, their housekeeper, always seemed to have her white cap askew and stains on her new ruffled white apron. Rebecca hoped she was doing it on purpose. Their driver, Rufus, looked like a cartoon character in his polished boots and fancy livery. They surely must want their old life back as badly as Rebecca did.

At times, she thought her life couldn't possibly become more dreary or meaningless. She was stuck in a boring school, mired in a lifestyle she hated, and unable to pursue her dream of traveling to exotic places. Worst of all, her sister and best friend, Flora, was becoming just like the empty-headed girls they used to disdain. Rebecca knew she needed to take action. It was time to plan another adventure.

She found her sister lounging on the settee in their newly renovated sitting room, paging through one of the widow's magazines. Beyond the French doors, which were also new, their exercise bars stood idle in the bright summer sunshine, beckoning to Rebecca. "Are you going to read ridiculous fashion magazines all day?" Rebecca asked. "We have more than enough dresses, Flora."

"I know. But I like looking at the new ones."

Rebecca reached down and closed the magazine. "Let's do something fun together. Why don't we put on our bloomers and get some exercise outside? We could practice speaking Greek to each other at the same time."

"It's too hot outside. And we already know enough Greek. Besides, we can't travel to Greece until the war ends, and who knows when that will be."

Rebecca's frustration with her narrowly constricted life had simmered for months. Now it boiled over. "I need to go on a marvelous trip right now!" she shouted. "Today!"

"But, Becky, we can't—"

"Don't tell me we can't! We used to have so much fun exploring together, remember? Now Mrs. Worthington has taken over our lives and you're no fun at all anymore." She started to leave, but Flora called to her.

"Wait! Don't be mad, Becky. . . . What would you like to do today—besides exercise?"

Rebecca remembered something their Greek teacher had told them and an idea started forming in her mind. "Let's explore parts of the city we've never seen before—like the section of Chicago where the Greek sailors and their families live. It will be almost like visiting Greece, and we can practice listening to them talking."

Flora wrinkled her dainty nose. "Oh, dear . . . foreign sailors?"

Her reaction made Rebecca all the more determined to rescue her sister from frivolous boredom. "Why not? Mr. Vasilakis told us where the sailors' boardinghouses are, remember?"

Flora seemed to sink deeper into the sofa cushions as if taking root there. "I don't know . . . is it safe to wander around Chicago by ourselves? Shouldn't we have a chaperone? I don't think it's proper to—"

"For heaven's sake, Flora! If we want to have a marvelous adventure, we can't worry about propriety! Let's have some fun for once! Let's learn about new things, explore new places, meet exotic people." She grabbed Flora's hand and yanked as if trying to uproot an oak tree, determined to rescue her. "Come with me. Please?"

"But Mrs. Worthington is coming later this afternoon to—"

"I don't care! I've had enough of her. For nearly two years I've done every boring thing she wanted me to do, and everything you insisted that I do, for Father's sake. Now I want to do something different, something . . . thrilling!"

"But our reputations—"

"Bah!" Rebecca dropped Flora's hand and moved toward the door. "I'm going exploring, with or without you."

"Becky, wait!"

Rebecca halted and turned back, watching Flora squirm to

extricate herself from the sofa's plump grip. Her corset and voluminous skirts barely allowed her to breathe, much less move freely. Flora's struggles were a fitting metaphor for the hold that her indolent life was having on her. "Are you coming with me?"

"You need to think this through and—"

"I'll see you later." Rebecca raced up to her bedroom in a very unladylike way, taking the steps two at a time. She and Flora slept in separate bedrooms now, after Mrs. Worthington convinced Flora to move into one of her own so she would have room for her wardrobes full of gowns and accessories. It was another sign of the growing distance between Rebecca and her sister, and she hated it.

When she reached her room, she shrugged off the ridiculous wrapper the widow insisted she wear around the house and dug in the wardrobe for the dress she'd worn to France two years ago. She hoped it still fit. She laid it on the bed, then searched for her sturdy leather shoes, remembering the miles of wear they'd endured as she'd wandered through London's fascinating museums and strolled the charming streets of Paris and climbed the hills of Rome. She swallowed a lump in her throat. Would she ever be able to travel and explore the world again?

The dress was a little tight and two inches too short, but she could still wiggle into it. She couldn't walk far in the shoes, but they would do for now. In spite of her snug clothing, Rebecca felt comfortably dressed for the first time since the widow had invaded her life. She turned toward her bedroom door and saw Flora watching her with a mixture of anxiety and jealousy. "Are you coming with me or not?" Rebecca asked her.

"I . . . I . . ."

"Because if you are, you'll need to change your clothes and put on real shoes."

"Oh, Becky. I don't know what to say. . . ."

"We used to be partners in all our exploits until the widow

squashed you into her tight corsets and tied you up with her rules of etiquette. Remember how much fun we had when we explored Paris together? We never would have visited the Garden of Tuileries on a gorgeous summer day or seen the Egyptian obelisk if the widow had been around." Flora stared at her without speaking, and Rebecca sensed how torn she was. She pushed past her dithering sister into the hallway. "I'll tell you all about it when I get back."

"Wait! You aren't going to walk around the city by yourself, are you?"

"I won't be walking. I think I'll take public transportation. It'll be a new experience." She reached the end of the hallway and started down the stairs.

"Wait! . . . I-I'll go with you if . . . if you let Rufus drive us. And if we just explore a new part of the city instead of trying to talk to Greek sailors. . . . And if we're back before Mrs. Worthington comes . . ."

"Excellent!" Rebecca said before Flora could add any more *ifs*. "I'll tell Rufus to prepare the carriage while you change your clothes. . . . And no hoop skirts, Flora."

Rebecca began formulating a plan as she stood in the carriage house waiting for Rufus to hitch up their horse. The real Flora still lay buried somewhere inside, even though the widow had nearly suffocated her beneath mounds of fancy gowns and social expectations. Rebecca needed to unearth her—the Flora who used to carry a pocketful of change wherever she went so she could give alms to the poor. The sister who'd longed to find God's purpose for her life more than she longed for a full dance card or a successful husband. "Do you know which section of the city has the most Irish immigrants?" she asked their driver.

"Yes . . . but you don't want to go there, Miss Rebecca."

"That's exactly where I want to go, Rufus. And please don't change into your fancy driving jacket and trousers."

"But Missus Worthington says—"

"She isn't here, Rufus. Let's just drive around like we used to do in the old days."

He gave her a wide grin. "Yes, Miss Rebecca."

Flora emerged twenty minutes later looking uncomfortable in her plain, well-worn skirt and shirtwaist. The seams in the bodice looked as though they were about to burst, but at least Flora hadn't grown any taller during the past two years so her ankles weren't showing. She was carrying her reticule, which meant she probably had some money with her—although she probably had her smelling salts with her, too. Dainty young ladies were instructed to carry them everywhere.

Rebecca felt lighter—freer—as they rode away from the lake and their wealthy neighborhood. "You know, Flora, exploring Chicago might be nearly as much fun as exploring a foreign country. I should have thought of it sooner." She and Flora were together again, sisters and partners in their sensible skirts and unfashionable shoes, having an adventure.

The jumbled buildings crowded closer together once they bypassed the city center. The streets deteriorated into unpaved lanes. Rebecca held her breath to keep from gagging as the odors of overflowing outhouses and uncollected garbage intensified. She nearly vomited as they passed a dead horse rotting in the street. Flora pulled a lace handkerchief from her reticule and held it over her nose. Eventually, the narrow lanes became so crowded with people and activity that the carriage could go no farther. "Let us out right here, Rufus. We'd like to walk."

"This is no place for you, Miss Rebecca. Your father wouldn't like this."

"We're only going to walk down to the end of this street and back again. You can watch us from here. We'll be fine." She scrambled out as she spoke, pulling her sister behind her.

Flora stammered, "Um . . . I don't think we should . . ."

"Flora. The Lord knows when the end of our days will be. We don't need to be afraid."

"Yes, but I don't think the Good Lord would like us to put ourselves in danger on purpose."

"Look around you, Flora. This is a neighborhood, even though it's a very poor one. These homes are where families live and children play. It's very different from our neighborhood, but I don't see any danger here." She tugged her sister along as she spoke, gesturing to the rickety tenements webbed with strings of flapping laundry. They passed a pen with live sheep and pigs in front of a meat market. Bloody carcasses and un-plucked chickens hung from hooks in the window. The smell nearly overpowered both of them. They hurried on and came to a group of ragged children playing in a mud puddle beneath the community's water spigot while their older siblings lined up to fill pails and cooking pots.

"See? They're just like us, Flora—only poor."

They passed a little girl about four years old, struggling to care for an infant and a toddler, both with bare bottoms. "Oh, look at all these little ones!" Flora said, her soft heart already touched. "It's so sad that this is the only place they have to play!" The children watched them curiously as they passed, as if she and Flora were animals escaped from a zoological garden. They came to a battered, wooden street cart piled with fruit, and the old man pushing it looked up with hope in his rheumy eyes. "How much are your apples?" Flora asked. She purchased as many as she and Rebecca could hold, then returned to where the children were playing. "My name is Flora," she said, offering an apple to one of the little girls. "What's yours?"

"Maggie." She accepted the offered fruit as if it were made of glass. More children quickly gathered around, emerging from narrow alleyways and front stoops, giggling as they told Flora their names. They stared at the apples in wonder, savoring the smell and the feel of them before allowing themselves to take a bite. The little girl named Maggie put the apple in her pocket.

"Don't you want to eat it?" Rebecca asked.

She nodded shyly then said, "But I'll share it with Mama and my little brothers."

"Which school do you go to?" Flora asked. Maggie shrugged.

"We don't go to school," an older girl said.

"Why not?"

"We watch the babies while our mamas work." She sounded proud.

"Are your fathers away at war?"

Most of the children nodded, but one boy said, "Mine works in the leather factory." He pointed to a grim brick building with smudged windows half a block away.

"My sister used to go to school," another child said, "but now she works there, too."

Flora looked at Rebecca, clearly distressed. "Isn't there anything we can do to help these children? They need to learn to read and write if they're going to have a better life than this."

Rebecca gestured helplessly. "I don't know." She was as upset by what she was seeing as Flora was, but what could she do? What had begun as a chance to explore new places had turned into something quite different.

They continued down the street to the factory at the end of the block. A large hand-printed sign beside the open door read, *Now Hiring.* The noon whistle sounded inside, and workers spewed from the fire escape doors on the second floor for their lunch break. A dozen girls no more than eight or ten years old emerged first, clambering down the wooden fire escape with their newspaper-wrapped lunches. All of them were barefooted. The women and teenaged girls perched on the steps and rickety landings to eat theirs. Flora hurried over with the rest of the apples and passed them around to the girls. "Do you work in that factory?" she asked in astonishment.

"We're making uniforms for the soldiers," one of the youngest replied. She seemed excited and proud, as if she was helping to win the war at just eight years old.

"There's lots of jobs because of the war," another said. "I make four dollars a week!"

"Four—!" Tears filled Flora's eyes as she turned to Rebecca. "They're exploiting these children, Becky. Surely they can pay their workers more than that, considering the demand for uniforms."

"You're right. It's outrageous."

Between the two of them, Rebecca and Flora emptied their change purses, buying fruit for everyone until the apple cart was empty. Children trailed behind Flora as if she were a queen and they were her handmaidens. Flora was still wiping her tears as they returned to Rufus and the waiting carriage. "I'm so embarrassed when I remember how much money I just spent on a new summer gown," she sniffed on the way home. "Did you notice they were all barefooted? My new shoes, which I didn't even need, cost more than those little girls make in a month!"

Rebecca didn't reply. She was very glad to have her sister back, yet at the same time, visiting that neighborhood had revealed a side of herself that Rebecca didn't like at all. Her desire to explore and collect exotic experiences simply for the novelty of it seemed as wrong as Flora's desire to collect wardrobes full of clothes. How dare she gawk at others' misfortune in order to entertain herself? If she was going to spend time and money pursuing her love of travel, there should be more to her adventures than novelty and an escape from boredom. Flora's question continued to haunt her. *"Isn't there anything we can do to help?"* She needed to think of something.

She found Flora waiting for Mrs. Worthington in the downstairs sitting room later that afternoon, looking dejected. "I can't stop thinking about everything we saw today," Flora said as Rebecca sat down beside her.

"I know. Me either. . . . I wanted to explore, but it seems selfish to me now. It's wrong to just gawk at new things, then walk away without even trying to make a difference. We gave those children free apples, but who will feed them tomorrow?"

"What do you suppose it's like for those little girls to work in that factory?" Flora asked.

Rebecca shrugged. "The factory must have a government contract to make army uniforms, so the owners are probably making a good profit. Shouldn't at least some of those profits go to the workers? I don't think four dollars is a fair wage for a week's work, do you?"

"No. And those little girls shouldn't have to work at all! What do you suppose they do inside there all day?"

An idea struck Rebecca like a smack on the head. "I think I know how we can find out." Flora looked at her, waiting. "We can apply for jobs there ourselves."

"You can't be serious. Why would we do that? We don't need the money. Besides, we're older than those girls were."

"True, but I saw some girls our age eating their lunches on the fire escape. We could dress in old clothes and see if they'll hire us. That way, we'll get a good look inside."

"And then what?"

Rebecca scrambled to think. "Well . . . once we see what's going on, maybe we can figure out how to change things. Father can help us. He knows a lot of important people here in Chicago. Think what a difference it would make to those families if the parents could earn a decent wage and the children could go to school."

"Do you think we dare?"

"Would you rather look the other way?"

Flora shook her head, her tendrils dancing. "No. I can't look the other way. Jesus told His followers to be compassionate. He said if we've been given much, then much will be required of us. But . . ." Her voice hushed. "But do you think Father will be upset when he finds out?"

"No. I think he'll be proud of us. Let's go back there tomorrow."

"I don't know, Becky. Mrs. Worthington has our week all scheduled with social calls and—"

"We'll tell her we're sick or that we need a week's vacation or that we have something more important to do—which we do. She won't like it, but that's too bad. She's ruined our lives enough, already."

"That's not fair, Becky. She's only trying to help us."

"And now it's time for us to help someone else. Are you with me or not?"

"You wouldn't go back there by yourself, would you?"

Rebecca thought for a moment. "I would. But I'd much rather go with you."

"Well, if you really think we should . . ."

"I do."

Mrs. Worthington could barely mask her displeasure when Rebecca and Flora told her they wouldn't be making social visits or receiving callers for the rest of the week. She had arrived with their new calling cards, fresh from the printer, and her cheeks turned from pink to red as she stood in their foyer struggling to control her temper and remain ladylike. "Why in the world not?" she asked.

"There's something more important we need to do," Flora said. She didn't elaborate. Rebecca grinned at her sister for showing more gumption than she had in a long time.

"But you have social obligations. This simply isn't done!" The widow couldn't have been more outraged than if they'd told her they were joining the Confederate Army. Rebecca suppressed a smile, knowing she would faint with horror if she knew the truth. "Does your father know about your plans?"

"We'll be sure to tell him," Rebecca replied. *After the experiment is over*, she added to herself.

"But . . . how shall I explain your unusual absence?" Widow Worthington addressed the question to Flora, aware that she could be pressured more easily to spill the details.

"I don't think it's anyone's business but ours," she replied. "If someone wants to know more, she's simply being nosy." Rebecca wanted to cheer. Flora suddenly seemed to catch herself and added, "If you please, Mrs. Worthington."

They designed their disguises that evening after supper. That's what Flora called them—disguises. Rebecca liked the intriguing sound of it. They found skirts and shirtwaists they hadn't worn for several years and attacked them with scissors, cutting and ripping and unraveling them until they looked as ragged as the ones the street children had worn. "They still don't look quite right," Rebecca decided, so they carried them out to the carriage house and dragged them across the floor until they were filthy. Rufus watched in astonishment. Rebecca stopped in the kitchen on their way upstairs again and asked the cook for a dollop of lard. Maria-Elena looked as mystified as Rufus had. "We'll rub it through our hair tomorrow morning," Rebecca told her sister, "so it looks greasy and unwashed." She fell asleep that night feeling more excited than she had in a long time.

After eating breakfast with their father as usual the next morning, they hurried upstairs to put on their disguises. "Isn't this fun?" Rebecca asked as she combed lard through her hair.

Flora made a face. "No, it's rather disgusting. But I'm trusting that it will be worthwhile in the end." Rebecca felt like a fraud when she looked at herself in the mirror. But she often felt that way when she saw herself all dolled up in the widow's finery, too. Neither image was the real Rebecca. But what was?

Rufus' eyes grew very wide when he returned from driving Father to work and saw them waiting for him in the carriage house. "What're you two misses up to now? Your father know about this? For sure Mrs. Worthington don't want to see you looking like that!"

"We're going back to the neighborhood where you took us yesterday," Rebecca said, "but this time we want to blend in."

"That you do for certain, miss. But I don't think—"

"We'll be fine, Rufus. We promise."

He stared at them for so long that Rebecca wondered if they would have to take public transportation. But he finally sighed and reached to help Flora into the carriage, mumbling, "I just hope I ain't in trouble right along with you." He drove them to the same place they'd gone yesterday and parked the carriage. The rotting horse still lay in the street, smelling even fouler after another day beneath the summer sun.

"If we're not back in an hour, Rufus, you can go home and—"

"I ain't leaving you young misses here unless your father say so!"

Rebecca didn't know what to do. She had no idea if their disguises would work or if the factory would even hire them. "Wait here for us, then," she said. "We'll be back."

The scene on the street looked unchanged from the day before. No one seemed to recognize them as the fine ladies who had given away apples a day earlier. They walked the length of the block to the drab factory and stepped through the open door. The pungent odor of tanned hides and the loud clamor of machinery assaulted them from the leather factory on the main floor. Flora clapped her hands over her ears as they climbed the narrow wooden stairs to the uniform factory on the second floor. "How can people stand to work here?" she asked, nearly shouting.

At the top of the steps, bolts of dark blue wool for Union

Army uniforms lay stacked in the hallway, on the stairs, and in every available space inside the doorway. The summer heat and humidity remained trapped inside the factory, the breeze unable to find its way through the open windows since the factory was surrounded by other factories and tenements packed closely together. Row after row of tables for the seamstresses filled the majority of the factory floor, the young women never looking up as they sewed nonstop on their chugging machines. A balding man with a walrus mustache sat at a desk directly in front of them, smoking a pungent cigar. He looked up from his ledgers and piles of paperwork when he saw them. "What can I do for you girls?"

"We wanna work." Rebecca said. She had advised Flora not to give themselves away by speaking properly. "Heard you're hiring."

"Can you operate a sewing machine?" he asked.

"We can learn."

He smirked and shook his head. "Forget it. I don't have time to teach you. You're too old to snip threads," he said, pointing his cigar at Rebecca. "But you aren't." He pointed it at Flora, who was tiny and petite at age sixteen and could pass for a twelve-year-old in her disguise. "Job is yours, if you want it."

"Is there another job that I could do?" Rebecca asked.

He stroked his walrus mustache and gave the factory floor a piercing glance, a cat on the lookout for wayward mice. "You don't look strong enough to cut through several layers of wool," he said, gesturing to the cutting table. "Or handle a steam iron. Try the leather factory downstairs."

"But I'm very strong, and I can carry things—like she's doing." Rebecca pointed to a young girl, scurrying between the tables with armloads of garments. The boss looked Rebecca up and down, and for a moment she feared he had seen through her disguise and could tell she was seventeen years old.

"You do look well-fed," he finally said, opening one of his ledger books. "Tell you what. I'll give you a try and see how you do. Names?"

"I'm Becky and she's Flora. Last name is Hawes."

He scribbled in his book, then said, "Work starts at seven o'clock tomorrow morning. If you're late it comes out of your pay, which is four dollars a week—minus any money we take out if you snip the cloth and ruin it," he said, pointing to Flora. "Bring your lunch. Workday ends at six fifteen."

"That's a very long day!" Flora said as they filed down the creaking stairs again. "How do those little girls do it? Did you see them working around that big table? They didn't even have chairs to sit on!"

"I guess we'll find out what it's like when we start work tomorrow." Rebecca knew it was ridiculous to feel elated about working in such a place and for such a pittance, but she couldn't stop smiling at the prospect of a new quest. Suddenly her sister halted, and Rebecca nearly toppled into her. "What's wrong?"

"We must be insane for doing this." Flora looked frightened. Rebecca waited, hoping she wouldn't change her mind, but then Flora seemed to steel herself. "Even so, I'm going to do it, Becky. The Almighty has given us so much, and I have to try to make a difference."

Rebecca smiled all the way home. Their disguises had fooled the foreman. She thought she understood the guilty delight a criminal must feel, the rush of energy and thrill of excitement at getting away with something. Imagine! Wealthy debutantes Rebecca and Flora Hawes were going to work in a uniform factory.

So far, it had been easy. But Rebecca found out the next morning that the most difficult step in her scheme was convincing Rufus to drop them off in the run-down part of town before seven o'clock and return for them at six fifteen that evening. He pulled off his hat when she told him and scratched his grizzled head. "I watched you gals grow up, always keeping an eye on you, and I know that ain't no place for you little misses. No, sir. This just ain't right at all."

Rebecca tried explaining what they intended to do, and why. "We want to help those little girls, Rufus. Change things for them. You saw how they lived. If we were older, we could accomplish that in a different way, but we're too young. Going inside the factory for a firsthand look is the only way we can report on the working conditions. Please help us. We don't want to be useless rich girls all our lives."

Rufus continued to shake his head, blowing out huffs of air, like one of his snorting horses. After much persuasion, he finally relented. "I'll take you. But anything happens to you, I'll never forgive myself."

"Nothing will happen to us."

Rebecca could tell how nervous Flora was as they drove there. She didn't say a word the entire way, and she shifted on the seat as if the seamstress had left a dozen straight pins in her gown. They ordered Rufus to halt on a side street, a block from the factory, and they joined the stream of workers, mostly women and young girls, climbing the narrow, enclosed staircase to the second floor. The man with the walrus mustache was waiting for them beside his desk. "So. You came back," he said with a grunt. "Wasn't sure you would. Leave your lunches in the cloak room and follow me." He led them on a twisting route across the crowded factory floor, weaving between the rows of sewing machines where the women were scurrying to take their places. Stray threads and blue lint from the wool littered the floor and windowsills, adhering to nearly every surface in the sticky heat. Rebecca wondered why no one bothered to clean up. They passed the cutting tables, draped with layers of blue wool, where workers prepared to cut stacks of pattern pieces with huge shears. A young girl stood ready to deliver the cut pieces to the rows of seamstresses, then hurry back to the cutting table for more.

The boss stopped beside a large table that had a haphazard mountain of uniforms piled in the middle. The little barefooted girls Rebecca and Flora had seen the other day gathered around it, and when the whistle shrieked, they each snatched a garment from the mound and began snipping threads. The boss reached into a box on the table and handed Flora a small pair of scissors.

"Snip off all the loose threads that the seamstresses left," he told her. "I don't want to see anyone dawdling or hear any talking or it'll come out of your pay. And if you snip the cloth and ruin the garment, that'll come out of your pay, too. Last girl we had was so sloppy it ended up costing her more than she earned. Had to fire her. Understand?"

"Yes, sir." Flora's voice squeaked with fear. There were no chairs or stools around the table, so she would have to stand in place until the noon whistle blew, five hours from now. Then for five more hours until the day ended. Flora raised her hand as if she was in school. "Um . . . what if we need the privy?" she asked.

He glared as if she had asked to buy the factory. "That's what your lunch break is for." Rebecca was already regretting the two cups of tea she'd had for breakfast. "You—follow me," he said, pointing to her with his unlit cigar. He led her to a mound of uniforms on the far side of the room surrounded by more uniforms tied into bundles. "When the girls finish snipping," he said, "a runner brings the uniforms here. Tie them into bales of a dozen each. You do know how to count to twelve, don't you?"

"Yes, sir." Rebecca longed to tell him she had studied algebra and geometry with a private tutor, but she held her tongue.

"Someone will come for them by closing time and deliver them to the people who do piece work in their homes at night, sewing on buttons and hand-stitching hems. These bundles over here are the finished ones. Untie them, count them, make sure they have all their buttons, then take them to the pressers." He pointed to the corner of the room where men in shirt-sleeves stood behind ironing boards, sweating in the heat as they pressed the finished uniforms with steam irons. The smell of damp wool saturated the air and caught in Rebecca's throat. Steam clouded the air and fogged the windows. Most of the factory workers were women, and the men who worked at the cutting and pressing tables looked too old or too unfit to fight in the war.

By lunchtime Rebecca couldn't remember ever feeling so tired. Never before had she remained on her feet for five straight hours without a chance to sit down. And she still had five more hours to go until the workday ended. She retrieved their newspaper-wrapped lunches from the cloakroom and followed her sister and the other girls down the fire escape to eat outside. They waited in line to use the reeking privy, then found a shady place to sit beside the factory's brick wall. Flora moaned as she collapsed to the ground. "I don't know if I can do this for another five hours, Becky. I ache all over from standing in one place." Her face and the back of her blouse were damp with sweat. Lint and stray threads stuck to the lard she had combed through her hair. Rebecca tried to stifle a giggle.

"What's so funny?"

"You look very authentic. If the widow could see you now she would pop all her corset stays."

"I'm too tired to laugh," Flora said with a sigh, but she did manage a smile. "You look ridiculous yourself with blue fuzz all over your arms."

"That wool is so itchy! But I don't dare to stop to scratch my arms." They dove into the lunch Maria Elena had packed as if they hadn't eaten in days, careful to hide the contents from the other girls. "By the way, I figured out that we each earned about thirty-three cents so far this morning." Rebecca said with a mouthful of sandwich.

"That's all?"

"I'm afraid so." Flora closed her eyes, but whether it was from fatigue or discouragement, Rebecca couldn't tell. She gave her the last piece of apple and folded up the soiled newspaper like the other girls were doing as if she intended to use it again.

"I'm so thirsty," Flora said when they finished. "I'm going to get a drink from the spigot over there."

"No, don't!" Rebecca grabbed her arm to hold her back. "The water may not be safe to drink in this part of the city. Besides, you'll have to wait five more hours before you can use the privy. "

Flora groaned and slumped down again, her shoulders drooping. "I'm not sure I can work five more hours, Becky. Can't we just leave?"

"I suppose we could, but Rufus won't be back to pick us up until six fifteen. It's a long walk home."

Flora tried to pat her hair the way she normally did to check her hairpins and ended up with a greasy hand. She made a face and wiped her fingers on her skirt. "At least we have a nice home to return to, and a wonderful dinner to eat."

"Not to mention a warm bath," Rebecca added.

"What do these poor girls have to look forward to after working ten hours?"

"I figure they'll have about sixty-six cents and another long day of work ahead of them tomorrow."

"Oh, Becky. And the sad thing is, they're thankful for that."

"Listen, we need to write everything down tonight in our report for Father—how exhausted we feel, how terrible the working conditions are, and how hopeless life must be for all these women and girls. Maybe he can help us figure out what to do about it."

They made it to the end of the workday—barely. Rebecca's

feet and shoulders had never pained her so much in her life. Flora complained of aching legs and a stiff back. She fell asleep in the bathtub and was too exhausted to hold a pen or write a word in their report. Rebecca wrote it for both of them, fired by indignation and exhaustion and fury. They ended their report with a list of ways to solve the factory's terrible working conditions, such as providing stools for the girls while they snipped threads, and additional breaks in the morning and afternoon so the workers could get a drink or use the privy.

They presented their report to Father the following evening after supper, requesting a meeting in his study. His face darkened as he read, the creases in his forehead multiplying. He hadn't even turned to the second page when he set down his cigar and lowered the paper to stare at them. Their placid, dignified Father looked furious. "You went to this place? By yourselves? Without a chaperone?"

"Yes, but we had a very good reason to," Rebecca said. "Please keep reading, Father, and you'll see what we hoped to accomplish." He left his cigar smoldering in the ashtray and returned to the report. By the time he finished the last page and tapped the paper into a neat stack, he seemed less angry. Rebecca tried not to fidget as she waited for his response.

"You have made your point very well."

"Will you help us do something about it, Father?"

He paused for a long moment. "I can tell that you were moved by what you've experienced. I'm proud to know that my daughters have such compassionate hearts. But I'm sorry to say that what you witnessed takes place in cities and factories all across our nation, every day. At the same time, there are good-hearted Christian men and women in those cities—and here in Chicago, as well—who are working hard to change things. It won't happen overnight. There will still be plenty for you to do once you're older."

"But I want to do something now," Rebecca said. Flora nodded in agreement.

Father shook his head. "When you're older." He picked up his cigar and puffed it back to life. When the end glowed red again, he looked at them and said, "Your mother also had a tender heart toward the less fortunate. She would have been pleased." Rebecca started to speak, but he raised his voice, interrupting her. "However, I intend to put measures in place to ensure that you never do anything like this again. You acted foolishly. You were fortunate that you didn't encounter any danger. I'm instructing Rufus not to listen to you if—"

"Please don't blame him, Father," Rebecca said, scrambling to her feet. "He argued very strenuously against taking us, but we threatened to take public transportation if he didn't. He only agreed so he could watch over us."

Father continued as if she hadn't spoken. "I also intend to ask Mrs. Worthington to exercise a more active, guiding hand in your lives from now on and supervise you more closely."

Rebecca had sat down but she leaped to her feet again. "No, Father! Please! The only reason I wanted to go to that part of the city to begin with was because I was so bored with all the things she makes us do. I wanted to learn new things and use the good mind God has given me. Since we couldn't go abroad again because of the war, I talked Flora into exploring with me."

Father held up his hand. "We'll travel abroad again, Rebecca, all in good time. I know how fertile and curious your mind is. That's why I've been making arrangements for both of you to study at Northwestern Female College this fall—against Mrs. Worthington's advice, I might add. She fears you'll turn into bluestockings and intimidate all your suitors."

"Ha! What suitors?" Rebecca said with a laugh. "You mean her nephews?"

"That's enough, Rebecca," he said. But there was no anger

in his voice. His expression softened. "Believe me when I say that I have your best interests in mind when making decisions on your behalf. But I'm not going to live forever. It's my duty—my desire—to see you happily settled in homes of your own, with husbands I can trust to take care of you after I'm gone."

Rebecca nearly jumped up again to protest that she was capable of taking care of herself, but she remained silent. When she thought about it, she really didn't want to remain alone all her life. While she wanted to travel and study and learn as much as she could, she also longed to fall in love with a man who enjoyed exploring as much as she did, one who would be her companion as they traveled the world together.

Father wasn't finished. "Mrs. Worthington assures me that the lessons she is teaching you and the direction in which she is guiding you will lead to a fine future when it comes time to marry. That's why I'll be making sure she monitors you more closely from now on. Is that clear?"

"Very clear," Rebecca replied. She would be back to a cage that felt much too small.

Flora lifted her hand in the air, like a student asking for permission to speak. "I have one question, Father. Since most of those poor little girls had no shoes to wear, may I please have your permission to organize a charity drive to provide shoes and clothing for them?"

He looked surprised. And pleased. "Of course, Flora."

"And then—since we won't be allowed to go back to that neighborhood again—will you please help me find a way to distribute them?"

A brief smile flickered across his face before disappearing. "Yes, Flora. I support several reputable charities that can assist you. I'll pass the information on to Mrs. Worthington, and you two can work together on your project."

Rebecca excused herself and hurried from the study, not

waiting for her sister. Without meaning to, Flora had put her to shame with her last request. After everything they had witnessed in the factory and in that neighborhood over the past few days, Rebecca still thought only of herself and her need for adventure. Flora's soft heart led her to think of others first. Rebecca longed to learn new things, but as she bounded up the stairs two at a time so no one would see her tears, she thought that perhaps her best teacher would always be Flora.

CHAPTER 8

Rebecca couldn't stop grinning as she sat at the breakfast table on a rainy morning in April with the daily newspaper spread before her. She and Father and Flora had been anticipating this news for weeks, praying for it at home and in church. Now the headline made it official: The war was over. General Lee had surrendered the Army of Northern Virginia to General Grant. She held up the front page as Flora hurried into the morning room with an armful of schoolbooks and slid into her place across the table. "They signed a peace treaty, Flora, in a village in Virginia called . . ." She turned the paper around to read it again. "Appomattox Court House. I think I'm nearly as happy as the battle-weary soldiers."

Flora closed her eyes for a moment and gave an enormous sigh. "Oh, thank heaven. Think of what this means for all the former slaves. They can finally live their lives as free men and women." Flora thanked Maria Elena as she placed a plate of eggs and toast in front of her, then bowed her head to pray before eating.

"Yes, and our lives can get back to normal, too," Rebecca said after Flora finished. "We can take our long-postponed trip to Europe this summer." She spread strawberry jam on her toast and continued to read the related articles about the war until their carriage pulled up in the porte cochere outside.

Rufus waited at the front door and held an umbrella over their heads as he helped them into their seats for the drive to Evanston. Rebecca would graduate from Northwestern Female College with a Laureate of Arts degree in history in two months. Flora would earn her Laureate of Literature degree next year. What perfect timing for a trip abroad.

"I wish I knew how I could help," Flora said as the carriage jolted forward, then turned into the busy street.

"Help who? With what?" Rebecca had brought the newspaper with her, but she folded it and laid it in her lap.

"The former slaves," Flora replied, as if it should be obvious.

"Oh, yes, of course. I'm sure there will be ways for us to get involved. But to be honest, I want to travel first. I've been planning this trip abroad since before the war began." Flora didn't reply right away, and her lack of enthusiasm worried Rebecca. She waited, listening to the carriage wheels splash through puddles and the rain tapping on the carriage top like nervous fingers. "Well . . . ?" she finally asked.

Flora shook her head. "I don't see how we can travel now, Becky. Father seems so unwell. Haven't you noticed how winded he is after climbing the stairs?"

"Yes. I've noticed." Over the course of the war, Father's once-sturdy frame had withered, along with his appetite. Just last evening Rebecca had watched him push away his untouched dinner plate and had asked, "Should we be worried about you?"

"Not at all," he'd replied. "Just a bit of indigestion." Rebecca chose to believe him. After all, he was bound to start slowing down at age sixty-three.

"If he doesn't want to travel, he can always hire a chaperone for us. It can't be that hard to find a seasoned traveling companion, can it?"

Flora was still shaking her head. "I don't want to go anywhere until Father is feeling better. It wouldn't be right to leave him here all alone when he's unwell."

Rebecca turned toward the window, afraid to speak, afraid she'd be unable to hide her disappointment. The city looked gray and gloomy beneath the soggy sky, and she longed to get out of Chicago. She loved her father and would be devastated if anything happened to him, but she'd waited a long time to travel and she couldn't suppress her frustration to think she may have to wait longer. Flora also didn't speak again until the carriage halted in front of the college and Rufus appeared at the door with the umbrella.

"Mrs. Worthington is coming to the house today at four o'clock," Flora told Rebecca. "Don't forget."

"How could I forget?" The widow had hovered over them since they'd gone undercover in the uniform factory. Now at age twenty, Rebecca was sick of being guarded. But the widow was Father's constant companion, burrowing into his life like a backyard gopher.

"Well, don't get lost in the library with your head in a history book," Flora warned.

"Don't worry. I'll meet you here in time." Rebecca strode through the misting rain into the building, letting her sister use the umbrella since Flora was much more concerned about her appearance. Excited voices filled the hallways as the students cheered the news of the peace treaty. Rebecca didn't greet anyone, hurrying to the sanctuary of her classroom instead. She loved this world of academia with its lectures and term papers and exams. Her passion for history and research had flourished in college, but this chapter in her life would soon come to an end, too. She had no idea what was next. She had hoped that traveling abroad would give her a new sense of direction.

The school day felt like a holiday with students and teachers celebrating the end of the war and the return of their brothers, fathers, fiancés, and friends from the battlefield. Rebecca found it hard to join in, aware only of her frustration and the guilty knowledge that she was being selfish to want to travel when Father was ill. Should she ask him to consult a physician? Maybe she should ask Mrs. Worthington to intervene. It was in the widow's best interests that Father recover his health. But what if he invited her to join their excursion? Or worse yet, what if he married her? Rebecca had asked Father to wait until she'd graduated from Northwestern Female College before marrying the widow, and he had agreed. But now that time was drawing near.

The moment the widow arrived that afternoon, Rebecca raised the subject of Father's health. Mrs. Worthington had just entered the parlor and hadn't even removed her hat or cloak when Rebecca said, "We're concerned about our father. Have you noticed that he seems unwell lately? Remember how he had to cancel your dinner plans last week?"

The widow took a moment to reply as she removed her hat and gloves and set them aside. She perched with perfect posture on the edge of the horsehair settee. The newly remodeled parlor was dainty and frilly, suiting the widow's taste, but not Rebecca's or Flora's—and certainly not Father's. But the little table near the fireplace did provide a quiet, cheerful place for Rebecca to spread out her books and study on rainy afternoons.

"He has seemed tired, lately," the widow finally said. "I'll speak to him about your concerns. However, what we need to accomplish today is—"

"Now that the war is over, Flora and I plan to travel to Greece and Egypt this summer," Rebecca interrupted. "I've been studying *Murray's Guidebook to Modern Egypt and Thebes*, and our itinerary is all set. All we need is a departure date—and possibly a chaperone if Father isn't well enough to join us."

Mrs. Worthington leaned forward to rest her hand on Rebecca's arm. Rebecca knew by the forlorn tilt of the widow's head and the sad expression in her eyes, that bad news was on the way. "My dear, there won't be time for travel this summer. Now that the young men are returning from the war, the competition for husbands will be fierce. We need to make sure you two girls are at the very top of every eligible man's list."

"Not this again," Rebecca said with a groan. She slouched back in her seat in disappointment. She and Flora had enjoyed a reprieve from Widow Worthington's matchmaking plans after most of the eligible men had gone off to fight the war. Only those who were physically unfit or so cowardly they had paid for substitutes had been left behind. Everyone agreed they wouldn't make suitable husbands.

"Sit up straight, Rebecca, and listen to me. It's critical that we attend to your social calendars today to make certain your schedules are full of opportunities in the coming weeks."

Panic squeezed the air out of Rebecca like a too-tight corset. The glorious months of summer travel would be squeezed from her life like juice from an orange. "But I don't want a full schedule or—"

"Your father has assured me that this is what he wants for you."

"Surely it won't make any difference in our marriage prospects if we're away for two or three months."

"Rebecca, dear, you and Flora aren't the only eligible women in Chicago. I've known couples who have met, become engaged, and then married in two or three months' time. The returning soldiers will be eager to settle down and resume civilian life."

The sun had made a brief appearance that afternoon after

the stormy morning, but it slid behind a cloud at that moment, and it was as if all the lamps in the room had been snuffed out. All hope of traveling was being extinguished, too. When the sun failed to reappear after several minutes, Rebecca felt doomed.

They spent the rest of the afternoon planning a dinner party at Mrs. Worthington's house to welcome home what the widow called the "important" soldiers—the ones who would be high on every marriageable woman's list. Rebecca wasn't surprised to find two of Mrs. Worthington's nephews, Frederick and Thomas, topping the list. "Nothing like a little nepotism to sharpen Cupid's arrows," Rebecca grumbled to Flora as they dressed for dinner on the appointed evening.

"But don't you long to meet someone wonderful and fall in love, Becky? Love is the theme of every good story ever written. Think of *Romeo and Juliet* and—"

"Leave it to a literature major to point that out." Rebecca inhaled as her lady's maid yanked her corset laces tighter. Getting dressed had become an elaborate, drawn-out process thanks to Mrs. Worthington. Gone were the days when Rebecca could easily dress herself for special occasions.

"The theme of true love is in all of your history books, too," Flora said. She sat at the dressing table while her maid pinned up her golden hair. "What about Helen of Troy and Anthony and Cleopatra? Men have fought wars for the women they love."

Rebecca winced at the mention of Cleopatra and the bitter reminder of her foiled plans to visit Egypt. She lifted her arms as the maid slipped the corded crinoline over her head, then looked at herself in the full-length mirror. The face she saw was square and plain. No matter how many ruffles and flounces and rows of lace the seamstresses sewed onto her gowns, Rebecca wouldn't be pretty. Her hair might be elaborately coiled and curled and pinned but it was still an uninspiring shade of mud-brown. "Let's be honest, Flora. The only reason men are going to fight over me is because Father is wealthy."

"That's not true—"

"You, on the other hand, are not only smart and kindhearted, you're beautiful." Rebecca knew her sister couldn't argue against the pretty, dark-eyed image she saw reflected in the mirror. Her slender body would still look graceful and womanly if she wore nothing but a burlap sack. But what made Flora even more appealing was the fact that she had no idea how lovely she was. There was no pride in her beauty, no arrogance. She shone with an inner loveliness that few beautiful women ever achieved. Her kind heart brought sunlight to every room she entered, from the grim dining room at the county poor house where she volunteered to the stately ballrooms of Chicago's finest mansions. Rebecca might have been jealous of her sister if she hadn't loved her so fiercely.

"We'll both find someone special, Becky, I know we will. Maybe even tonight."

"That's fine with me. The sooner I find someone, the sooner we can be off on our travels abroad. The man who proposes marriage to me had better be prepared to see the world."

"And ready for an adventure, right? What fun is it to travel if nothing exciting happens?"

"Exactly." Rebecca bent so the maid could slip her striped silk gown over her head, then stood straight again while she fastened the tiny buttons and tied the bow in back. "I do want to find love and companionship, Flora, but I still don't know what God wants me to do with my life. I won't settle for a husband who won't let me find that purpose. I'm so frustrated because other people get to decide what I do every day, how I must act, and even what I wear. Why can't I make my own decisions?"

Flora rose from her seat and pulled Rebecca into her arms, their voluminous skirts and crinolines crushed between them.

"I know, I know. But this is only temporary, Becky. We'll take that trip to Egypt one day, I promise we will."

The widow's newly discharged nephews, Thomas and Frederick, stood waiting to greet Rebecca and Flora in the foyer of the Worthington home, looking lean and fidgety after their years in the army. They reminded Rebecca of thoroughbreds at the starting gate, poised to race to the finish line. It unnerved her to realize that she and Flora were the prizes. She remembered Freddy Worthington from before the war, when he'd been languid and pale, and she had envied his studies at Yale University. She also recalled struggling to find a topic of conversation that would be of interest to both of them.

They exchanged greetings before Rebecca and Flora excused themselves to shed their wraps and freshen up in the same upstairs cloak room they'd used five years ago—and at many events since. They were better prepared for an elegant dinner party this time and certainly better dressed, thanks to the widow. But Rebecca still felt as uncomfortable as the tabby cat she and Flora used to dress up in doll's clothing. The reflection she saw in the mirror didn't resemble her mental image of herself at all.

"Well, it's obvious that the widow has arranged for her nephews to be the first ones in line to court us," Rebecca said as she watched Flora pinch her cheeks to bring color to them. "We could be on our way to Cairo or Athens right now, and I'm quite sure those two would wait for us—and for Father's piles of money."

"I know you don't enjoy these fancy affairs, Becky, but we're doing this for Father's sake, remember? He wants us to be well taken care of."

"I'd rather take care of myself, thank you very much."

"You need to give love a chance. It can't walk through a door that's tightly closed. But it might surprise you and sneak inside if you leave it open a crack."

Rebecca frowned. "What novel did that come from?"

"None. I just made it up!"

They mingled in the drawing room, making pleasant conversation until the dinner bell rang. Fredrick Worthington offered his arm to Rebecca as he had the first time they'd met, escorting her to the dining room. Freddy's cousin, Thomas Worthington, had obviously won the luck of the draw or the flip of the coin or however it had been decided, and served as Flora's escort for the evening.

"Tell me about the war," Rebecca said as the first course was served. She reached without hesitation for the proper fork, the rules of etiquette second nature now. "It must have been fascinating to get out of Chicago and travel someplace new, even if it was under difficult circumstances."

"I was stationed in Washington for the duration of the war, working in the office of the Quartermaster General."

It seemed to Rebecca that a less able-bodied man than Freddy could have handled a desk job, leaving him free for combat, but she refrained from saying so. "How interesting. What did you do there?

"I procured supplies, negotiated government contracts with manufacturers, arranged for shipping—"

"Did that include uniforms?"

"Among other things."

"Flora and I visited a factory here in Chicago that made army uniforms. The working conditions were appalling. They had girls as young as eight years old working there, earning a mere four dollars a week."

"I wouldn't know anything about that."

Nor did he seem to care. Rebecca waited for the footman to remove her fish plate and for her indignation to cool before speaking again. "Were you able to visit any interesting places in the Washington area while you were there?"

"I had no desire to, nor could I spare the time."

"Well, how about now? Surely you must have plans to travel now that the war is over."

"I'm quite happy to be back in Chicago and eager to settle down and resume work in the business world."

"Have you ever traveled abroad?"

"I've never cared to. Mind you, if my work took me abroad, I would go. But to travel merely to see the sights is a waste of time and money."

Rebecca's burning cheeks betrayed her rising ire. She battled a fit of impatience at his ignorance. *Waste of time indeed!* "Travel can also be educational. There's so much one can learn by visiting foreign lands and observing different cultures. And there are so many great works of art and architecture to see, the visual evidence of the world's past history. The last time I traveled abroad I gained an entirely new perspective on our own country." She waited for him to reply and ask her about her experiences, but he didn't. The conversation had meandered down a road that led nowhere.

Rebecca had little appetite for the platters of delicacies the footman offered her, caused in part by the pinch of her whalebone corset stays and partly by indignation. She pretended interest in the food to keep from voicing all the insulting comments that came to mind—such as how Freddy might become a less boring person if he got out of his office and traveled someplace new.

He wasn't bad-looking—some might call him handsome. But he had a way of lifting his chin and looking down on everybody that annoyed Rebecca. He had dark curly hair, fair skin, and the same greedy look in his deep-set blue eyes as his aunt, Mrs. Worthington. He was close to six feet tall but was already tending toward plumpness beneath his well-tailored evening suit. Freddy had a high-strung nervousness about him that might have been attributed to battle weariness if he had actually gone into combat instead of sitting out the war in Washington. His fingers drummed when he wasn't holding something in them, and his leg jiggled continuously when he was seated as if he was waiting for someone who was late. How could such a boring man be so fidgety?

But maybe she wasn't being fair to Freddy. Instead of talking about her own interests, she should be exploring his. When it was time for a new course to be served, she politely chose a new subject. "Tell me about your work."

"I'm in the field of finance and investments. I would hate to bore you with the details. Besides, you probably wouldn't understand."

Rebecca laid down her fork to keep from stabbing him with it. "Try me," she challenged. "I'm about to graduate *summa cum laude* from North Western Female College. My professors assure me that I'm very intelligent for a woman."

He gave her a condescending smile, missing the irony in her tone. "My aunt has told me. But I'd rather not spoil her special dinner by discussing my work."

Rebecca tried several more avenues of conversation as they worked their way through the five-course meal, but each avenue ended much the same as the others. She heard Flora and Thomas laughing together at the other end of the table and guessed that her sister was better at making conversation than she was. Or else Thomas was less dour than Freddy. Rebecca saw little chance that a spark of attraction might be kindled between them since Freddy was about as interesting as a soggy handkerchief. Yet she had been taught that it was the woman's task to keep conversation going by raising fascinating topics and asking probing questions—provided they weren't too personal. As the waiter served the fluffy, strawberry dessert, she decided one last time to inspire his imagination.

"If you did have the opportunity to travel, what place would you most like to visit?"

"I have no desire to travel at all."

Rebecca had had enough. Against all advice to the contrary, she decided to talk about herself. "Well, I've thought about it a lot. I would leave tomorrow, if I had a chance, and visit the lands of the Bible—Egypt, Jerusalem, the Sea of Galilee. I would explore—"

"I understand those places are very backward and only half-civilized. I doubt they would have any of the amenities we're accustomed to."

"I wouldn't care about amenities. I would love to walk in the land where Jesus walked and absorb the centuries of history in the Holy Land. One of the missions our family supports is a Protestant church located right in Old Jerusalem, right where Christianity first began. Their missionaries visit here from time to time, to talk about their work in that part of the world. I always find their reports fascinating."

Like a carriage without a hand brake, Rebecca was rolling forward on a topic that interested her and she couldn't stop. "I would also love to visit the part of the world where all the archeological discoveries have been made and see the sites that Layard and Botta have unearthed, places like Khorsabad and the Palace of Sargon." She glanced at Freddy, who looked as though he had no idea what she was talking about, then continued on, gaining momentum, wondering what his response would be when she finished. He would either admit that he was bored with her and move on to court someone else, or he would prove by his interest in her passions that he would make a suitable husband.

"What I've found so fascinating in my history studies is that no one believed that the people and places mentioned in the Bible were real—people like King Nebuchadnezzar and places like Assyria and Babylon. It was just as the prophet Jeremiah had predicted: Babylon had become a heap of ruins without inhabitants, where owls lived and jackals prowled." She thought she saw Freddy stifling a yawn and continued just for spite. "But no one can dismiss the Bible as myths and legends anymore because Layard's discoveries proved that those people and places did exist and that therefore the history in the Bible is indeed based on fact. I would love to travel there and take part in making such astounding discoveries. Wouldn't you?"

"No. It isn't safe to travel anywhere in the Ottoman Empire." His tone of voice was so cold she nearly shivered. Thankfully, the footman had removed her dinner fork and with it the renewed temptation to stab Freddy with it. She decided she would end his interest in courting her once and for all.

"I've been told by my tutors that I have a gift for languages. I dream of being able to do what Champollion did in interpreting a priceless find like the Rosetta Stone. Imagine the thrill of deciphering hieroglyphics. It would be like unlocking a secret code and opening up an entire world of discoveries to historians—a firsthand look into the past."

"But what would be the point, Miss Hawes? How would it improve anyone's daily life here in Chicago?"

"There's a verse in Romans that says everything that was written in the past was written to teach us, so that we might have encouragement and hope. Isn't that why we read the Bible? So that we'll know about the past and learn from it? We can look at the ruins of Babylon and study the reasons why it was ultimately destroyed and learn from them, so we don't repeat past mistakes. When Flora and I were growing up, the pastor of our church filled his sermons with people and places from the Old Testament: Abraham leaving Ur of the Chaldees to follow God; Moses hearing God's voice at the burning bush and confronting Pharaoh with his command to 'Let my people go.'

We heard about the Egyptian army drowning in the Red Sea, the Ten Commandments at Mount Sinai, Joshua conquering Jericho. Our pastor applied lessons from these examples that we could use in our daily lives."

"I suppose there would be some validity to those stories in the context of a sermon. But your clergyman made his point without the risk of traveling to Egypt, didn't he?"

Rebecca released her frustration in an unladylike sigh. "Don't you find history interesting for its own sake? I do."

"Frankly, I'm more interested in looking toward the future than in gazing behind me at the past. Now that the war is over, this country will grow and change very rapidly. The new cross-country railroad has joined east with west, and Chicago sits right in the middle of our nation. I want to work with brilliant men like your father and learn how to invest in America's future."

There it was. Freddy had finally revealed his motive for courting her, whether he had intended to or not. She rested her folded hands on her lap to keep from pointing an accusing finger at him and shouting, *Aha!* When she was calm again, she said, "If you spend any time at all working with my father, you'll find he is every bit as fascinated with the study of history as I am. His library is filled with volumes on the subject. I suppose that's where my interest originates." Rebecca realized her mistake too late. Freddy might feign an interest in history merely to win Father's favor.

She found she had nothing more to say. When the excruciating dinner came to an end, she moved with a sense of relief to the drawing room, which had been cleared for dancing. Rebecca was much better prepared to waltz this time, thanks to the widow's lessons, and she felt lithe and graceful compared to Freddy, who danced as if standing at attention at dress parade. Across the room, Flora and Thomas seemed made for each other, waltzing and whirling as if gliding on ice. Her sister was so vibrant, so pretty. Rebecca hoped Thomas Worthington was worthy of her.

By the time the evening ended, Freddy had bored Rebecca into a stupor—and she had likely bored him, too. After tonight, he would move on to court someone else's wealthy daughter, which was fine with her. But as he stood in the foyer to help her with her wrap, he surprised her by saying, "Would you be kind enough to accompany me to my regimental dinner next week?"

Why? she nearly blurted out. *We have nothing in common.* But then she saw her father watching them. Dark circles rimmed his eyes. He looked as pallid as when he'd suffered from seasickness. Rebecca wanted to help him get well by pleasing him. He was an excellent judge of character and must see something good in Freddy. She turned to him. "I would be delighted to," she lied.

CHAPTER 9

Rebecca attended one event after the other with Freddy Worthington that spring, each time hoping that he would reveal an interest in what she was thinking, what her hopes and dreams were, or who she really was at heart. He didn't. But she continued to play her part for her father's sake, a well-mannered mannequin who was there to be seen but not heard. Occasionally Freddy revealed a charming side, such as when he showed up with a bouquet of flowers, or when he presented her with an elegant gold bracelet engraved with her initials to celebrate her college graduation. "I enjoy your company, Rebecca," he told her. "You're not as giddy as most women I know." If only he had a sense of humor, Rebecca thought with a sigh. Or even a tiny pinch of curiosity. She would much rather he asked about her history dissertation than bring her flowers.

She longed to tell Father that she wanted to court someone else, but each time she gathered up her nerve, she would see him and Freddy talking together and would realize two things: how happy Freddy seemed to make her father, and how very ill Father seemed to be. The summer of 1865 arrived and once again, Rebecca's travel plans remained in her dresser drawer along with a scrapbook filled with news clippings about Egypt. The Prince of Wales had made a tour down the Nile three years ago, and she had filled the pages with weekly reports of his travels, along with articles detailing the progress being made on digging the Suez Canal. Egypt had become an exotic destination for Europe's wealthiest tourists, and it frustrated Rebecca that they were viewing the pyramids and she wasn't. If Father's health would improve, Rebecca felt certain Flora would agree to travel with her even if he didn't care to go. Yet she felt callous for fussing about his illness simply because she wanted to be free to travel.

To ease her boredom, Rebecca planned a Fourth of July picnic with Freddy in nearby Lake Park. She recalled the picnickers in the *Jardin des Tuileries* in Paris and hoped that spending a romantic afternoon together beneath sunny Chicago skies would draw them closer. She also hoped to pique his interest in Egypt and turn him into the traveling companion she longed for. As they sat on a blanket spread on the grass, eating Maria Elena's fried chicken and squares of corn bread, Rebecca unfolded a newspaper article. "Have you been reading the news about the Suez Canal, Freddy?" He shook his head, swatting at a fly buzzing around his head. "They've been digging for five years and are halfway done. Imagine how much time it will save once it opens. Ships won't have to sail around the entire continent of Africa to get to India or the Far East." She laid the clipping in front of him, but he showed no interest. He was much more concerned with the colony of ants that marched with great determination toward their hamper.

"Listen, is there any way to be rid of all these insects?" he asked. "They're swarming everywhere."

"Not that I know of. They're part of the charm of an open-air picnic. We're invading their territory, so it's only fair that they investigate us."

"I don't find insects charming."

"Forget about them, Freddy. We're surrounded by beautiful trees—and look at what a lovely color Lake Michigan is today. I love hearing the birds singing and watching the squirrels chase each other, don't you? I would eat all my meals outdoors if I could."

Freddy shivered as if the ants had crawled up his pant leg. The picnickers in Paris hadn't looked disgruntled and uncomfortable. But perhaps Freddy felt as awkward as she did at a formal occasion with her corset laced up tightly and her crinolines itching. She sighed and tried again.

"When Father is feeling better, I still plan to visit Egypt, the Holy Land, and Greece. Flora and I studied Greek so we'll be able to converse with people. And I recently located a tutor to teach us Arabic for our visits to the Ottoman Empire."

"I'm sure you've also read the news about the unrest in Europe between Austria and Prussia. I don't think it's safe to travel there."

"Europe is a big continent, Freddy. I'm certain it's possible to travel and still avoid any unrest." She watched him pick up a chicken drumstick with his thumb and forefinger as if reluctant to get his hands dirty. He had searched the hamper in vain for plates and cutlery, and had finally settled for spreading his napkin across his lap.

"As for visiting Egypt and the Ottoman Empire," he continued, "there is a continual threat of contracting cholera and dysentery in such backward places. I would think that would dampen your enthusiasm."

"Not a chance. There have been outbreaks of cholera right here in Chicago, too." Rebecca watched Freddy nibble at his lunch while waging a futile battle against the ants and flies and a pesky yellow jacket that seemed determined to annoy him. She had trouble picturing him sipping coffee at a romantic outdoor café in Paris, let alone sailing down the Nile River on a dahabeeah.

The afternoon didn't get any better as time passed. Freddy declined a walk along the lakeshore, fearing the damp sand would ruin his shoes. He didn't want to wait for the fireworks display, complaining of mosquitoes once the sun set. Rebecca's hope that she and Freddy would grow more comfortable with each other in a more relaxed setting had failed. But she did let him steal a kiss in the foyer when he brought her home. She saw him moving close, bending his head toward her, and she closed her eyes in anticipation, wondering what it would feel like to be kissed. It was described in literature as something wonderful. Freddy's arms encircled her, and he pressed his damp lips to hers for a long moment before pulling away again. She could see by the light in the foyer that his cheeks had turned as red as ripe apples. Sadly, the only emotion Rebecca felt was embarrassment. "Good-bye," she said abruptly. "Thank you for a nice afternoon." She pushed him out the door.

Their courtship continued throughout the fall and winter months as the opportunity to travel abroad remained out of reach. The widow had arranged Rebecca's social calendar and her dates with Freddy weeks in advance, and Rebecca didn't know how to explain to Mrs. Worthington—or to Freddy, for that matter—that she would like to try courting someone else. Someone who shared an interest in the things she did. Someone funny and spontaneous and witty. Someone who liked talking about the same things she did. Where was the steady stream of eligible suitors that were supposed to be lining up at her door after the war? With no way out, Rebecca allowed herself to be dragged along, listening with envy as Flora chattered on and on about Thomas, who seemed to be everything her sister dreamed of in a partner. Flora barely took an interest in her final year of studies at North Western College, while Rebecca spent every spare moment learning Arabic with a private tutor and auditing every university history or theology course she could cajole her way into attending.

By spring of 1866, her boredom with Freddy began tilting dangerously toward dislike. His only interest seemed to be in learning how to make more money. Rebecca knew that good manners required never mentioning religion but she decided to wade into theological waters as they rode home from church one Sunday. Freddy had been attending church with her and Father—and Mrs. Worthington, of course—for several months.

"We've never spoken about God or our faith," she began, "but I wondered what you thought about today's sermon and Jonah's reluctant response to God's call. Have you ever heard God's call in your life?"

The nervous jiggling of Freddy's foot sped up. "As a Christian, I feel that the church plays an important role in people's lives."

"Does *God* play a role in your life?"

"I don't understand the question. What's the difference?"

"There's a huge difference! The church is composed of all of us, and God is . . . well, He's God! He created me the way I am for a purpose, and I want to obey Him when He asks me to do something for Him, instead of running the other way like Jonah did. But I'm still not clear what, exactly, He's calling me to do."

Freddy uncrossed his right leg and switched to his left one. It immediately began jiggling as fast as the other one had. "I've always tried to follow the church's teachings and to be a good person . . ."

"But what if God asked you to—"

"To be honest, Rebecca," he interrupted, "this is not the sort of conversation I'm very comfortable with."

She let it go. But that was the day Rebecca decided that she couldn't keep up the façade of interest in Freddy a single day longer. Their courtship had reached a dead end. Marrying him was out of the question. She couldn't imagine spending a lifetime with a man whose faith was as tepid as Freddy's or who led such a narrowly constricted life. Rebecca couldn't remember ever laughing out loud when she was with him, pouring her heart out to him, or engaging in an interesting discussion with him on any topic. She made up her mind to tell Father about her decision and to end her courtship once and for all, regardless of how ill Father was or how upset it made him. She had tried to like Freddy, truly she had. But she was beginning to dislike herself in the process.

The opportunity came the following evening when Father summoned her and Flora into his library for a meeting. The familiar scent of his cigars and his worn leather chairs filled the dark-paneled room. Rebecca drew courage from the shelves of books surrounding her. Her father's love of learning was as insatiable as hers, and he wouldn't ask her to settle for a man who never opened a book. But Father looked as small and as pale as a ghost as he sat down behind his mahogany desk, facing her and Flora. "I know you girls have been concerned about my health," he began, "so I'll tell you the truth. The doctors say I have a leaky heart."

"Oh no!" Flora's hands flew to cover her mouth. Rebecca's own heart seemed to skip a beat.

"The reason I sometimes experience trouble breathing is because fluid is gathering in my chest as my heart grows weaker."

Rebecca wondered how the books stayed on the shelves as the room seemed to shift and tilt. Father was the pillar of her life, the source of her independent nature, her encourager, her inspiration. He couldn't be dying! She gripped the armrests to steady herself as something deep inside her felt shaken loose. "Can they do anything to help you?"

"I've been assured that I'll have the best care possible." He took a fresh cigar from his humidor, snipped off the end and held it to his nose to smell it before placing it between his fingers. The familiar ritual, part of Rebecca's life since childhood, pierced her heart. But Father never completed the final step of lighting it, and the dead cigar seemed like an omen. He cleared his throat and said, "Now, what I also want to discuss with you girls tonight is—"

"Wait!" Rebecca said. "Tell us everything the doctors said, first." She wanted to ask if he was dying, and if so, how much time she had left with him, but she was afraid to say the words out loud.

"The doctors have prescribed some remedies that may help. And they've advised me to cut back on my work, perhaps by hiring an assistant. Which brings me to Frederick Worthington." Rebecca's stomach made a slow turn. "He asked me for your hand in marriage, Rebecca. He's a fine young man from a good family, and not only would he make an able assistant to me, but a fine husband for you."

Rebecca gripped the chair even tighter, fighting the urge to shake her head in refusal. She saw no way out without disappointing her father—and who knew how much longer he had to live? He wanted his household in order before he died, she understood that. But the cost to her was much too great. "It's just that I . . . I still want to travel and see the world, and Freddy doesn't want to. Isn't there some way I could go abroad and get it out of my system first before committing myself to marriage?"

"Perhaps. But right now it's urgent that I find a partner for you who is bright enough and trustworthy enough to manage your money. You and Flora will become very wealthy women after I die, and I fear I haven't adequately prepared you for the responsibility of handling so much wealth. I don't expect you to be knowledgeable about investments and trust funds and things of that nature, but I feel that the wealth I've acquired was entrusted to me by God, and so I'm obligated to leave it in capable hands."

"But you aren't dying now, are you Father?" Rebecca asked. Panic rose and swirled like flood waters. "Why is it so important that I marry Freddy and not someone else?" *Anyone else!* A man who would laugh with her, dream with her.

"Because your inheritance will pass to your husband when you marry, and I want to be sure that the men you and Flora marry understand how to handle it. According to the laws of this state, your husband takes full control of your inheritance, your property, and your estate once you're married, and—"

"Wait! Full control?" Helplessness filled Rebecca with rage. "Does this mean I can't control my own life or make my own decisions after I marry? I can't even claim my own inheritance? That's outrageous!"

"It's the law, Rebecca."

"Does Freddy know how much you're worth?"

"He has a fairly good idea."

"Then how do you know he isn't marrying me for your money?"

"Because he's Mrs. Worthington's nephew. She has vouched for his outstanding character."

"Don't you think she might be just a little biased?"

"Don't be unkind, Rebecca."

A crushing weight pressed down on her, making it hard to think, to breathe. Freddy Worthington sat atop that suffocating weight. She struggled against rising despair as she searched for a way out.

"I'm sorry, Father, but I don't think I can accept Freddy's proposal right now. He doesn't think I should travel and explore the world, and that's what I long to do. He has also made it clear that he doesn't want to travel with me."

"Perhaps something can be worked out—"

"Haven't you always taught Flora and me that we need to pursue God's purpose for our lives? I can't believe that it's my purpose to marry Freddy Worthington and give dinner parties for his important clients for the rest of my life."

"What do you plan to do with your life, Rebecca?"

"I don't know. That's the problem. I need to find out why God made me so interested in history and languages and travel. Why He gave us so much wealth, when most of the world is so poor. He must have something He wants me to do with what I've been given."

"I think—"

"And what about love?" she interrupted. "Shouldn't two people be in love with each other if they're going to spend the rest of their lives together?"

"Frederick assures me that he's very fond of you—"

"*Fond?* You want me to spend the rest of my life with a man who is merely *fond* of me? Were you in love with our mother when you married her or merely *fond* of her?"

He looked down at his cigar, still clenched between his fingers. She heard him draw a wheezing breath and realized with a shock that the reason his cigar remained unlit was because he couldn't breathe deeply enough to light it. "I loved your mother very much," he said softly.

The tenderness in his voice brought tears to Rebecca's eyes. "I want to fall in love, too, Father."

He nodded and laid down his cigar. "I won't force you to marry Frederick. But I will ask you to give his proposal more thought before you turn him down. Frederick is going to approach you in the very near future. Please pray about your answer."

"I will." The words came out choked as she swallowed a knot of grief.

"Now, what about you, Flora?" he said, turning to her. "Frederick's cousin Thomas has asked me for your hand, and—"

"Wait—what?" Rebecca interrupted. She knew how soft-hearted Flora was, how eager to please their father. She couldn't let her sister rush into a marriage that she might one day regret. "You're barely twenty years old, Flora. You haven't finished your college degree yet. What's the big hurry?"

Flora stared at her as if surprised by the interruption.

Father replied before Flora could. "I don't think there's any hurry for either of you to set a wedding date. It will take time to educate both Thomas and Frederick about the intricacies of my estate. Neither of them is ready to handle it at this point. But I don't want to begin the apprenticeship until you're both committed to marriage."

"I can't imagine myself with anyone but Thomas," Flora said, her voice dreamy.

"That's because he hasn't given you a chance to court anyone else!" Rebecca shouted, infuriated. "Tell me, have you talked with him about your charity work? Do you know how he feels about the fact that you donate so much time and money to the poor?"

"Thomas knows that I volunteer at the county home, but we haven't talked much about it or—"

"Then you'd better do it soon, Flora. Once he's in charge of all your money, he'll be the one who decides which causes you can contribute to and which ones he thinks are a waste of your money—I mean *his* money. Because it will all become *his*! He'll—"

"That's enough, Rebecca." Father said. "You don't need to make Flora unhappy just because you are."

She refused to back down. "I'm sorry, Father, but this is a huge decision for both of us. I'm worried that Flora will be blinded by Thomas' charm and swayed by her desire to please you. Flora doesn't know how to say no to anyone."

"Becky!" Flora sounded more hurt than angry.

"I'm sorry, but this conversation has me very upset. Not only have I just learned that Father is gravely ill, but I feel like I'm being forced to hand over control of my life to a man who doesn't even love me, and who bores me to tears!" She rose to flee to her room.

"Just a moment," Father said before she reached the door. "There's one more thing I would like to say." Rebecca turned around in the doorway, tears burning her eyes. "I've asked Mrs. Worthington to marry me. It'll be a quiet ceremony, no fuss or frills. And it will take place next summer, after Flora finishes college."

"You don't need to wait for my sake," Flora said.

He looked past Flora at Rebecca, who stood trembling in the doorway. She shook her head. "I think it's best that Mrs. Worthington and I wait," he said.

Rebecca turned and ran upstairs to her bedroom, stumbling over her petticoats as they tried to trip her on the way up. Freddy Worthington was going to propose to her. It was what her father wanted, what he believed was best for her. She locked her door and threw herself onto her bed, sobbing into her pillow and ignoring all of Flora's pleas to let her come inside.

⟫⟪

Two weeks later, Rebecca and Freddy attended a birthday celebration for Mrs. Worthington, a date that had been arranged weeks earlier. She dreaded the evening, fearing he might use the festive occasion to propose to her. Rebecca watched Freddy's ever-tapping fingers on the tablecloth as Mrs. Worthington cut her birthday cake and felt his jiggling foot shaking the floor, and she wished he would propose and get it over with. Instead, he waited until the evening ended and they sat in his carriage parked outside her home. Freddy took her gloved hand in hers, cleared his throat, and said, "Rebecca . . . will you marry me?"

He made no romantic gestures, such as falling on one knee or professing his great love and devotion. There was no heirloom brooch or ring from the Worthington family to dignify the occasion. Freddy lacked the imagination for such meaningful gestures. Rebecca heard his foot tapping the floorboards as he waited for her reply.

She had thought endlessly about what she should say, praying for guidance as her father had requested. She had rehearsed dozens of conversations in her head, practicing each one, debating between her duty and her heart. In the end, she decided that her answer would depend on Freddy's response to one question. He still held her hand, so she gave it a gentle squeeze and asked, "Will you let me go on the excursion to Egypt I've planned for this coming summer?" He looked baffled, and then irritated that she hadn't responded to his proposal with a joyful *yes!*

"What would be the purpose of such a trip, Rebecca? Especially when there will be so many details to attend to before the wedding? And I believe we've already discussed how dangerous and foolhardy it is to travel to that part of the world."

"You're telling me I can't go?"

"As your fiancé, and especially as your husband, I would have to forbid it." His voice was stern, like a parent correcting a child.

She slipped her hand out of his, and the relief she felt was as if she had lifted a noose from around her neck. "Then I'm sorry, Freddy, but my answer to your proposal has to be *no*. I can't marry you."

His body jerked back in surprise, as if it had never occurred to him that she might refuse. She watched his face and saw his expression transform from shock to anger, and then to panic, as he seemed to realize how much wealth had slipped from his grasp in a few brief moments. Rebecca had to turn away. This glimpse of the true motive behind his proposal brought tears of humiliation to her eyes. There were no declarations of undying love, no pleas that he couldn't bear to live without her. "I should go," she said, reaching for the door handle.

"Rebecca, wait." She turned back, swiping her tears, hating that he saw them. "I didn't mean my answer to sound so harsh, but you need to understand that I have a duty to protect you. That is . . . I *want* to protect you, and—"

"I've been under my father's protection all my life, and he has always encouraged me to explore the world and to follow wherever my interests take me."

"Well . . . perhaps under the right circumstances . . . with the proper chaperones and escorts, something might be arranged for you to travel and—"

"But you have no interest in joining me?"

"I-I . . . It would be a waste of my time."

"I see." It would be a waste of his time to be with her, to make her happy. "And once we're married, would I be free to travel wherever and whenever I wanted to? Because I know from past experience that the urge to travel isn't something I can get out of my system. Each journey has left me hungry for more. And there are so many places I long to see as I search for my purpose in life."

"It's just that . . . it may not be very practical to travel once we're married, with all of your social obligations as my wife and—"

"To the devil with my social obligations!" she shouted.

"Rebecca!"

"There! I've shocked you. You need to know, Freddy Worthington, that the real Rebecca Hawes is outspoken and short-tempered and opinionated. I don't know why I've allowed myself to become molded into this . . . this phony persona your aunt has created of a demure, high-society debutante. But it's not the real me." She pulled off her hat as she spoke and tossed it onto the carriage floor, then yanked her fingers from her gloves, tearing the delicate lace in the process. She threw them onto the floor, too. She would have ripped off her petticoats and discarded her scratchy crinolines if it hadn't been impossible to free herself without her maid's help. "The life you're offering me isn't the life I want, Freddy. It's as suffocating as this stupid whalebone corset I'm forced to wear!"

"Rebecca . . . please . . ." His face was turning red at her impromptu striptease and the inappropriate mention of her intimate undergarments.

"I hate that my clothes are so complicated that I can't even undress myself. And that my hair has to be brushed and combed and curled and pinned for me. You can't imagine how much I long to pull out my hairpins and strip down to my bloomers and run out to our backyard and swing from the parallel bars Father built for us."

"I've heard quite enough."

"Good. Then you understand that I don't want anything to do with the wealthy social world that you love so much. I've gone along with everything your aunt has forced me to do for my father's sake. It was what he wanted for me. But I've let myself become trapped like a wild bird in a gilded cage, and now it's time for me to escape and fly free."

Panic seemed to make Freddy short of breath, as if he saw the life he'd envisioned flying away with her. "Perhaps you need more time to—"

"No. I don't need more time. You're a nice man, Freddy, and I'm certain you'll find the wife you need. One who shares your values and ambitions. But it won't be me."

Rebecca climbed from the carriage, trampling on her gloves and crushing her hat, leaving them behind. She strode through the front door of her home, kicked off her delicate shoes at the foot of the stairs and skipped up to her bedroom, feeling enormous relief. The weight that had pressed down on her for so long was gone. Rebecca pulled out her hairpins and shook her head to free her hair. Maybe she would have her hair cut short. Maybe she would cut it short herself. Tomorrow she would tell her seamstress to create some simple dresses from ordinary fabric, dresses that didn't require crinolines or corsets or an entourage of servants to help her button them. And from now on, Rebecca Hawes would not allow herself to become imprisoned in a cage of etiquette and social obligations, especially with a man who didn't know her. Or love her.

When Flora returned home from the widow's birthday party, Rebecca told her about Freddy's proposal. And her refusal. "I'll probably never marry—and that's fine with me. If I can't find a husband who loves me the way I am, then I'll look for a university somewhere that will allow me to study and learn. I don't need a husband in order to make something of my life. I can do it on my own."

"Are you sure about this, Becky? It seems like a very drastic decision."

"Very sure. Ever since Mrs. Worthington came into our lives, I've been going along with her coaching, letting her turn me into someone I'm not—and hating it! Now that I've finally come to my senses, I can get on with my life the way I was meant to live it."

"I can't imagine what Father will say."

Rebecca's bubble of euphoria popped. "I know. He'll be so disappointed. I dread telling him. He can still hire Freddy to manage my inheritance if he wants to, but I can't marry him."

Flora took Rebecca's hands in hers. "Maybe it will soften the blow for Father when I tell him my news."

"Oh, Flora, you didn't . . ."

"Please don't think less of me," she said, squeezing her hands tightly. "But I've accepted Thomas' marriage proposal."

Rebecca closed her eyes for a moment. "Does he make you happy?" she asked when she opened them again.

"Yes," Flora said.

But Rebecca glimpsed tears in her eyes before Flora enveloped her in an embrace. She hoped they were tears of joy. "Then I'm happy for you, too," she said.

At least one of the caged birds had escaped.

CHAPTER 10

Rebecca was dressing for breakfast the next morning when she heard Griffin, their butler, receiving a caller in the front hall. She finished buttoning her shirtwaist and went down in her bare feet to see who it was. Going without shoes and stockings was a delicious luxury that would appall Mrs. Worthington, who probably would dress in crinolines if she was dying of the plague. The foyer was empty except for Griffin, who stood holding the silver tray containing their caller's engraved name card. "Who was at the door?" Rebecca asked.

"Mrs. Worthington, miss. She's waiting for you and Mr. Hawes in the library."

"I've been summoned to court?"

"Apparently." A wry smile flickered on the butler's face. He wasn't fond of the widow either, or the uppity "improvements" she'd demanded from him and the other servants.

Rebecca hurried upstairs to fetch her shoes and to warn Flora, who was getting ready for school, of the coming confrontation. "Mrs. Worthington is here," she said after knocking on Flora's door. "I'm guessing she heard that I refused Freddy's proposal."

"Oh dear."

"I've been summoned to the library. Come with me, Flora. I need your support."

Father had been eating his breakfast in bed and going to work late for the past few weeks, but he came downstairs in his robe and slippers—the first time Rebecca could ever recall him doing so—and sat down behind the desk in his library, facing Mrs. Worthington. Rebecca was too nervous to sit and let Flora take the chair beside the widow's.

"Did Rebecca tell you what she did, Edward?" Mrs. Worthington asked without preamble.

"I haven't had a chance to—" Rebecca began.

"She turned down Freddy's proposal last night."

Father looked surprised. He frowned at Rebecca as he waited for her explanation. "It's true, I did turn him down. I had to refuse him because . . ." She stopped. It was too early in the morning, and she was much too relieved to be free of Freddy to launch into all the reasons why. Nor did she wish to start a war with Mrs. Worthington by enumerating Freddy's faults. She exhaled and said, "Because I don't love him. I tried, but I just don't. And he doesn't love me. I believe love is important in a marriage, don't you?"

Father leaned back in his chair. "I'm disappointed in your decision, of course, but—"

"Flora, on the other hand, very graciously accepted Thomas' proposal," the widow interrupted. She looked pleased with herself, as if she had won at least one victory.

"I was going to tell you the news this morning, Father," Flora said.

He looked from one of them to the other, and Rebecca held her breath as she waited for his reply. "Well, you're both bright, sensible girls," he finally said, "which is why I've always allowed you to make your own decisions. That's especially true when it's something as important as marriage. Perhaps there will be someone else for you, Rebecca."

She felt relieved—but only for a moment. The widow wanted the final word. "But don't you see how selfish Rebecca was to lead Freddy along, all this time?" She presented the perfect picture of genteel anger, sitting with absolute composure, refusing to raise her voice, even though Rebecca could tell she was furious. "You've wasted his precious time, Rebecca. He is quite downhearted."

"Is he downhearted because he loves me or because he'll never inherit my money?"

Father cleared his throat. "Rebecca . . ."

But she wasn't finished with the widow yet. "Didn't you promise Flora and me that dozens of eligible suitors would line up to court us? Where are they?"

"Well, it's too late now. Everyone assumes you and Freddy are a couple."

"You can inform them that we're not. And while you're here, Mrs. Worthington, you can cross off all the social events from my calendar for the rest of the month. In fact, for the rest of the year. If I'm going to court my future husband, I don't want it to be at some stiff, dull affair where I have to get trussed up in corsets and petticoats. I would like to meet someone who enjoys walking along the lakeshore with me, strolling through the park on a Sunday afternoon, or taking a train ride out to see the countryside. Most of all, I would like to meet someone who longs to travel abroad as much as I do."

"I can't help you with that," the widow said coldly. "Not if you're going to insult our way of life."

"Please, don't fight," Flora said, ever the peacemaker. "Let's talk about this again after our tempers have cooled. Have you eaten breakfast, Mrs. Worthington? Would you like to join us?"

"No, thank you," she said, rising to her feet. "I must be on my way. I just wanted to make sure that you knew what your daughter has done, Edward."

"It's not as if I murdered Freddy in cold blood. . . ." Rebecca mumbled, and Flora covered her mouth to hide a smile.

⇒· ⇐

Rebecca enjoyed her freedom for two months. Then her world fell apart on a sunny day in May, and finding a husband no longer seemed important. Two weeks before Flora graduated from college and a month before Widow Worthington would become their stepmother, Father's law clerk found him lying dead on his office floor. Rebecca and Flora were inconsolable.

"It's too soon," Rebecca wept as she clung to Flora. "We were supposed to enjoy many more years together."

"He was supposed to walk me down the aisle when I marry Thomas," Flora said.

"I feel so guilty for disappointing him. He wanted so much to know we would be taken care of after he was gone."

"But he didn't want you to marry someone you didn't love."

"I don't know, Flora . . . I just feel so bad that he passed away before this was resolved."

Father had left written instructions for his funeral and burial, which was a good thing since neither Rebecca nor Flora was able to think past her grief. Rebecca had to close the door to his library at home, unable to look inside and see his vacant desk or catch the scent of his cigars and books. She heard the servants weeping for him and knew they had loved him, too. Rufus was still wiping his eyes as he drove everyone to Father's funeral at the overflowing church. Rebecca barely heard the eloquent eulogies from Chicago's leading citizens. She didn't need other people to tell her what a fine Christian man her father was. Etiquette dictated that she remain in control and save her tears for private moments as Mrs. Worthington was

143

doing, but Rebecca didn't care. She wept throughout the funeral and graveside service, barely noticing the lilacs blooming in the cemetery as they buried their father beside their mother.

Rebecca longed to finish mourning in private with her sister, but the Worthingtons and all the other mourners returned home with her for the funeral luncheon that the servants had prepared. It was part of the grieving process to play the role of a hostess and accept condolences, but all she really wanted to do was run outside to the garden and weep. Rebecca fell into bed that night, exhausted with grief. What would she do with the rest of her life now that she'd finished college and had no prospects for marriage?

A week after the funeral, she and Flora went to Father's law office for the reading of his will. "What are they doing here?" she asked the executor of the estate when she saw Thomas and Mrs. Worthington also arriving.

"Your father wanted them here," the lawyer replied. "Thomas Worthington is engaged to Miss Flora, and Mrs. Worthington is mentioned in the will." At least Freddy hadn't come. Rebecca had no choice but to sit down with them in Father's office as the clerk read the distributions from his sizable estate.

Generous portions went to Father's church and several other charitable institutions. He had died before marrying Mrs. Worthington, but he rewarded her years of patient waiting with a handsome annuity. The vast remainder of his estate would be divided equally between his two daughters—with Thomas Worthington to inherit all of Flora's portion once they married. As the clerk read the long lists of bank figures and investment holdings, Rebecca was astounded to discover how very wealthy she and Flora were. If only she knew what she was supposed to do with all that wealth.

Afterward, she hurried outside to be alone while Flora spoke with Mrs. Worthington and Thomas. Rebecca feared she would lose control if she saw something other than grief in their expressions. She removed her hat and mourning veil as she stood beside the carriage and let the warm breeze ruffle her hair. As she watched Flora embrace the Worthingtons before saying good-bye, Rebecca worried that with so much wealth at stake, they would pressure Flora to marry Thomas quickly. The moment her sister reached the carriage, Rebecca said, "Promise me you won't set a date for your wedding until after our mourning period ends."

Flora gripped her hat as a gust of wind threatened to carry it away. "But Thomas wants to—"

"Never mind what he wants. I'm begging you to wait, for my sake. Please?"

Flora lifted the black mourning veil from her face and her expression turned soft with love. "Yes, of course I'll wait, Becky."

Rufus opened the carriage door, and Flora ducked inside. Rebecca mounted the step, but when she looked inside the black-draped enclosure, she felt as though she were suffocating. She stepped down again. "I think I'll walk home."

"But it's such a long way."

"I don't mind. I need time to think."

"Would you like me to come with you?"

Rebecca looked at Flora's dainty shoes and shook her head. "No, thanks. I want to be alone." Her own shoes weren't much sturdier than her sister's, thanks to Mrs. Worthington's meddling, but Rebecca set off down the avenue, not caring how many blisters she got. Weekday traffic rushed past as Chicagoans went about their business, unaware of Rebecca's loss. She grieved not only for her father but for the emptiness that threatened to fill her life in the days ahead. She longed to find meaning in it all.

A train whistle warbled in the distance as it approached the station. It seemed to beckon to Rebecca, a siren-song that offered hope. Her longing increased as she strode down Michigan

Avenue and found herself in front of Cunard's shipping office, the same one she and Flora had visited as schoolgirls. She opened the door and went inside. Rebecca emerged an hour later with two steamship tickets from New York City to France and strolled the rest of the way home, a tiny spark of hope rekindled.

That evening, she and Flora sat side-by-side in the dining room, trying not to stare at their father's empty chair. Rebecca forced herself to eat three times a day while she mourned—not because she had an appetite, but because the servants insisted. And because Flora said they shouldn't let Maria Elena's hard work go to waste. Rebecca waited until Griffin set the dishes of food on the table, then pulled out the steamship tickets and laid them in front of her sister.

"What is this, Becky?" Flora asked.

"Read it." She gave her sister a moment to peruse the tiny print, then said, "Staying in Chicago while we mourn for Father won't bring him back. I've decided that I'm finally going on our long-planned trip to Egypt. Maybe I'll add the Holy Land, too. And Greece. You once dreamed of seeing all those places, remember? I would love for you to come with me."

"Just the two of us?"

"Well, I won't need a lady's maid when I'm sailing down the Nile River in a dahabeeah, but you may bring your maid along, if you wish."

"Would we be part of a tour group?"

"I'd rather not. The clerk at Cunard's said we can hire a traveling agent to make hotel reservations and arrange ground transportation once we settle on an itinerary. We'll hire a local tour guide for each place we visit—like we did when we went to France and Italy with Father, remember?"

Tears filled Flora's eyes at the mention of their father. Rebecca knew her sister very well, and knew before she spoke that she would refuse. "Thomas wouldn't like me to travel all that way without a chaperone."

"I'm willing to hire one, if you'd like. But Thomas has no right to make decisions for you. You aren't married to him. You haven't even officially announced your engagement, yet."

"I would hate to displease him."

"I doubt he would risk losing your inheritance—or your love—by arguing with you. I'm not asking you to cancel your engagement to Thomas. Just take one last trip with me before you marry him."

Flora laid aside the ticket as if it burned her fingers. She stared down at her empty plate, her hands folded in her lap. "It seems so strange that we can't ask Father for advice. Maybe I should talk to Thomas or Mrs. Worthington first."

Rebecca resisted the urge to shake sense into her. "We're on our own for the time being, and we need to think for ourselves, make our own decisions."

Flora finally looked up. "Why do you want to go so badly, Becky?"

How could she explain it? Rebecca knew she had to try. "The urge to travel has never gone away—never!—despite all of our etiquette lessons, my disastrous courtship with Freddy, and even earning my college degree. It's like a voice in my heart that won't stop nagging me. And so I've come to believe that the voice must be important. That it's leading me to something important."

"What do you suppose that might that be?"

Rebecca took a moment to reply. "Remember when I talked you into going to the poorest part of Chicago? And how that led to our crazy scheme to work in the factory? Those experiences were what made you realize that you had a calling to help the poor, and you've been pursuing it ever since. I know I have a passion for history, but I need to find out what

I'm supposed to do with it. That's what I hope this trip will accomplish."

Flora was truly listening to her. She was the only person besides their Father who ever had. "I understand," Flora said. But she still looked hesitant.

"Look, I'll find someone else to go with me if you don't want to. But there's no one else in the whole world I would rather share this journey with than you. You're my sister, my best friend. The trip will give us a chance to mourn Father without any distractions. He would love that we're finally going. And it will give us the gift of time together before you leave home to marry Thomas."

Flora picked up the ticket again. She studied it for a long moment before looking up at Rebecca again. "If I'm reading this right, our ship sails in less than a month. We'd better get packing if we're going to be ready on time."

Rebecca let out a very unladylike cheer.

CHAPTER 11

THE ATLANTIC OCEAN

Their ship encountered a storm three days at sea, but while the other first-class passengers hunkered in their cabins or huddled on deck chairs, swaddled in blankets, Rebecca and Flora gripped the rail on the passenger deck and watched the waves crash against the side of the ship. Each time the wind brought a spray of salt water that dampened their faces, they laughed aloud. "I love the freedom of the open seas!" Rebecca shouted above the wind. "This invigorates me, Flora! I'm thriving out here! Yet I can't wait to get to shore and start exploring new places!"

"You were right to plan this trip, Becky. I'm glad we're doing this together. It brings back so many good memories of traveling with Father. And I can have one last adventure before I settle down with Thomas."

"Have you talked with Thomas about traveling after you're married? Is he interested?"

"I mentioned it, but he doesn't care to. He complained about how terribly hot it was in Atlanta during the war, and he has hated warm climates ever since. Besides, I hope to have children right away. Dozens of them. I want so much to be a mother."

Rebecca watched the churning waves and gray water for a long moment. "We don't really know what a mother is like, do we? And yet I never felt as though I missed anything."

"I did. And I want to be the very best mother in the world to the children Thomas and I will have."

"I hope that means letting them go off and explore the world. You won't tie them down with all the things they 'must' do, will you?"

"No, I'll be sure to let them travel the world with their wonderful Aunt Becky."

A huge spray of water caught both of them off guard, drenching their faces and the front of their coats. Flora squealed and Rebecca gasped, then they hugged each other, laughing like schoolgirls. "We're on our way to Egypt!" Rebecca shouted. "We're going to see the pyramids—just like we dreamed of doing."

According to *Murray's Guidebook to Modern Egypt and Thebes*, which Rebecca consulted religiously, there were three main routes for travelers to get from France to the pyramids. She chose the most adventurous one so they could see as much of Europe as possible. After landing in France, they traveled east by passenger train and carriage to the Danube River. From there they took a steamboat downriver to the Black Sea, pausing to spend time in beautiful Vienna before entering the Ottoman Empire. A local steamer took them across the Black Sea to Constantinople, where they stayed and explored the city for three days. They hired a guide to show them the best sites, ate in authentic local restaurants, and slept in the best hotels available. They didn't worry about running out of money since they'd arranged for their father's attorney to wire funds to them along the way.

"I've loved traveling through the Ottoman Empire," Rebecca said as they finally boarded another ship to cross the Mediterranean Sea to Alexandria, Egypt. "Freddy was so against it, saying it would be dangerous." They stood at the stern, watching until Constantinople's skyline with its many domes and minarets faded from view. "It's so exotic here! Doesn't it remind you of *The Arabian Nights*? I remember reading that book when we were schoolgirls, and now we're finally visiting these strange lands."

"I'm going to read the book all over again when we get home," Flora replied. "Now I can really picture everything."

The first thing that struck Rebecca when they disembarked from the ship in Cairo was the stench, a potent mixture of stale sweat, human filth, rotting melons, and fish left out too long beneath the sweltering sun. Flora yanked her handkerchief from her sleeve and held it over her nose. The abundance of flies was the second thing Rebecca couldn't help noticing. She tied her bonnet tighter around her face, grateful for the veil netting as fat black flies swarmed and buzzed around her head. "Well, this is certainly an adventure!" she said as they waited for the porter to fetch their baggage.

"Do you suppose we'll get used to the smell?" Flora asked.

"Try not to breathe too deeply," Rebecca replied. She scanned the fascinating array of people, the ships in the harbor, the carriage drivers clamoring for their business, and said, "Let's hire that open carriage, Flora. I want to see everything!"

"Are you sure you want that one, Becky? That poor horse looks ready for the glue factory." But Rebecca hurried over to it and allowed the toothless driver to help her onto the seat.

"Take us to Shepheard's Hotel, please," Rebecca said when their baggage had been piled high onto the narrow ledge behind them and tied down with ropes. The raggedy driver cracked his whip and the ancient horse lurched forward.

The crowded streets of Cairo contained more enthralling sights than Rebecca ever dreamed of seeing. They passed a display of Turkish rugs for sale, the owner seated on a wooden chair smoking a hookah. Barefooted girls in long robes and winding head-coverings carried earthenware jars on their heads. Bearded men in turbans trotted past on child-sized donkeys, their feet nearly dragging on the ground. She heard a drum banging and turned to see a dark-skinned man leading a donkey with a monkey on its back. "A monkey, Flora!" she said, laughing. "And it's wearing a little fez!"

"You don't see that on the streets of Chicago."

"Nor that," Rebecca said, drawing Flora's attention to a group of soldiers on horseback, dressed in the baggy trousers and headgear of Zouaves. "They look like they just arrived home from the Crusades."

The streets became broader, the buildings more European-looking as they neared Shepheard's Hotel. "I'm a little embarrassed by our transportation," Flora said when they halted in front of the elegant hotel where men and women in Western dress lounged on the broad veranda.

"I'm not. This hardworking man and his horse need to earn a living, too." But when three hotel porters came running to help, she guessed it was to prevent the ragged Egyptian from stepping his sandaled feet in their fashionable hotel. Rebecca paid the fare, adding a liberal tip. The driver looked shocked, but whether it was from her generosity or the fact that she thanked him in Arabic, she couldn't tell.

"I believe you just gave him enough money to buy a new horse," Flora whispered.

"I believe he could use one," she whispered back.

They stepped into the hotel and into a different world. The exotic streets of Cairo might have been hundreds of miles away. The porters and waiters spoke English and French, the guests wore Paris fashions, and the food and accommodations had been tailored to Western tastes. Rebecca hated it, but tolerated it for Flora's sake. At least they could have a hot bath.

The first thing Rebecca did after settling her sister in their room was speak with the concierge about visiting the pyramids. "Certainly, mademoiselle. We have a carriage tour leaving the hotel tomorrow morning after breakfast if—"

"I don't want a tour or a carriage. My sister and I would like to travel by camelback to see the pyramids. And we would like to leave before breakfast so we can watch the sunrise."

His obliging smile seemed to slip a bit but he said, "Very well, mademoiselle. And will there be others with you? A gentleman, perhaps?"

"Just the two of us." She could see she had shocked him and knew it wouldn't be the last time that she would do so.

The timing the next morning turned out to be perfect. The sun was just bursting above the horizon, setting the eastern sky aflame, when Rebecca saw the great pyramids of Giza for the first time. The sight, from her perch atop a camel, took her breath away. "I had no idea how enormous the pyramids are, Flora! Aren't they magnificent?" They arrived before any of the other tourists and had the vast, rocky plain and towering views all to themselves. Flora swiveled around in the saddle as if trying to take it all in.

"I can barely speak, Becky!"

They asked the guide to take them closer, and as the sun continued to rise above the distant Nile, they reached the base of the Great Pyramid. "I feel as small and insignificant as an ant," Flora breathed. "How in the world did they build something this enormous?"

"Let's try to climb it," Rebecca said. They dismounted, and Rebecca asked the guide and one of the camel drivers to take their hands and lead the way up the huge, step-like stones. Many of the blocks were nearly as tall as she was. They climbed only to the height of a rooftop when they had to stop. "Confound these useless skirts!" Rebecca fumed. "We could make it all the way if we had worn our bloomers."

"Wouldn't that have shocked Cairo society!" They sat down on one of the huge stones, their feet dangling, and gazed down at the Plain of Giza. The colossal head of the Sphinx sprouted from the ground in the distance, its body trapped beneath the rocky earth.

"I can't believe we're finally here, Becky. We've dreamt about this all our lives. I only wish Father could see this."

"I know. I do, too." Rebecca felt dizzy with joy as she pondered what a significant moment this was for her. "I have a degree in history, yet I still can't comprehend how very ancient these pyramids are. They were already here when Abraham and Sarah traveled to Egypt. Joseph might have seen them when he labored here as a slave and when he saved Egypt from the famine. The Hebrews would have seen them when they worked to make bricks—and Moses, too, when God ordered him to challenge Pharaoh's power and deliver the Hebrews from slavery. Even the infant Jesus may have seen them when Mary and Joseph fled here with Him to escape from King Herod. I can't grasp all those thousands of years of history, can you?" Flora shook her head.

Rebecca had believed that seeing the pyramids would bring satisfaction—and it had, to a certain measure. Yet something more still called to her. "I feel like this is only the beginning, Flora," she said, stretching her arms wide. "There's something I'm supposed to do in response to this. Something meaningful. I just have no idea what it might be."

"Then we'll simply have to keep asking and searching until you figure it out."

They spent all day exploring the pyramids and returned to

Cairo late that afternoon sticky, hot, and coated with a layer of dust. After a warm bath and a dinner of English-style roast beef and potatoes, they decided to explore the open-air souk on their own tomorrow. The concierge seemed alarmed when Rebecca asked for directions, and offered to send a guide along to accompany them. She relented for Flora's sake, and the three of them set off to see the market after breakfast, she and Flora wearing their sturdy shoes. They smelled the souk before they saw it. The blended aromas of cumin and mint, baking bread and donkey droppings, strong tobacco and even stronger coffee filled the narrow, shop-lined streets. Buyers and merchants shouted angrily as they bartered for wares, and Rebecca halted in front of a silk shop to eavesdrop on a conversation, trying to see how much she understood. At first it sounded as though the two men might come to blows any minute, but when she finally deciphered what they were saying, she laughed out loud.

"What's so funny?" Flora asked. "What are they so angry about?"

"They're bartering over that bolt of silk, but the amount they're dickering over is a matter of pennies." The same scene played over and over as they wandered down the street, whether it was for a turquoise necklace or a bag of pistachios.

"Bartering seems to be a way of life here," Flora said.

"Yes, and I'd love to try my hand at it." The opportunity came a few minutes later when an oily little man approached with what looked like a page from a very old book. Their guide tried to wave the man away, but the ancient-looking document aroused Rebecca's curiosity. The souk's dark alleyway didn't offer much sunlight, and Rebecca had to squint to get a good look at it. "This writing isn't Hebrew, but it's similar. I'd like to know if this is parchment or maybe papyrus, but I have no idea how to say either word. It certainly looks old, though."

"It could be a clever fake."

"True. I don't think I've ever seen real parchment. It's supposedly made of animal skins." She held the page to her nose and sniffed, then laughed and made a face. "Oh, my! That smells rotten! But I think I'll try bartering with him." Their guide offered to do the bartering for her, but Rebecca declined. "I need to make good use of my Arabic lessons."

"How will you know if you're paying too much?" Flora asked.

"I won't. But he'll probably start exorbitantly high, so I'll start ridiculously low, and maybe we'll meet in the middle." A curious crowd of Egyptian men in turbans and fezzes and small boys in long tunics and skullcaps gathered around to watch, amazed to hear a young Western woman speaking their language. Judging by the expressions on their faces, they were shocked that she dared to barter with a man—and with her face uncovered, no less. To Rebecca, the process was great fun. "I can see why these people enjoy haggling so much," she told Flora after she'd agreed on a price several minutes later. It was much closer to the Egyptian's starting price than to hers, but Rebecca felt elated as she walked away with a lighter purse and a scrap of something that looked and smelled very old. When they returned to their hotel room late that afternoon to wash off the dust and sweat of Cairo, Rebecca examined it more closely.

"Can you tell what it is? Is it authentic?" Flora asked.

"I have no idea. I'll try to find out when we get home. But that was fun, wasn't it? I might try bartering for everything when we get back to Chicago."

They spent a week in Cairo, exploring the city on foot or sometimes by carriage, eating warm bread from street vendors and sipping coffee in tiny cafés. The other hotel guests seemed shocked when Rebecca described their exploits over dinner in the evening. "This has been the trip of a lifetime, Becky," Flora said at the end of a wonderful week. "I'm so glad you talked me into coming. I won't forget the sight of those magnificent pyramids as long as I live. Or how poor and filthy this part of the world is. The slums of Chicago seem clean in comparison— and that's saying a lot."

Rebecca went over to the window where her sister stood gazing down at the street in front of the hotel. "Listen, Flora, I've been thinking. . . . I'm not ready to return to Chicago, are you? We've only been traveling for a little more than a month."

"Well . . . I am enjoying myself immensely. I would be willing to stay a little longer, but I should send Thomas a cable to let him know we changed our plans."

Rebecca didn't reply. Flora's response reminded her that soon she'd be losing her sister. Their lives would diverge in opposite directions once they returned home and Flora became Mrs. Thomas Worthington. Rebecca neither wanted nor expected to be invited to Worthington family events after refusing Cousin Freddy's marriage proposal; she would need to steer her life in a different direction.

"Let's pack up tonight and leave for the Holy Land, Flora. We'll send Thomas a cable before we go." Rebecca hoped to be in Jerusalem by the time Thomas read the message. He would have no way to voice his displeasure or pressure Flora to return. "The easiest way to get to Jerusalem," she continued, "would be to take a boat down the Nile and across the Mediterranean to the port of Joppa—"

"And risk getting shipwrecked like the Apostle Paul?" Flora asked with a grin. "Or swallowed by a giant fish like Jonah? That sounds dangerously fun!"

"Yes, it does. But I also think it would be fun to travel by land like Abraham and Sarah did when they went back and forth from Egypt to the Promised Land. It would be more authentic, and we'd have more freedom to stop and see things along the way."

"Wonderful! Let's do it!"

Rebecca asked the concierge to engage the services of a

traveling agent the next morning while Flora sent a telegram to Thomas telling him their plans. "I can arrange for you to travel with a touring group—" the concierge began, but Rebecca cut him off.

"No, thank you. You must know by now that my sister and I don't do things the conventional way."

"Yes, mademoiselle. I do. But the road to Gaza can be very dangerous and—"

"Thank you for your concern. I'm certain we'll be fine." It took an extra day to arrange storage for all but their most basic clothing and necessities at the hotel, and for Habib, the guide the concierge hired, to gather supplies and assemble a caravan of horses and mules. Rebecca and Flora left Cairo at dawn, riding sidesaddle on a pair of pretty white horses, grateful for the riding lessons Rufus had arranged.

With Cairo behind them, they passed through a few scattered villages and settlements along the Gaza Road before it became desolate and deserted. After a while it seemed as though they'd traveled for hours since passing through a town, and they'd seen no other travelers or caravans during that time. Rebecca decided not to mention to Flora that the concierge had called this road "very dangerous." She had begun to wonder how fast her horse could gallop if trouble arose, and if she could stay in the saddle if it did, when a distant heap of rags alongside the road suddenly leaped up and began frantically fluttering its arms. The drivers seemed wary of the man as they approached, and Rebecca was, too, until she realized that he was shouting in English.

"Hello, there! . . . Hello! Oh, thank heaven!" he said with a sigh when she drew her horse to a halt. Beneath the dust and sweat was a tall, lean, pleasant-looking man in his thirties, with sandy hair and eyes as blue as the desert sky. "I wonder if you would be kind enough to help me?" he asked in a crisp British accent.

"What's wrong?" Rebecca asked from her perch atop her horse.

"I'm terribly embarrassed to admit it, but it seems I've been swindled. The agent and caravan I hired in Cairo to take me to Jerusalem stole all my cash and equipment, then abandoned me along the roadside. I might have known that the price we agreed on was too good to be true, but I was hoping to save a few quid, you see—and now they've taken off like Ali Baba and the forty thieves, except there were only a half-dozen of them."

Rebecca covered her mouth to hide a smile. The poor man wasn't trying to be funny, and his situation wasn't at all humorous, but there was something comical about finding a proper Englishman in the middle of nowhere wearing khaki shorts and the kind of hat that explorers wear when making great archaeological discoveries. She couldn't help smiling.

"I've been alternating between walking and resting for the longest time," he continued, groping in the pockets of his shorts. "Well, it seems they've stolen my pocket watch, too, so I'm not exactly sure how long it's been. Certainly since before mid-morning. I've been praying that the Lord would forgive my foolishness for trusting myself to brigands and rescue me in spite of it . . . and finally! You're the first travelers to come along in hours."

"You look very hot," Flora said. "Would you like a drink of water?"

"Yes, if you'd be so kind. The bit of water they left me is nearly gone." He pulled a water skin from the canvas bag he wore slung over his shoulder and smiled shyly as he shook it. The water made a faint sloshing sound.

"Help us dismount," Rebecca commanded the driver in Arabic, "and give the man some water." The driver gripped her waist as she slid to the ground, then helped Flora dismount. Habib untied an extra water skin from their mule's supplies and offered it to the stranger. The Englishman held it to his lips and drank long and deep. He looked like the very definition of an exotic explorer. He had rolled up his shirtsleeves, and the sun had toasted every inch of exposed skin on his arms, face, and bare legs. He might pass for a Cherokee Indian if he'd hidden his sun-bleached hair beneath a feathered headdress. He was pleasant-looking, Rebecca decided, and his blue eyes seemed kind.

"Ah. Thank you, my dear ladies," he breathed as he wiped his lips. "I do believe you have saved my life. You are fortunate to speak Arabic. My lack of foresight in learning the language was what led to my being swindled. I've traveled this part of the world many times, but this has never happened before."

"How unfortunate that it happened now. My name is Rebecca Hawes," she said, extending her hand. "And this is my sister, Flora. We're from Chicago, Illinois."

"Edmund Merriday from Cambridge, England. How do you do?" His grip was strong as he shook hands.

"We do very well, thank you," Rebecca said, "While you, Mr. Merriday, seem to be having a hard time of it."

He laughed heartily, as she'd hoped he would. "I was reading the parable of the Good Samaritan as I was sitting here, and I decided I fared a little better than that ancient traveler did. I may have been robbed, but at least I wasn't beaten and left for dead."

"Nor did you lose your sense of humor, I see."

"Would you like to join us, Mr. Merriday?" Flora asked. "We would be happy to help you along to the next village or perhaps to Ashkelon, if you'd like. We certainly can't leave you stranded all alone out here."

"That would be very kind of you," he said with obvious relief.

Rebecca ordered the driver to reposition the saddles and the loads so she and Flora could ride the same animal, leaving a horse for Mr. Merriday.

"What brings you ladies along just in time to rescue me?" he asked.

"We're indulging our love of travel," Rebecca replied. "After visiting Egypt and the pyramids, we decided to see the Holy Land."

"Are you with a tour group?" He shielded his eyes to look down the road behind them. "Where's the rest of your traveling party?"

"It's just Flora and me. Our agent, Habib, takes care of the horses and supplies and hires drivers for us."

"Bravo for you!" He didn't seem the least bit shocked that they were traveling unescorted. "You were fortunate to find a good agent. The one I hired in Cairo turned out to be a scoundrel."

When the horses were ready, Habib boosted Flora into the saddle, then helped Rebecca mount behind her on the horse's rump. It wasn't the most comfortable arrangement, but Rebecca had wanted an adventure. Mr. Merriday hoisted himself onto the horse as if accustomed to riding. They started on their way again, their horses walking side by side.

"What brings you to this part of the world, Mr. Merriday?" Flora asked.

"Please, call me Edmund," he said with a grin. "Mr. Merriday sounds much too stuffy, don't you think?"

"Then you must call us Flora and Rebecca," she replied.

"Very well, Flora. To answer your question, I'm on summer holidays at the moment from Cambridge University, where I work as a research librarian. I dabble in amateur archaeology on the side, so I've been poking around this part of the world looking for items to add to my collection."

"What sort of collection?"

He opened his dusty canvas bag again, and pulled out bits of broken pottery, stones, and scraps of paper, holding up each

item for them to see. "I collect potsherds like these. And fragments of biblical scrolls. I'm interested in ancient manuscripts,
in particular. Thank heaven the thieves didn't see any value in
these relics and took only my money."

"Most men I know would be horrified at the thought of
losing 'only' money," Rebecca said with a laugh. "But those
pages of yours . . . they look a lot like something I purchased
in Cairo. May I show it to you?"

"Certainly."

Rebecca gripped Flora's jacket to keep from falling off
the horse as she dug through the saddlebag for the page of
parchment she'd purchased. She unwound the wrappings and
held it out to him. "Can you tell me anything about it?" He
studied it carefully, holding it up to the light, squinting at
the tiny writing, scratching the edge of it with his fingernail,
sniffing it as she had done, all while balancing on the moving
horse. He seemed very athletic for a man who worked in a
library all day.

"I'm very impressed," he said at last. "I think this may be
ancient parchment, but I would have to examine it with a magnifying glass to be certain."

"Do you know what it says? Can you read it?"

He rummaged in his bag and produced a pair of horn-
rimmed spectacles. "The writing appears to be Syriac. I'm
guessing from what's left of the binding that it's a page from
a very old codex. May I ask where you purchased it?"

"Flora and I were exploring one of the back streets in Cairo
when an oily little man asked if I wanted to buy it."

"Do you remember which part of Cairo?"

"Yes, it was in the souk near Shepheard's Hotel. Why do
you ask?"

"I would love to know if there are any more pages from this
codex. Fragments like this have been showing up for sale on the

streets of Cairo ever since tourists started visiting Egypt and the pyramids. Local scavengers and thieves find or steal priceless scrolls and codices, and slice them up to sell piecemeal to tourists. Valuable artifacts are destroyed in the process."

"Is there a way one might save these documents from destruction?"

"Yes, by purchasing them—hopefully before they're cut into pieces—and bringing them to a proper university or museum for scholars to study. I would buy them myself if I could afford it."

Rebecca's heart sped up at the thought of saving precious historical documents. "I would love to learn more about it from you if you can spare the time," she said, "I would especially like to learn how to tell if something is authentic. I'm a student of ancient history, so I understand their importance."

He smiled, and the wrinkles on his tanned face fell into place around his eyes and mouth as if he smiled often. He was very charming in a bumbling sort of way. "I would be happy to teach you everything I know," he said. "It's the very least I can do in return for your kindness."

"You're traveling on your own, obviously," Flora said. "But do you have a family back home in England?"

"Two married sisters and a father who is a country rector. But I'm married to my passions, a quality not many ladies appreciate in a husband. I spend all of my holidays on treks like this one, sleeping in tents and exploring ancient ruins. I have yet to find a woman who is interested in joining me."

"It sounds heavenly to me," Rebecca said. "Flora and I have no family back home. Sadly, our parents have both passed away."

"I'm sorry to hear that. But if you ladies enjoy trekking from Egypt to Gaza on horseback, you are the exception to the rule, I assure you. I typically travel alone. That way I can wander wherever I like, stay as long as I like, and see what I want to see without anyone slowing me down. Although I do miss engaging in intelligent conversations in the evening. I envy you ladies for having each other for company."

"I couldn't agree more about enjoying the freedom to wander," Rebecca said. "That's why Flora and I set our own itinerary without all the bother of a tour group. We've wanted to travel to this part of the world for some time, but the American War Between the States made it impossible until now. May I ask where you're headed in the Holy Land?"

"I was hoping to visit Galilee and see the ruins of the first century synagogue in Capernaum, but that's clearly out of the question until next year. Those vandals stole everything but my traveling papers and my steamship ticket home."

"We read about those ruins in the newspaper. There are so many wonderful things to see and places to explore. Our list grows longer all the time, doesn't it, Flora?"

They talked all afternoon and arrived at their destination shortly before sunset. Rebecca's knees felt wobbly after dismounting, and Edmund had to grab her to keep her from falling over. "I'm sorry. I guess I'm still not used to riding a horse all day. The swaying made me a little dizzy."

"I can't thank you dear ladies enough for your help. I fear I would still be sitting under an acacia tree and perishing from thirst if not for your kindness."

"What will you do now?" Rebecca asked.

"I have an acquaintance in Joppa who might loan me funds to return to Cairo. I trust I can exchange my steamship ticket once I'm there and sail back to England."

"So this is the end of your vacation?"

"I'm afraid so. For this year, at any rate."

"Where will you sleep tonight?" Flora asked. "What will you eat?"

He lifted his shoulders in a helpless shrug, but before he could reply, Rebecca said, "Our agent has booked a room for us in this inn. Let me see if he can arrange another one for you."

"I couldn't possibly accept. I have no way to repay you."

"Don't worry about that. We can't have you sleeping in the street. You might get robbed again."

"That's very kind of you. I promise to repay you as soon as I arrive home. But you must promise to keep an account of my debt."

"For now, you may repay me by telling me more about ancient manuscripts in general and mine in particular," Rebecca said.

Habib had unloaded their overnight bags and stood ready to escort them into the squat, fieldstone inn while the drivers took the horses away to be boarded for the night. He was casting suspicious glances at Edmund, and his dark brow furrowed in disapproval when Rebecca asked him to book another room for him. Habib was still scowling as he led the way inside, carrying their bags.

"This building looks like something right out of the New Testament," Flora said. It was made entirely of beige stone, with stone walls and floors and an open-air courtyard in the middle. The innkeeper led them to their room, which had a colorful Turkish rug on the floor and two wooden beds, piled with Moroccan blankets. "You don't suppose these beds have fleas, do you?" she asked.

"This is an adventure, Flora. You can't worry about fleas. "

The innkeeper led Edmund to a much smaller room with a straw-filled pallet on the floor that likely served as a servant's room. "Are you sure this will do?" Rebecca asked him.

"It's much better than I dared hope for. Thank you."

Before they parted, he turned to them and asked, "Do you ladies enjoy Moroccan food? The last time I was here I found a wonderful place to eat, and I would love to have dinner there again—if it's still in business, that is."

"I don't think we've ever had Moroccan food, have we, Flora?"

"I'm willing to try it if you are."

"I am," Rebecca said. "Give us an hour to rest and wash up, Mr. Merriday, and we'll meet you downstairs in what passes for a lobby."

Edmund reached into his pocket as if to pull out his watch, then sighed when he remembered it had been stolen. "Oh, dear. . . . In any event, I'll meet you out front in about an hour's time."

The sun had already set an hour later as Edmund led them through the narrow, winding streets and past a souk that was closing for the day. The smells were amazing—foul and delicious and rotten and spicy all at the same time. Edmund could have been leading them to some out-of-the-way place to rob them or accost them, but Rebecca didn't think so. His tanned face looked honest, and the evening promised to be unique.

"Ah, here it is!" he said at last. He led them through a dark, dingy room that might well have been someone's house, then into an outdoor courtyard open to the sky. The proprietor smiled and bowed as he seated them on a rug on the stone floor near a low table. Edmund did all the ordering for them in French, and they watched the cook prepare their meal in a wood-fueled oven across the courtyard. The oven also provided light and heat as they ate.

It was a marvelous dinner, the best Rebecca had eaten on the entire trip. They watched the stars come out as they consumed fluffy flatbread spread with mashed chickpeas and a deliciously spicy chicken served with something called couscous. The meal came in a brightly-colored earthenware bowl with a conical lid, and they all ate from the same dish, using their fingers and pieces of bread for scooping. How different this was from the stuffy, formal dinners Rebecca had endured with Freddy Worthington, juggling a multitude of cutlery. She listened as

Flora laughed at Edmund's colorful stories and wondered if her sister also noticed the difference between dining with Edmund and with the Worthingtons. They talked about where Rebecca and Flora were headed next until late into the night, with Edmund describing all of the places they must see. No one wanted the evening to end.

"I suppose we have no way of knowing if Edmund Merriday is telling the truth or swindling us, do we?" Rebecca asked after they'd returned to the inn for the night. "It's much like this fragment of parchment I purchased—is it real or fake?"

"He carries a Bible in his bag, Becky. He was reading it when we found him."

"Maybe he stole the Bible, and he carries it around as a ruse."

Flora smiled and dismissed the thought with a wave. "I have a good feeling about him, don't you? He seems very kind. And he has a wonderful sense of humor."

"And most scoundrels don't have a sense of humor, I suppose?"

"Most of the people I know don't have a sense of humor," Flora replied. She was thoughtful for a moment, then said, "Listen, Becky, I think we should invite Edmund to travel with us. I really don't see what harm it could do. He can't be too disreputable if he works at Cambridge University."

"You're assuming he's telling the truth about Cambridge?"

"Well . . . yes, I suppose I am."

Rebecca laughed, then said, "I agree. I believe he's genuine, too. After all, he couldn't have stranded himself out there, could he? And I do like him. He's not only intelligent and knowledgeable, but quite charming."

"Good. Although I suppose Thomas would be very displeased if he knew we were inviting a stranger to join us. Especially one with short trousers and hairy legs."

"The horror of it!" Rebecca said with a laugh. "But Thomas

doesn't have to know about Edmund. I won't mention him if you don't."

"Then please don't tell him I rode on a camel to see the pyramids, either. I'm sure he's imagining me in a fancy carriage with matched stallions."

"Aren't you glad you're not?"

"Yes, but Thomas would be—"

"Stop worrying about Thomas and just have fun. Tomorrow we'll invite Mr. Merriday to join us and be our guide in Jerusalem. And for the record, I hope he agrees."

Rebecca blew out the lamp, plunging the room into total darkness. A moment later, she heard Flora's voice from a few feet away. "Becky? This bedding is really scratchy. You don't suppose it has bedbugs, do you?"

"Well, if so, it will be another new experience. And we can't have an adventure without some sort of trouble, can we?"

CHAPTER 12

Edmund Merriday looked rested the next morning as he slid his lanky body onto the bench to join them for breakfast in the inn's courtyard. "Good morning, ladies. I want to thank you once again for—"

"We have a proposition to make," Rebecca interrupted. "We would like you to come to Jerusalem with us and show us the sights. Perhaps we could even add the synagogue in Capernaum to our itinerary."

He stared at them for a moment, his blue eyes wide with surprise. "But I have no way to pay for my expenses, and I couldn't possibly impose on—"

"You're not imposing. You can earn your way by serving as our guide."

"We were going to hire one anyway," Flora added. "And you seem very knowledgeable. You also have the added advantage of speaking perfect English."

Edmund looked from one of them to the other. He seemed incapable of forming a reply.

"If you come with us," Rebecca continued, "you could travel for a few more weeks instead of cutting your vacation short.

And I would love to learn more about ancient artifacts and manuscripts from you."

Edmund raised one eyebrow. "Are you certain you're not going to regret it? One might think me a bumbling liability, considering the sad condition I was in when you found me. What sort of reputable guide wanders around penniless and on foot, for heaven's sake?"

"Nonsense. We could use an interesting traveling companion."

"Oh, I do hope you'll agree," Flora said. "If so, we'll ask Habib to hire another horse for you."

Edmund took a moment to consider. "Very well, but only if you promise to send me on my way the moment I become a nuisance."

"It's a deal." Rebecca shook hands with him, sealing the contract.

Flora extended her hand in a proper, ladylike manner. "Take us through Jerusalem and the Holy Land, Edmund. Teach us everything you know."

They spent the following three nights sleeping in the tents Habib had packed as they made their way through the hill country to Jerusalem. The terrain became greener and more mountainous as they neared the ancient city. Rebecca's heart seemed to skip a beat as her horse reached the top of a rise and she saw the golden walls of Jerusalem in the distance for the first time. "It's magical!" she said. "Like a castle from a fairy tale."

"Perhaps from this distance," Edmund said. "I don't want to disillusion you ladies, but up close it's much like all the other run-down, neglected cities in the Ottoman Empire. None of Jerusalem's conquerors have been able to make the city thrive since the Romans exiled the Jewish people from it."

"Then let's sit here and gaze at it for a moment longer," Flora said. "I can't believe we're seeing the same city where Jesus walked."

"See that large gray dome behind the walls?" Edmund asked, pointing. "That's a Moslem shrine built about twelve hundred years ago on the site where the Jewish Temple once stood. I'll show it to you, if you'd like."

They toured the Temple Mount and the Church of the Holy Sepulcher, where Christ's tomb supposedly stood, and visited the mission church in Jerusalem that Rebecca's church had supported all these years. Edmund took them on a hike up the Mount of Olives, then down the other side to the village of Bethany, where Jesus had raised Lazarus from the dead. As they rode astride the squat little donkeys Edmund had hired, laughing uproariously, their skirts hiked up and their bare legs dangling, Rebecca was relieved to see the change in her sister. Flora had finally let go of all the rules that kept her tightly bound these past few years and no longer seemed concerned about her clothes or her hair, let alone propriety. Rebecca hadn't seen her sister so relaxed and happy since they were schoolgirls. Edmund was proving to be a delightful guide, finding amusement in every situation, entertaining them with stories, and narrating centuries of history at every site they visited. She began to hope that Flora would see the differences between charming Edmund and her fiancé, Thomas, and raise her standards for a lifelong partner once they returned home. Surely there were more men in Chicago for the two of them to choose from than Thomas and Freddy Worthington.

Edmund knew all the best places to eat, and Rebecca had never seen anyone enjoy sampling new food as much as he did. He ate each meal as if it might be his last, and the food fueled his boundless energy. He bounced around each site in his khaki shorts, curiously peering into every niche, asking hundreds of questions of the people they met using Rebecca as his interpreter. Rebecca had never met a man quite like Edmund and knew she probably never would again. She loved watching his elegant hands while he ate and as he gestured whenever he talked, as if painting each sentence with his fingers. She longed to brush her fingers across the golden hairs on his sun-bronzed arms or comb his thick, sandy hair when it fell into his eyes like a mischievous schoolboy's. He badly needed a proper haircut and trim for his beard and mustache, which had grown full since they'd met him, but Rebecca wouldn't change a single thing about this wonderful, remarkable man. Was she falling in love with him? She quickly dismissed the thought. They had learned that he was thirty-six, which made him fifteen years older than her, sixteen years older than Flora.

He took them to Bethlehem to see the church built by Constantine the Great in AD 333 over the traditional site where Jesus was born. Afterward, they bought a lunch of bread, olives, cucumbers, and dates and sat on a hillside on the edge of the village to eat while their horses munched on tufts of grass nearby. Her tour of the Holy Land had barely begun and already Rebecca felt full nearly to overflowing from all she'd seen and experienced. She watched a shepherd leading a ragged flock of sheep in the distance and thought of the angels bursting through the sky with their announcement on the night of Christ's birth. If only God would send even one angel to announce His plans for her life. She sighed and reached for another plump date as she brought her attention back to the conversation that Edmund and Flora were having.

"So you believe the Church of the Nativity might house some ancient manuscripts?" Flora was asking him.

"Undoubtedly. But I believe that the true gold mine for ancient manuscripts is the Monastery of St. Catherine on Mount Sinai."

"The same Mount Sinai where God gave Moses the Ten Commandments?"

"Well, according to tradition it's the same site. But how can anyone really know for certain?"

"I don't suppose Moses marked the spot with an enormous sign, did he?" Rebecca added.

"I once visited St. Catherine's Monastery and toured their library," Edmund continued. "It was quite disorganized with everything in disarray, nothing catalogued or sorted. Some scrolls had simply been stashed inside chests and boxes and left to crumble into dust. I volunteered my expertise to help the monks organize it all, since they didn't seem to have any idea what they possessed, and they agreed. But I'd barely made a start when the summer ended, and I had to return to Cambridge. I promised to return and help them catalog everything the following year. But before I had a chance, the huge scandal caused by a German scholar named von Tischendorf came to a very nasty ending, and the doors to St. Catherine's were closed to even harmless librarians like me."

"That sounds intriguing," Rebecca said, scooping up a handful of olives. "I love a good scandal. Tell us more."

Edmund leaned forward to tell the story. "Well, it seems von Tischendorf visited the monastery and saw the large number of early manuscripts in their library, just as I had. He returned to the University of Leipzig with forty-three parchment pages from an Old Testament codex, written in Greek, which he claims the monks were about to burn in the fireplace. Scholars were astonished to realize that these pages were part of one of the oldest Bibles ever discovered. Of course, von Tischendorf wanted to get his hands on the rest of the codex. He visited Russia and got support for his research from the Russian czar. The czar and his ancestors had long supported the Monastery of St. Catherine, so the monks had to welcome von Tischendorf for the sake of their Russian patron. He somehow convinced the monks to let him 'borrow' the complete Bible, known as the

Codex Sinaiticus, to show to the Russian emperor—but it was never returned. The monks felt robbed, of course, and so the library at St. Catherine's has been closed to scholars ever since."

"Oh my. What a black mark for Christian scholars."

"If the Codex Sinaiticus is any example, I believe the monks may unknowingly possess more ancient manuscripts just as valuable. The library could prove to be a treasure-house if scholars ever had the opportunity to study there. Unfortunately, von Tischendorf ruined that chance for everyone."

"What would be the importance if someone were to find these manuscripts?" Flora asked.

"They would prove to all the skeptics and naysayers that the Bible we have today hasn't changed in the thousands of years since it was written. Christ's words haven't been embellished or altered over the years but are nearly the same as when He spoke them. Authenticating the Bible is really the goal behind all my travels and my collection of artifacts."

"What do you mean?" Rebecca asked.

"My Christian faith is very important to me," Edmund said, his eyes shining as he spoke. "It's part of who I am. Because of that, I've been compiling a record of recent archaeological discoveries in this part of the world and noting how each discovery sheds new light on Scripture."

"Flora and I have been following the news of these discoveries, too. Please continue."

"Well, with the growing interest in scientific inquiry, many people in England scoff at miracles and ridicule the Bible. They don't believe, for instance, that angels could have burst forth from heaven and into our world in a field like this two thousand years ago. Or that a virgin could bear a son as the prophet foretold hundreds of years earlier. Their skepticism is playing havoc with people's faith in the accuracy of Scripture. But if I can show that the Bible can be believed as a historical document, accurate in every respect, then perhaps the skeptics will concede that the Bible's spiritual message may have validity, as well."

"That's fascinating!" Rebecca said. "When I read Henry Layard's book, *Discoveries in the Ruins of Nineveh and Babylon*, I realized that Jeremiah's prophecy had been fulfilled. Babylon had been completely buried."

"Yes! Jeremiah chapter fifty-one!" Edmund jumped up from the rock where he'd been sitting, dancing with excitement as he quoted the Scripture. "'Babylon will be a heap of ruins, a haunt of jackals, an object of horror and scorn, a place where no one lives.' I thought I was the only person in the world who was interested in all of this."

"So did I!" Rebecca felt like dancing, too. "Flora and our father were the only people in Chicago I could even talk to about it." She felt a growing excitement as she laid down her bread, too keyed up to eat. Edmund's work combined travel and study and ancient history and faith—all of her passions! And he planned to combine them in a book—a potentially life-changing book. "How far along is your project?" she asked.

He sighed and removed his hat to run his fingers through his hair. "I have piles and piles of notes and observations and artifacts that I've collected during my holidays, but each time I return home and the school term begins, I have little time to compile my findings, much less write them up in a coherent narrative. Besides, I'm a researcher, so my writing style tends to be rather pedantic. Certainly not something the general public would appreciate—and that's the audience I hope to reach. At any rate, I don't have nearly as much time to devote to the project as it requires, so it's a mere daydream at this point. And there are financial considerations, as well. I must work to pay for my flat, of course, and fund my travels."

Rebecca knew she had the finances to support Edmund's

work. Was this how she could use the gifts and resources God had given to her?

They gathered up the remains of their picnic and returned to their inn in Jerusalem, but the more Rebecca pondered Edmund's book, the more intrigued she became. She couldn't stop thinking about it, trying to figure out a way she could offer to sponsor his work without insulting him. She barely tasted her food that evening, imagining the manuscripts that may lie hidden in dark, dusty churches like the Church of the Nativity or the Church of the Holy Sepulcher, imagining how Edmund's book could shine light into the minds and hearts of skeptics.

"You've been quiet all afternoon, Becky," Flora said as she braided her long hair before bed. "Are you unwell?"

"I've never felt better. But I can't stop thinking about Edmund's project."

"What project?" It hadn't struck a chord with Flora the way it had with Rebecca.

"The book he described to us today." The stones felt warm beneath her bare feet as she paced the floor of their tiny room, too excited to sleep. "I've been imagining how wonderful it would be to research a book like his about archaeology and history and the Bible—all of the things I'm interested in. I would love to work on it with him, and in a way I feel it may be what I was meant to do. What if everything in my life has been leading up to this—all my studies, our travels, the languages we've mastered, the way Father raised us with a fascination for archaeology?"

She paused, waiting for Flora's reaction to her excited musings, and saw a look of interest on her face. "Go on, I'm listening."

"Ever since Edmund told us about his book, I've been looking back on my life, all I've experienced and struggled with, and I can see all those things converging in this project—and God's hand directing it. I feel like Paul meeting Jesus on the road to Damascus when his eyes were finally opened."

"Why don't you talk to Edmund about it some more?"

Rebecca barely heard her. "When I recall how we just happened to run into Edmund in the first place, it has to be more than a coincidence, doesn't it? It can't be pure chance that we took the same road on the same day. Or that our agent was honest and Edmund's wasn't."

"You believe God arranged it?"

"I do. Just for me, Flora. I want to help Edmund with his book . . . but . . ."

"Why are you hesitating?"

"I'm afraid he'll question my motives and think I'm trying to steal his idea."

"He knows us better than that by now. Just come right out and ask him tomorrow. Tell him everything you told me. The worst he can do is say no."

Rebecca would be devastated if Edmund did turn her down. And then what would she do? Plunge into the research herself, stealing his idea the way von Tischendorf had stolen the codex? She admired Edmund Merriday too much to do such a thing. Yet she felt she was meant to work on this book. "Yes . . . maybe I will discuss it with him," she finally said. "Good night, Flora."

Rebecca climbed between the sheets and tried to settle down on the narrow bed. She didn't know what the proprietor had used to stuff the mattress, but it poked through the sheet and the canvas ticking like millions of tiny dress pins. She spent the long night trying to get comfortable and praying that Edmund would agree to let her help with his book. Surely this was God's purpose for her, wasn't it?

"What shall we see today?" Edmund asked as they drank tea together the next morning.

"If we've seen everything here in Jerusalem," Flora replied, "I would love to travel north to the Sea of Galilee."

Rebecca forced herself to wait, listening to the morning small-talk between Edmund and Flora, waiting for the right moment to make her proposal. When the time finally came, she shoved aside the teapot and cups and plates, careful to speak calmly so her enthusiasm wouldn't frighten him away. "Before we begin our day, Edmund, I have a proposition for you. You don't need to give me an answer right away—take time to think it over . . . But Flora and I are also Christians, as you know. I have a college degree in history and a fascination with the ancient world. I've been told by my teachers that I'm an excellent writer—as is Flora, who has a Laureate of Literature degree. I love history and I can read Greek and Hebrew and French and a little Italian. I love to travel and explore, and our financial situation allows us the freedom to do it. And so I wonder if . . ." She drew a deep breath. "If you would consider allowing me to collaborate with you on the book you're writing?" She wished she could decipher the puzzled expression on his face as he scratched his forehead.

"You mean you want to help me turn my disorganized pile of notes into a coherent book?"

"Yes, that's exactly what I mean." She rushed on without giving him time to reply. "I share your love of Scripture and your outrage at what's being done to the Christian faith by so-called scientists. Scientific inquiry was made possible in the first place because the people studying the natural world believed they would find patterns and rules and laws that had been put there by the Creator. They weren't seeking to undermine Scripture but to unravel the mysteries of Creation. As for Charles Darwin's theories, it takes more faith to believe we evolved from apes than to believe that a loving God created us in His image." She paused to take another breath to continue, but Edmund reached across the table and covered her hand with his, stopping her.

"Say no more, Miss Rebecca Hawes! For a second time this summer, you are the answer to my prayers. I cannot believe that an intelligent woman like yourself would truly want to collaborate with me on this wild project, but if you're serious . . ." He looked like a child who was afraid to believe that the gift before him was really his.

"Of course I'm serious!"

"Then, yes! I would love your help!"

"Thank you!" Rebecca knew as surely as the sun shone in the blue Jerusalem sky that she'd found her purpose at last. She leaped up and threw her arms around him, planting a kiss on his shaggy, sun-browned cheek. The smell of his fresh, clean skin and the damp warmth of his body beneath his khaki shirt left Rebecca feeling light-headed. Even more surprising was the longing she felt to feel his tanned arms surrounding her in return, holding her close. He had granted her wish to allow her to work with him, yet she found herself wishing for more, to feel the touch of his lips on hers. Rebecca could no longer deny that somewhere between the Gaza Road and Jerusalem, she had fallen in love with Edmund Merriday. Had she just revealed that truth to him and to the rest of the world? Her impulsive act seemed to surprise Edmund as much as it did her.

"Well . . . my goodness . . . um . . . you're certainly very welcome. . . ."

Flora saved her from further embarrassment by pushing back her chair and saying, "Well, now that it's settled, let's go. There's so much more I want to see."

Rebecca traveled the dusty roads from Jerusalem to the town of Tiberius overlooking the Sea of Galilee in a daze. Her emotions seemed to rise and fall as much as the rocky terrain did, climbing to heights of joy because she had found her purpose at last, working with the man she loved, and then descending into melancholy at the hopelessness of that love. Not only did she and Edmund live separate lives an ocean apart, but it became more and more apparent once she acknowledged her feelings for him, that he didn't share them. The truth struck her like a blow as she stood with Edmund and Flora on the shore of the Sea of Galilee, gazing out at the sparkling water dotted with tiny fishing boats.

"Oh, it's even more beautiful than I imagined," Flora said.

Edmund murmured in reply—but he wasn't looking at the lake. He was gazing at beautiful Flora. And no wonder; Flora's natural beauty was enhanced by the sunshine that gilded her hair and turned her complexion the color of peaches. Back home in Chicago, rules of etiquette and whalebone corsets made Flora seem stiff and cold. But her chilly reserve vanished as she relaxed in the summer sunshine. Flora's beauty had blossomed a little more each day like a rosebud bursting into flower. *This is my real sister*, Rebecca thought, *not the phony version the widow created*. No wonder Edmund Merriday was falling in love with her. For the first time in her life, Rebecca wished she was beautiful, too.

In the days that followed as they explored the region where Christ performed miracles, Rebecca became aware of how much time Edmund spent gazing at her sister. He always managed to sit beside Flora and look out for her comfort. Slowly, a subtle change took place, and by the time their trip to the Holy Land ended and they were sailing back from Joppa to Cairo, Rebecca noticed Flora looking at Edmund the same tender way he looked at her.

In the end, Rebecca was forced to pull out an imaginary white flag and wave it in surrender. Edmund would never love her the way she loved him. It would have to be enough to work with him on his book—their book. She would find joy and contentment in that. Yet as hard as she tried—and Rebecca did fight with everything in her—she couldn't stop loving Edmund Merriday. She was twenty-one years old, thousands of miles from home, and helplessly in love for the first time in her life. She knew her heart would be broken, but like a runaway freight train on a mountain slope, she could do nothing to stop it.

CHAPTER 13

I f the manager of Shepheard's Hotel in Cairo was surprised to see Rebecca and Flora returning from their travels with a strange man in tow, like wild game hunters carrying a trophy of elephant tusks, he was too well-mannered to show it. He never blinked as they reserved a room for Edmund and had it added to their account. But as they waited outside the elegant dining room for Edmund to join them for dinner the first night, Flora and Rebecca were informed that Edmund would not be welcome in his rumpled khaki shorts.

"Let's take him out and buy him some clothes," Rebecca suggested. "Or better still, the concierge can have them delivered." She started across the lobby toward the concierge's desk, but Flora stopped her.

"Edmund will never agree, Becky. He already feels bad about all the money we've spent on him this summer. He's been keeping track of it in that little notebook he carries in his rucksack."

"He hasn't!"

"I've seen him writing down the cost after we've eaten together, and the prices at all the inns where we've stayed. That's why he balked at staying here. It took a lot of convincing to talk him into it."

"He has no idea how wealthy we are, does he?"

"I don't think he could imagine that much money even if we did tell him. Nor would he want any of it."

"Well, if that's the case, we'll simply have to eat someplace else while we're in Cairo."

Edmund knew all the best places, of course, ones that didn't require a jacket and tie. He had acquaintances everywhere he went—Egyptians and Moroccans and Syrians and Abyssinians—and he asked them to spread the word on the street that he and his American friends were interested in purchasing ancient manuscripts for souvenirs. They didn't have long to wait. As they drank tea in a café near the souk one day, a man wearing baggy Oriental trousers and a fez told Edmund to visit the Turkish carpet booth in the souk. Edmund scrambled to his feet, spilling the tea and nearly knocking over the table in his haste to leave. Then he turned to Flora and said, "It might be better if you took a carriage back to the hotel."

"Not on your life, Edmund Merriday! I go wherever Becky goes. And you need her to translate."

"But my dear, it may be dangerous. They know we're carrying money, since we're interested in buying souvenirs and—"

"The danger is what makes it so exciting."

Edmund reluctantly agreed when it became clear Flora wouldn't back down. "You should know that Middle Eastern men have a great deal of pride," Edmund said as they walked through the souk to the rug merchant's stall. "They refuse to deal with women on any sort of equal basis."

"It was a man who sold the page to me," Rebecca pointed out.

"Even so, it might be best if we pretend you're interpreting for me and that I'm the one who's bargaining with him."

Rebecca handed him her little purse. "In that case, here's our money pouch."

The Turkish rug merchant sat on a pile of cushions outside

his booth, wearing a white turban and smoking a hookah pipe. When Edmund told him why he was there, he clapped his hands and summoned his servant to bring more cushions, a small table with a mosaic top, and tiny cups of strong coffee. Rebecca grew impatient with the ritual formalities and annoyed that no cushions or cups of coffee had been offered to her and Flora, but she dutifully played the part of interpreter. Eventually, the same oily man who had sold Rebecca the parchment page joined them. "Good," Edmund said when she told him. "Maybe now the little thief will sell us the rest of the codex." Edmund showed him the page Rebecca had purchased and said, "Ask him if he has any more pages like this to sell."

Rebecca did, then waited for his reply. "He says he might . . . he's being very cagey, Edmund."

"Tell him that if this was taken from a folio, with many pages, I would like to buy the entire thing. I don't care what condition it's in. But we need all of it, not loose pages. They're worthless."

Rebecca frowned at Edmund. "I thought even the scraps were valuable."

"They are. But he doesn't need to know that."

She turned back to the man and relayed Edmund's words. He told them to wait, then disappeared. The men drank more coffee, and the merchant offered Edmund a puff on his hookah pipe, which he politely refused. Meanwhile, Rebecca and Flora remained standing in the narrow alleyway, choking on clouds of smoke.

The little man returned a quarter of an hour later carrying a filthy cloth bag. He pulled out what appeared to be a book without a front cover. At least half the pages were missing, but the remaining ones were the same size and shape and condition as the page Rebecca had purchased. Edmund looked it over as if examining a piece of trash that he'd found littering the street. She wondered if he was deliberately disguising his true opinion or if it really was worthless. "So, what do you think?" she asked when she was unable to stand the suspense.

"We may be about to rescue a priceless manuscript," he said, still frowning. "But you should also know that we may be buying a worthless fake. I would hate to waste your money."

"I'll take that chance. Let's barter with him." The haggling began, growing louder and more vigorous as time passed, with Rebecca taking her cues from Edmund. At one point, the little man snatched the book from Edmund's hands and strode away, insisting he could go no lower in price. "Shall I call him back?" Rebecca asked in a panic.

"No. Just wait." Before he reached the end of the alley, the man turned back, and they settled on a price. "Tell him if he has any more books like this one, I would be interested in buying them," Edmund said. The little man shook his head and hurried away.

Edmund rose, and after exchanging a few more pleasantries with the rug merchant, he offered Flora one arm and Rebecca the other as they walked back through the souk toward the main street. Rebecca wanted to linger, perusing the shops, experiencing the splendor and vulgarity of the marketplace and the souk's noisy clamor, enjoying Edmund. But he continued walking until they reached the lobby of the hotel. He halted and handed the book to Rebecca. "Congratulations," he said, "You've just purchased the very first artifact for your collection."

"Isn't she amazing?" Flora asked.

"Yes, quite!" Edmund agreed. "Rebecca and I are going to be full partners in our writing endeavor, with her name on the cover of our book right alongside mine."

Rebecca couldn't have said which was the greatest thrill—knowing that he viewed her as an equal partner or carrying what was possibly a priceless artifact . . . or simply being close to Edmund. Yet the moment was bittersweet. While he viewed her as a fascinating companion whose ideas he valued and whose collaboration he welcomed, Flora was the sister he loved. And his devotion to Flora was also bittersweet; Edmund knew she was engaged and that he had no hope of winning her away from her fiancé in Chicago. Even so, he seemed content to love Flora in silence until it was time to part, enjoying each remaining moment with her the way a man stranded in the desert treasures each precious drop of water. Rebecca understood exactly how he felt.

"I wish we could find out where he got that codex," Edmund said as they lingered in the lobby.

"I asked him," Rebecca said, "but he wouldn't tell me."

"If we can spare one more day here, I would like to wait and see if he turns up with more artifacts."

"That's fine with me," Rebecca said. "But realistically, Edmund, what should I do with this new codex, other than stash it on a shelf in my father's library?"

"If you truly don't mind parting with it for a while, I would like to show it to the document experts at Cambridge. They can study it and tell you what you have. I'll make certain it's returned to you in due time."

"If it's worthless, I would like it for a keepsake. But if it's valuable, I'll be happy to let the experts study it for as long as it takes."

"I'll see that you're given credit for the discovery, and for making a charitable contribution to the university or the British Museum."

Two days passed without a word from the shifty little man with the manuscripts. Edmund could no longer delay returning to his job at Cambridge for the fall term. "Flora and I have decided to take you up on your offer to return with you to Cambridge," Rebecca told him. "You can give me all the notes you've gathered for your book."

"Splendid! But it will be *our* book, Rebecca. Yours and mine."

She couldn't bear it when Edmund smiled at her that way. She was trying so hard not to feel anything for him except brotherly affection, but it was impossible. How she wished Edmund loved her instead of Flora. But he didn't, so that was that. She was grateful for the wide expanse of ocean that would soon stand between them.

The voyage from Cairo across the Mediterranean Sea to France was an exotic vacation in itself, with so many interesting people aboard that Rebecca found welcome distraction from her feelings for Edmund. Late one starry night, after lingering to talk with one of their dinner companions, Rebecca went in search of her sister on the passenger deck and found her in Edmund's embrace. He was kissing her.

Rebecca fled back to their stateroom in tears. She would still research and write a book with him, even if she couldn't marry him. But Edmund had set a new standard for her, and she would never marry, she decided, unless she found a man who respected her intelligence and shared her love of travel. A man who would look at her the way Edmund looked at Flora.

She closed the stateroom door behind her and hugged herself, longing to feel his tanned arms around her. When she heard Flora unlocking their door a few minutes later, she quickly wiped her tears.

"I'm sorry for staying out so late," Flora said, "but I won't get to enjoy Edmund's company much longer. I'm going to miss him terribly."

"He's fascinating, isn't he? And intelligent? And open-minded about women and their roles?"

"Yes, he's all of those things," Flora said with a little frown. "Why are you bringing it up?"

"There's quite a difference between Edmund and Thomas, isn't there?"

Her frown deepened. "It would be very unfair to compare the two—"

"Because you know Thomas would come up short."

Flora turned away and started preparing for bed. "Maybe it's the novelty of Edmund," she said, "and the fact that I've been away from Thomas for so long, but I feel like I'm a different person when I'm with Edmund. He sees me as a partner rather than a mindless little ornament who isn't allowed to think."

"I've been hoping you would reconsider your engagement to Thomas while you're apart. To be honest, it's one of the reasons I wanted you on this trip."

Flora sank down on her bunk across from Rebecca, their knees nearly touching in the tiny stateroom. "There have been times this summer when my life with Thomas in Chicago seems like a dream I once had. But I suppose that when I'm home with Thomas, this trip will seem like the dream."

"You need to decide which one is real and which isn't and make a choice, Flora. Never mind what others expect you to do or what you feel obligated to do. What do you feel in your heart? Marriage is a lifelong commitment. You'll have to live with your choice for a very long time."

"It sounds like you think I should choose Edmund. He hasn't proposed to me, you know. I doubt he ever will. He has his own life to live. And he's sixteen years older than me."

"Any fool can see he's in love with you. I saw him kissing you tonight."

Flora lowered her head as if she wanted to hide. "Edmund and I got a little carried away in the moonlight. Please don't tell Thomas."

"Of course I won't."

Flora stood again and walked to the tiny porthole, gazing at her reflection in the dark circle. "It's just that Edmund is so much more . . . *exciting* than Thomas."

"Then why settle for less?"

"Because I already accepted Thomas' proposal. We're going to be married when I return home. If I break our engagement, Thomas could sue me for breach of promise."

"So? Let him sue you. Would paying him off be the very worst thing that could happen? Or would marrying a man you're not sure you love be much worse?"

"Oh, I just don't know. I can't think!" She lowered her face again and covered it with her hands. When she looked up again she asked, "What do you think I should do, Becky?"

"My opinion doesn't matter. It's your life."

"You never liked Thomas, did you? Don't shrug your shoulders, Becky, I know it's true."

"Very well, I admit it. I think Thomas Worthington lacks an imagination, and that he's marrying you for your inheritance. It grieves me to think that you might spend the rest of your life with him. You deserve so much better. He'll drench all the golden sunshine in your spirit beneath a monsoon of obligations and expectations. You're so much happier when you're with Edmund. . . . See? You blush like a rose every time you hear his name."

Flora felt her cheeks as if to see if it was true, then grew serious again. "But so do you, Becky. I can see by the way your eyes light up when you talk to him, the way you hold tight to his arm and glow in the light of praise. . . . You're in love with Edmund, too. Maybe you're the one who should marry him, instead of me."

A fist squeezed Rebecca's heart.

"Edmund isn't in love with me," she said quietly. "He's in love with you. I couldn't marry him knowing I was his second choice. That he wished you were the woman in his arms every time he held me. I would feel like I'd won second place—like ugly Leah to your beautiful Rachel. And every time we visited

189

you and stuffy old Thomas, I would see Edmund longing for you . . . and I couldn't bear it."

"Edmund has never spoken about marriage. He's been a bachelor all these years—"

"He would propose to you in a heartbeat with a little encouragement. I'm certain of it."

"But I'm also fond of Thomas, and I promised him—"

"We all have to make choices in life, Flora. This is a very important one."

"Oh, I wish I knew what to do!"

"Take your time thinking it over, and don't do anything until your mind is clear. You'll have the rest of your life to regret it."

PART II

Flora

CHAPTER 14

For the past week, Flora had been traveling across the Sinai Desert on camelback with her sister, remembering the first time she ever rode on a camel. It was the summer she visited the pyramids, the summer she and Becky met Edmund Merriday. But that was twenty-five years ago, and she was very much out of practice riding one now. When their agent, Mr. Farouk, announced that it was time to take a lunch break after a long morning's ride, Flora was glad to climb off the beast. The place where the caravan halted looked as desolate as every other place they'd seen that morning, and the sun pressed down on her like a dome of heated brass. Mr. Farouk led her and the other travelers to a sliver of shade beneath an overhanging rock and said in his patchy English, "You must now eat. And drink much water. I think sleep a little." He left them with water and a box of provisions—dates and figs and flatbread—and joined the sheikh and the caravan drivers as they bowed down to pray.

Flora was grateful to be here in spite of the heat and barren terrain. Years ago Becky had convinced her to travel after their

193

father died, and it had turned out to be just the change Flora had needed. They had met Edmund Merriday, and what had begun as a tour of Egypt and the Holy Land had become life-changing. This time Flora had agreed because her sister needed her. After everything that Becky had done for her over the years, it was the least Flora could do. "I've never been so hot in my life," she said as she eased down to the rocky ground to rest.

"Me either!" Becky dug into the provision box and offered a clump of figs to Flora. "As eager as I am to get to the monastery, I'm still glad we stopped to rest just now. I was getting saddle-weary."

"So was I. . . . Come and have something to eat, Kate," she called to their maid. The girl ignored her, embroiled in another argument with Petersen. They argued every day, day after day, over every little thing. "I do wish they would stop bickering," Flora said. "They make my head ache."

"They're like jackals snarling over their prey." Becky pulled out a container of olives—the shriveled little black ones that Flora loved. "Petersen is right to assert his authority over her, but Kate resents any authority at all."

"I'm very proud of Petersen and how much he has matured during this trip. He has become like a son to me, you know."

Becky groaned. "Please don't tell me Kate is like a daughter to you. I would sooner tangle with an entire nest of vipers than with that girl."

"I think this trip has already softened her a little, don't you?"

"Not in the least. If anything, the heat has brought her temper to the boiling point. There have been times when I've been sorry you ever talked me into hiring her. Sorrier still that we brought her along."

Their servants' argument ended with a shout. Petersen wrapped the end of his white turban over his face and stalked away. Kate flopped down in the shade beside Flora with a huff, her face fiery with indignation. Flora pushed the box of food toward her. "Have something to eat, Kate. And don't forget to drink plenty of water."

"I'm sick of this same old bread, day after day," she said. "And pretty sick of *him*, too!" But Flora watched Kate gobble two rounds of flatbread just the same.

"According to the sheikh, we'll arrive at the monastery tomorrow afternoon," Becky said. She had finished eating and was leaning back against the rocky outcropping. "It's been a long week of travel, hasn't it? I know it's been tiring for you, Flora, but we're nearly there."

"I haven't minded. I've had plenty of time to daydream along the way and do some reminiscing."

"I can barely wait to get to that library and have a look at those manuscripts—assuming the monks will even let us near them, that is. I've been thinking about the St. Catherine library ever since Edmund first told us about it years ago, remember? The idea of finding an ancient copy of the Bible is what keeps me going through this heat and desolation. It's fun to travel, yes, but this trip has a greater purpose. A big one for me. And I'm so glad you're with me, Flora. I can't thank you enough for coming."

Flora smiled at her older sister. All her life, Becky had hungered for adventure—and she usually managed to convince Flora to come along. Here they were in the Sinai Desert, riding camels, journeying to Mount Sinai like the ancient Israelites. Flora hoped this quest would lead to happiness for Becky in the end. She had always been unlucky in love, yet now, when she'd finally stopped looking for it, romance had found her at last. "You've sacrificed so much for my sake," Flora told her, "the least I can do is repay you by coming on this trip. Besides, it has given me a chance to ponder what's next for my life. Our journeys together have always given me a larger perspective."

"I've been reminiscing along the way, too, and I recalled a secret that I never told you, Flora. The only secret I've ever kept from you."

"This sounds intriguing!"

"Yes, well . . . I'm feeling guilty after all these years, so I want to confess." Becky drew a deep breath, then let it out in her usual dramatic fashion. "Remember Widow Worthington?" she asked.

"How could I forget her?"

"Well, it's my fault Father never married her. I asked him not to."

"You didn't!"

"I did. I made him promise to wait until we both finished college and were married and on our own. I didn't want our life disrupted."

"Oh, Becky. I always wondered why he didn't marry her. I think he really cared for her. She added spice to his otherwise dull life, and he seemed so much happier in the years after they met, remember? I never understood why you didn't like her."

"Because she kept trying to change me, Flora, and turn me into someone I'm not. That's why I fought back so hard. If I hadn't discarded everything about the Worthingtons and their values and their way of life, I never would have become the woman God created me to be. As far as I'm concerned, Mrs. Worthington nearly ruined my life by trying to turn me into a socialite and marrying me off to her nephew."

"She was right about one thing, though. Our manners did need polishing. And I don't know about you, Becky, but I longed for a mother back then. I think that's why I went along with everything she wanted us to do. Mrs. Worthington was the closest thing we ever had to a mother."

"She disappeared from our lives pretty quickly after Father died. On the prowl for another wealthy widower, perhaps."

"I don't believe that. But tell me, does it bother you that

Father kept his promise and then died before he had a chance to marry her?"

"He didn't have to give in to me . . . but I'm glad he did. We would still be stuck with her as our stepmother if he had, not to mention stuck with all her dreadful relatives."

"Like Freddy Worthington? You nearly married him."

"I'll tell you exactly how I feel about Freddy Worthington. Remember all those stories that circulated after the war about how a soldier dodged a bullet by mere inches or avoided a deadly wound because he had a Bible or a packet of love letters in his pocket? I made a miraculous escape where Freddy is concerned—and dodged a bullet that surely would have killed me."

"You're outrageous. But I love you for it."

"I doubt if either of us would be here today if I had married Freddy."

"That's for certain!" Flora said, laughing.

They finished eating and settled back in the stingy patch of shade to nap and let the camels rest. Flora quickly fell asleep and was dreaming about Mrs. Worthington when something awakened her. She sat up and looked around, listening for any sound. The utter stillness of the camp struck her as unusual. She'd become accustomed to the near-constant jingling of the little brass bells on the camels' harnesses and the low muttering voices of the drivers. Now the total silence seemed ominous.

Becky and Kate were still asleep, so Flora stood and walked around the campsite by herself, the hot air moving against her skin like a wool blanket. The first thing she noticed was the heap of equipment piled on the ground where the camels had been tethered. The drivers never unloaded the caravan when they paused for a noon break. Never. They always left it intact until they camped for the night. But the tents and equipment and food supplies had been unloaded and piled in a heap. Flora walked a little farther and saw Mr. Farouk, Petersen, and the cook napping beneath another band of shade, but there was no sign of the drivers. And where were the camels?

Flora climbed a small rise for a better view, slipping and sliding in the dry, crumbling dirt. Perhaps the drivers had found a larger patch of shade on the other side of the hill. But when she reached the top, sweating and winded, her shirtwaist glued to her skin, Flora saw nothing but desolate scenery and wrinkled brown mountains fading into the hazy distance. The camels, the sheikh, and the Bedouin drivers had vanished.

Her stomach went hollow with fear. She understood how Edmund had felt all those years ago when he'd been robbed and abandoned on the Gaza Road. At least he'd been stranded along a caravan route. There were no discernable roads in this wasteland, no markers to point the way. The sandstorm had been disconcerting, but now, for the first time since beginning this journey, Flora felt truly afraid. She hurried down the hill, the loose dirt filling her shoes, and nudged Rebecca awake.

"Something's wrong, Becky. Wake up." She spoke in a breathless whisper so she wouldn't disturb their maid. "The drivers and camels are gone."

"Gone? What do you mean?"

"They're not here! Look—they unloaded everything over there, but the sheikh, the camels, and the drivers are nowhere in sight!"

"I'm sure there must be a logical explanation." Becky leaned against the rock face for support as she rose to her feet, then turned in a circle as she scanned the area just as Flora had done. She wouldn't see any sign of them, either. Flora watched a trickle of sweat roll down Becky's face. Her fearless sister looked shaken. "Did you talk to Mr. Farouk?" she asked. "Does he know what's going on?"

"No, maybe we should wake him." They walked to where Mr. Farouk lay dozing, his head-covering pulled over his face like a curtain. Petersen and the cook snored nearby. Flora shook Mr. Farouk's arm, and he jolted to attention with a loud cry, waking the other two men. "I'm sorry for startling you, Mr. Farouk. But do you know where the sheikh and all the drivers went?"

He surveyed the campsite with a glazed look in his eyes, as if still disoriented from sleep. "They must be here. . . ."

"But they aren't. They unloaded the caravan and piled our belongings over there. See?" Mr. Farouk continued to blink and shake his head as if the scene might change if he stared long enough.

Petersen, on the other hand, leaped to his feet. "What's going on? Where are the camels? How can they be gone?" He bounded around in circles as if he might find the animals hidden beneath a rock. Flora would have found the butler's efforts amusing, like a child playing a game of hide-and-seek, if she weren't so alarmed.

"When did you last see the sheikh, Mr. Farouk?" Rebecca asked.

"We finish praying . . . the sheikh say to let everyone sleep. He say too hot to travel . . ."

"Perhaps the cook saw them leave?" Flora suggested. The little cook sat on the ground looking bewildered, but he jumped to his feet, flinching as Mr. Farouk shouted at him in Arabic. Flora thought the Arabic language made everyone who spoke it sound angry, but this time Mr. Farouk's frantic shouts could probably be heard for miles. The cook took a few steps back, shaking his head so hard Flora worried it might come loose. It was clear that the cook knew nothing. He was as frightened as they were to learn they'd been abandoned in the desert.

Mr. Farouk stormed away from the man and scuttled up the same rise Flora had climbed, Petersen right behind him. Becky thought Mr. Farouk resembled a beetle with his short legs, stocky build, and glistening black hair—and at the moment, he was a very frightened beetle. Flora and Becky followed the two men up the hill to scan the horizon with them. Not even a speck of movement was visible in any direction. As she made a slow turn, Flora spotted a mirage shimmering in a low spot in the distance, the earth reflecting the sky like water. These phony pools of water had fooled her nearly every day of their journey, and only after eight days of travel and disappointment was she convinced that the pool she saw now was a mirage.

"I do not understand," Mr. Farouk mumbled. "Where they go . . . ?"

Petersen grabbed the front of Mr. Farouk's robe, giving him a little shake. "You were supposed to be in charge of those people! You're supposed to know where they are and what they're up to!"

Flora hurried over to soothe him. "Let's not panic, Petersen. I'm sure they can't be far."

"Leaving us all alone out here is a death sentence, Miss Flora," Petersen said, releasing Mr. Farouk's robe. "And he knows it!"

"We still have water, and it looks like all our supplies are here. I understand we're nearly to the monastery, isn't that right, Becky?"

"Yes. Less than a day's ride away."

"For all the good it will do us," Petersen said. "Even if we could walk there, we have no idea which direction it is!" He strode down the hill again, kicking up a cloud of dust and dirt as he went.

Flora refused to panic. "I'm certain the Bedouin will return. After all, we're paying them for their services in increments, and they won't receive the full payment until we're back where we started."

"Mr. Farouk," Rebecca said, "if you have any idea what might be going on, you need to tell us."

"Has there been any trouble with the Bedouin that you're aware of?" Flora added. "Has the sheikh mentioned anything to you?" She had seen the two men arguing several times over the past few days but didn't know the source of it.

Farouk wouldn't meet her gaze. He closed his eyes and lowered his chin. Flora felt her skin prickle. Becky started to speak, but Flora held up her hand to shush her. She linked her arm through her sister's, dragging her down the hill away from him. "What are you doing, Flora? He thought of something, I could tell."

"I know. But Edmund once warned us that Middle Eastern men like Mr. Farouk have a great deal of pride. He'll never admit his failings, especially to two women. He might be more forthcoming if Petersen speaks with him."

They found Petersen sitting on a rock, his shoulders hunched with defeat. "This is a desperate situation," he mumbled. "Desperate! I promised to protect you and—"

"Petersen," Flora interrupted, "we believe Mr. Farouk has thought of something, and he may prefer to explain it to you rather than to us."

Petersen rose and looked up the hill where Mr. Farouk stood alone. "Try not to yell at him, dear. It will only make matters worse."

The broiling sun and hot air made it difficult for Flora to breathe, especially after marching up and down the hill twice. She and Becky returned to the slender patch of the shade where they'd napped, while Petersen climbed the hill to talk with Mr. Farouk. Flora couldn't see the butler's face, but his rigid posture and Farouk's flailing arms told her that whatever news the little agent was relating wasn't good.

"I'm so sorry for dragging you here with me, Flora," Becky said. "I never should have involved you."

"Hush. I'm sure everything will be fine."

Kate awoke from her nap and stretched like a cat as she sat upright. "What's all the whispering about? What's going on?"

"We're not exactly sure," Flora said.

"Well, isn't it time to move on? Why are we still here?" Before Flora had a chance to reply, Kate leapt to her feet, saying, "Hey! Why's all our stuff heaped up in a pile? We aren't camping here for the night, are we? Where are the camels? And all the drivers?"

"We're not sure of that either, Katie dear. We're waiting for them to return—"

"Return? Where did they go?"

"We don't know, but—"

"I knew it! I just knew it! We're all going to die out here, aren't we? Aren't we!"

"And . . . she's off!" Becky mumbled as they listened to their hot-tempered maid's panicked tirade.

"We never should have trusted those sneaky Bedouin! I told you so, didn't I? I told you! Now look what's happened!"

Flora rose and took Kate's arm, trying to pull her back into the shade. "Listen, dear. It won't help to get overly excited, especially in this heat."

"But what are we going to do? Are they really gone without a trace?"

"I suppose they left a trail of camel droppings we could follow if we put our noses to the ground," Becky said.

Flora couldn't help laughing as she pictured Petersen and Mr. Farouk sniffing the dirt like bloodhounds. "How can you laugh at a time like this?" Kate shouted.

"Well, it certainly doesn't help to weep and wail," Flora said. "Come, sit down and have a drink of water while Petersen and Mr. Farouk discuss it. Try to calm down."

"Do we have enough water? Shouldn't we ration it or something?"

"It seems they left all the water and other supplies here. We have plenty."

"It can't last forever, though. And that's how long we're going to be here—forever! Even if we knew which direction to go, we have no way to get there."

"Oh, do sit down and be quiet," Becky said, exasperated. "I'm sure this will be resolved soon."

"God knows when the end of our days will be," Flora said, patting Kate's hand. "We have nothing to fear."

Flora had no sooner spoken when Petersen's angry shout echoed off a nearby ridge. He slid down the hill and hurried toward them, his pale face as dark as a thundercloud. "I need to speak with you in private, Miss Flora and Miss Rebecca."

"Hey! I have a right to know what's going on, too!" Kate yelled.

He frowned at the maid, who stood with her hands on her hips as if itching for a fight. He shook his head at her and turned to Flora. "I really think we should speak about this in private."

"No! You're not leaving me out of this—"

"Oh, for goodness' sake," Becky said. "Just tell us what Mr. Farouk said."

He gave Kate a wary look and exhaled. "Mr. Farouk says it's *her* fault that they're gone." He pointed to the maid.

"Me? What did I do? You're just saying that because you hate me!" She lunged at the butler, but Flora grabbed her around the waist and held her back. Kate was so slender that Flora could feel all her ribs.

"Katie, stop it. Let Petersen tell us what he knows."

"It's hard to understand Mr. Farouk's terrible English," Petersen said, "but evidently the sheikh has been asking questions for days about the 'fiery, red-haired servant girl.' He's been pressuring Mr. Farouk to speak to you ladies about . . . um . . ." He cleared his throat. "About bartering for her."

Flora felt Kate's body go limp, sagging against her for support. Flora felt a little weak herself. "Bartering . . . ? That's outrageous," she said.

"The sheikh became furious with Mr. Farouk just this morning because he refused to negotiate with you on his behalf."

Rebecca stood and called up the hill, "Mr. Farouk. Come down here, please." He slouched down the rise to stand before them like a condemned man, his head hanging. "What exactly did you tell the sheikh this morning?" Rebecca asked him.

"I explain that things go differently in your country. Servants not to be owned by you."

"Wait. You mean he wants to buy Kate for his servant?" Rebecca asked.

"Not for servant. He wants for his harem."

Flora pulled Kate close and held her tight, something she had never dared to do with the prickly girl before. "Over my dead body!"

"Oh, Flora," Rebecca said. "I'm afraid that may be exactly what they have in mind."

Kate twisted out of Flora's arms and stalked off. Flora watched her bend to scoop up a handful of stones and throw them, one by one, as far into the distance as she could.

"What would you like me to do?" Petersen asked. He pulled off his turban and ran his hand through his pale hair, obviously distressed by his helplessness.

"Let's all sit down in the shade," Flora suggested. She led the way back to the overhanging rock and waited until Becky and Petersen were settled. Mr. Farouk had climbed the small rise again with the cook. Kate was still throwing rocks at imaginary targets but was close enough to hear Flora. "Remember when we met Edmund on the Gaza road all those years ago, Becky? He was stranded just like we are."

"Yes, and thankfully we came to his rescue."

"He was praying when we found him, remember? And that's what I think we should do." Petersen looked doubtful, but Flora reached for his hand. It felt gritty with sweat and dirt. She took Becky's hand in her other one to create a small circle. "Lord, you see us right now. You know we're here. We're never out of your sight or out of your care. You know how frightened young Kate is—"

"I'm not scared! I'm mad!" she shouted from a dozen feet away. "I told you I didn't like the way they kept looking at me! I told you!"

"Lord, send someone to rescue us, we pray. Show us the way out and what we should do. Calm our hearts with the assurance that you will never leave us or forsake us."

Flora continued praying aloud for several minutes until everyone was calm again, including Kate, who finally stopped throwing rocks and settled down with them to wait.

"Help will come," Flora said. "You'll see." Just as help had arrived in answer to Edmund's prayers when he'd been stranded along the road on that long-ago day. . . .

CHAPTER 15

CAMBRIDGE, ENGLAND
1865
TWENTY-FIVE YEARS AGO

Flora couldn't get over how lush and green the British countryside looked as the train neared the town of Cambridge.
After three months in arid lands, it was as if she had returned to the Garden of Eden. She thought it would be lovely
to stay and explore the English countryside with Edmund, but
then she remembered her fiancé, Thomas, and was struck by an
arrow of guilt. According to their original plan, she and Becky
should have returned to Chicago more than a month ago, but
they were still a long way from home. Flora had sent cables to
Thomas from Cairo and France, then another one from London
explaining their delays and assuring him they were fine, so he
wouldn't worry.

"Come with me to Cambridge," Edmund had pleaded when
they'd arrived in France after their long trek through the Holy
Land. "I don't want to say good-bye yet."

Flora hadn't wanted to say good-bye to him, either, but she
knew she shouldn't stay any longer. She needed to return to

Thomas and her life in Chicago before she lost her heart completely to Edmund. The longer Flora traveled with him, laughed with him, and talked with him, the deeper she fell in love with him. In the end, Becky had decided the issue.

"Yes, please let's go to Cambridge, Flora. I'll need a week to look over Edmund's notes for our book and pack all his materials to ship to Chicago. Then we'll sail home, I promise."

Flora fell in love with Cambridge the moment she stepped off the train. She could easily imagine living here. "It's like a page from a storybook, Edmund," she said as she gazed at the historic town.

"Yes, it is lovely this time of year, isn't it? As much as I love traveling, I'm always pleased to come back." He showed them around the village and the university campus and found rooms for them to rent in an inn. Edmund's tiny apartment near the library was as interesting and exotic as he was, with boxes and bins and dusty shelves filled with pottery shards, old scraps of parchment, and even a stray bone or two, brought back from his many travels. He had wonderful stories to tell about each item in the room, and he entertained them with tales of his journeys as they sat on the floor sipping tea together. And books! Rows and rows of interesting books filled Edmund's shelves. The extras lay piled on the floor or stacked beside the bed or heaped haphazardly around the cluttered room.

Flora couldn't help comparing his collection to the tidy, well-dusted library that Thomas Worthington had once shown her in his family's home. She also recalled her shock when Thomas admitted he'd never read a single one of those books. "Not one," he'd repeated. He had sounded proud.

"But why not?" she'd asked. "There are so many wonderful titles here."

Thomas had laughed, making light of her astonishment. "Because I have neither the time nor the interest in reading them. You may borrow them if you'd like. My father collects them, but he doesn't read them." Flora still felt sad when she recalled that conversation. Now, as she perused Edmund's books, many with markers and papers stuffed between the pages, she could see that his collection was well-used.

"Have you read all of these books?" she asked.

"Most of them. That pile over there contains the ones I hope to read this fall. Why?"

"No reason." She hated herself for comparing the two men; it wasn't fair to Thomas. Edmund's life was free from the enormous responsibilities heaped on Thomas' shoulders. Managing money was a very weighty matter, he'd informed her.

Flora and Becky worked all week with Edmund, sorting through his notebooks and papers. Becky wrote pages of notes as Edmund explained what he'd planned for each chapter, and the proposed book grew in size and scope as Becky came up with even more ideas to add to his. "That's a wonderful idea!" Edmund would say as they sat at his table with their heads bent together. "I wouldn't have thought of that, Rebecca."

"It will require more research, but I would love the chance to tackle it."

"Superb!"

Becky came alive when she was with Edmund. In fact, Flora had never seen her so happy. Her sister had fallen in love with Edmund Merriday, too. But Edmund didn't gaze at Becky the way he did at her. The knowledge that he preferred her filled Flora with guilt. Perhaps if she went home to Thomas, as she knew she should, Edmund would see Becky in a different light. Maybe he would marry her. They worked so well together.

Much too soon, their time in Cambridge came to an end. One day remained before they would return to London for the voyage home, and that day was the Sabbath. "If you're not too tired," Edmund said, "and if you're willing to get up early, I would love to show you the work I'm doing with the poor."

"We would love that," Flora replied.

Edmund came to the inn to fetch them early the next morning with a hired carriage. As they drove down Mill Road, leading out of Cambridge, Edmund explained how the growth of the railways had caused a surge of population in this area. "And poverty along with it," he added.

"It's much the same in Chicago," Flora said as she gazed at the rows of disheveled housing, the ragged, dirty, working-class children playing in the streets. Many weren't wearing shoes. Smoke from locomotives and factory chimneys hung low in the gritty air, even on the Sabbath. The carriage halted, and they walked to an old stone church built centuries ago. Flora felt out of place among so many impoverished people, even though her skirt, shirtwaist, and bonnet were ordinary compared to the fashionable dresses in her wardrobe back home. But the parishioners sang the hymns with spirit, and the pastor preached about Jesus' love for the poor. When the worship service ended, Edmund led them outside again.

"You didn't bring us here simply to attend church, did you?" Flora asked. She didn't say so, but she would have preferred to attend the magnificent Kings College Chapel.

"No, the service was merely for starters. Now the fun work begins. You see, some colleagues and I have established a Sabbath school in this part of town so we can teach the poor, working-class children how to read and write. We also teach them about the Bible and who Jesus is."

Flora's heart gave a little skip of excitement. "What a wonderful idea!"

"A Christian named Robert Raikes started the first Sunday school because he wanted to do something about the poverty and illiteracy he saw all around him. The idea has grown since then, and we now have more than 100,000 volunteer teachers reaching more than a million children each week."

"I would love to help you," Flora said. As the sisters followed him to the building where the classes were held, Flora told Edmund what she and Rebecca had once done, dressing up in rags and dirtying their faces in order to see inside the garment factory.

Edmund laughed at her descriptions. "You didn't really!"

"Yes, it's a true story. But we only lasted one day in that factory—and we never did go back for our wages, did we, Becky?"

Her sister laughed and shook her head. "Why bother? It amounted to less than a dollar."

"I can't imagine you beautiful ladies in raggedy clothes and with dirt on your faces."

"It wasn't just a lark, Edmund. Once we saw how those people lived and how little they earned, we wanted to do something to help. Like you're doing here. This is such a wonderful idea. Remember those girls we worked with in the factory, Becky? And the children on the street? I would love to teach little ones like them to read and write."

"I think you would be very good at that," Becky replied.

Dozens of wiggling, chattering children were already pouring inside what looked to be a factory shipping room. They sat on the stone floor, using shipping crates for desks. Flora worked side-by-side with Edmund as he taught the eager students who seemed thrilled to be learning to read. They clearly loved Edmund, who poured all of his bumbling energy into teaching. Flora tried to imagine Thomas here and couldn't. Again, she was angry with herself for comparing the two men. Becky joined in, too, using her most dramatic voice to tell Bible stories to the enraptured children sitting in a circle around her. When it was time to leave, the entire group of children skipped down the road alongside them, hugging them and waving good-bye.

That evening, as Edmund and Becky finished packing materials from his apartment, Flora walked outside to sit on the grassy riverbank alone. She loved watching the boats drift by, rowboats and punters and a rowing team from the university straining against the current as the coxswain called the signals. As the sun began to set, Edmund came outside and silently sat down on the grass beside her. "Is the packing all done?" Flora asked him.

He nodded and plucked a few blades of grass, twiddling them between his fingers. She heard him sigh. "For the first time in my life," he finally said, "I find myself regretting that I have so little in the way of worldly possessions and wealth. Regretting that I've spent all of my meager resources on travel and research."

"But why would you regret that, Edmund? You clearly love your life."

He gently turned her face so she would have to look at him. "Because I've fallen in love with you, Flora, and I have nothing to offer you. It pains me to send you back to America and to your fiancé, and yet I know he'll give you the life I only wish I could provide. And your happiness is my deepest wish."

Flora opened her mouth to speak, to tell him she had more than enough money for both of them, but he stopped her with a gentle kiss. "No, don't say anything, Flora. Let me remember this beautiful moment just the way it is."

What else could she say? Did she want to break her engagement with Thomas and move to England to marry a man she'd known for only a few months? She thought she did, but the chance to speak had passed. They returned to Edmund's flat to fetch Becky.

That night in their room at the inn, Flora felt a deep sadness she couldn't name. Becky couldn't seem to settle down to sleep and paced the narrow space between their beds as if propelled by an inner clock spring that had been wound too tightly. She gestured to the crate full of Edmund's books and notes and said, "I can't begin to describe how excited I am about the work ahead of me. I'm meant to write this book with Edmund, I know I am. It was no accident that we met him on the Gaza Road that day and . . . What's wrong, Flora? Why are you crying?"

Flora had hoped Becky would continue talking and pacing and never notice the tears running silently down her face. Flora couldn't seem to make them stop. "I'm going to miss Edmund and . . . and all of the exciting things we did this summer and . . . oh, I really don't know why I'm crying!" She wiped another tear and said, "Yes, I do. . . . I'm crying because Edmund told me he loved me tonight."

"Well, of course he loves you. Haven't I been saying that?"

"He said he wished he had money so he could provide for me, but since he doesn't, he's sending me home to my fiancé. I didn't know what to say. He has no idea how wealthy we are, Becky. He doesn't know that I don't need Thomas or anyone else to provide for me."

"Do you love him, Flora?"

"I . . . I do. But I thought I loved Thomas, too, a few months ago." Becky handed her a handkerchief to blow her nose. "I'm sorry for blubbering. I need to be sensible about this and not let romantic notions carry me away. Edmund is like . . . like a hero in an adventure novel. And everything was so exotic in the Holy Land this summer, with the moon shining down on the Sea of Galilee and the scent of rosemary and cedar filling the air. I shouldn't have allowed Edmund Merriday to sweep me off my feet."

"Is that such a bad thing?" Rebecca asked. "Don't we all need a little romance in our lives?"

"I let him kiss me, Becky. I'm engaged to Thomas, and I betrayed him. I don't know what I'll say to him when I return home, but I need to tell him I'm sorry for allowing my heart to get the best of me. I should have followed my head, not my heart. I've done a terrible thing, and I feel so guilty about it. I need to confess everything to Thomas and—"

"Wait. Whoa! What would be the point of confessing? You would only injure Thomas' pride. Remember how Edmund warned us that Middle Eastern men are prideful? The truth is, all men have too much pride."

Flora's tears continued to fall. "I don't know what to do."

"Then don't do anything. Take time to sort out your feelings. You won't be with either man on the voyage home, so you'll have a chance to gain some perspective. Think about all the lessons we learned on this adventure—and it was an adventure, wasn't it?"

"The best one of my life! I can't wait to follow Edmund's example and start working with local churches back home to start Sunday schools. You're excited about the book you're writing, and I'm just as excited about the work ahead of me. I can't wait to tell Thomas all about it, so he can show me how to set up a charity."

"So, you've decided to return to Thomas?"

"We're engaged. . . . I think I should . . . don't you?"

"Do you really want to know what I think, Flora?"

"Yes. Tell me the truth." But Flora already knew what her sister would say. She squeezed her eyes shut as she waited to hear it.

"Edmund Merriday is ten times the man Thomas is. And he loves you for yourself, not for your money."

"You always think everyone is after our money—Mrs. Worthington, Freddy, and now Thomas."

Becky folded her arms across her chest. "You'll never convince me they're not."

Flora spent the long voyage home thinking about the two men she loved. Was Becky right about the Worthingtons? Were they only interested in her inheritance? Flora couldn't make herself believe it. In the end, she decided that she would never forget the long, eventful summer with Edmund and harbor a secret joy when she thought of him, but her place was with Thomas in Chicago.

Thomas showed up at Flora's home before Mrs. Griffin even had a chance to unpack her steamer trunks. She still wore her wrinkled traveling clothes, her hair pulled back in a messy knot, but she hurried downstairs so she wouldn't keep him waiting. "How wonderful to see you, Thomas! If I had known you were coming—"

He pulled her close and kissed her. "I couldn't wait a moment longer," he said. Flora inhaled the clean scent of his soap and cologne and thought of Edmund—the rugged, outdoor smell of his khaki clothes, his callused hands, sun-bleached hair, and browned skin. She pulled away from Thomas with alarm.

"Forgive me, dear Flora," he said, misunderstanding her reaction. "It's just that I've missed you so."

"Let's go into the morning room. I'll ask the servants to bring tea . . . or whatever you'd like," she said, remembering that it was Edmund who drank tea, not Thomas. She held his smooth, well-manicured hand in hers as she led him into the morning room and sat beside him on the settee.

"I couldn't wait to tell you how the plans for our wedding have been moving forward while you were away," he said. "Aunt Priscilla has arranged for a seamstress to sew your gown, and—"

"But we haven't even chosen a date, yet."

"I've chosen several dates for you to pick from. You don't need to decide right this minute," he said with a little laugh, but he went on and on about the wedding dinner, the hundreds of invited guests, and all the other arrangements he'd made. Flora felt dizzy. Thomas clearly envisioned a lavish and very expensive affair. After a while the details bored her, and she began daydreaming about Edmund's Sunday school. She remembered how he'd laughed out loud when she'd told him about working in the uniform factory. She had never told that story to Thomas, but she could easily guess what his horrified reaction would be. His aunt, Mrs. Worthington, had become their unofficial governess—Becky called her their jailor—after that escapade. "What do you think?" Thomas asked, finishing at last. Flora hadn't been listening for several minutes.

"Must we have such an elaborate affair?" she asked. "I would feel more comfortable with a simple wedding, with just our families, perhaps. And a simple buffet luncheon."

"Our society friends will feel snubbed if they aren't invited. It might cause a scandal if they think we're hiding something."

"I don't much care what they think. We have a right to plan our own wedding."

Thomas took both of her hands in his. "Don't be cross, Flora. I'm trying to establish myself in Chicago and build a future here in the business world. An event like our wedding offers the perfect opportunity to build the social connections I'll need. And speaking of building, I've decided where our new home will be. I've made inquiries about purchasing the lot and talked with an architect about—"

"But I love this house. It's my home. I don't need any other house." She thought of the tiny, dusty rooms where Edmund lived, how wonderfully chaotic and inviting they were. She felt panicked at the thought of living in a monstrous new mansion with a library full of books that no one read, room after room of gaudy possessions that someone else had chosen, and shelves full of knickknacks that held no meaning or memories for her. In fact, as she looked around this fussy sitting room created by Mrs. Worthington, her panic soared. She pulled her hand free from Thomas' and tugged at the neckline of her shirtwaist, unable to breathe.

"Why not sell your half of this house to your sister?" Thomas asked.

"*Sell* it to her?"

"Yes. We'll need a much grander home for entertaining. I want to build a ballroom on the third floor for you and fill it with music and dancing—you love to waltz, don't you? It's not as if we can't afford to build a new house. After all, we are very wealthy."

Was that greed she saw sparkling in Thomas' eyes? He certainly had elaborate plans to spend money that wasn't even his yet. Flora suddenly recalled that every dollar of her inheritance would become Thomas' once they married. She would forfeit all control. Was this how Thomas would use her wealth, wasting it on lavish living?

"What's wrong, Flora?" Thomas rubbed her hand between his. "You aren't usually this pensive. You must be exhausted from your trip."

"No, I'm merely thinking about something . . . I want to tell you about an idea I saw in England. They've created schools that child workers can attend on Sundays, their only day off from work, so they can get an education and perhaps a better job. They're taught reading and arithmetic, but also the gospel. I've decided to do the same thing here in Chicago. I want to support local churches in the poorest areas of the city so they'll have the materials and the teachers they'll need to set up Sunday schools. Will you help me organize a charity to do that and arrange and distribute the finances? . . . Why are you frowning like that, Thomas?" she asked when he didn't reply right away.

"If you start giving away money to those sorts of people, you won't be able to stop. No matter how much you throw at them, they'll say it's never enough."

"Thomas! What *sorts* of people?"

"People who have no idea how to handle money. They get

paid a week's wages, and the first thing they do is head to the saloon. They have endless numbers of children like litters of puppies, children they can neither afford nor raise properly."

"And you know *these people*, Thomas? Personally know them?"

"I know what I'm talking about, Flora. You've been sheltered all your life—and rightly so."

"I know much more than you think. I've seen the way *these people* live, and sometimes I believe they're much happier than our society friends. I also know how much money I have inherited. I was there when my Father's will was read. I know that I could easily give away half of it to charity and still be a very wealthy woman."

"Give away—?" Thomas looked alarmed.

"In fact," she continued, "I understand that my inheritance will remain under *my* control as long as I remain unmarried. So I truly could give all of it away tomorrow if I wanted to."

"Flora, you don't understand—"

"I understand that even though we can afford this extravagant wedding that you're planning for us, it would be a sin to waste so much money when there are people here in Chicago without shoes or food or a roof over their head."

"You're still tired from traveling. You're allowing your emotions to get the better of you. Why don't you rest for a few days, and I'm certain you'll agree that I'm right." He tried to take her hand again, but she pushed him away.

"I also understand that we show our love for Jesus when we help the poor. I'm responsible before God for what I do with my inheritance, Thomas."

"But you must admit that you need guidance. Be reasonable, Flora. You can't get carried away."

She stood and took a step back. "I can't marry you, Thomas. I'm sorry." But she wasn't sorry. She felt a tidal wave of relief. She knew with certainty that if she married Thomas Worthington, he would dominate every area of her life, just as he was trying to do with their wedding and the big mansion he wanted. She couldn't allow that to happen. "We disagree on too many fundamental things. I believe God gives us wealth so we can use it to build *His* kingdom, not our own. I don't want a lavish wedding or an enormous house with a ballroom. I want to help little girls who have to stand on their feet in a factory all day earning four dollars a week."

"Flora, listen . . ."

"I think you should leave now."

"But . . . can't we talk about this—?"

"There's nothing more to say. Good-bye, Thomas. I wish you well."

She felt shaky as she walked from the sitting room, leaving Thomas to see himself out. She knew Rebecca was working in their father's library, unpacking Edmund's boxes, so she walked in and closed the door behind her. Becky was kneeling on the floor sorting through stacks of notebooks, but she looked up when Flora entered. "Goodness, Flora! You look like you've seen a ghost."

"Thomas was just here. I-I ended my engagement with him."

Becky's eyes went wide. "Really? Why?"

"He doesn't want to support my Sunday school idea. He has nothing but disdain for the poor—no compassion, no tenderness. He wants all my money for himself." Flora's knees gave way, and she sank onto one of the chairs in front of the huge desk. "I can't comprehend such a coldhearted attitude, can you? Especially when we have so much money to spare."

Becky stared at her for a long moment. Then she began to laugh. Giddy, boisterous peals of laughter rocked her body, bringing tears to her eyes. Flora didn't know how she had expected Becky to react, but she hadn't expected laughter. Becky rose from where she knelt in the middle of the boxes and enveloped Flora in a hug. "Bravo, little sister! I'm so proud of you! That was a huge decision. Are you going to be all right?"

"I-I think so. I feel . . . reborn!"

Flora began her charity work the next day. If her sister could learn to speak Arabic and organize mountains of research into a book, Flora could certainly learn about finances and organize a Sunday school. She hired one of the lawyers from her father's firm to teach her about endowments and investments and dividends and charitable trusts so she could manage her inheritance wisely. "If Thomas and Freddy Worthington can learn about such things, I certainly can, too," she told Becky. Instead of spending time and money planning an extravagant wedding and building an enormous mansion, Flora worked with three Chicago churches to set up Sunday schools. She even expanded the original idea so that working men and women could also learn to read and write. Along with teaching literacy, the schools taught the gospel.

Flora turned away a barrage of messages and letters and visits from Thomas and their former society friends, including Widow Worthington—all who pleaded with Flora to change her mind. Thomas promised to set up an annuity for her charity and give her free reign over the funds, but Flora refused. "I'm learning how to manage my own money," she told Becky. "What makes him think I'd settle for one measly annuity?"

"Do you regret not marrying Thomas?" Rebecca asked her one Sunday afternoon as they rode home from teaching together.

Flora smiled and shook her head. "Not even for a minute."

Four months later as Christmas approached, Rebecca emerged from Father's library, which she had taken over with her book project, and found Flora poring over her financial accounts in the sitting room. Rebecca wore her coat and bonnet and was carrying Flora's winter coat over her arm. "Come for a ride with me," Becky said.

"Right now? I'm in the middle of something."

"We need a break from our work and some fresh air. I've decided we should go on a tiny adventure."

Flora wasn't in the mood for an adventure, and besides, Becky's adventures were never tiny. But she couldn't refuse her sister, so she finished adding her sums and rose and put on her coat and gloves. She was a little surprised to see the carriage already waiting outside, but she climbed in beside Becky. They had recently purchased a new carriage to replace the squeaking, rattling one they used to drive to school. They had a new team of horses, too. But it was still Rufus who insisted on driving them everywhere, even though he'd allowed them to hire a young groom named Andrew to help him in the carriage house.

A sharp wind blew off the lake as the carriage headed north on Michigan Avenue. The trees were bare, and Flora knew the first snowflakes would fall soon. She was wondering how she could make sure Chicago's poorest children had shoes and warm coats for winter when the carriage made a right-hand turn toward the lake, just before the Rush Street Bridge.

"Why are we heading toward the train station?" Flora asked. "Don't tell me you've purchased tickets again, because as much as I would love to travel with you, Becky, I can't drop everything and go this time."

"Don't worry," she said as they halted in front of the depot. "We aren't going anywhere. Just humor me and come inside."

The commotion inside the echoing station brought back memories of last summer's trip, especially the train ride through the lush English countryside to Cambridge. Becky towed Flora by the arm as they pushed through the holiday crowds, finally halting on one of the platforms. Steam and smoke and winter air swirled around them. Nothing happened for several minutes as they waited. Then a locomotive whistle shrieked in the distance and a shouting conductor announced that the train rumbling toward them was arriving from New York. Flora got swept up in the excitement as she stood on the platform, watching people emerge from the train, running to greet loved ones, laughing and embracing. Busy porters unloaded trunks and suitcases from distant destinations.

"Why are we here, Becky? We aren't expecting guests—" Then she saw him stepping down onto the platform, tall and lanky and sandy-haired and wonderfully disheveled. Flora gripped Becky's arm to steady herself. "Edmund? . . . Is it really him?" Before Becky could reply, Edmund saw Flora, too, and he dropped his suitcase on the platform and sprinted toward her. The next moment she was in his arms, and he was lifting her from the ground, crushing her to himself. It was a good thing he was holding her, because her knees had gone so weak with joy she might have fallen over. Flora knew it wasn't proper for an unmarried couple to embrace in public for all the world to see—right on the platform no less! Widow Worthington would have needed smelling salts to revive from such a sight. Flora didn't care. She hugged Edmund with all her strength until he finally set her on the ground again. Flora turned to Becky to thank her and saw her sister wiping a tear. "Did you arrange this, Becky?"

"Um . . . I may have mentioned in one of my letters to Edmund that you had ended your engagement to Thomas."

"But it was my idea to come," Edmund said. His eyes were bright with love and tears. "I'm afraid I invited myself. Terribly improper, I know. And I promise to reimburse you for my travel expenses, Rebecca," he added with a worried look.

"I'll deduct it from our first royalty check after our book is published," she said with a wry smile.

"What about your job at the library in Cambridge?" Flora asked.

"I requested a leave of absence in addition to my Christmas holidays, and hopped on the very first ship I could find. I couldn't let you walk out of my life for a second time."

Flora hugged him again, afraid to believe he was real. "Let's go home, Edmund," she said. "We have so much to talk about. And I can't wait to show you the work Becky and I are doing with our three new Sunday schools."

Edmund paused to gaze out at Lake Michigan before stepping into the carriage, shielding his eyes from the bright winter sun. "I can't believe that's a lake. It's immense! Like an ocean! One can't even see the other side of it."

Flora wasn't looking at the lake. She couldn't take her eyes off Edmund, unable to believe he was really here. "There's an entire inland-waterway of Great Lakes. I'll show you a map when we get home."

"Everything looks so new here in America," he said as they drove home down Michigan Avenue.

"It is new. Unlike Cambridge, which is hundreds of years old, Chicago wasn't even incorporated until 1837."

"This must be where the landed gentry live," he said when they reached their neighborhood. "How many families live in each of these homes?"

"Just one. And this home is ours," Flora said as they pulled to a halt.

"You're joking."

"No, this is where Becky and I live."

Edmund seemed unable to move as he stared up at the house. "Oh my . . ."

"Ours is by no means one of the largest or fanciest homes."

"You ladies kept telling me not to worry about finances last summer, but I had no idea you were this rich!"

"I'll leave you two to talk," Becky said as she ducked out of the carriage.

"I-I don't believe I can speak . . ." Edmund murmured. "I'm incredulous."

"It's just a house, Edmund. My parents built it. What difference does it make how grand it is?"

"It was my intention to convince you to marry me and return to England with me, but now that I've seen your home, I'm embarrassed to think of asking you to move to my cramped little flat."

"Let's go inside. It's too cold to sit out here. And Rufus needs to put the carriage away."

"You—you have servants, too?" he mumbled as Rufus helped them from the carriage and Griffin opened the door and took Edmund's coat and suitcase. Flora led Edmund into the little sitting room so he wouldn't be further overwhelmed, but even that room, decorated to Mrs. Worthington's taste, would seem pretentious to him. "You must be royalty," he said as he looked around.

"Don't be silly. We don't have royalty here in America." Flora gestured for him to sit, but he didn't move, so she remained standing, as well. "You once said that you loved me, Edmund. Is that still true?"

He turned his gaze to hers. "Yes. With all my heart. I've been living in an agony of moroseness since you left, and I've kicked myself a thousand times over for letting you leave. Yet I knew I couldn't give you the life you deserve. I still can't. Look at all of this! You must be millionaires!"

"We are, to put it bluntly. Our father made some very wise investments before he died, leaving Becky and me with an enormous inheritance. I've begun studying the intricacies of banking and finance these past months so I can manage that inheritance wisely, but money won't be a concern for us for the remainder of our lives." She gave him a moment to digest her words, but the look of surprise and shock never left his face. "Do you enjoy your job at Cambridge, Edmund? Because if you still want to marry me, you would never have to work again."

"I long to marry you, Flora! That's why I jumped on the very first steamship to America that I could find. It's why I wanted to go down to the engine room and shovel coal into the boilers myself to make it go faster. I love you more than I ever dreamed I could love someone. But I won't live off your inheritance like a slacker. And you obviously have a much better mind for handling finances and investments than I do."

"You could learn. I did."

He moved close to her and held her face between his hands. "You're such a dear, sweet girl. You have no idea how brilliant you are, do you? Or how hopeless I am when it comes to money."

"I can understand if you don't want to live the life I do. I didn't want it either, which is why I didn't marry Thomas Worthington. But the Lord gave Becky and me this inheritance, and I believe that Christ's words apply to us: To whom much has been given, much will be required. I have an obligation to be a good steward over what's been entrusted to me."

"I admire you so much for that. And I understand why you need to stay here in America. The work you're doing among the poor sounds amazing."

"But . . . ? It sounds like you're about to tell me why you can't marry me."

"Flora, listen . . . I'm sixteen years older than you. And I'm just a vagabond scholar, the son of a country clergyman—"

"What difference does that make? Why does your stupid pride have to ruin everything? It was pride that made you send me back to America last summer because you didn't think you could provide for me. Well, the truth is, I don't need you or anyone else to provide for me. If we love each other, why can't we just accept our roles the way they are? You and I aren't ordinary people, Edmund. Neither one of us follows society's rules. Why can't our marriage be unconventional, too?"

"Are you proposing marriage to me?"

"I am!" Flora said, stomping her foot. "And you'd better not turn me down, Edmund Merriday, if you know what's good for you!"

He laughed and pulled her into his arms. "Then I accept your proposal, darling Flora, on one condition."

"And what would that be?" She wasn't in the mood for any more arguments.

"I insist on finding a job here in Chicago and earning an honest living, rather than being supported by my wife and doing nothing all day."

"What about the book you're writing with Becky?"

"That's hardly a full-time job, and besides, she'll be much better at writing it than I would be."

"Fine! Get up every morning and go work for a living if that's what makes you happy—you wonderful, ridiculous man! But I'm going to marry you if it's the last thing I do!" Flora stood on her tiptoes, and they sealed the bargain with a kiss.

The sound of clapping interrupted them. Rufus, Griffin, Maria Elena, and Mrs. Griffin all stood in the doorway with Becky, watching them—and applauding.

Flora's joy seemed boundless and complete—except for one problem. Becky was in love with Edmund, too. After everyone went to bed that night, Flora knocked on her sister's bedroom door. "May I come in, Becky? I want to talk." Her sister was sitting up in bed, reading, but she laid the book aside as Flora climbed onto the bed and sat cross-legged, facing her. "I'll never be able to thank you enough for writing to Edmund and paying his fare to get here. I know you love him, too, and yet you did such a brave, unselfish thing—for me. Thank you, with all my heart."

"What are sisters for?" Becky attempted a smile, but Flora could tell she was battling tears.

"What can I do for you in return? I don't want there to be any awkwardness between us, or for there to be heartache in your life whenever you see Edmund. Please, tell me what we should do. Edmund and I can find our own home if that would make things easier, but that isn't what I want. I want you to live with us, always. Just tell me what would be best and easiest for you. I can only imagine how difficult this must be for you."

"It is hard," Becky said, closing her eyes for a moment. "But the fact that Edmund doesn't have a clue about my feelings for him makes it a little easier. I've had time to adjust, to heal. And I know how deeply he loves you—and you him." She attempted another smile. "In the end, God has given you a wonderful husband, and me a coauthor and a book to write. It's more than enough to be thankful for."

"But what about our living arrangements? Shall I make plans to move?"

"Let's leave things the way they are for now, and take it one day at a time."

Flora rose to her knees and hugged Becky tightly. "Thank you," she whispered. "If there's anything in the world I can ever do for you . . ."

"Well, I did have one thought," Becky said as Flora sat back again.

"Anything!"

"Since Father isn't here to walk you down the aisle on your wedding day, would you let me give you away to Edmund?"

"Yes, why not?" Flora said, laughing. "You've never done anything conventional in your life, so why start now?"

Flora married Edmund a week later. A small gathering of their closest friends and faithful servants helped them celebrate. Any acquaintances of Flora's from Chicago's fashionable circles who would have gossiped that Edmund was too old for her, or that he was a foreigner, or that he didn't have two pennies to rub together, hadn't been invited. That included the Worthingtons. The widow would have gasped in shock to see Flora getting married in last year's gown, shorn of all but the simplest frills and lace. Edmund wore the only good suit he had packed, which also happened to be the only good suit he owned. Neither he nor Flora was willing to wait for a tailor to sew him a new one.

Flora thought she might burst with joy as she linked her arm through Edmund's and walked from the church with him to begin their new life. She was now Mrs. Edmund Merriday. After hosting a reception in their home so everyone could get to know this wonderful man who brought her so much joy, Flora sailed to England with him for their wedding trip. They spent their nights at an inn in Cambridge and their days exploring the area and packing Edmund's belongings and books and artifacts to be shipped to Chicago. They hosted another small reception so Edmund could say good-bye to his family and his Cambridge friends and colleagues, then they sailed back to America where they would live with Becky in their childhood home. It had more than enough room for all three of them.

"Tell me what you wish for, my dear Flora," Edmund said as they stood at the ship's rail on a blustery evening at sea. They had wrapped themselves in layers against the cold air and salt spray. Flora had to hang on to her bonnet as the wind threatened to snatch it off her head. Edmund gave up and clutched his hat in his fist, his sandy hair blowing wildly in the wind.

Flora smiled and said, "This would be so much more romantic if we stood beneath a full moon with clear, starry skies above us."

"Yes, but why expect a fairy-tale evening or a peaceful crossing when our life together is certain to be unique in every way?" They were both startled when a rogue wave spilled water over the deck, soaking their shoes. They retreated from the rail and sank, laughing, onto a deck chair, squeezing close together, pulling a blanket over their legs. "But besides moonlight and starlight, my dear Flora, what else do you wish for when we arrive home again? I stand ready to grant your every wish."

"I wish for children. Dozens of them, filling our home with their giggles and running feet. I want to read stories to them every night, all of the wonderful tales that I enjoyed as a child."

"I suppose you'd like to pack them all onto camels and take them with us on our many travels, too?"

"Absolutely! I can't wait to share our travels with them, can you? I'm certain they'll be as curious and fearless as their father is."

"And as adorable and resolute as their beautiful mother."

"And as bright and adventurous as their aunt Becky. But what do you wish for, Edmund?"

He sighed and reached for her hand. "Right now, my life is filled with so much joy I wouldn't dare ask for more. I know we will also experience sorrow in the years ahead. But through it all, I wish for a life filled with meaning and purpose, a life lived for God."

How Flora loved this man!

CHAPTER 16

CHICAGO
1871
NINETEEN YEARS AGO

The celebration on a mild Saturday evening in October was a grand one. Six years after her wedding and two days before Edmund's forty-second birthday, Flora watched in pride as her husband and sister presented copies of their newly released book to their departing dinner guests—longtime friends from church and from Flora's many charities, as well as colleagues of Edmund's from Northwestern University in nearby Evanston, where he'd been employed for the past five years. More boxes of the book he and Becky had co-written were stacked in Father's office, the authors' names listed on the cover alphabetically: *R. Hawes and E. Merriday*. Invitations for them to speak were already streaming in.

"Any idea what all the commotion was about tonight?" Flora asked their butler, Griffin, as he closed the door behind the last of their guests. "It sounded like a good many fire alarm bells were clanging in the distance while we were eating dinner."

"They say there's a big fire on the West Side, near that large grain warehouse. Rufus said the sky was glowing in that direction."

"I'm not surprised. Everything is so dry. I can't recall when it rained last. I trust the fire is under control now?"

"The firemen have been hard at it all evening, Miss Flora. I haven't heard any more alarm bells in the last hour, so they must have put it out."

Edmund had come over to stand beside Flora and heard the last of their conversation. "Isn't one of the Sunday schools we support located in a church on the West Side?" he asked.

"Yes. That's what has me worried. Maybe Rufus can drive us over there tomorrow so we can see if—"

"The only place any of us is going tomorrow is to church." Edmund wrapped his arm around Flora's shoulder and steered her toward the stairs. "I think our servants deserve a full day off tomorrow after working so hard on this grand celebration for our new book, and that includes Rufus."

"He's right," Becky said, climbing the stairs behind them. "Even with all the extra help we hired for the party, everyone must be exhausted. I know I am."

The wind was strong as they walked to church the next day. It clawed at Flora's bonnet and blew fine dust into her eyes, making them sting. "This must be ash from last night's fire," she said. She stood on tiptoes to brush the fine powder from the shoulders of Edmund's dark suit before entering the church.

"It's a good thing the fire was last night," he said, "and not on a windy day like today."

Worry gnawed at Flora throughout the day of rest. She needed to see if the West Side church still stood, if the children were safe, if the needs of all those families were being taken care of. Shortly before it was time to return for the evening church service, she went in search of Becky to ask if she wanted to go with her to the West Side tomorrow. She found her sister in

Father's office with his chair turned toward the window, staring out of it. "Becky, I wanted to ask you if—" She halted when Becky turned around. She had been crying, something Becky almost never did.

"Tell me what's wrong," Flora said, sitting in one of the chairs in front of her desk.

"It's nothing," Becky said with a wave of dismissal. "Just me being silly, that's all."

"It isn't silly to feel a little sad now that the work you've labored over for the past five years is finished."

Becky blinked in surprise. "How did you guess?"

"Because we know each other so well. I still remember the moment in Bethlehem when you knew you were meant to work on this book with Edmund. I had the same experience when I saw Edmund's Sunday school in Cambridge."

"I know you did. And I can tell you're worried about last night's fire on the West Side. I'll go there with you tomorrow if you want."

"Thank you. I do." One of the new books rested on the desk, and Flora watched as Becky ran her hand over the cover like a mother caressing her child's face. "You're wondering what's next, aren't you, Becky?" She nodded and slid the book to the side. "We both know there will be more books. And just as God showed you the work He had for you by stranding poor Edmund along the Gaza Road, He will surely show you what's next if you trust Him and wait." Becky nodded, too full of emotion to speak. "Come on," Flora said, rising to her feet. "It's time to leave for church."

That night, the fire bells began sounding another alarm on the way home from the evening service. "I wonder if the fire has started up again from the ashes of the first one," Edmund said as they undressed for bed. Flora's worries had retreated during the day, but now they returned in force as the clanging bells sounded in the distance.

"Those poor people. All the buildings in that part of town are made of wood, you know. They were slapped together haphazardly because the city grew so fast during the war." She climbed into bed beside her husband, but after tossing for an hour, unable to sleep, she finally rose again and put on her dressing gown.

"What's wrong, darling?" Edmund asked with a yawn.

"I can't stop thinking of ways to organize a relief effort to help the fire victims. I may as well get up and write some of them down. Those people have so little as it is, the very least I can do is sponsor a fund-raising drive to help them replace things like bedding and household items."

"Would you like me to help you come up with ideas?"

"No, dear man. Go back to sleep. You have to go to work tomorrow." She went downstairs to the little sitting room at the back of the house and sat down at her table with pen and paper. She had gotten rid of Mrs. Worthington's useless frills and gewgaws and transformed the room into a comfortable office where she managed the finances and oversaw the trust funds from her and Becky's inheritance. She worked for more than an hour, choosing two charitable foundations to draw upon, then turned out the gaslights to return to bed. She got as far as the stair landing when she noticed the glow in the sky beyond the huge, arched window. It looked like the sun was about to dawn in a storm-red sky—but the clock in the hallway had just struck midnight. And the sun rose in the east, not in the west. She hurried to her room and shook Edmund awake.

"Come look at the sky, Edmund. It's all aglow." He struggled out of bed and followed her down to the landing, rubbing sleep from his eyes.

"Good heavens," he breathed. "The fire must be huge to light up the sky that way! And it doesn't seem to be confined to the area where last night's fire was."

"I'm not surprised that it's spreading. Listen to that wind howling. It won't jump to our side of the river, will it?"

"I shouldn't think it could cross the water. But we'd better wake Rebecca and the servants as a precaution. Tell them to get dressed and to start thinking about what to pack in case it gets any worse."

They spent half an hour doing that. All the while alarm bells rang in the distance, and the wind wailed outside the house like the furies, rattling the window glass as if trying to come inside. As Flora placed a box filled with important papers in the foyer where they were collecting their valuables, Rebecca emerged from the library with a box of research documents she and Edmund had used to write their book. "I'm going up to the attic to see if I can see anything from the window," Becky said. "Do you and Edmund want to join me?"

"I think that's a good idea." Flora fetched Edmund, and they climbed up to the attic, carrying a lamp.

"I remember exploring up here when we were children," Becky said as they entered the shadowy space.

"I don't think anyone has been up here since." Flora was surprised to see how much discarded furniture and household items and old clothing were piled beneath the cobwebbed rafters. "I see a great deal of items we can donate to the poor when this is over. I'm guessing most of our friends have attics filled with useful things, too." Her mind spun with ideas as the three of them balanced their way across the rafters and loose floorboards to the west-facing window. The wind shrieked around the gables above their heads. "We can hire wagons and deliverymen to bring all the donations to one of the churches on the West Side. We should ask for food donations, too, and organize hot meals for the people to eat."

They reached the window, and Flora dimmed the lamp to peer out. What she saw made her stomach roll in horror. Tongues of flame leapt into the sky in the distance, reaching all the way to the clouds. A sickening, orange-yellow glow lit up the heart of the city. "Dear Lord, help us," she breathed. Edmund slipped his arm around her shoulders.

"We'd better keep packing our things," he said.

Flora's heart raced as they hurried down from the attic. What should they pack? Where should they take it all? When she reached the foyer and saw the pile of boxes they'd already accumulated, she had another thought. "Edmund! If the fire reaches the city center, Father's office will be in danger. All our important business papers and stock certificates and the deeds to his properties are in the office safe."

"Is the safe fireproof?"

"It's supposed to be . . . but I would hate to put all my trust in it."

"Would you like me to go there and retrieve them for you?" he asked.

"No, I need to go there with you and help."

"But, Flora, darling, it's much too dangerous for you—"

"Don't coddle me, Edmund. It's just as dangerous for you as it is for me. I would be in an agony of worry if I stayed here and let you go by yourself. Besides, I know where to find everything quickly, and I could gather them much faster than you could."

"Well, you two aren't having an adventure without me," Rebecca said. "I'm going with you."

They decided to walk after instructing Rufus and Andrew to prepare the carriage in case they needed to evacuate in a hurry. The heat and smoke intensified as they neared the city's center. So did the throngs of desperate people cramming the streets, dragging trunks and suitcases and carrying bundles on their backs as they hurried to escape the approaching flames. Discarded items littered the streets, abandoned by people in their haste to flee. Showers of sparks and chunks of flaming debris filled the air, hurled by the hurricane-like winds.

"Look!" Becky shouted, pointing up. "The courthouse is on fire!" Flames were devouring the cupola of the building only a few blocks away. They leaped so high into the sky and were spreading so fast to the adjacent rooftops that Flora didn't see how anything could stop them. The skyline to the west was a towering wall of fire.

"We need to hurry," Edmund said, "before it spreads to your building."

Flora's hands shook as she fumbled with her key to unlock the main door. When it finally opened, they raced up the stairs to Father's law and investment offices on the second floor, taking them two at a time. She was relieved to see that several of her father's partners and associates were already there with the safe open, working to save their valuable records. The rooms were so bright from the light of the flames that they didn't need a lamp. Edmund helped Flora stuff deeds and stock certificates into the rucksacks and canvas bags that he'd wisely thought to bring.

"Enough, Flora," he said when they were full. "We need to get out." They raced down the stairs and out of the building again, heading east toward the lake and home, the heat of the fire warming their backs.

By the time they reached their street, Flora felt weak with exhaustion. Edmund was pale with fatigue and wheezing from the smoke. "This fire is unbelievable," Becky murmured. "I keep wondering if I'm dreaming." They saw many of their neighbors hastily loading goods and children into carriages and onto wagons. Others had ripped up their carpets and soaked them with water, and were now spreading them on their rooftops to protect them from flying sparks.

"Do you think we should cover our roof, too, so the fire won't catch?" Becky asked. She always had been fearless in the past, but Flora could tell that the eerie horror of this strange night had shaken her.

"I don't see how we could manage it," Edmund said. "We can't climb all the way up to the roof, and we have no one to help us. Rufus and Griffin are too elderly, and I'm certainly not going to allow you ladies to do it. Besides, our house is so close to all the others that we couldn't possibly stop the fire from spreading once it comes this way."

"God help us," Flora said.

Becky squeezed her hand. "He's the only One who can."

They went inside to gather their wits and try to decide what to do next. "I think we all need to leave and go someplace safe," Edmund said. "The fire has already jumped to our side of the river and could spread this way next. I want everyone to get into the carriage so Rufus can take us north across the main branch of the Chicago River. Gather your most important possessions, and let's go."

Flora saw fear in her elderly servants' eyes as they hurried to collect their things. Rufus had parked the carriage near the door, and he and Andrew began loading it. Flora drew Edmund aside, away from the others and said, "We won't all fit, Edmund. That carriage is much too small. Let's send Becky and the servants on their way first. Rufus or Andrew can return for us if there's time. "

"But I want you to be safe, darling Flora. You saw how quickly the fire is spreading through the city."

"I can run fast, and they can't—I'm a good thirty years younger than the Griffins and Maria Elena are. Besides, I need to make sure all these documents and your research papers make it out safely, and they're going to take up a lot of space in the carriage."

"Then let's get everything loaded so Rebecca and the servants can leave."

"I'm not going anywhere without you two," Becky said. She stood in the doorway and had overheard Flora's plan. "I can run just as fast as you, Flora. Probably faster. We're in this together. All three of us."

Edmund dragged their boxes and sacks outside and helped Rufus strap them to the back of the carriage. Flora had been right—the servants barely managed to squeeze into the carriage with all of their things. "Where shall we meet up?" Flora asked as Rufus prepared to leave.

"My sister works for a family up on LaSalle Street," Mrs. Griffin suggested. Flora copied down the address and tucked it into her pocket.

"I sure don't like leaving you folks behind," Rufus said. He wore the same worried look that he'd had years ago when he'd left Flora and Becky at the uniform factory.

Flora reached up to the driver's seat to squeeze his arm. "We'll be fine, Rufus. Don't worry. We have God and Edmund to watch out for us." Rufus nodded and tipped his hat before driving away. Flora marveled at the commotion taking place on her normally tranquil street. Her neighbors and their servants were dragging expensive pieces of furniture and wardrobes filled with clothing through the streets toward the shore of Lake Michigan, then hurrying back for more. "Is there anything we should try to save?" she asked Becky as they watched the frantic activity.

"None of it matters. Let's leave it all in the Lord's hands." The three of them returned inside, and as Flora gazed around the enormous drawing room filled with furniture and bronze statues and oil paintings, she knew Becky was right. It was useless to try to save all their possessions, no matter how valuable they were. Either their home would be spared—or it wouldn't.

She turned to Edmund. "Thank goodness your books and artifact collections are in your office in Evanston. The fire won't spread that far, will it?"

"Twelve miles? I don't think so. But what about your Father's library? Is there any way to save all those wonderful books?"

"We could bury some of them in the backyard for safekeeping," Becky said. "There's already a large hole out there where the gardener removed a dead bush the other day. I don't think he planted the new one yet."

They hauled an empty steamer trunk down from upstairs and Becky filled it with the best volumes from his collection. Flora went from room to room gathering a few of their most treasured mementos, including the tiny oil painting of their mother and a few pieces of her jewelry. Edmund laid a blanket on the dining room floor and piled the family silver in the middle of it and tied the bundle closed. He had to dig the hole a little deeper to fit everything in, including a box of the book they'd written, and he was sweating with the effort by the time he'd covered the hole with dirt again. They went inside to wash the ash and dirt off their hands.

"Now what?" Becky asked as they gazed around the disheveled rooms. The clock in the foyer struck three thirty as if in reply.

"It's still the middle of the night," Edmund said, "and look— it's as light as day in here. We can't wait for Rufus to come back. We need to get out." His face was smudged with soot like a laborer's, and a layer of ash had turned his hair gray. Flora went to him and held him tightly, knowing she would sooner lose the house and everything in it than lose him and Becky.

"You're right. Let's go."

They stuffed their pockets and Edmund's knapsack with all of the cash they had in the house. Becky added bread and apples and a few pieces of chicken from their celebration dinner. Then they walked out the door, hoping it wasn't for the last time, and headed north toward the bridge that crossed the Chicago River, joining the tidal wave of fleeing people. "Rufus will never be able to make it back for us with the carriage even if he wanted to," Flora said. The wind tore at their clothes and brought showers of flaming sparks down on them like rain. Some of the larger pieces burned through the fabric of Flora's blouse and stung her arms and back like wasp bites. She removed her hat, fearing the straw would ignite and set her hair on fire, and the wind promptly snatched it from her hand. The smoke that blinded them and stung their eyes was so thick at times it threatened to suffocate them. A surge of panic pressed against Flora's chest. They had waited too long to leave. The fire was about to overtake them. She gripped Edmund's and Becky's hands to keep from being separated in the running mob.

But a gang of rough-looking men who obviously didn't belong in this well-to-do neighborhood was moving in the opposite direction. Flora saw looters running out of several homes with armloads of valuables. One man wore several layers of fine gentlemen's clothing and carried a bundle of silk dresses. "Do you think they'll loot our house, too?" she asked.

Becky squeezed her hand. "There's nothing we can do."

There were only so many bridges to the north side of the river, and the entire population of Chicago poured toward them. Panicked people clutching all sorts of belongings jammed the roadway, many of them dragging trunks and suitcases, pushing wheelbarrows, or driving wagons and carriages and carts of every shape and kind. Children screamed in terror, and their fear nearly broke Flora's heart. She had longed for a baby these past five years, but as she saw the terrified little ones being carried and herded through the streets, she was grateful that she didn't have a child to experience such danger and horror.

At last she saw the arches of the bridge up ahead in the fire-bright sky. But the crowd suddenly halted and the press of people pushed against her from all sides. She and Edmund and Becky struggled to hang on to each other. "What's going on?

Why have we stopped?" she asked. Then she heard the clanging, grinding gears of the swing bridge and saw the tips of several masts up ahead on the river. They were opening the bridge to let ships through, forcing all of these people to wait! After what seemed like a lifetime, the bridge swung closed again and the mob surged forward to cross it.

The fire was right behind them, gaining on them. Flora saw the wind-driven flames leap across the river to the west of them as they hurried over the bridge, and for the first time that night, she wondered if they would survive. Piles of belongings littered the road ahead, abandoned by their owners in their haste to flee. "I don't think we can outrun this," Edmund shouted above the melee. "We need to get to the lakeshore!" He dragged them by the hand toward the lake beneath a hailstorm of burning cinders. Flora had just spotted the black void of the water ahead of them when a flaming ball of canvas tumbled down the street behind them and ignited the hem of Becky's dress. Edmund turned at the sound of her screams and tore a portion of her skirt free, stomping on it to extinguish the fire. "Are you all right?" he breathed.

"Yes. But we need to run!"

Thousands of people had reached the lake ahead of them— rich and poor, young and old, muttering in a babble of languages. Some wept, many prayed, but most huddled on the shore beside their bundles of belongings, gazing at the city in disbelief. "Look," Becky said, pointing to the Great Central Depot. It lit up the night as it burned across the river.

At times the choking smoke became so bad they could barely breathe. The heat sent them wading into the chilly water, and as they stood with their arms wrapped around each other's waists, Flora said, "I wonder if we're going to die?"

"God knows when the hour of our end will be," Becky said. "We don't need to fear. . . . But I truly hope it isn't tonight." She and Flora looked at each other and began to laugh. It bubbled up from deep inside Flora, and she let go of her husband for a moment to cling tightly to her sister.

"This has been an adventure, hasn't it, Becky?"

"One I wouldn't have chosen—but, yes, it has."

They waded out of the water again after a while and sat on the ground, shivering with all the other refugees. Edmund left them for a few minutes, and when he returned he looked worried. "I hate to say this, but we can't stay here. Everything along these docks is going to burn—the brewery, all of that lumber, those warehouses and piles of coal. If the flames don't kill us, the smoke will. We have to move farther north."

Flora's heart began to thump. "Back into the fire?"

"I think we can stay ahead of it if we zigzag through the streets. . . . Ready?"

They plunged back into the maelstrom to outrun the firestorm. Sometimes they saw it a mere half-block away, as if it were pursuing them, taunting them. Edmund had to pause several times, overcome by fits of coughing, and they sat down on the curb to rest. At dawn, with the fire behind them for now, they staggered into the cemetery near Lincoln Park. At least Flora thought it was dawn—the sky was so bright with flames it was difficult to tell. Thousands of people had reached the safety of the cemetery ahead of them, and it was a scene of despair and desolation. Where would all these people live? How would they survive in the coming days once the fire's fury spent itself? If it ever did.

The three of them sank down on one of the graves, leaning against the tombstones, and ate the food that Becky had packed earlier that night, grateful for it. Flora longed for a drink of water, her mouth and throat parched and dry, but there was none. Weary with fatigue and sorrow, she closed her eyes and dozed.

When she woke again, clouds of black smoke swirled over the city, which was still in flames. "As if one night of this hell on earth wasn't enough," she heard Edmund telling Becky, "it seems we're in for more. The fire shows no signs of dying out."

"Do you think we'll be safe here?"

"I don't know. For now, maybe. But I'm worried about our servants. The fire is burning a path straight north through that part of the city. Will you take care of Flora for me while I try to find them and warn them to leave?"

Flora sat up straight, every part of her body aching. "Nothing doing! We all go or none of us does."

They set off again, weaving west toward LaSalle Street, the roads still crowded with fleeing people. How many thousands would be homeless when this nightmare ended? Would she and Edmund and Becky be homeless, too? As they neared LaSalle, Flora thought the neighborhood looked familiar, then she realized that Mrs. Worthington lived nearby. Flora had tried to remain friends with her for Father's sake after ending her engagement to Thomas, but the widow had turned her away.

"Edmund, wait," she said as he started to turn north on LaSalle. "Can we go down one more block to Wells Street? Mrs. Worthington lives on Wells, and I want to make sure she's safe. She doesn't have any children, so she may need help. Do you mind, Becky?"

"No, I don't mind. But we'll need to be quick. The fire is right behind us, and we haven't found our servants yet."

The scene on the widow's street was the same as the others they had witnessed on this endless night and day—people loading household goods into carts and wagons, cramming into the homes of friends and strangers as they waited for the danger to end, wondering if they'd have to flee again. Flora halted in front of the stately Georgian-style home Mrs. Worthington had bought with the inheritance Father had left her. "I'll wait out here," Becky said. "I don't think she will approve of my attire." She gestured to her half-torn skirt and bare leg, visible through the charred edges. Flora grinned at the sight, then walked with Edmund through the widow's wide-open front door and found her in the middle of a chaotic mess. Half-packed boxes lay strewn in every room as if she was trying to move the home's entire contents. The widow herself looked wild-eyed, her hair in disarray, her cheeks hectic with feverish color. "Flora, the gaslights all went out!" she said without greeting. "And now it seems the water is off, too."

"That's because the gasworks and water pumping station are on fire. The flames are coming this way, Mrs. Worthington. You need to get out."

"I'm waiting for my driver. I sent him to my cousin's house with the first load of goods, and he hasn't returned. The rest of my servants got tired of waiting for him and the cowards all abandoned me."

"I doubt if your driver can make it back," Flora told her. "The roads are filled with people and wagons all moving in the opposite direction. You'd be wise to leave everything and get out while you can."

"Leave a lifetime of memorabilia? My dear, how can I? Besides, I can't get anywhere without a carriage. I'm quite unaccustomed to walking."

"Would you like me to see if I can secure a place for you on someone's wagon?" Edmund offered. "In this wild time, people will do anything if the price is right."

"Don't *you* have a carriage?" she asked.

"No, ma'am, we—"

"You forced your wife to walk all this way?" Flora saw disdain for Edmund in her expression and heard it in her voice. "You live miles from here!"

Flora felt every one of those miles in her aching feet and

weary body. "He isn't making me walk, Mrs. Worthington. We sent our servants off to safety in our carriage last night. We're on our way now to meet them. Please come with us."

"I am not leaving my home and all my things." She placed the silver teapot she'd been holding into one of the open boxes.

"Can't you smell the smoke, Mrs. Worthington?" Flora asked. The widow didn't reply. Flora tried one last time. "Please, Mrs. Worthington. I know how much my father cared for you, and I don't want to leave you here. Come with us, for his sake. Please."

"No, thank you. The ties between our families were severed years ago when you married *him*." She lifted her chin as she nodded at Edmund—wonderful, brave, exhausted Edmund who would risk his life to save her and Becky. "Good day," Mrs. Worthington added curtly.

Flora brushed away tears as Edmund closed the front door, and they rejoined Becky in the chaos-filled street. She knew by the dense smoke filling the air and the rain of cinders falling down on them that the fire was getting closer. Flora tasted grit in her mouth and rubbed it from her burning eyes. "At least you tried," Edmund told her. "Come on, let's find our servants."

Unlike Mrs. Worthington's deserted house, the home where their servants had taken refuge overflowed with people. Many of them were acquaintances of the owners who had fled north from the city center, but just as many were strangers who had spent the long night there. The homeowners had opened their pantry and Maria Elena, Mrs. Griffin, and the others were making sure everyone had something to eat. Rufus tried to comfort a weeping man who had lost his family in all the confusion. Another distraught mother came to the door searching for her children. She had sent them ahead with their nanny after arranging to meet again at a relative's home—but that home also stood in the fire's path, and her family had been forced to leave. She didn't know where her children had gone. A man told

Edmund how he had loaded a wagon with all his valuables, but when he went inside his house for the final load, a thief stole the wagon and drove away with his goods.

Flora sat down in the dining room with Becky long enough to eat something and quench her thirst and rest her throbbing feet, while Edmund warned everyone else that they needed to flee father north or west. "The fire is coming this way, and you're right in the path."

The homeowner's father was gravely ill and bedridden. Edmund made room for him in their carriage by removing the satchels and rucksacks with their important papers, deciding that he and Flora and Becky could carry them to safety themselves. After arranging with their own servants to meet back home when this ordeal ended—if indeed they had a home to return to—they said good-bye once again.

"Which way, Edmund?" Flora asked.

"West, I think. The wind is blowing from the south."

They managed to stay ahead of the fire throughout the day on Monday, resting often and relying on the kindness of strangers. When night fell, Flora slept for a few hours on the front porch of a stranger's home and was awakened before dawn by the sound of rain on the roof. She sat up, careful not to awaken Edmund who lay curled beside her, and saw her sister standing out in the rain with her smudged face and soot-covered hands lifted to the sky. Becky and her ragged clothing were getting drenched, but she didn't seem to care. God had rescued them at last.

CHAPTER 17

Flora stared at the mound of ash and bricks that was once her home. It was unrecognizable, apart from the crumbling chimney in their former drawing room. "I expected our house to be gone," she said, "but seeing this is still a terrible shock." She searched the pockets of her scorched skirt in vain for a handkerchief to wipe her tears.

"So much loss," Edmund said, his arm around her shoulder. "But at least we're all safe."

He had flagged down an empty freight wagon late Tuesday afternoon when they were certain the fire was out and paid the driver handsomely to take them home. The devastation they passed along the way was incomprehensible—miles and miles of burned-out homes and businesses and churches. Only one arched wall of the Great Central Depot remained standing. The entire city had been destroyed with only charred remains of walls and chimney stacks rising above the rubble. Even the trees had been reduced to charcoal. Chicago's bewildered citizens milled around in the still-smoking ruins, searching for even the smallest remnant of their past. Flora didn't have the heart to drive through the city center where Father's office had once been; she knew from viewing the gutted buildings in the distance that it was gone, too.

"All Father's business investments," she lamented. "All those properties that he owned—that we owned—are gone!"

"Were they insured?" Edmund asked.

"Some were. And we still own the land. I suppose we could rebuild and start all over again. It's just too overwhelming to think about right now."

Their neighborhood, all the way to the lakeshore, was a scene of desolation. The piles of furniture that her neighbors had dragged to safety still lined the waterfront, but where would the furniture go? Everyone's home had been lost.

"Let's look for the things we buried in the backyard." Becky said. Flora followed her as she picked her way through the fallen bricks and charred beams that filled the driveway. The kitchen wall had fallen in, and she could see the twisted, melted remains of the cast iron cookstove. Flora knew she needed to rise above her shock and despair and figure out how they would eat, where they would live. Their only clothes were the filthy, raggedy ones they'd been wearing since Sunday night, pocked with burn holes. The soles of her shoes, ruined and threadbare from walking, were about to separate from the uppers. Why hadn't she at least packed a change of clothing?

Flora surveyed the remains of the carriage house and Rufus' apartment. Where would he live? Where would they board their horses? So many questions and no answers.

Becky found the mound of dirt where their only remaining possessions lay buried, but their shovel no longer had a wooden handle, and the melted, misshapen blade was useless for digging. "So much for that," Becky said, tossing the blade on the ground again. "I suppose there's no place to store our belongings even if we could dig them up. We may as well leave them buried for now. Besides, I doubt if there will be much interest in my new book."

"Oh, Becky—I forgot about your brand-new book. I hate that this has overshadowed all the joy in your accomplishment."

"We've lost so much, Flora, my book is the very least of it." Flora could always rely on her sister to be tough and matter-of-fact, but tears rolled down Becky's cheeks, making trails in the layer of soot that covered her face. Flora went to her and held her tightly.

"We'll survive this," she murmured. "God has a plan. . . . He always has a plan." She released her again when she heard Edmund calling to her from the driveway.

"Flora! Come see who's here."

She and Becky walked around to the front—and there was Rufus standing beside their carriage with his hat in his hand. "Just tell me where you thinking to go," he said, "and I'll take you there." Flora couldn't resist hugging him.

"You dear, sweet man. You've lost everything in the world, too."

"Don't matter much. My real treasure is waiting for me up in heaven."

"It's too demoralizing to stand around here looking at this mess," Edmund said. "There's nothing we can do about it anyway, for the time being. Rufus says that Maria Elena, Andrew, and the Griffins are staying with friends and relatives. I say we drive there to see them and give them some cash for their immediate needs, then head to Evanston. I'm sure one of my colleagues will be willing to take us in until we can find a place to rent." Those friends had toasted Edmund and Becky at their book party—was it only two days ago? It felt like a lifetime to Flora.

The chaotic days that followed were no less wearisome for Flora as she and the others tried to piece their lives back together. Soldiers arrived in the city to prevent further looting. Help poured in from all across the United States and Canada.

Flora's immediate concern was learning the whereabouts of friends and colleagues in all the chaos, and after posting notices in the reborn *Chicago Tribune*, as hundreds of other people were doing, she found Mrs. Worthington. Her home and all her possessions had burned, but her nephew had returned in time to rescue her. Some three hundred people had lost their lives. Flora, Becky, and Edmund were among the more than 100,000 who were homeless. The fire had destroyed a path four miles long and nearly a mile wide. More than one million dollars in cash had gone up in flames inside banks and the Federal Reserve building that had burned downtown.

After staying with friends for more than a week, Edmund found a house for them to rent in Evanston, near his work. On a brisk day in late October, Rufus and Andrew drove Flora and Becky back to where their home once stood to sift through the ruins and dig up the buried items in the backyard. The steamer trunk with Father's books, their family silver, and the crate with Becky's new books were damp and heat-scorched, but salvageable. Becky laughed as Andrew lifted the sheet filled with their parents' silver from the hole in the yard. "What in the world do we need a silver teapot for?"

"Only the Good Lord knows," Flora replied with a smile. When Andrew and Rufus finished unearthing them, Flora stared at the depressing mound of rubble from her former home. "Is it worth trying to pick through this mess to see if anything survived?" she asked.

Becky shook her head. "No. I don't think it's safe to dig around in there."

"Well, this serves as a lesson, doesn't it? I guess we didn't need all those things to begin with. I'm grateful we didn't base our lives and identity on them."

"If we had, we would be overwhelmed with despair, like so many others are."

Rufus and Andrew asked for time to sift through the ruins of the carriage house when they finished loading the rescued possessions. "Of course. But please be careful," Flora begged. She and Becky sat on the stone stoop where their rear door had once stood and watched from a distance. Their exercise bars in the middle of the yard were bent and twisted from the heat. "What do you suppose the city will do with all the debris from the fire?" Flora asked.

"I read in the newspaper that they're going to plow it all into the lake and create a park along the lakeshore on top of the new land they'll create."

"That will be nice . . . Edmund thinks we should sell this property and build a new home in Evanston, but I told him you and I needed time to think about it."

"I don't need time, Flora. I think it's a good idea. But it's going to take a while to build a new house since there's such a huge demand for lumber and supplies and workers right now. In the meantime, we need to decide what's next for us."

"I'm hoping you'll help me with my relief work. All three of our Sunday school churches were destroyed and will have to be rebuilt. People need food and housing and—"

"I know, I know. And I'm happy to help you. But there's something else I think we should consider. I know you'll probably disagree, but please hear me out." Becky paused, and the somberness in her tone made Flora turn from watching Rufus and Andrew and meet her sister's gaze. "I think we need to travel abroad."

"Oh, Becky! How can you even think of traveling at a time like this?"

"No, listen, Flora. Now that everything we once had is gone, it's as if we don't know where we belong. Yet every trip we've taken and each escapade we've had in the past has helped us find another piece of the puzzle of our lives. That first trip we took to France helped me discover my gift for learning new languages, and it's also where we came across Mr. Darwin's book. Both of those things became important keys to the work God has given me. We also met Mrs. Worthington on that journey and embarked on the quest of learning how to behave in society. Knowing how to get around in her elite circles has been very helpful in your charity work."

"That's true, but—"

"You found your passion for helping others after we worked in the uniform factory—another of our adventures. And we never would have met Edmund if we hadn't done the illogical thing and traveled to the Holy Land after Father died. Now the fire has taken everything away from us, and we have to start all over again. Before we build a new house and try to replace a lifetime of possessions, we need to get away from the devastation and all its distractions and ask God for direction. Otherwise we'll simply keep meeting needs and doing whatever work lies directly in front of us, and we'll rebuild our lives without ever seeing the bigger picture. What if God wants to show us a much larger world filled with needs beyond the city of Chicago?"

"But our Sunday schools . . . I need to stay and work—"

"God is very capable of getting the work done without you, Flora. We both need to get away. We're emotionally and physically exhausted. Why not step away for a few weeks and listen for God's voice before we do anything else? I need to hear from God. I need to know if He has another book in mind for me to write."

"But Edmund has his work at the university. He wouldn't be able to travel with us."

"We're perfectly capable of traveling abroad without him. Besides, have you forgotten the letter he received from Cambridge right before the fire?"

Indeed, Flora had forgotten. It said that the codex Becky and

Edmund purchased in Cairo was a rare, tenth-century copy of the Gospel of Matthew. The University begged them to return to Egypt and search for others like it.

"I think Edmund would want us to pursue such important work," Becky continued. "Rescuing manuscripts was his passion long before he met us, remember? We have the time and the knowledge and the financial means to pursue it now."

"I would feel cowardly, running away from all this."

"You're not running away. And even if you are, no one would blame you. It's going to take a long time to get this city back on its feet. And we're homeless ourselves. What we need is time away to figure out what's next. God never would have taken everything away from us if He didn't have something wonderful to give back to us in return."

"I'll need to discuss it with Edmund—"

"Well . . . please don't be angry, but he's the one who came to me with the idea to travel. He thinks you need a rest, and I agree."

"Ha! Since when have your adventures ever been restful?"

Becky grinned. "We'll have a long, leisurely voyage across the ocean to rest."

"Ha!" Flora said again. "With our luck, our ship will sail into a storm!"

CHAPTER 18

THE MEDITERRANEAN SEA

Flora sat on the floor of the stateroom with her sister, clinging to their luggage and their bunks. It was the only way they could keep their trunks and themselves from sliding back and forth across the floor as their steamship battled the ferocious waves of a winter storm on the Mediterranean Sea. The room pitched upward as the ship climbed a mountainous wave and Flora braced herself as she waited for it to shudder down into a trough again. "I don't know, Becky," she said, "but I think this journey might be the end of us."

"I know. We've gone from fire to flood. Do you think God is trying to get our attention?"

"Well, He certainly has mine! This was supposed to be a relaxing trip, as I recall, not one in which we're forced to face our own mortality." Flora wondered if she looked as pale and ill as Becky did. They had shared the same bucket for the past two hours, overwhelmed with nausea and seasickness for the first time in all of their travels. She couldn't imagine ever eating again.

Becky let go of her bunk for a moment and pulled the bucket

closer, as if she might need it again, bracing it between her knees. "When I consider all that we've been through these past few months," she said, "it might seem like God has turned against us. But you know what? He has never felt closer to me than through all these trials."

"I know. I've prayed more than ever before, too."

"I think He's trying to teach us something, Flora. To trust Him, for one thing."

"Yes. But it's easier to trust Him when life goes the way we want it to than when it doesn't. Maybe—" She cried out as the ship suddenly leaned so far to one side she feared it would tip over. Flora's body was crushed against the wall as her bulky steamer trunk pinned her there. When the ship righted itself a moment later, Becky shoved the trunk away, freeing her.

"Are you all right, Flora?"

"Yes, I think so." They both took a moment to steady their nerves and secure their luggage again.

Becky exhaled. "God knows when the hour of our end will be," she said in a shaky voice. "But I sincerely hope it isn't tonight."

"Me too." Flora waited until her heart was no longer beating in her throat and said, "I have a new appreciation for what Paul and Luke experienced in the book of Acts when they were shipwrecked. Didn't their storm last a long time?"

"Fourteen days, I believe." Becky crawled on her hands and knees to retrieve the bucket that had slid away during the upheaval and braced it between her knees again. "And I also have a new appreciation for what our poor father suffered before the widow gave him her magical medicine."

"I wish we had some of it now," Flora said with a groan.

They remained awake throughout the long night, hanging on and praying. Eventually the sky grew light, and the sea calmed enough to allow them to crawl onto their beds and sleep. Thankfully the storm lasted only one day. But it took Flora and Becky two days to recover once they reached Cairo and checked into their room at Shepheard's Hotel. They were bruised and battered from the rough seas and weak from not eating, but very happy to be alive. The concierge told them that another steamship following the same route had sunk in the storm that night.

Becky rebounded faster than Flora did, claiming that the experience hadn't dampened her enthusiasm for traveling in the least. "But you should rest some more," Becky told her. "I'll go hire a private sailboat for our journey down the Nile."

"Wait. I thought Murray's tour book said they have regular steamship excursions to all the sites along the Nile."

"They do. But if we take a tourist ship, we'll have to adhere to their timetable instead of following our own."

They hired a two-masted sailing vessel called a dahabeeah, complete with a captain, crew, and cook. The vessel was a sailing barge with four cabins, a dining room, and a sitting room clustered on the main deck. The crew slept in the hold belowdecks, where the luggage and supplies were stored. The ship was much larger than they needed, but it would be their home for several weeks as they traveled up the Nile to Saqqara, Abydos, and Thebes. Flora liked to sit with Becky on the roof of the cabins where the best views were, beneath the shade of a canopy. They watched the flat, green fields and waving palm trees slip past, marveling at the distinct dividing line between the green swath of fertile land along the Nile and the desolate wilderness just beyond the Nile's reach. They enjoyed views of abundant wildlife—cranes and herons and pelicans. And crocodiles! Egyptian women in robes that might have been in fashion during biblical times did their wash along the riverbank while their naked children swam nearby, seemingly oblivious to the danger.

After their stormy steamship voyage, Flora was thankful

that their adventures on the Nile were very few—although one of them involved rats. The ship was plagued with them until Becky forced the captain to stop at a village along the way and acquire three cats to keep them under control. And there were several days on the journey upriver when the wind died; Flora and Becky sat in the doldrums with slackened sails, waiting for a breeze. They passed the time by reading aloud from the book of Exodus.

"I realize now why the Israelites grumbled against Moses and looked back on their days in Egypt with such fondness," Flora said as she waved a paper fan to cool herself. "Look how lush and green everything is along the Nile. And remember how desolate the Gaza Road was where poor Edmund was stranded?"

"We must be careful not to do the same thing that the Israelites did," Becky replied. "After losing so much, it's going to be hard for us not to look back at what we lost instead of moving forward."

"You're right," Flora said. "Although I confess that I keep thinking of things we lost in the fire. Nearly every day something pops into my mind—like Father's old desk. It always reminded me of him and brought him back to life whenever I looked at it."

Becky looked away as if she were seeing it, too. "We must think of this upheaval as a new beginning," she said, "just like the new beginning the Israelites had when they left Egypt. That temple we saw yesterday with all the Egyptian idols made me wonder if I have idols I need to leave behind, too."

Flora closed her eyes, remembering her wardrobes filled with gowns and accessories, now nothing but ash. "I won't need nearly as many gowns and shoes and hats as I had before. Goodness, what a waste of time and money. You were right about that, Becky." She watched a tourist ship chug toward them and glimpsed the well-dressed people lounging in style on the main deck. Becky grinned at them and waved. "I'm glad we're not traveling in luxury like they are," Flora said, "even if we are stuck here with slackened sails. You're always so wise, Becky."

At last the wind picked up, and they landed at Thebes, where they spent hours exploring the sprawling ruins of Egyptian temples. Flora walked with Becky down a long avenue lined with hundreds of statues of rams. They reached the immense hall in the Temple of Amun-Re, impressive even in its abandoned state. Becky darted around the dusty space, running her hands over the carved walls and towering columns, her eyes dancing with excitement. "What's going on in that mind of yours?" Flora asked. "I can almost hear your gears turning like the inside of a clock." That was another thing Flora would miss—the tall clock that had stood in their foyer, patiently announcing the hour with its deep, resonant chime.

"I think it's coming to me, Flora! I think I'm starting to see what my next book project is supposed to be."

"Sit a minute, and tell me about it." Flora found a seat on one of the huge stone blocks, leaving room for her sister, but Becky had too much restless energy to sit.

"It's going to be about all of this," she said, spreading her arms. "The kingdom of Egypt, the grandeur of these temple complexes and elaborate tombs, the power of pharaoh—and how very different idolatry is from what God revealed about Himself. The walls of these temples describe the elaborate rituals the people performed in order to placate their gods—"

"But weren't we just reading in Exodus about all the laws God gave the Jewish people, and the intricate details of the sacrifices they were supposed to make?"

"Yes, but there's a huge difference between the two. None of this," she said, twirling in a circle, "brought the Egyptians closer to their gods. The rituals were performed in order to keep the gods happy and to avoid disaster. And whenever we work to try to please God, we're thinking just like the Egyptians. God gave us the Temple sacrifices—and eventually the sacrifice of His Son—in order to draw us closer to Him. We don't serve Him to avoid disaster."

"Ever since the fire," Flora said, "I've heard people asking how a loving God could allow us to suffer through that nightmare and experience such loss."

Becky gestured to the wall-carvings again. "Egyptian thinking would say that we must have angered Him. That He's punishing us. But our faith asks us to trust Him and to believe that He has a plan for our good, even in the midst of disaster."

"I wish I could see His plan," Flora said. "I keep thinking about our Sunday schools, of all the books and supplies that were lost. It doesn't make sense when we were accomplishing such good things with those children."

"And the Israelites might have looked back at Egypt and mourned everything they left behind," Becky said, "even though they were slaves to it. But God brought them into the wilderness to rebuild them into a nation that would serve Him. Maybe the lesson for us will be in the rebuilding, Flora. Maybe God wants to teach us to work together and share what we have. Maybe seeing His church in action will be a greater lesson to those children than a dozen Sunday school lessons."

"I never thought of that," Flora said. "Now I wish I was back home so I could be part of it."

"Don't worry, they'll still be rebuilding Chicago when we get home. But I think God shakes things up sometimes just to show us our faulty thinking. The Israelites lived here in Egypt for hundreds of years, so they probably began to think like Egyptians and adopt their gods in order to get what they wanted. I want to write a book that shows how God used the plagues and the long journey in the wilderness to change the way His people thought and to restore them to Himself."

"So the disaster in Chicago might be God's way of teaching us something, too?"

"Yes, if we take time to listen to Him."

Flora was quiet a moment, considering her sister's wise words. "Becky, I'm glad you talked me into coming."

They went outside again, stopping in the doorway. Becky pointed to the barren mountains and desolate wilderness in the distance. "We've seen the clear dividing line between the green fields along the Nile and the wasteland beyond it. Now imagine that you've lived in the lush part all your life, and God suddenly asks you to leave it behind and head into the desert to worship Him. Would you trust Him?"

"Probably not," Flora said, laughing. "I would ask, 'What will we eat? Where will we get clothes?' The same questions we all asked after the fire."

"But God said, 'Trust me.' And those sound like Jesus' words, don't they? He said don't worry about what you'll eat or what you'll wear, but seek His kingdom first, and all those other things will be added on."

"You and I are wealthy enough not to worry about food and clothes," Flora said. "And I know that the charities we've set up will help the poor get a new start. But I still feel like there's something more I should do, some other way to show His love besides giving money away."

"He'll show you what's next, Flora."

They returned to the boat after a long day beneath the sun and ate dinner aboard their ship, watching the sun sink into the desert in flames of red and gold. Flora guessed that her sister longed to go into her cabin and make notes for her new book, but Becky took her time eating, slowly winding down as they sat together in the stillness, listening to the croaking frogs and buzzing insects. After dinner, they stood outside on the deck to gaze up at the stars.

"Do you think Edmund will be willing to work on this new book with me?" Becky asked. "I wouldn't dare tackle it without him."

"I'm certain he will. He's always been fascinated with Egypt. And the story of the Exodus is one of his favorites."

"Flora, look!" Becky said, pointing up at a shooting star. "Make a wish!"

The stars blurred through her tears as Flora wished for a child. After six years of marriage, God still hadn't answered her prayer. "Tell me yours first," she said.

Becky sighed. "Well . . . here it is. . . . I long for what you and Edmund have. But as an old spinster of twenty-seven, I suppose it's too late to find love now. Mrs. Worthington was right when she called me a bluestocking and said I'd never find a husband if I continued my studies."

Flora heard the deep sadness in her sister's voice and pulled her into her arms. "Oh, Becky! I had no idea you felt that way. You seem so strong and independent, not caring what anyone thinks. And you've been so successful as you've followed your passions. I always thought you were content with your life."

"I am—most of the time. But sometimes I wonder what it would be like to have a companion to share my life with. Someone to talk with at the end of the day. Someone to love."

"Oh, Becky . . ."

"Let's not get maudlin," Becky said, freeing herself from Flora's embrace. "That's enough self-pity from me. Tell me your wish."

Flora felt embarrassed to admit it now, but she knew her sister would hound her until she confessed. "Well . . . I wished for a child. My life is so complete and rich and full, and yet . . . why has God denied me this one thing?"

"We're just like the Israelites, aren't we? God gives us manna from heaven and water from the rock, and we want the leeks and melons of Egypt. Why aren't we ever happy with what God gives us?"

Flora couldn't answer that question. She sat down on a crate as the boat rocked gently on the waves, listening to the mumbling voices of the crew, the scratching of the rats below deck. She caught a whiff of the captain's strong tobacco as he puffed on his cigarette, blending with the fishy aroma of the Nile. "Becky? . . . Shall I ask Edmund if there's someone at the university you could meet—"

"No, please don't. The Egyptians used their rituals to try to manipulate the gods into giving them what they wanted, and I need to leave my life in God's hands and be content. I admit I haven't found contentment yet, but I'm trying. Meanwhile, I need to keep doing His work without expecting to be rewarded with all of my wishes in return."

Becky's words pierced Flora's heart. Was she trying to use God that way? She thought of all her hard work for the poor, especially for poor children, and her hours of volunteer work in the Sunday schools. Was she doing it to win God's approval so He would give her and Edmund a baby? Deep in her heart, she had to admit that was part of her motivation. "I'm going to bed now," she told Becky. "You've given me a lot to think about. And I have a feeling you want to start outlining your ideas. Am I right?"

Becky turned to her and smiled. "You know me so well. Good night, Flora." But Flora hadn't known her well after all. She'd had no idea that her brilliant, independent sister still longed to find love.

The next morning Becky told the captain he could turn the ship around and begin the journey back up the Nile to Cairo. The river's current would carry them now, and the return trip would be much faster since they no longer relied on the wind. As Flora sat with her sister beneath the canopy on the upper deck, wrestling with her will versus God's will as she had all night, she wondered what was next for her when they returned to Chicago. Becky had found a renewed purpose with an idea for her next book, but Flora continued to wonder what God had in store for her. She was daydreaming about the long, hard work of rebuilding when she heard shouts and the sound of splashing water nearby.

"Flora, look!" Becky said. She stood and pointed to several bare-chested Egyptian men who were trying to haul a crocodile they had snared onto the riverbank. The beast snapped and thrashed wildly as it tried to break free, revealing rows of sharp teeth in its wide-open mouth. Flora winced when one of the men barely missed being snatched into the animal's jaws. "That strikes me as a very perilous occupation," Becky said. They continued watching the dangerous battle until the men finally prevailed, driving a spear into the crocodile and killing it.

"You know," Flora said as they continued sailing, "for years I've been reading the story of baby Moses floating in the Nile in his little wicker basket, yet it never occurred to me that crocodiles lived in this river. It makes his mother's faith in God even more amazing."

"I can't understand the cruelty of the Egyptian culture—or any culture—that fails to value their children," Becky said. "That's another area where Egyptian thinking is so different from how God wants us to think. When He gave His law on Mount Sinai, He made sure there were provisions for society's most vulnerable members and affirmed the dignity of all people because we're made in His image. Jesus emphasized the same things when He blessed the little children and said that when we meet the needs of the very least, we do it for Him."

Something stirred in Flora's heart as she listened to her sister. "Those children who worked in the uniform factory and who come to our Sunday schools . . . it's as if society has tossed them into the Nile to die. But what if we built a lifeboat for them, Becky? A place where orphans could find new homes, like baby Moses did? A place where families in need could safely leave their children for a while and know they'd be fed and clothed and have a warm bed to sleep in at night?"

"You could build that place, Flora."

Flora stared into the distance as countless fears and objections quickly rose to the surface. "I—I wouldn't know how to begin."

"Nonsense! You begin by taking one step forward, trusting God to part the waters."

"Will you help me, Becky?"

"No," she said with a grin. "I have my own work to do. But I'm certain God will."

The scenery went past Flora in a blur as they traveled downriver to Cairo. She couldn't stop thinking about the idea of starting an orphanage in Chicago, planning all of the things she needed to do to bring it to life. But as eager as she was to start the journey home, she also knew how important it was to spend time in Cairo searching the black market for ancient manuscripts and codices like the one Becky and Edmund had rescued.

"I can't think of a better use for my inheritance than buying lost biblical documents," Becky said as they waited to meet with a seller in the rug shop where they'd made the purchase five years ago. Flora tried to quiet the unease in her stomach, knowing how vulnerable they were without Edmund to protect them.

"Maybe the reason God made you and me so different," Becky continued, "is because the needs of His kingdom are so different. You have your work with the poor, while my task is to write books for intellectual historians who've rejected the Bible."

"That's a beautiful way of looking at it," Flora said. She

scanned the dark shadows for movement, wishing her heart would slow down, wishing Becky wasn't so oblivious to the danger they might be facing while carrying a purse full of money. In the end, Flora's fears were unfounded. Becky purchased several ancient-looking manuscripts and parchment fragments, then returned to the safety of their hotel.

"I have no idea if I just threw my money away on worthless fakes or not," Becky said as she studied them beneath a lamp.

"Is it time to head home now?" Flora hoped the answer was yes, but judging by the serious expression on Becky's face, she feared it wasn't.

"Well . . . I've been thinking. . . ."

"Oh, dear. I'm not sure I like the sound of that. Please don't tell me you're planning another trip for us."

"No, but I think it may be time for you and me to go our separate ways. Would you mind terribly if you sailed home by yourself?"

"I am not leaving you alone in Cairo, Becky. Don't even suggest such a thing."

"No, nothing as foolish as that," she said, waving her hand. "But I don't want to keep buying artifacts in ignorance. I need to learn more about identifying a document's age, and how to tell a real one from a fake. What I'd really like to do is spend the winter in Cambridge learning from the experts. I can afford private tutoring. And they can repay me for my purchases by indulging my academic pursuits for a few months."

Again, Flora felt afraid for her sister, a young woman traveling and living alone in a foreign country. And for herself, traveling alone to Chicago. It simply wasn't done—and probably for good reason. But if she'd learned any lesson on this trip, it was to trust God. Whether she was running from the flames in Chicago or suffering through the violent storm at sea, God remained in control. It was up to Him to decide when or if she would have a child, and when or if Becky would find a husband. Flora could trust Him to part the seas for her sister in Cambridge and to make a path for her to start an orphanage in Chicago.

"So what do you say?" Becky asked, still waiting for her answer.

"I say we travel together as far as Southampton, then each get busy with God's work."

CHAPTER 19

THE SINAI DESERT
1890

Well, I wonder what's going to happen next," Flora said as she sank down in the patch of shade beside Becky. The blinding sun hung high above them, baking them like biscuits. The view of brown rocks and wrinkled mountains was the same no matter which direction she looked, so she finally stopped looking. Petersen and Mr. Farouk had climbed the hill again and were scanning the horizon in all directions for any sign of the Bedouin. The cook sat alone on a nearby rock, shaking his head and mumbling in Arabic. And poor Kate Rafferty walked around in circles, kicking stones and stirring up dust.

"I don't know why or how it's possible," Becky replied, "but I feel calm in spite of our circumstances. I do feel responsible for this turn of events, since I'm the reason we're all out here to begin with. But God led me on this quest and opened many doors so far, so I have faith that we'll reach the monastery, one way or another."

"Without selling Kate to the Bedouin, I hope?"

Becky looked at her and smiled. "I'm guessing you'd never agree to that—although Petersen might be tempted."

"Shh!" Flora gave her sister a nudge to quiet her as Kate shuffled over to where they were sitting and sank down beside them.

"I don't understand why the sheikh wants me," she said.

"Oh, dear," Flora said, fanning her face with her straw hat. "Has no one ever explained the facts of life to you, Kate?"

She made a face, as if swallowing a lemon. "If you mean what I think you mean, of course I know what men always want—but why pick me?"

"I think the sheikh is attracted to you because you're young and pretty," Flora said.

"Then why didn't he talk to me himself? Not that I would be interested in him—or that I would even understand a word he was saying."

"Women are treated differently in his culture," Flora said, placing her straw hat on her head again. "In this part of the world, a man negotiates with the girl's father when he wants her for his wife. It's more of a business deal. There's no romance involved, as when an American man courts a woman."

"*Some* American men, you mean," Becky added. "Remember Freddy Worthington? That was a business deal if I ever saw one."

Flora nudged her again. "You're not helping matters, Becky."

"Well, what's going to happen to us?" Kate asked. There was something in her voice that Flora had never heard before. The rough, tough, thieving street girl was scared after all.

"We'll just have to remain calm," Flora said, "and wait and see. Worrying won't help matters but praying will." She was trying to convince herself as much as Kate. A few minutes later, Petersen returned from the top of the hill and stood in the shade beside them. "Any sign of our friends?" Flora asked him.

"None." He slid his head covering off and ran his fingers

through his pale hair, which had darkened with sweat. "This still doesn't make sense to me," he said. "Why didn't the sheikh just kidnap Kate and disappear if he wanted her?"

"Thanks a lot!"

"Why would they leave her behind with us and all the supplies?" he continued, ignoring Kate. "They could have grabbed her while we slept and took off with the caravan, and no one would've ever known what became of us."

"He's right," Becky said. "It doesn't make sense. Unless they're angry with us for refusing to sell her."

"Then why leave all the supplies?" Petersen asked, shaking his head.

"Maybe they're coming back with more men," Kate said.

"That doesn't make sense, either. They already outnumber us."

"I guess we'll just have to keep praying for help," Flora said. "And trust our lives to God's hands."

"In the meantime," Petersen said, as if dismissing any help from God, "maybe we can figure out which direction the monastery is from here. The men prayed facing in that direction when we stopped to rest," he said, pointing. "If Mr. Farouk has a map or something, I could start walking and try to find help—"

"Oh, no, no, no," Flora interrupted. "You would never make it, Soren. These mountains all look alike. You'd be searching for a needle in a haystack, isn't that right, Mr. Farouk?" He had descended the hill while they'd talked and stood nearby, wringing his hands. He looked as lost as a turtle without a shell.

"Only sheikh knows where monks live," he replied.

The little agent was no help at all. Flora was grateful when Petersen suddenly took charge. "Let's set up the tents. They'll provide shade so we can stay out of the sun. And we need to ration our food and water to make it last." He prodded the cook and Mr. Farouk into moving, and they began unpacking the equipment. The tents wouldn't change their situation, but Flora knew that Petersen needed to keep busy rather than sitting here helplessly. Sweat soaked through his clothes in no time as he cleared stones from the largest level area he could find, creating a place for the tents. He probably wished he could strip off his bulky robe, but his fair skin would burn within minutes. As the men worked, Flora decided to recite Scripture to make everyone feel better, particularly herself.

"'I will lift up mine eyes unto the hills,'" she began, "'from whence cometh my help. My help cometh from the Lord, which made heaven and earth. . . .'" The words did seem to lift everyone's spirits. Even Kate seemed to relax a bit, so she continued. "'The Lord shall preserve thee from all evil. He shall preserve thy soul. The Lord shall . . .' How does that last verse go, Becky?"

"'The Lord shall preserve thy going out and thy coming in from this time forth, and even for evermore.'"

Flora recited her entire repertoire of memorized verses as the tents were set up and the supplies put away. Then Petersen, Mr. Farouk, and the cook took turns standing on the little rise and scanning the horizon for signs of life.

Flora was looking forward to sunset and the end of the searing heat and blinding sunlight when Petersen, who was taking his shift, called to them from the top of the hill. Becky scrambled to her feet and offered Flora a hand to help her up. "Come on, we'd better see what it is."

"Does that look like a dust cloud in the distance to you?" he asked when they reached the top. "See it? Could another sandstorm be coming?"

Flora blotted sweat from her face with her handkerchief and shaded her eyes. "If it is, I'm glad you set up the tents, Petersen." The growing disturbance sped closer. When Flora was finally able to distinguish what it was, she felt as though she'd been kicked in the stomach. It was worse than a sandstorm. A large mob of people were approaching on camels.

"The Bedouin are coming back," Petersen said. "Lots of them."

"I don't know if that qualifies as good news or bad," Becky said.

"The Lord knows when the hour of our end will be," Flora said. "We don't need to fear." But she was afraid nonetheless. Her heart thudded in time with the hoofbeats.

"I think we should all go down to our campsite to wait," Petersen said when the approaching band was close enough to be seen distinctly. He led the way down the hill, taking charge again. Normally either Flora or Becky would have issued orders, but they both knew how much it meant to Petersen to be their protector. "Kate, get inside the tent and stay there," he ordered. "Don't come out unless I tell you."

She dug in her heels as he tried to push her toward the opening. "Hands off me! Who made you the boss of everyone? Don't I have any say in this?"

"Do you want to be the sheikh's wife?" he asked.

"'Course not. I want to tell him to get lost."

"And that's exactly where your answer would leave the rest of us—lost!"

Flora draped her arm around the girl's shoulders and nudged her forward. "Petersen is right, Katie. You'd better stay out of sight for now."

"But I want to know who's coming and what's going on."

"I'll stand right outside the tent and tell you everything that's happening, but you need to stay inside." Flora tied the tent flap closed behind Kate—as if that would keep intruders out, or Kate in.

They could hear the jingling bells on the Bedouin camels now. Petersen dug through the supply crate and pulled out three knives, keeping the largest butcher knife for himself and handing the other two to Mr. Farouk and the cook. "I'll take a knife, too," Becky said when she saw what he was doing. He gave her the cleaver that Cook used to chop the heads from the chickens.

The caravan halted in a plume of dust a short distance away. Flora's heart pounded like galloping horses when she recognized the sheikh barking orders to the others. Dozens and dozens of others. "The sheikh is back, Katie dear," Flora told her. "With what looks like an entire village of people. I see Bedouin women in their long robes and gold jewelry, and little children, too. They seem to have animals with them—sheep and goats."

"Are they coming here?" Kate asked. Once again, Flora detected fear in her voice.

"No, not at the moment. They're all staying about a hundred yards away."

Becky came and stood beside Flora, and they watched the activity for several minutes. Flora's shoulders ached with pent-up anxiety and fear. "Just what exactly are you planning to do with that silly cleaver?" she asked Becky, trying to diffuse the tension.

"Protect you, of course. After all, this misadventure is my fault."

"Do you really think a cleaver is going to do much against a dozen Bedouin men?"

"No . . . that's why I'm praying, too."

"My fierce big sister," Flora said, shaking her head.

At first the Bedouin seemed to be doing little more than milling around and talking amongst themselves. Then Flora saw the first tent go up, a hulking, black mound held up with low poles. Then a second one appeared, and a third.

"It looks like they're setting up camp, Kate," Flora told her. "They have several black goat-hair tents."

"Petersen, fetch the stools," Becky said after a while. "We may

as well all sit down while they build a little village over there. I
don't think they'll start negotiating with us or slaughtering us,
whichever the case may be, until they're finished."

She turned out to be right. An orderly Bedouin settlement
sprang up in the desert with a cluster of tents and makeshift
pens for the animals. Smoke rose from cooking fires and the
tantalizing aroma of exotic spices drifted over to Flora's camp.
Along with the sheikh, she recognized several of the drivers
who had traveled with them. Moments before sunset, the men
gathered to pray, bowing down toward the east. Flora made a
mental note of the setting sun's position. If nothing else, it told
her which direction to walk to return to the gulf. Mr. Farouk
and the cook went behind their tent to pray, too—and they were
likely the most fervent prayers those two men had ever uttered.

Petersen sat down to talk with Flora and Becky. "With all
due respect, I think we should tell the sheikh that I'm in charge,
not Mr. Farouk. It's his fault the sheikh is mad at us, and from
what you've said, I'm guessing the Bedouin won't negotiate
with you because you're women."

"You're right," Becky said. "We'll let you do all the talking,
Petersen. I'll stay close by since I understand the language and
make sure Mr. Farouk is translating everything accurately."

Flora's stomach rumbled with hunger and unease. She grew
more and more apprehensive as they waited for evening prayers
to end. "When can I come out?" Kate whined. "It's like an oven
in here."

"Not yet," Petersen said. "Not until we find out what's going
on." He bent to whisper to Flora, "We can't take a chance that
she'll do something stupid."

"I know."

When their prayers ended, the Bedouin men gathered in a
huddle for a moment, then the sheikh led the band of men across
the desert toward Flora and Becky's camp. Petersen rose to his

feet, the butcher knife tucked beneath his robe. "Tell the sheikh I'm in charge, Mr. Farouk." He prodded the little man forward to meet them, with Becky and Flora close behind. Mr. Farouk looked as though he might pass out, but he did as was told. The sheikh looked somber, his dark face half-hidden behind his head covering. But his words, after being translated, were surprisingly friendly.

"Come. A meal has been prepared for you. Enjoy my hospitality."

"All of us?" Petersen asked.

Mr. Farouk translated his question and then the sheikh's reply. "Yes. The women will eat in the tent with our wives. And bring the red-haired woman."

"Can we trust them?" Petersen whispered.

"We have no choice," Becky replied. "We're badly outnumbered. Besides, they could have murdered us by now if that was their intention."

"Well," Flora said with a sigh, "let's go."

"It's about time," Kate said when they fetched her from inside the tent.

They crossed the rocky desert to the Bedouin encampment where a banquet of food and fresh bread was spread on a rug in front of one of the tents. The sheikh invited Petersen and Mr. Farouk to sit down with him, while Flora, Becky, and Kate were ushered inside one of the low black tents where a second banquet had been spread. The Bedouin women gestured for them to sit, reserving the largest pile of cushions for Kate. They offered each platter of food to Kate first, as if she were a queen, urging her to eat her fill. Since there was no cutlery, everyone used her fingers and pieces of bread to scoop from the common platters. Flora found the food surprisingly delicious, seasoned with a mixture of spices that she'd never tasted before. The centerpiece of the banquet was a platter of roasted meat.

"What are we eating?" Kate asked. "What kind of meat is this?"

Flora guessed it was goat, but said, "Don't ask, dear. You're better off not knowing."

"It's delicious," Becky said, licking her fingers. "The bread is wonderful, too. Warm and smoky and crisp on the outside, yet soft on the inside."

Flora heard the men's voices outside and wondered what was going on. "Can you hear what the sheikh is saying?" she asked Becky.

Becky tilted her head and listened. "He's bragging about how rich he is. How he can offer Kate a good life."

"So this is all a show? To convince us to let him have her?"

"It seems so."

"Ha!" Kate said. "As if I'd want to live here! This tent stinks like dead animals."

"And what will happen if we refuse?" Flora asked.

"Who knows?" Becky said with a shrug. If she was as frightened as Flora was, Becky was putting on a brave front to hide it, eating heartily and smiling pleasantly at the gathered women. The tent grew dark as time passed and the Bedouin women lit oil lamps. Most of the food was gone when one of the women presented Kate with a lavish array of golden neck ornaments, earrings, and bracelets like the Bedouin women wore. Kate's eyes widened as she fingered the gold as if tallying their value. "Are these for me?"

"Don't take them, Kate," Becky warned. "We don't know what it means in this culture to accept such gifts."

Flora saw the reluctance in Kate's eyes as she pushed away the glimmering jewelry. She had likely never seen such wealth in her life. The Bedouin women persisted, grabbing Kate's hands and trying to push the jangling bracelets onto her wrists. Flora feared they soon would have her arrayed like one of them if they weren't stopped.

Suddenly Becky rose to her feet and spoke firmly to them in Arabic. The women froze, staring at Becky as if she had just risen from the dead. She spoke again, and the women dropped Kate's arms, letting the jewelry fall on the carpet in front of her. Flora wasn't sure if she should be alarmed or relieved.

"What did you say?" she asked her sister.

"I told them to stop. I said to tell the sheikh we can't accept his gifts." Becky laughed and added, "But I think the look of shock you see on their faces has nothing to do with the jewelry. In a million years, they never expected to hear me speaking their language."

Kate looked like a frightened child as she silently gazed from one woman to the other, and Flora had to resist the urge to hug her. No one seemed to know what to do next until one of the Bedouin women rose, and everyone else quickly followed. They pushed Kate and Flora and Becky from the tent and out to the campfire where the men sat, the remains of their meal still spread before them. All conversation halted as the sheikh stood, his men quickly rising to their feet with him. "What's going on?" Flora asked as the sheikh spoke to Mr. Farouk.

"He said he'll take us back to our camp now," Becky translated. "It's time for the men to pray before sleeping."

"Just like that? We still don't know what's going on?"

"No. But I'm glad you didn't put on that jewelry, Kate. It might have meant you're now his wife."

Once they moved away from the campfire, the moonless night was so black that Flora could barely see her own feet. She gripped Becky's and Kate's hands as the Bedouin men formed a circle around them to walk them back to their tents, warning of any rocks or holes in their path. "The sheikh wishes you good rest," Mr. Farouk translated before the men left.

Flora's heart had been racing for so long she didn't think she could settle down to sleep. After groping her way to a camp stool and sinking down, she looked up at the night sky and prayed for guidance. The huge band of the Milky Way stretched from one end of the horizon to the other, filling the heavens with more stars than she'd ever seen in her life. "Just look, Becky," she said, pointing up. "Isn't that magnificent?" Becky, Kate, and Petersen joined her while Mr. Farouk and the cook prayed nearby.

"What was that meal all about?" Petersen asked, not noticing the jewelry box of stars overhead.

"I think they wanted to impress us with what a good life they're offering Kate," Becky replied. "Did the sheikh try to bargain with you for her?"

"No. Unless Mr. Farouk wasn't telling me the truth. All we did was eat. Did you learn anything from the women?"

Becky shook her head. "They spoke in such low voices most of the time that I couldn't understand them."

"Well, they haven't harmed us," Flora said with a sigh, "so that's a good sign. We've been treated very well, in spite of the suspense."

"Yes," Becky agreed. "I imagine the sheikh will be back to bargain for Kate in the morning. You'd better be ready, Petersen."

"What should I say?"

"Tell him I ain't for sale!" Kate said.

Flora patted her arm. "Yes, of course he'll tell them that, Kate. But it may not be that simple. Becky and I will pray for wisdom. In fact, I suggest we all take our cue from the Bedouin and get down on our knees and pray before we go to sleep tonight."

"Petersen did so well tonight, didn't he?" Flora said when she and Becky were in their tent undressing for bed. "I'm so proud of him for taking charge the way he did."

"I hope he isn't putting himself in danger," Becky said.

"We need to pray for him."

Kate had been uncharacteristically quiet as she had undressed and climbed onto her cot, wrapping the covers around herself like a cocoon. Flora longed to hold the girl close and reassure her that God was in control, but Kate would never accept such comfort. "We won't let anything happen to you, Kate," she said as she blew out the lamp. "I promise." *Or to Petersen either*, she added to herself.

Flora stretched out on her camp cot and pulled the blanket up to her chin, remembering the day she first met Soren Petersen and his brother Gunnar. And with those memories came a caravan-load of regrets. . . .

CHAPTER 20

The children's laughter created a deep ache in Flora's heart. She watched the Easter party that was well underway in the dining hall of the orphans' home and wished she felt genuine contentment. She had founded the home nearly sixteen years ago after returning from her trip up the Nile with Becky, and it was a happy place, considering the tragedies that had brought the children here. She was proud of the work she and her board of directors had accomplished. Yet the yearning for her own child had never gone away.

The matron and her volunteers cut the special cake Flora had brought and set out bags of candy for the children. Becky entertained the children with a mixture of Bible stories and modified tales from *The Arabian Nights* as they gathered around her, seated on chairs and on the floor at her feet. Becky had a knack for dramatic storytelling, peppering her tales with details from their own travels. The children cheered whenever she walked through the orphanage's doors on special occasions like this.

Outside, the green buds dotting the tree branches were a sure sign that new life was springing up in chilly Chicago. But inside, the orphanage seemed drab and cold to Flora no matter how hard she tried to keep the walls freshly painted, bright curtains on the windows, and fresh flowers on the dining tables. The institution looked gray and colorless to her, as barren as her empty womb.

She had returned home from her trip to Egypt with a renewed determination to help Chicago's children, and after arranging an endowment and gathering a board of directors, Flora had created the Chicago Orphans' Home. She envisioned it not only as a place where homeless orphans could find adoptive parents, but a safe place where families in distress could leave their children for a while, knowing they would be cared for until the family could be reunited. And her vision had succeeded. She'd lost track of the number of children who had found refuge here or new adoptive families. Yet Flora's prayer for a child of her own remained unanswered. Yes, she had placed the matter in God's hands—over and over again as she and Edmund consulted physicians and prayed together. But she knew in her heart that she resented God's will because it contradicted her own.

The children sat spellbound as Becky told the Easter story, describing the women walking to the tomb, finding it empty, seeing Jesus. As Flora scanned the children's faces she saw two new ones—a beautiful little boy about four years old sitting on the lap of a young man in his teens. They looked so much alike with their blond hair and fair skin that they had to be brothers. She noticed the tender way they held on to each other, their love and devotion apparent with every gesture. When Becky finished her story and the children lined up for cake, Flora asked the head matron, Mrs. Miller, about the newcomers.

"They came to us two weeks ago," she replied. Mrs. Miller was a warm, plump woman who showed affection freely to these children who so desperately needed it. Even when she was firm with them, she always did so in a loving way. She lived at the orphanage with her husband, who was the handyman and groundkeeper. "Those boys were so dirty and ragged when they first arrived," she continued, "we had no idea how blond and fair-skinned they were. Their names are Soren and Gunnar Petersen, so we assume they have a Scandinavian heritage."

"They're so thin. Are they eating well?"

"They are now. I made sure of that. But from the way they wolfed down their food, it seemed they hadn't eaten a proper meal in a good, long while."

Flora watched as the new boys waited in line for their cake and a bag of Easter candy. Instead of joining the other boys his age, the older brother stayed with the younger one, sitting close beside him and helping him with his cake. The little one seemed skittish. While the other four-year-olds ran around the dining hall, laughing and playing, he clung to his brother. Flora fought the urge to take the little one on her lap and bury her nose in his golden hair. "Do they always stick this close to each other?" she asked the matron.

"Always, and it's a bit of a problem. We find Soren sleeping on the floor in Gunnar's dormitory every morning. He's supposed to sleep with the boys his own age, but he won't stay there. He's devoted to that child."

"Then let them stay together, Mrs. Miller, regardless of their ages. Don't send them to different dormitories."

"But the house rules say—"

"Rules need to be bent sometimes. Anyone can see that it would be cruel to separate them. Give them time to settle in together."

"Yes, Mrs. Merriday."

Becky joined Flora and Mrs. Miller with a piece of cake for

each of them and one for herself. "What happened to their parents?" Becky asked as the older one tucked his own bag of candy into his brother's pocket.

"They won't tell us much. The landlord who reported them to city officials said they'd been living with their mother until she died. There didn't seem to be a father or any next of kin that he knew of. He hated to kick them out on the street, but they had no way to pay the rent. He sent for us."

"They're beautiful children," Flora murmured. They could be Edmund's sons with their fair hair and slender builds. She imagined herself rocking the little one in her arms, kissing him good-night. Then she stopped. How many times had she fought this battle? Each time the longing for a child threatened to undo her, she surrendered it back to God, knowing that if it was His will for her and Edmund to have a baby, He could easily have given her one over the years. But now that she was forty-one and Edmund fifty-eight, the time to bear children had passed.

Becky finished her cake and set down the plate. "It shouldn't be too difficult to find a family to adopt those boys, I would think," she said.

"Oh, we could easily place little Gunnar in a home," Mrs. Miller replied, "but Soren won't agree to let him go."

"Why would you even ask such a thing of him?" Flora said. "Isn't it our policy to always keep families together?"

"Yes, of course it is. It's just that there's such a large age difference between the two. Gunnar is four, and Soren is six-teen—nearly old enough to leave the orphanage and find a job. We tried to explain to him that it would be better for Gunnar to get a new start with a loving family than to stay here in this gloomy place, but he insisted that they stay together."

"Surely you can find a family willing to take both of them, can't you?" Becky asked.

"I wish we could, Miss Hawes—and we'll keep searching for

one. But nearly all of the families want to adopt very young children. They fear the older ones will have bad habits that are difficult to break."

"Is that why there are so many older children here?" Becky asked.

"Yes, Miss Hawes. We'll probably never find homes for them. We try to teach them to read and write, but they're often far behind in school by the time they come here, and they don't want to sit in a classroom with children half their age. Once they turn seventeen they go off on their own."

Flora stayed until the cake and lemonade were gone and the children had bundled up to play outside in the yard behind the building. She wished she could do more as she watched them stream outside into the sunlight, but at least they each had a warm jacket and shoes that fit. They would have three good meals every day and a warm bed to sleep in at night. But no amount of money could give them what they needed most of all—love.

"You're very quiet," Becky said on the ride home to Evanston. "Are you all right, Flora?"

"Yes, I'm just thinking."

"Well, I'm thinking that if visiting that place and hearing such tragic stories is difficult for me, it must break your heart. I don't know how you do it."

"It does break my heart." She closed her eyes for a moment, still picturing Gunnar, the little blond-haired boy. Hundreds of orphans had walked through the doors of the orphan home over the years, but she had never felt such an instant, soul-deep longing for a child the way she had today.

"May I ask you a delicate question, Flora? . . . Why haven't you and Edmund ever adopted a child?"

"I've thought about it. But I can't take all of them, and to choose one over all the others would be impossible. And so unfair. I decided it would be better if I continued to find loving families for them and to make the orphan home a cheerful place, where those who aren't adopted can have a good life. Besides, I wouldn't have time for my charity work if I adopted children of my own."

"But I can clearly see the longing in your heart. The way you looked at those two new boys today . . . Maybe God is asking you to adopt them and—"

"I was warned when I began this work, as well as my work with the Sunday schools, that I mustn't allow myself to get emotionally attached to the children. I believe the work I'm doing will improve their lives, and that's reward enough. Of course, I continue to look for new solutions to poverty and illiteracy, but—"

"Are you trying to convince me or yourself?"

Tears stung Flora's eyes, but she fought to keep them from falling. "I can't lose my heart to each and every child, Becky. If I do, I'll collapse beneath the load and die of a broken heart. There are just too many suffering children here in Chicago, too many needs for me to carry them all on my shoulders."

"Are you certain you're able to remain detached? Because even I had trouble hardening my heart today."

"On days like today, when I look into those children's eyes and see their longing for a mother's love . . . well, that's when I have to leave and go home." She dabbed her handkerchief at a tear that escaped.

"I worry about you, Flora. Your work takes a huge emotional toll on you, especially since you want children of your own—"

"It's up to God to decide whether or not I'll have children, and He has clearly decided that I won't." She wanted to end this painful conversation; thankfully they arrived home a moment later. As Flora walked into the house with her sister, she hoped Becky hadn't detected the bitterness in her heart.

❧ ❦

A month later Flora, Edmund, and Becky left Chicago on a long-planned trip to Greece. They traveled the hilly countryside by horseback with pack mules to haul their baggage, reading the book of Acts and the writings of St. Paul along the way. Since there were few inns available in the remote villages, they often spent the night in monasteries, making friends with the Greek Orthodox monks who welcomed them and enjoying long, interesting discussions about the Scriptures. Flora and Becky still hadn't forgotten their Greek after all these years or their childhood fascination with Homer's *Odyssey* and *Iliad*.

One of Becky's goals had been to see the ruins of Mycenae, where a thousand ships had been launched to attack Troy, according to the *Iliad*. Flora was breathless by the time they reached the top of the hill. The three of them stood together inside the crumbling citadel walls, row after row of terraced green hillsides rising toward the clear blue skies in the distance. "This is breathtaking," Flora said. "That goes for the view as well as the climb."

"It's so inspiring," Edmund said. "Just look at these immense building stones, hauled into place thousands of years ago. Such industry and ambition!"

"I'm even more inspired by the perseverance of Mycenae's archaeologist," Becky said. On the climb to the top of the hill, she had shared the story of the self-made millionaire, Heinrich Schliemann, who had made the discovery. Convinced that Homer's poems were based on historical facts, Schliemann had begun digging here nine years ago, unearthing the walls of the citadel and a wealth of gold and silver artifacts, including what he claimed was the mask of Agamemnon, who had led the attack on Troy.

"I love that every time there's another archaeological discovery, it adds to the story of mankind's past," Becky said. "And while Mycenae doesn't have any bearing on the Bible, it does show that what we once believed was myth may have a basis in historical fact. The discoveries in the Holy Land and the ancient scrolls we're finding are going to do the same."

"I like that Schliemann pursued his passion," Flora said, "and didn't let critics stop him. I hope we can look back someday and say that we've lived a life of purpose, too."

"Hey, now," Edmund said. "We're much too young to talk this way. I'm certain we have many more years ahead of us."

"And many more years of travel," Becky added.

Flora smiled at her sister. "Here's to us!" she said, making a mock toast with her canteen of water. "The Adventure Sisters!"

"Hear, hear!"

The leaves were changing color the day Flora visited the orphanage again after being away in Greece for more than three months. She hadn't forgotten her interest in the Petersen brothers and went around to the backyard to scan the playground for them. The yard was deserted. It seemed unusual to find it empty on such a warm fall afternoon, but perhaps there was a special event going on inside. Flora bumped into the matron just inside the door and almost didn't recognize her. Mrs. Miller was wearing a drab, gray uniform, of all things, with a starched white apron and a cap on her head.

"Why, Mrs. Merriday! Welcome back," she said when she saw Flora. "I trust you had a nice trip?"

"Yes, very nice, Mrs. Miller." Normally the matron would have enveloped Flora in a long hug, but she held back for some reason. She seemed nervous and as stiff as her new uniform. She had always dressed like a beloved grandmother, wearing comfortable dresses and calico aprons with her gray hair askew. Her spectacles usually perched on her head instead of a fussy, white cap. "Why are you wearing a uniform, Mrs. Miller? It looks new."

"It is new. A lot has happened while you've been away." She reached up to tuck a stray curl beneath the cap. "The director fell ill a week after you left for Greece and had to resign."

"Oh, no. I hope he's recovering."

"I'm sorry to say he passed, ma'am. The board did a quick search and hired Mr. Wingate to replace him. He's around here somewhere, if you'd like to meet him."

Before Flora could reply, a group of five young schoolgirls came out of their dormitory room and walked down the hall to the kitchen in a straight line. None of them spoke a word, let alone giggled. Flora noticed other changes as she followed Mrs. Miller into the deserted lounge. The orphanage seemed too quiet, the living areas too prim and neat considering the large number of children living there.

"Please tell me about the new director before I meet him, Mrs. Miller. I can't help noticing a different atmosphere around here. Everything seems so rigid, and the children are unnaturally quiet. Why aren't they playing outdoors? And why are you dressed in a uniform—?" Before she could finish, Flora heard shouts and the sound of a fight in the hallway on the second floor.

"Oh no!" Mrs. Miller said. She hurried up the stairs with Flora right behind her. Two teenaged boys were on the hallway floor, fighting and wrestling and calling each other names. Mrs. Miller waded into the middle of it and began pulling them apart. "Stop! You boys have to stop fighting! I don't know what this is about, but you're going to get into terrible trouble if you get caught!" She spoke in a whisper, as if she didn't want to be overheard. Then a voice thundered from behind Flora, making her jump.

"That's enough!" A bearded man with the ramrod posture

of a soldier marched forward with a riding crop in his hand. "This behavior will not be tolerated!" He grabbed one of the boys by the arm and yanked him to his feet, then struck him with his crop. Before Flora could draw a breath to stop him, he did the same to the second boy. Flora felt Mrs. Miller's arms surrounding her as if to shield her or perhaps hold her back as the man continued his tirade. He ordered all of the other boys to come out of the dormitory room and line up in the hallway, including the ones who were crowding in the doorway to watch. Then he shoved the two brawlers inside and locked the door behind them with his key. "I'll be back to deal with both of you shortly," he shouted through the closed doors. It sounded like a threat. "The rest of you, go downstairs to the lounge and wait."

"You . . . you can't do that!" Flora said in outrage when she finally found her voice.

"Who are you?" Mr. Wingate was breathing hard as he straightened his vest and smoothed his dark hair back into place.

"I'm Mrs. Edmund Merriday, and I've been on the board of directors of this orphanage since its founding. I will not have our children treated this way."

"Come to my office." He marched down the stairs as if to a drumbeat and led the way into the director's office. "Have a seat, Mrs. Merriday."

"I will not sit! I'm appalled at what I just witnessed! That was a highly inappropriate way to handle an everyday spat. We do not beat our children—for *any* reason!"

"We're grateful for all you do, Mrs. Merriday. All of the orphanage's board members are much appreciated. But I'm the new director here, and I have a great deal of experience in dealing with young ruffians. Those boys must learn to obey the rules." He laid his riding crop on his desk as if it were a trophy. Flora had the urge to snatch it up and use it on him.

"They aren't ruffians, Mr. Wingate. They're orphaned children in need of love and affection."

"And sometimes discipline." He sat down behind his desk, straightening a pile of papers that was already neat. "Was there something in particular you wished to discuss with me, Mrs. Merriday? As you can see, I have work to do."

Flora turned without saying another word and fled outside to her carriage. "Take me home," she told Andrew. She was much too upset, too shocked to spend another minute with that abusive little martinet. He must be fired immediately. She would call a board meeting and tell them what she'd witnessed. Edmund was home when she arrived, and she told him about the new director and her instant dislike for him. "If he treated the children that harshly right in front of me, what must he be doing when visitors aren't present? I still can't forget the sound of that riding crop on those poor boys' shoulders."

"My dear, you must report this to the board immediately. But in the meantime, I suggest you pay another unexpected visit and see for yourself if he is always so abusive. Get more ammunition for the battle, you might say."

Flora returned the following afternoon, waiting until the children had all returned home from school. Once again, the yard was deserted, the building unusually quiet. She went in search of Mrs. Miller and found her in the little girls' dormitory, quietly reading a story to them as they sat stiffly on their beds. "What's going on, Mrs. Miller? Where is everyone?"

She closed the book and led Flora out to the hallway. "The children are being kept in their rooms as punishment. We've had runaways, Mrs. Merriday. The two boys you saw fighting yesterday—"

"Did they run away because of Mr. Wingate?"

"Most likely . . . and because of what happened after you

left." She had lowered her voice to a whisper and paused to glance around as if afraid of being overheard.

"You can trust me, Mrs. Miller. I have the highest regard for you and the wonderful work you do here. Please tell me the truth."

Tears filled Mrs. Miller's eyes. "Mr. Wingate beat those boys after you left."

"No . . . !"

"Then he locked them in the coal cellar as punishment. They climbed out through the coal chute and ran away."

"Oh no . . . no . . ." Flora felt so shaken she had to lean against the wall. She shouldn't have left in such a hurry yesterday. She should have stayed and taken charge of the orphanage. She should have ordered Mr. Wingate to leave immediately. "What are the boys' names?" she asked, wanting to know them as individuals with names and personalities.

"The two you saw fighting are Ronald Darby and Daniel Nobel. They're best friends, Mrs. Merriday. The argument was just their rough-and-tumble way of getting along. They come from terrible backgrounds and don't know any better. And there was a third boy who ran away with them. Mr. Wingate had locked him in the cellar the night before. His name is Soren Petersen."

Flora felt dizzy. "*What?* I don't believe it. He would never run away and leave his little brother. Did Gunnar run away, too?"

"Oh, Mrs. Merriday . . . I thought you knew." A chill went through Flora as Mrs. Miller rested both hands on Flora's arms. "The younger Petersen boy has been adopted."

"Adopted! That's impossible. Our policy in this orphanage is very clear—we do not separate siblings. Ever!"

"It happened last summer, while you were away. The new director arranged it—"

"Where is he?" Flora hadn't known she was capable of such

fury as she strode into his office with the matron hurrying behind her. Mr. Wingate sat behind his desk, writing something. He looked irritated at the interruption.

"Good afternoon, Mrs. Merriday."

"First of all, it is completely unacceptable to punish all of the children in this home just because three of them have run away."

"Punishment acts as a deterrent against future runaways. The children learn that such behavior won't be tolerated and that their actions adversely affect those who remain behind."

"That's outrageous!" Flora turned to Mrs. Miller. "Go let those children out of their rooms at once so they can play outdoors."

The director was on his feet. "It's not your place to override my decisions—"

"Do it!" Flora said. She saw a faint smile on Mrs. Miller's face as she hurried off to obey.

"You have no right, Mrs. Merriday—"

"Secondly, if it's true that those boys ran away because you beat them and locked them in the coal cellar, I will have you arrested and thrown into jail for assault. We do not use physical punishment in this home—ever! Do you understand?"

"My contract clearly states that I have the right—"

"I'm not finished! I've been told that one of the runaways is Soren Petersen, and that his brother has been adopted. How is that possible when our charter clearly states that we do *not* separate families?"

"It turns out that they were only half-brothers. They had two different fathers, and apparently their mother was never married to the second man. Since that makes the younger one a bas—"

"Don't you dare say it!" Flora shouted. "No one in this home will ever use that terrible word to describe one of our children. These little ones are children of God! And given the circumstances of our Savior's birth, He might well have been called by the same name."

Mr. Wingate looked defiant. He drummed his fingers on his desk, refusing to give in or to offer Flora an apology. "I examined the Petersen boys' records, and saw no reason to keep them together since the younger one—"

"We keep them together because they are a family!" She had to grip the back of the chair as her entire body trembled with rage. "Soren took care of that child for his entire life! The only family either one of them had left in the world was each other!"

"Happily, that's no longer true. Gunnar now has a new family. I'm convinced it will be much better in the long run for the younger boy to be raised in a good Christian home. I'm sure you can understand that, Mrs. Merriday."

"I neither understand nor agree. My sister and I are also orphans. We lost our mother when I was an infant and our father when I was twenty. My sister and I have been together all our lives, and I can well imagine how devastated we would be if someone separated us. It would be even more devastating if Becky and I were as young as those boys are."

"Nevertheless, my mandate here at the orphanage is to find homes for all the children. That's what I've done. The adoptive family had no interest in taking a boy as old as Soren. Experience has shown that older children have too many ingrained behaviors. They cause problems and can disrupt a well-settled home. Soren's behavior here has proven that to be true."

"I've been told that you locked him in the coal cellar."

"To separate him from the other children, yes. He couldn't control his anger."

"No wonder he ran away!" Flora was appalled. She couldn't believe that Wingate wasn't backing down in the face of her outrage. He remained unmoved by her anger and her arguments, unconcerned that he was being reprimanded by a founding board member and benefactor. "What you've done to those two brothers is a terrible injustice! One that I'll make sure you pay for!" She was shouting, but she didn't care.

"You're entitled to your own opinion, Mrs. Merriday, but I'm simply doing what the board of directors hired me to do." He sat down in his chair again and picked up his pen.

She was getting nowhere with this obnoxious man. She would deal with him later, but for now she had to try to repair some of the damage he had done. "What's being done to find Soren and the other boys?" she asked.

"We've notified the police, but Chicago is a big city. They'll bring the runaways back to the orphanage if they find them, but they won't waste time searching for them."

"Waste *time*? That's completely unacceptable!"

"What would be the point in bringing them back? All three boys are nearing the age when they would be released. We try to find jobs and housing for the young men before they leave the home, but Darby and Nobel showed no interest in getting a job, let alone an education."

"Your disdain for the children in your care is despicable! You haven't heard the last of this, Mr. Wingate." She slammed his office door on her way out.

Edmund saw her distress the moment he arrived home from work. "My poor darling," he said when she'd told him the story. "He has no right to treat you or those children that way. How soon is the board of directors able to meet? That man must be fired."

"I'm trying to arrange a meeting as soon as possible. But it's still too late for those poor brothers. The younger one has been in his adoptive home for three months already. And the older one is . . . well, who knows where he is? Living on the streets of Chicago."

"You did everything you could."

"But I still won't be able to reunite them." Or to adopt them herself. She should have listened to Becky. She should have followed her heart and taken those two boys home with her. Now it was too late.

Flora convened a meeting with the orphanage's board of directors, but the chairman wasn't convinced of the need to fire Mr. Wingate. "We had a difficult time finding someone with his experience—and someone who was willing to work for such a meager salary. Besides, Wingate asked for and was given a one-year contract, which we would have to pay out in full if we were to let him go."

"That's outrageous! He should be in jail!"

"He had it written into his contract that he has the right to use corporal punishment in extreme cases."

"I never would have allowed that," Flora said.

The chairman simply shrugged. "You weren't here, at the time—"

"I would offer to pay out his salary myself, just to be rid of him, but I can't bear the thought of rewarding him for what he has done to those two boys—not to mention the Petersen brothers."

"I agree that Wingate must be reprimanded," the chairman concluded. "But it looks as though we will either have to pay him or give him a second chance."

The board chairman went to the orphanage with Flora the following afternoon to tell Mr. Wingate of their decision. "Make no mistake," Flora told Wingate, "I wanted to have you fired. The other board members didn't witness your abuse the way I did. Instead, they've voted to issue you a warning and put you on probation. But from now on there will be absolutely no beatings or confinement of our children. And if I hear even a whisper that you're being harsh, I will have you fired and make certain you never work with children again."

"Yes, Mrs. Merriday." At least this time he seemed contrite.

"And you cannot separate siblings, even half-siblings. *Ever!* Is that clear? From now on, the board and I reserve the right to review every adoption proceeding before it becomes final."

"Yes, Mrs. Merriday."

The word *final* pounded into Flora's heart like a spike. Little Gunnar's adoption was final. He was gone, and so was his brother, Soren.

CHAPTER 21

The knock on Flora's front door at two o'clock in the morning awakened her from a sound sleep. She went with Edmund to answer it and was surprised to see Fergus Miller, the orphanage's handyman and husband of the matron, standing on her front step. Her heart sped up. "Mr. Miller, please come in." He stepped through the door far enough for it to close but no further, as if he had no right to be inside such a fine home. Given the late hour and the worried expression on his face, Flora feared the worst. She swallowed and asked, "What brings you here, Fergus?"

"I'm sorry to disturb you, Mr. and Mrs. Merriday, but I thought you would want to know that there has been a terrible incident at the orphanage tonight."

Edmund tightened his arm around her shoulder. "What happened?"

"Not a fire, I hope?" Flora asked, holding her breath. Fire was the institution's greatest fear. They tried to provide ways of escape and to teach the workers and children what to do in an emergency. But Flora knew how quickly a building like the orphan home could go up in flames and how many lives would be lost if it happened when the children were asleep.

"No, Mrs. Merriday, thankfully not a fire. Three intruders broke into the office tonight and tried to rob it. When Mr. Wingate confronted them, he was attacked and brutally beaten. Two of the robbers got away, but the police managed to catch the third. He was the most vicious of the three and wouldn't stop beating the director. The police had to pry him away."

Nearly a year had passed since Flora and the board chairman warned Mr. Wingate about physically punishing the children. He'd been forbidden to bring his riding crop into the building or to lock anyone in the coal cellar. She'd heard of no other incidents since then, but the atmosphere at the orphanage still felt oppressive to her. "Was Mr. Wingate badly injured?" she asked.

"Some broken bones, cuts, and bruises. But the police think he'll survive."

Flora noticed a look of hesitation on Mr. Miller's face and asked, "Is there something more I should know?"

"Well, the thing is, the youths who attacked him used to live in the orphanage. It will give our young people a bad name when the public hears about it in the news tomorrow. They won't like their kids going to the same neighborhood schools as our orphans."

"Do you know the boys' names?" she asked with a sinking feeling.

"We believe Daniel Nobel and Ronald Darby were the two who got away."

"I'm not surprised. They both held grudges against Mr. Wingate for beating them and locking them in the basement last year." She was reminded of the saying that those who lived by the sword would die by the sword. Wingate himself had taught those boys that violence was an acceptable form of punishment. "What about the third boy?" she asked, dreading his reply.

"The one who got caught is Soren Petersen."

"Oh no." Flora needed to sit down. She backed away and sank onto the bottom step in the foyer.

"Is he the young man you told me about?" Edmund asked. "With the younger brother?"

Flora nodded. "Mr. Wingate arranged for Soren's brother to be adopted. It was a huge injustice."

"That's why he kept beating Mr. Wingate after the other two boys fled," Miller said. "He was demanding to know where his brother was and threatening to kill Wingate if he didn't tell."

"Where is Soren now?"

"In jail. He'll be charged with assault and attempted murder."

Flora closed her eyes. She couldn't imagine the patient, tenderhearted young man she'd watched with his little brother a year ago doing such a vicious thing. But she understood it. "Do you know which jail?" she asked, rising again. "I want to see him."

"Not tonight, dear Flora," Edmund said. "I'll take you to see him first thing tomorrow, I promise. But it's too late now. Besides, if the young man was in a murderous frame of mind, he may need a night in jail to settle down."

They thanked Mr. Miller and sent him off. Flora returned to bed but didn't sleep. Edmund tried to comfort her, but even he couldn't ease the guilt she felt. "I blame myself for not helping Soren . . . and for not firing Mr. Wingate a year ago. I should have adopted those two boys, Edmund. I longed to, and I could picture them living here with us so clearly, but . . ."

"Why didn't you say something to me, darling? I would have been willing."

"I don't know. . . . I can't explain it. I thought adopting was a sign that I lacked faith. That I didn't believe God would give us a baby of our own. I kept rationalizing all the reasons why I shouldn't adopt a child from the orphanage because I wanted to prove to God that I had enough faith to believe I would get pregnant. When He didn't honor my faith, I got angry with Him—and all along He was showing me an orphanage full of children who needed our love."

"Oh, Flora. I'm so sorry. I wish I had known."

"When I first saw Soren and little Gunnar, I instantly felt as though they were ours. But I didn't act because . . . because . . . I stubbornly insisted on having my own way, my own child, instead of accepting what God was offering me. Am I making any sense?"

"You should have come to me, Flora. You could have talked with me about how you felt."

"I know, I know. I guess I didn't want you to know how mixed up I was, how badly I still wanted my own way. We had both agreed to accept God's will for us."

"I don't know what to say. How can I make all of this better for you?"

"I don't know. I just wish . . . I wish I hadn't ignored my instincts. I wish I had adopted those boys when I had the chance. Now look at the mess I've created."

"Don't place the guilt on yourself, Flora. This Wingate fellow is the one to blame, and it sounds like he paid the consequences for it tonight."

Edmund rode with Flora to the jail the next morning. They arrived just in time to hurry into court for Soren's preliminary hearing. It had been a year since Flora last saw him, and she barely recognized him at first. Soren was filthy and ragged and obviously hadn't bathed in months. The cuts and bruises on his face and hands from last night's fight hadn't been doctored and were crusted with dried blood. But the biggest change Flora saw was the deadness in his eyes, the look of hatred on a face that had once showed such tenderness and love. She understood why the police had shackled his wrists. He did indeed look frightening.

The bailiff read the charges against him: breaking and entering, assault and battery, attempted murder. There hadn't been time to hire an attorney, so Edmund stood beside the court-appointed one when the judge asked Soren how he pleaded. Edmund advised him to plead not guilty.

"Your honor, the state requests that no bail be set," the state's attorney said, "and that Mr. Petersen be remanded to the county jail as a danger to society. The victim, Mr. Wingate, suffered a vicious beating at the defendant's hands. What's more, the defendant has no fixed address and no family ties, making him a flight risk."

Flora could no longer remain silent. "Your honor, may I please speak?"

The judge frowned. He knew Flora and Edmund from the society functions and fund-raisers that he and his wife attended with them. Flora had remained active in many of the social circles that Mrs. Worthington had introduced her to in order to persuade Chicago's wealthiest citizens to give generously to the poorest ones. "Yes, Mrs. Merriday?" he asked.

"I know Soren Petersen. He used to live in the orphanage that my charitable foundation supports and where I work as a volunteer. If you will kindly set bail, my husband and I will take Soren home with us and be responsible for him."

"Are you sure you know what you're doing? He may pose a danger to you."

"I'm quite confident that he won't." Even so, the judge set a very high bail amount and slammed down his gavel. Flora made arrangements to pay, and Soren was released by noontime. As they stood on the street outside the jail, Soren spoke for the first time since pleading not guilty.

"Are you taking me back there?"

Flora knew he meant the orphan home. "No, Soren. You're coming home to Evanston with us."

"Why? What do you want with me?" The bitterness simmering behind his cold blue eyes made Flora shiver. He still looked as though he wanted to murder someone. She had acted on impulse when she'd stood up for him in court and hadn't determined what the next step would be.

"You can work for us in return for your room and board. After all, we just put up a great sum of money for your bail. Unless you'd prefer to remain in jail?"

He stared down at his bruised knuckles, massaging them. "No."

"Then let's go home." Flora gestured to her carriage and saw Soren hesitate. "It's all right, Soren. Get in." He smelled as though he hadn't bathed or washed in months, and the odor expanded to fill every inch of the confined carriage. Flora resisted the urge to cover her mouth and nose with her handkerchief. "I'm taking a huge chance on you, Soren," she said as they began to move, "because I don't believe you're a vicious murderer. I was very sorry when I heard that you had run away with the other boys."

"I had no reason to stay. Wingate took my brother."

"I understand. I saw you with your brother, and you were always so gentle and loving, not at all like those other two boys. Why did you run away with them?"

"They said they'd help me find Gunnar. And they wanted to get even with Wingate, too. I wouldn't have beaten him if he'd just told me where Gunnar is."

"I understand that your brother is living with a good family. Mr. Wingate believed it was better for him than growing up in an orphan home."

"Do you know where Gunnar is?"

"No, I don't. I'm sorry."

"Can you find out for me?"

Flora sighed. "The adoption records are sealed by the court. But right now we need to take care of your situation. Attempted murder is a very serious charge." Soren didn't reply. He continued staring down at his hands on the long ride home. When the carriage halted outside Flora's house, he lifted his head for the first time. She saw him take the measure of it, and although it wasn't a mansion by any means, he seemed to shrivel back in his seat.

Edmund asked him to climb from the carriage first, then took Flora's hand and held her back for a moment. "Are you two going to be fine together, or would you like me to stay?" he asked softly.

"Of course we'll be fine. You need to go to work. Becky is here with me." She kissed Edmund and stepped out, then led Soren through the back door into the kitchen. They had a new cook and housekeeper now that Maria Elena and the Griffins had retired, and the servants sat at the table eating lunch with Becky, who often joined them for the noon meal when she didn't want to eat alone. "This is Soren Petersen," she told everyone.

Becky smiled and said, "How do you do? I'm Rebecca Hawes," but the others looked him over warily. Flora saw the housekeeper prop her elbow on the table and discreetly pinch her nose shut.

"Soren is going to be staying here and working for us, but right now he needs a bath, and his injuries need to be tended. Please find him some clothes to wear, too—perhaps some of Edmund's old ones. He can sleep in the servants' rooms on the third floor."

"Yes, Miss Flora." The housekeeper pushed back her chair and started poking the coals on the stove to heat the bath water. Flora smiled up at Soren, but he remained somber.

"Why are you doing this?" he asked. "What do you want with me?"

"Nothing. I simply want you to have a second chance. I'll try my best to keep you from going to prison by explaining that you suffered a terrible injustice at Mr. Wingate's hands. But if you run away and disappear, I'll forfeit all my bail money—and it's a considerable amount. That money could have gone to help other children in need. Do you understand what I'm saying?"

"Yes, ma'am."

"I would like to give you a chance to travel a different road than the one you've been on. I hope you'll be wise enough to take it."

After the housekeeper led Soren off for his bath, Becky exhaled dramatically and fanned her hand in front of her nose. "Phew! I don't know how that boy can live with himself!"

"He does smell pretty bad."

"Sit down and have some lunch, Flora—if you still have an appetite, that is. Then you can tell me what your plans are for this latest project of yours."

"I really don't know," she said as she sank onto a chair. "I told Soren he can work for us, so I suppose I'll need to find him a job to do." The cook set a bowl of soup in front of Flora, then poured her a cup of tea. "Maybe Soren can work with Edmund. . . . I don't think that boy has had a father in his life for a long time."

Becky laughed. "Well, it will be more fuel for society gossip when people learn we have an accused felon living in our home. But I'm proud of you, Flora. You did the right thing."

Flora spent the next week trying to find a job around their house for Soren to do. The servants were less frightened of him once he was cleaned up, and they accepted him as one of their own—even though Soren, who they now called Petersen, rarely spoke. He didn't know anything about horses and seemed uncomfortable around them, but he did have a knack for anticipating the needs of everyone he worked with and rushing to help them. He was especially attentive with Edmund, and so even though Edmund had never wanted a personal valet, the job became Petersen's. With everything working out well so far, Flora decided the time had come to deal with Petersen's legal issues.

"I'm going to speak with Mr. Wingate tomorrow," she told Becky after knocking on her bedroom door one night. Becky sat at her dressing table, brushing her dark hair. "I plan to ask him to drop the charges against Petersen. Will you come with me, please? You're much tougher than I am—and much more convincing when it comes to confrontations."

"Why, thank you. Most people wouldn't consider toughness a very desirable trait for dainty women like us, but I consider it a compliment."

"I meant it as one."

"Shall I arm myself with a weapon?" Becky asked, brandishing the hairbrush.

"No, just prayer."

Flora felt nervous as she and Becky arrived at the director's office the next morning. This meeting was so important. A young man's future was at stake. Mr. Wingate remained seated behind his desk, still showing the signs of the beating he'd taken, his face swollen and bruised, his broken wrist in a splint. Flora wasted no time with pleasantries. "You know you treated Soren and Gunnar Petersen unfairly. They were as close as any two brothers could be, even if they did have different fathers. I understand that it's too late to undo the adoption. Gunnar has been with his new family for more than a year now, and it would be unfair to everyone. But Petersen told me you didn't even give him a chance to say good-bye."

"I knew he would cause a scene. His violence proves that my assessment was correct."

"Any one of us would create a 'scene,' as you call it, if we were cruelly torn away from someone we loved! Have you ever lost a loved one that way? I imagine you haven't, or you wouldn't have done what you did. What's more, you imprisoned him in the coal cellar!"

"Are you finished, Mrs. Merriday? I have work to do."

"No, I am not finished. I have come to tell you that I will pay all of your medical expenses, and whatever restitution you're seeking, but I would like you to drop the charges against Petersen."

"I can't do that. He's a danger to society. He should be taken off the streets and kept in prison."

"He's a seventeen-year-old boy who's all alone in the world. He has lost every person who was ever important to him. We can't change the terrible past that he was forced to endure, but if you drop the charges, we can offer him a new start and a chance to have a future. You know, Mr. Wingate, that I would have fired you a year ago. But I decided to give you a second chance. Now you owe it to both Petersen and to me to extend the same opportunity to him. A second chance. That boy will die if he's sent to prison."

"He nearly killed me."

"But he didn't." Flora's shoulders ached with tension as she waited. They had reached a stalemate.

Becky took a step toward him. "What will it take to change your mind, Mr. Wingate? A raise in salary? A cash payment? Stop acting so sanctimonious and tell me how much money you want."

Flora feared for a moment, that Becky had gone too far. Instead, it turned out that she had said the magic word—money. After a bit of haggling, Wingate agreed on a price, and Becky got him to sign an affidavit, formally dropping all the charges and testifying that Petersen had acted in self-defense.

On the way home, Flora managed a smile for the first time since waking up that morning. "You're my hero, Becky. Do you know that?"

"Bah! What are sisters for?"

Petersen was in the pantry, polishing Edmund's shoes to a glossy shine when Flora returned home. When she told him the news that he wouldn't have to return to jail, he staggered backward against the wall, then covered his face. Flora longed to hug him but didn't. "I can't imagine how hard this has been for you, having prison hanging over your head. But it's over now, Soren."

He looked up, wiping his eyes. "Wingate deserved it, though."

"Let's not dwell on revenge anymore," she said. "We need to decide what's next for you. You're welcome to continue working for us, but you're not obligated to do so. We can help you find a job and a place to live if there's some other type of work you'd like to do. Or perhaps you'd like to learn a skill." She found herself holding her breath, hoping he would stay. She wanted a second chance to win his trust and maybe, someday, his love.

Petersen stared down, not meeting Flora's gaze. "I can't read or write. I went to school for a few months when I lived in the orphanage . . . before . . ."

"I'm sure Edmund would be happy to tutor you if you'd like to learn. He enjoys having you work for him. In fact, you've been a huge help to all of us. You're very bright, Petersen, and I'm certain you'll learn quickly. Would that be agreeable to you? Please say yes." When he nodded, Flora longed once again to hug him.

"Good news," she told Becky a few minutes later when she found her in her office. "Petersen has agreed to stay with us."

"I'm glad."

"I'm going to ask Edmund to tutor him since Soren has never

had an education, but will you help him, too? You're a wonderful teacher."

"Of course. . . . But you do realize that the only reason he's sticking around is because he hopes you'll help him find his brother."

"I know he is. But the adoption records are sealed by the courts, Becky. There's nothing I can do to help him."

Except show love to Petersen, help him heal, and do whatever she could to atone for the part she had played in his tragic life.

CHAPTER 22

When Edmund's and Becky's third book was published, Flora arranged to hold the gala celebration for them at the Northwestern University library. She invited scholars from other Chicago-area universities to attend the reception, including faculty members from the University of Chicago, still in its formative stages. Edmund stood tall and proud beside Flora as they waited for the event to begin, but she could tell by the way Becky fidgeted, tugging at her new gown and poking at her hair, that she was nervous. Flora saw no reason for it. The first two books she and Edmund had co-written had been honored and acclaimed. Flora was about to remind her sister of that fact when Becky leaned toward Edmund and said, "You're very brave to host our book launch here at Northwestern. Aren't you afraid you'll face the scorn of your university colleagues for my lack of credentials?"

"Not at all," Edmund replied. "You're a remarkable scholar, Rebecca, and highly skilled at deciphering ancient languages, even if Cambridge isn't wise enough to award you a degree for all your studies there because of your gender. What's more, you're a much better writer than I am. If anyone has a problem with that, I'll be happy to let them have a piece of my mind."

"You'll have to be quick," Flora said, "or Becky might give them a piece of hers first."

The doors finally opened, and one of Edmund's colleagues introduced him and Becky to the surprisingly large audience. He praised their book as "a fascinating and fresh contribution to the historical debate." Flora thought she would burst with pride as the room echoed with congratulations and applause.

"Thank you," Edmund said, tilting his head in his charming, self-deprecating way. "Now please enjoy the wonderful refreshments my wife has been kind enough to provide."

Flora stood in the receiving line between Edmund and Becky as they greeted their guests and signed copies of their book. She was so proud of her husband and more in love with him than ever. Edmund would be sixty soon and his thick, sandy hair was turning gray and his shoulders beginning to stoop. But he was the same wonderful, energetic man she had fallen in love with. How many times during their twenty-three years of marriage had Flora thanked God that she had married Edmund Merriday instead of Thomas Worthington?

Flora greeted all of Edmund's colleagues, knowing them well after hosting them for dinners in her home. She enjoyed the academic banter and lively conversations they brought to her table. None of them had the means to return the invitations, but they loved accepting them—and Flora loved extending them. These were her and Becky's kind of people, much more so than the wealthier guests that Flora also entertained in an effort to squeeze support from them for her charities. She often thought how grateful she was to Mrs. Worthington for teaching her the social graces, which allowed her to raise funds for the work she loved. Flora even managed to recruit several of the wealthy matrons who shared her passions to serve on her charities' boards of directors. Now, as she listened to the laughter and conversation in the university library, Flora was thrilled to have her foot in both worlds—the wealthy social world that supported her passion for the poor, and the academic world that offered support and camaraderie to Edmund and Becky. What different yet strangely intersecting paths she and her sister had taken.

Just as the number of guests in the receiving line was starting to taper off and Flora thought she might be able to sneak away to the refreshment table, she saw a determined-looking gentleman in his fifties approaching. He had a copy of their book in his hand that was already underlined and stuffed full of markers. "Uh-oh," Flora said, nudging Edmund. "I hope he's not a critic on the warpath, looking for an argument."

But the stranger broke into a wide grin when he finally reached the front of the line and offered his hand. "Good evening Miss Hawes, Mr. and Mrs. Merriday. I'm Professor Timothy Dyk from the University of Chicago, and I have a few questions for you, if you don't mind." He was a short, compact man with bushy gray hair that needed a trim. His suit was baggy and wrinkled, but his round, friendly face and cheerful grin were so disarming that Flora felt ashamed for noticing his disheveled state. Edmund had also been shaggy and rumpled when she'd first met him.

Flora listened as her husband responded to a few of the professor's questions, but Edmund finally gestured to Becky and said, "You're asking the wrong person, Professor Dyk. That's Miss Hawes' area of expertise. The ideas in that chapter are purely hers."

Flora held her breath, wondering if the man would insult Becky by refusing to take her seriously, but Professor Dyk never missed a beat as he turned to her and repeated his question. A few minutes later, he and Becky wandered away from the reception line, deep in conversation. Flora linked her arm through Edmund's and steered him toward the refreshment table. She lost sight of her sister as she and Edmund filled their plates and chatted with friends, but when Flora finally went in search of Becky more than an hour later, she was surprised to find her still deep in conversation with the professor. It didn't look as though they were arguing, and he seemed to be listening intently to Becky and nodding. Yet Flora kept her eye on them for a few minutes, waiting to intervene if necessary. When Becky laughed at something the professor said, Flora returned to Edmund's side, relieved.

Much too soon the refreshments were gone and the event started winding down. Flora stood at the door with her husband, saying good-bye to their friends and guests. Professor Dyk was among the last to leave, having talked with Becky the entire time. "It looked as though you and that professor were having an interesting discussion," Flora said to her on the short drive home. "In fact, he monopolized your evening."

"Why bother talking with anyone else," Becky replied, "when he asks such fascinating questions?"

"I'm happy to hear that," Flora said. She nestled close to her husband with a sigh. "I'm so glad the evening was a success. Maybe tomorrow we could—"

"I've invited Professor Dyk to come for dinner tomorrow," Becky interrupted. "Remind me to let the cook know." Her earlier nervousness had vanished, replaced by a strange look of satisfaction that Flora rarely saw on her sister's face.

Flora stole a glance at Edmund, trying not to smile. "Wonderful," she said. "Shall I see if any of our other friends are free to join us?"

"If you'd like," Becky replied. But Flora could tell that her sister's thoughts were miles away.

Petersen answered the door with a polite bow when Professor Dyk arrived the following evening. Flora had been teaching him to serve as a butler in addition to his duties as Edmund's valet. The professor halted just inside the door wearing the same suit as the night before, his hair and beard still in need of a trim. He gazed around the foyer with a look of amazement. "Goodness! If I had realized that publishing books paid so handsomely, I might have considered writing one myself."

"Don't be absurd," Becky said with a laugh. "Our father made some very wise investments during his lifetime. Take his coat and hat, Petersen. Follow me, Professor, and I'll show you that book I mentioned last night." She led him to her study, talking a mile a minute about her research and her conclusions.

"Do you know this Professor Dyk?" Flora whispered to Edmund as they remained behind to greet their other guests.

"Never met him before. I think he said he's from the University of Chicago. Should we be worried?"

"I don't think so. Becky is a pretty shrewd judge of character. After all, she convinced me to get rid of Thomas Worthington and marry you, remember?"

An hour later, Becky and the professor were still in her study. Flora poked her head inside the door and saw them bending over the desk examining a parchment that Becky had purchased on her last journey to Jerusalem, studying it closely with a magnifying glass. "I hate to interrupt," Flora said, "but all of the other guests have arrived and dinner is ready."

Professor Dyk looked up at her in surprise. "Oh, dear! Please forgive me, Mrs. Merriday. I've been terribly rude spending all this time with Miss Hawes when I should have been more sociable."

"Nonsense. We're a very unconventional family. Follow me, Professor." She led the way to the dining room where a simple table had been spread for their university guests. Flora had instructed the housekeeper not to lay out all of the intimidating forks and spoons, fearing that the obvious display of wealth might make her guests uneasy.

The conversation around the table was thoroughly engaging and fun, as it always was when they hosted Edmund's colleagues. And there was nothing at all stuffy about Professor Dyk either, even though it was clear that he was a very intelligent man. Edmund introduced him to their other guests, then said, "Tell us a little about yourself, Professor."

"Please, I hope you'll call me Timothy. I recently moved to Chicago from Pennsylvania, where I taught ancient history at the university. I've been offered a faculty position at the new University of Chicago, and thought it would be a marvelous challenge to help found an academic institution from the very beginning. I find this series of books Mr. Merriday and Miss Hawes have coauthored quite intriguing. Their scholarship and research is second-to-none, yet any well-educated layman could read and enjoy them. Of course, that's not to say I agree with all your conclusions—"

"Here we go again!" Becky said. But she was laughing as she said it, which Flora saw as a good sign. Becky looked very pretty tonight, her face flushed with color. Flora thought it was rouge at first, but it wasn't. It was happiness.

"I have to confess something," the professor said as Petersen offered him and all the other guests second servings of the meal. "When my department chairman heard that I'd been invited here tonight, he asked me to charm my way into your good graces, Mrs. Merriday, so the university could solicit your financial support in the future. He said if I did, he would put me on the fast-track to a tenured position. But I told him that I was very uncomfortable with such subterfuge. I would rather earn tenure the honest, old-fashioned way and leave the fundraising to the experts."

Flora found his confession amusing as well as refreshing. "Well, thank you for your honesty," she said. "As you can imagine, Becky and I get quite a few requests for financial support. Please tell your department chairman that he's welcome to visit my foundation and talk with me himself about funding. And perhaps Becky would like to endow a scholarship in ancient history sometime in the future."

"Thank you. That's very kind of you both—and it lets me off the hook. I would love to see the University of Chicago become a world-renowned institution. Since my specialty is ancient Near Eastern history, I would love to help the university develop a world-class museum where scholars could study the artifacts that are being unearthed from the Babylonian and Assyrian Empires."

"Edmund has collected some wonderful artifacts," Becky said. "And I've made a few interesting purchases myself over the years."

"I would love to see them."

They retired to the parlor for coffee after the meal, and once again Becky and the professor ended up deep in conversation. "I truly do admire your books," Flora heard him telling her. "But I'm sorry to say I don't share your religious views."

"What religion do you ascribe to?" Becky asked.

"I'm what you might call a contented agnostic. I've learned in my study of ancient history that religions come and go over the centuries—and most of them have gone. No one worships Baal or Moloch or the sun god Amun-Re anymore."

Becky was quick with her retort. "It's not quite true to say they've all vanished. How would you explain the amazing endurance of the Jewish faith? Against all odds and in the face of horrendous persecution and exile, Judaism still survives today. And I would also argue that Christianity is an outgrowth of Judaism." Her tone had grown sharp, and Flora feared for a moment that the professor would take offense. Instead, his expression seemed to brighten at the prospect of a lively debate.

"Hmm. I suppose I would have to concede that they are exceptions to the rule."

"Might I suggest that they have survived while the others haven't because they are the one true religion and the others all counterfeits?"

"Well, let's think about those assumptions for a moment," he began. The debate that followed between him and Becky lasted until late in the evening and quickly left Flora, Edmund, and the other guests unable to get a word in edgeways. It was like competing in a horse race and being left far behind as the lead horses sprinted ahead. When Becky and Timothy finally stopped debating and looked around, they seemed surprised to find that the other guests had all gone home. The professor scrambled to his feet. "Oh, dear! I've overstayed my welcome. Not a very good first impression, is it?"

"You've been a very interesting guest," Flora said. "We're delighted to meet you."

"And I've thoroughly enjoyed myself," he said as he made his way to the door. "Thank you for a very enchanting evening. But I still have questions for you, Rebecca. And there are so many other topics I'm eager to debate with you. I find your perspective is such a fresh, unique way of looking at history."

Becky put her hands on her hips as if challenging him. "Are you trying to wrangle another dinner invitation out of me, Professor Dyk?"

"If I am, I'm doing a very clumsy job of it, I'm afraid."

"Is there a Mrs. Dyk?" Flora asked. "If so, please tell her that she's welcome to come next time, as well."

"Sadly, no, there is no Mrs. Dyk. I seem to want too much in a companion—a meeting of the minds as well as the souls. I was once engaged to a lovely woman—a match engineered by our fathers. I was eager to marry, but my fiancée decided we had little in common. In truth, I suppose we didn't. I couldn't understand why she had no interest at all in Homer or Herodotus."

"What a jolly man Becky's new friend is," Flora told Edmund later that night after they'd gone upstairs to their bedroom. "I liked him very much."

"I did, too. And jolly is the perfect word to describe him."

They all enjoyed Timothy's company in the weeks that followed, and he quickly became such a frequent guest that it seemed as though he'd always been part of their life. He and Becky went to concerts and plays together, and he invited Becky to sit in on some of his lectures at the university. And although he agreed to attend church with Becky one Sunday, it seemed to Flora that it was more of an experiment to satisfy his curiosity than a true spiritual quest. Even so, it was the happiest that Flora had seen her sister in a long, long time. She recalled the conversation they'd had on that starry night in Egypt years ago and hoped that Becky had found her heart's companion at last.

"I think my sister is falling in love," she told Edmund one night after spending the evening at a symphony concert with Becky and Timothy. Edmund had just sat down on their bed to pull off his shoes and socks and Flora watched him perform his familiar, nightly ritual from her seat at the dressing table. They shared the same room and bed, even though Flora's rich friends would think them very strange for doing so. Most mansions had separate bedrooms for husbands and wives, as if marriage had nothing at all to do with love and friendship. "What do you think of their relationship, Edmund? Does it seem to you that Becky and Timothy are in love?"

"Hmm," he said, loosening his tie. "They do seem very relaxed and comfortable with each other. Not that they never have disagreements—they certainly do! Very loud ones, at times."

"Yes, but their debates are intellectual arguments, not

personal ones. And when one of them fails to persuade the other, they usually end up laughing together and agreeing to disagree. And have you noticed how they interrupted each other at dinner tonight and finished each other's thoughts?"

"You have a keener eye for that sort of thing than I do, darling."

Flora turned to her mirror and began pulling out her hairpins, shaking her head to loosen her hair so she could brush it. She recognized the love in Edmund's eyes as he watched her—even after all these years—and thought she had seen Timothy gazing at Becky the same way tonight during the concert. Oh, how she hoped it was true!

"Have you asked Rebecca how she feels about Timothy?" Edmund asked.

"I'm afraid to. I so hope she finds happiness with him, yet I don't want to see her get hurt. If she is falling in love with Timothy and he doesn't return her feelings . . . if he is simply leading her along for her money or for any other reason—"

"I'll murder him," Edmund finished. "It's as simple as that. Would you like me to talk to him alone? Man to man?"

"No, we'd better wait a bit. They've known each other for less than a year. Let me talk to Becky first. Maybe I'm reading things wrong. Although I don't think so."

After a few days of dithering, torn between helping her sister and minding her own business, Flora decided to talk to Becky and offer her advice and perhaps consolation if she needed it. She went into Becky's room after an evening out and sat down on her bed. "Can we talk?"

"I figured this was coming," Becky said, sinking onto a slipper chair and kicking off her shoes. "I'm surprised you waited this long. You want to ask me about Timothy, don't you?"

"Anyone with a pair of eyes can see how fond you are of each other and—"

"I'm in love with him, Flora. Against all the odds, especially at my age, I've finally found a man I could happily spend the rest of my life with."

"Do you know how Timothy feels? I would hate to see you get hurt. . . ."

Becky laughed out loud. "He loves me, too, Flora. He told me so. He says he loves my brilliant mind and says I am an equal partner in every way. He asked me to marry him."

"Timothy proposed?"

"Several times."

"That's wonderful!" Flora said, leaping to her feet. "Why didn't you tell me? Should we start planning the wedding?"

Becky held up both hands, stopping Flora before she could give her a congratulatory hug. "How can I marry him, Flora? You know Timothy isn't a believer. The Bible says, 'Be ye not unequally yoked together with unbelievers.' I can't deliberately go against Scripture. That law was given for a very good reason. Marriage is a union of spirits and souls, not just bodies."

"But he's such a good man . . . and you love each other."

"Would you have married Edmund if he wasn't a believer?"

Flora sank down on the bed again and thought for a moment. "I see your point," she finally said. "Sometimes love just isn't enough, is it?"

"Timothy and I have talked about how wonderful it would be to be married, and we long to travel together. There are so many places I would love to show him, places he has always wanted to see and never dreamt he could afford. It would be a dream come true for me, too."

"I admire him for not pretending to have faith just to win your hand and your bank account."

"Unlike some other men we've known?" Becky asked with a wry smile. "No, Timothy is honest to his core and would never lie about what he believes. But how can we be true partners if we disagree about the most important thing in life—our faith in God? And how can I bear to share my life with him, to love him fully, while knowing he won't spend eternity with me? As a Christian, my chief aim in life is to serve God, but Timothy doesn't share that goal. And that keeps us worlds apart."

"The obvious solution is to persuade him to believe."

"That's what I've been trying to do—and getting nowhere."

"I'll ask Edmund to enter the debate. I'll make sure he brings up the subject of faith whenever they're together. We'll wear Timothy down, Becky. Sooner or later he'll have to concede if we offer enough convincing arguments and proofs."

"I hope you're right. In the meantime, Timothy has agreed to come with us and be a volunteer tutor at the Sunday school next time we go."

"Wonderful! That's a great start." Flora smiled and added, "I hope the children can understand him. He loses me half the time when I try to discuss anything with him."

"Maybe their simple, childlike faith will convince him," Becky said. "Didn't Jesus say that we must become like a little child to enter the kingdom?"

Timothy seemed delighted by the swarms of excited children the following Sunday at the downtown church, though slightly befuddled when it came to handling them all. He helped tutor two older boys who were struggling to read and watched in fascination as Becky retold a Bible story in her unique, dramatic fashion. But as Flora watched him, she suspected that he was enthralled with her, not the story.

Flora was searching for a tactful way to ask Timothy's opinion of their Sunday school mission work on the ride home when Becky suddenly came right out and asked, "What did you think of the lesson of the Good Samaritan?"

He thought a moment, stroking his still-shaggy beard—which Becky apparently never noticed or cared about. "The notion of using a story to emphasize a moral lesson was an interesting one," he finally said. "It reminded me of the way other ancient cultures often used fables for teaching purposes."

Becky gave an exasperated sigh. "But what about the content of the story, Timothy. The point that Jesus was trying to make?"

"Be kind to your neighbor?" he asked with a shrug. "It's a valid point."

"It's more than that. Jesus is using the parable to teach us how to live." She looked as though she wanted to shake him. Flora nudged Edmund with her elbow.

"I have seen Rebecca and Flora live out this truth," Edmund said. "Did we ever share the story of how we all met?"

"I don't believe so," Timothy replied.

"Flora and Rebecca found me along the side of the Gaza Road after I'd been robbed by an unscrupulous caravan driver and left to fend for myself beneath the broiling sun. They were two young women, traveling on their own, yet they stopped to offer their help, oblivious to any danger I may have presented. They were quite fearless."

"We weren't completely oblivious, Edmund dear," Flora said, "but you seemed harmless enough."

"As for being fearless," Becky added, "we believe that God knows when the hour of our end will be, so we don't need to fear. But the true reason we stopped is because we believe that the Bible is God's inspired Word, and we must live our lives by it."

"Hmm. As a historian, I have a problem with that," Timothy said, scratching his chin. "I'm surprised you don't, Rebecca. How do we know that the Bible represents a true, historical record of what Jesus did and taught? Every author begins with an agenda, something they hope to prove. Are you and Edmund completely objective when you research and write your books?"

"Of course not. We intend our works to persuade, and we're

quite clear about that. But we don't alter the historical or archaeological records to fit our thesis. "

"Well, the men who wrote the books of the Bible all had agendas, too. The Gospel of John clearly says that he wrote his Gospel 'so ye might believe that Jesus is the Christ, the Son of God.' In other words, it was written to convince and—"

"You didn't finish the verse, Timothy," Becky interrupted. "John goes on to write, ' . . . and that believing ye might have life through his name.' John is trying to convince his readers because he believes that what he's saying is a matter of life and death. It's the same reason that I'm trying to convince you. I long for you to share in the fullness of life we have in Christ."

Timothy leaned toward Becky and took her hand. "There is no doubt in my mind about how much your faith means to you—to all of you," he added, nodding at Flora and Edmund. "But it just isn't a logical step that I can take."

Flora was about to tell him that taking a leap of faith requires more than logic, when Becky said, "Fine. Leaving the Bible aside for a moment, what about Mr. Darwin's book? He clearly had an agenda when he wrote *On the Origin of Species*. He wanted to disprove the biblical account of creation, even though he offers very little scientific proof aside from a few scattered fossils, and a great deal of speculation. Yet you suspended logic in order to believe his theory of evolution."

"Well, Mr. Darwin's explanation for the origin of life on earth is a very logical thesis. Much more logical, you must admit, than that a supernatural being scooped up a pile of mud to make a man then removed one of his ribs to create a woman."

"Listen to yourself! You're focusing on the details and not on the broader message of the Bible's creation account—which is that God created mankind with a specific intention and gave him a purpose. Yet you read Darwin's book and do the exact opposite—swallowing the broader message instead of focusing on all of his nonsensical details. Can a fish really grow legs and a pair of lungs all by itself and crawl onto dry land? Can an ape develop a brain, somehow, and write brilliant symphonies and exquisite poetry? It requires a gigantic leap of faith, in my opinion, to believe that theory." Becky was raising her voice and gesturing wildly, which she always did when she grew excited. Flora glanced at Edmund, but he simply shrugged as if to say, *she's doing fine without my help.*

"All of the books of the Bible, written over several centuries, share a common theme and a common thesis," Becky continued, "and they paint a composite picture of the God we serve. He's revealing to us that there is a Creator who loves us, who created this earth and all its creatures for us, and that He has intervened in history because He wants to restore us to Himself."

Timothy captured one of Becky's gesturing hands and held on to it. "The issue I have with the Bible is that it surely has been edited over the years. It's like a thread of gossip that becomes altered a little bit each time it gets passed along to the next person. Jesus started off as a kindhearted rabbi centuries ago, and over the years He was gradually credited with more and more miracles, such as curing a man born blind, until pretty soon this ordinary rabbi was being described as the Son of God."

Flora expected another theological lecture from Becky but instead, she lowered her voice and quietly said, "What if I could prove that the Bible hasn't changed? That it's the same document it was when it was first written down?"

"How would you do that?"

"You've read the research Edmund and I did on the Codex Sinaiticus. Edmund believes there may be more copies of very early manuscripts at the Monastery of St. Catherine on Mount Sinai. Complete ones. So far, we've only been able to find and purchase fragments of books and scrolls over the years, but as the experts have studied these fragments, they've concluded that they are virtually identical to the same passages we have in our Scriptures today. Suppose we could find more ancient Gospels, ones that were intact, and what if they also proved to be identical to our Bible?"

"I suppose if the weight of proof tilted in that direction . . ." Timothy conceded. But their discussion was interrupted when their carriage arrived home. Since he was unable to stay for dinner, Timothy and Becky agreed to continue the debate another day.

"What am I doing wrong, Edmund?" Becky asked as they shared a light meal in the breakfast room later.

"Nothing that I can see," he replied.

"I'm sorry we weren't more help," Flora said. "But sooner or later you'll wear him down, don't you think?"

"No one has ever been 'argued' into the kingdom," Edmund said. "It requires a leap of faith, a change of heart. And that's the work of the Holy Spirit." Flora knew he was right, but Becky didn't seem to hear him.

"Timothy seemed open during the discussion today, didn't he?" she asked. "We need to find more manuscripts, some very early ones, and show Timothy that the Scriptures haven't been altered by man's hand. And I think we all know where we might find them."

"You want to go to the Monastery of St. Catherine on Mount Sinai, don't you?" Flora asked. She could see how much her sister longed to not only spend her life with the man she loved, but to have him come to Christ. Becky had once brought Edmund and her together, and now Flora longed to do the same for her and Timothy. "How can I help?" she asked.

"Figure out a way for us to visit the monastery."

"It has long been my dream to return to the Sinai, too," Edmund added.

"Maybe the monks we befriended in Greece will give us letters of introduction to the archbishop in Cairo," Flora said. "Edmund could ask for letters from Cambridge and Northwestern."

"Good idea," Becky said. "We aren't scholars, and we don't have any ties to czars and kings, so we shouldn't be seen as a threat like that von Tischendorf fellow who stole their manuscript."

"Photography is going to be the key," Edmund said. "We need to assure the monks that the manuscripts will remain in the monastery where they belong. We'll simply take photographs of the important documents so scholars can study and translate them. No harm will be done to the artifacts, nor will they be removed."

"That's brilliant, Edmund," Becky said. "Timothy is a scholar with a deep respect for the historical record. He'll have to concede that the Bible is a valid, historical document when faced with the overwhelming proof."

"The things we do for love . . ." Flora said, shaking her head. "Edmund and I are with you, Becky. Let's start planning a trip to the Sinai."

"Wonderful. But first, I need to study photography."

PART III
Petersen

CHAPTER 23

THE SINAI DESERT
1890

Soren Petersen never could have imagined traveling halfway around the world to the Sinai Desert, far from the slums of Chicago. Nor could he have imagined being abandoned here, with no idea where he was or how to get back to civilization. He tried not to panic at the thought he might die. He had to find a way out. He had promises to keep. *No trees grow to the sky*, he told himself. The wait would come to an end, one way or another.

"We need to pray," Miss Flora said before she and Miss Rebecca retired for the night. Petersen was relieved when they didn't ask him to join hands and pray with them again. Each time they did, it made him feel doomed. He groped in the dark tent until he located his cot, but he didn't undress. He needed to be ready—for what, he didn't know. He still had the cook's knife.

Mr. Farouk and the cook rustled around for a while but eventually they both began to snore. Petersen had no idea how they could sleep under these circumstances. He was afraid to sleep, wondering if he would die tomorrow at the hands of the Bedouin. The unnerving dinner he'd eaten in their camp tonight, sitting among the men, separated from the sisters, had proven how helpless and far from home he really was.

When it came down to it, Soren was afraid to die. He'd been attending church with the sisters ever since he'd started working for them, and he'd accompanied them to Sunday school, too. But he still didn't know if what he'd learned about God and heaven and hell was true. Either way, if his life was about to end, he hated that it would be because of Kate Rafferty. He wished he could sell her to the sheikh tomorrow and save the sisters' lives, but Miss Flora would never allow it.

Why would anyone want such an ill-tempered woman for his wife—or even his servant, for that matter? Kate had been nothing but trouble since she'd barged into their lives a year ago. Miss Flora and Miss Rebecca were kindhearted women, taking pity on Kate when they should have called for the police and tossed her into jail. But since the sisters had taken him into their lives under similar circumstances, Petersen could hardly complain. If only they could have foreseen the trouble Kate would cause them, stranding them in the desert this way—well, they might have thought twice.

He remained awake, listening for sounds in the darkness until Mr. Farouk's snoring grew so loud that Petersen feared he'd never hear any intruders until they were upon him. He gave up trying to sleep and went outside to sit under the stars in front of his tent, dragging his blanket with him for warmth. Fear squeezed the air from his chest at the thought that the sheikh and his thugs might sneak over in the night and murder them all. Petersen couldn't bear it if anything happened to the sisters. They had rescued him from jail and helped him start a new life, and he had vowed to protect them in return. He hated his helplessness. And to think that the reason they might all die was because of that disagreeable girl. It made his blood boil.

What would his life be like tonight and tomorrow if he had stayed home in Chicago? Petersen couldn't answer that question. He looked up at the endless stars and remembered gazing up at them as he'd huddled with Gunnar in a cold Chicago alley, hungry and alone. His parents' faces were little more than hazy blurs in his memory, unless he looked at his own reflection in a mirror and saw the same pale hair and blue eyes that they'd had, the same fair skin. If he was going to pray, as Miss Flora had suggested, it would be for his brother, not for himself. He would pray that Gunnar was safe and warm in his bed tonight.

And happy.

More than anything else, Petersen hoped his brother was happy.

He managed to doze a little during the night and awoke just before dawn when both camps began to stir. Petersen stood guard, watching the Bedouin closely while the rest of his camp ate breakfast. He continued watching as the other men bowed down for their morning prayers. But he made a mental note of where the sun had risen, knowing that if he walked in the opposite direction, the desert would eventually end at the gulf. Miss Flora had convinced him that they had no hope of finding the monastery by themselves, but they could follow the sun west, couldn't they?

"Here they come," he warned when the sheikh and his men finished their prayers and started walking the short distance to the sisters' camp. "Kate needs to get inside the tent and stay there." He hoped the ladies couldn't detect the fear that raced through his body and knotted his gut.

"We're praying for you, Soren," Miss Flora said, resting her hand on his shoulder. "God will be with you."

The Bedouin halted a few feet away, and one of them rolled

a rug out on the stony ground. The sheikh beckoned for Petersen and Mr. Farouk to sit down on it with him. The other men crowded behind the sheikh, while the two sisters stood behind Soren. If it came to a fight, the two teams were greatly mismatched.

The sheikh began to speak, gesturing broadly, his hawk-nosed face tilted with pride. "He offers you many gifts for the girl," Mr. Farouk translated. "Sheep . . . camels . . . goats . . . gold, and more."

"Tell him she isn't for sale or for trade—or whatever it's called," Petersen replied. He waited, growing anxious while an animated conversation passed between the two men. At last the sheikh finished, and Mr. Farouk translated for Petersen.

"He say his wives give him only daughters. He say a flame-haired woman of such fire surely gives a strong son."

"That's absurd," Petersen mumbled, shaking his head. Once again the sheikh began to speak, his voice growing louder, his gestures broader as he pointed to the empty desert, the endless sky.

"He say to name your price, no matter how high."

"We're getting nowhere," Miss Rebecca said from behind Soren. "The Bedouin think bartering is part of the game. He's going to keep offering more and more, isn't he, Mr. Farouk?"

"It takes many days until deal is made."

Petersen tried not to groan.

"Mr. Farouk," Miss Flora said. "Is there any way to convince the sheikh that he can't have Kate for his wife?"

He thought for a moment. "Only if price you ask is too high."

"We don't dare do that," Miss Rebecca said. "What if we name one and he agrees to pay it?"

Mr. Farouk thought again, scratching his shiny head. "If the girl already is promised as a wife—"

"You mean, engaged to another man?" Miss Flora asked.

"Yes . . . But even then he may offer more for her."

Petersen gazed up at the sisters as they digested this information. "We could tell him she is betrothed to me," he said after a moment.

Miss Rebecca gave a short laugh. "The sheikh has seen the way you two fight. We all have. He'll never believe it."

"But no," Mr. Farouk said, holding up his hand. "The sheikh say he admire the golden man for keeping the girl her in place."

"Should we try it?" Miss Rebecca asked. "Do you think it will work?"

"No, no, no. It's too risky," Miss Flora said. "What if he views Petersen as a rival and challenges him to a duel or something?"

Petersen had thought of that, too.

"Well, I don't think we have any other choice, at this point," Miss Rebecca said. "I think we should try it."

"I don't like this at all," Miss Flora said, shaking her head. "We brought these two young people all the way out here with us, and I don't want to lose either one of them."

An idea suddenly occurred to Petersen. "I'll tell him that Kate is betrothed as my wife, but that I'll consider selling her if he takes us to the monastery, as he promised."

"Then what?" Flora asked.

"Then we'll hope the monks will protect us until we figure out how to get out of this desert again."

"Soren, that's brilliant!" Miss Rebecca said. "It just might work."

"I guess it's worth a try," Miss Flora agreed.

Petersen knew he would need to put on a convincing show, and he hoped the stubborn girl would have sense enough to play along with him. "Miss Flora, would you please go into the tent and tell Kate she has to do exactly what I tell her to do. Her life and everyone else's depends on it."

"I'll try."

He waited, then turned to Mr. Farouk, who looked worried and confused. Petersen wanted to shout at him and tell him this was all his fault for hiring these Bedouin in the first place. And he never should have allowed the sheikh to come along with the caravan drivers. But Soren held his temper and waited until he was calm again.

"Mr. Farouk, you need to apologize to the sheikh and explain that you were at fault for not telling me about his offer from the very beginning. Tell him I am the one he needed to approach concerning the girl, but you didn't realize my relationship to her. Tell him that Kate has been promised to me as my wife." Soren waited for Farouk to translate, glancing at Miss Rebecca to see if he was saying what he was supposed to. She gave a slight nod.

The sheikh's face darkened at the news. He glared at Petersen, which made Petersen's heart race, but he forced himself not to react. "Tell him I will call for the girl now, Mr. Farouk. And then make sure you go along with everything I do and say, understand?"

"Yes." Farouk's life was on the line, too. As soon as Farouk finished translating, Petersen stood and turned toward the tent.

"Kate! Come out here at once!" he called as loudly as he could. The sheikh wouldn't understand his words but there was no mistaking his authority. Petersen held his breath, hoping Kate would do what she was told for once in her life.

Thankfully, she did come out, but she couldn't quite manage to look submissive. Petersen was peeved to see that she was as defiant as ever, standing with her hands on her hips as she asked, "What do you want?"

"Stupid girl! Don't you realize the sheikh sees your stubbornness as a challenge? He'll want you all the more!" He reached for Kate's arm and yanked her toward him. "Tell him you're going to be my wife."

"When pigs fly," she replied.

"Don't translate that, Mr. Farouk," Petersen said quietly.

"I have an idea," Miss Rebecca said. "We'll tell him Kate's father sold her to you against Kate's will to repay a debt before he died. We'll say that you've been waiting for her time of mourning to end before you claim her."

"Good. That's good," Petersen said. He gestured to Farouk to translate. The sheikh narrowed his eyes and folded his arms across his chest as he listened. Then he began to shout.

"He's asking Mr. Farouk why he didn't explain this sooner," Miss Rebecca whispered. "He's asking for proof that it's true."

Petersen had to think fast. He wrapped his arm around Kate's shoulder and drew her close beside him. "Don't fight me, Kate, or we're all dead," he whispered to her. He could feel her body trembling, but knowing Kate, it was probably from anger, not fear. "Now, Mr. Farouk, tell him I'm willing to consider his generous offer to buy the girl from me, but not under these circumstances and not out here in the middle of nowhere. First, he needs to honor his side of the bargain and take us to the monastery, as he promised to do."

The sheikh listened to Mr. Farouk's translation but didn't reply. Petersen stared at the man, not flinching, a battle of wills. He wondered if he had earned the sheikh's respect by standing up to him—or if this would be the moment when the Bedouin would murder him, grab Kate, and disappear into the vast desert. He decided to give one last show of authority and hope Kate would play her part. He released her and spun her around, pointing to the tent. "Get back inside!"

She immediately started one of her tirades. "You think you're the big hero, don't you? But you're not! You're no better than me, and you know it. I don't have to take orders from you, Petersen. . . ." On and on she ranted as she walked to the tent, but she lifted the flap and went inside with a huff. Petersen exhaled.

The sheikh finally spoke, and Soren waited for Farouk to

translate: "The sheikh say she may be promised to you but she is a wild mare that has yet to be broken. He wants her for his wife." The sheikh spoke again, then nodded his head. "He will take us to the monastery."

Petersen tried not to sag with relief. "When?" he asked, narrowing his eyes.

"Today. They pack caravan now and go." The sheikh rose and returned to his camp with his men, taking the rug with them.

There was a flurry of activity in both camps as the tents were struck and the camels loaded. Petersen was carrying the sisters' baggage out of their tent when Miss Flora stopped him. "You did a very brave thing today, Soren. We're grateful and very proud of you." She turned to address Kate, who looked sullen. "You need to show him some gratitude, Kate. He's risking his life to try to save you and the rest of us." Kate didn't reply—but Petersen hadn't expected her to. The girl seemed incapable of being pleasant. "And we all need to thank Almighty God for answering our prayers," Miss Flora finished.

"Amen!" Miss Rebecca said.

Within the hour the Bedouin had the caravan loaded, and Petersen was swaying in the saddle as the camels plodded toward the monastery beneath the desert sun. At least he hoped that was where they were going. Their lives had been spared—for now. Maybe there was a God who had created all the stars, and maybe He did answer the prayers of good people like Miss Flora and Miss Rebecca. But when Petersen thought about his past and all the terrible things he'd done, the deaths he was responsible for . . . he doubted that God would ever be willing to answer his prayers.

CHAPTER 24

CHICAGO
1876
FOURTEEN YEARS AGO

No trees grow to the sky," Soren repeated to himself as he sat in the dark stairwell outside his family's apartment. Tears streamed silently down his face. He was five years old and certain that his mama was dying. He wiped his nose and cheeks with his fists, then tried to cover his ears, but he still could hear her terrible screams. "Go wait out in the hallway, Soren," their neighbor, Mrs. Donovan, had said when he'd begun to cry. "You can come back inside after the baby is born."

Mama gripped her belly, her moans growing worse, but she'd managed to say, "Be a good boy now, Soren." He'd done as he'd been told. The two rooms he shared with his mama and papa were on the third floor of a crowded tenement. With Mama in the first room and Papa asleep in the second, there was no other place for Soren to go but out to the hallway. The stench of mold and urine filled the windowless space. People weren't always careful when they carried their slop buckets down the steep, dark stairs every morning to empty them in the privy outside.

"No trees grow to the sky," he whispered again. That's what Mama always told him. And as he waited, he wondered if she was thinking of those words, too. There weren't many trees in the Chicago neighborhood where he lived because most of them had burned up in the Great Fire five years ago. But Soren knew what Mama meant when she said it: *Nothing lasts forever.* When he and Mama were hungry or cold, "No trees grow to the sky" meant that the bad times would end soon. And when they did have food and coal for the fire, "No trees grow to the sky" meant that they should enjoy the food and the warmth while they could.

The door behind him rattled open. Soren turned and was surprised to see his papa. "Pretty hard for us fellows to catch a nap, isn't it?" he asked, raking his hand through his tawny hair. Before Soren could reply, Papa said, "Any room for me on that step?" Soren slid over as Papa sank down beside him with a huge sigh. For most of the hours that Soren was awake, his papa was asleep. He didn't leave for work early every morning like all the other fathers in his apartment building did. Soren would wake up as they clomped down the wooden stairs in their thick shoes, but his papa was just coming home at that hour. The other men in his tenement wore work clothes that were stained and torn, and they came home at the end of the day smelling of the stockyards or the docks or the railyards. Papa didn't leave for work until after the stars came out, and he dressed from head to toe in clothes that were as black as the night.

"Hey, now. There's nothing to cry about," Papa said when he saw Soren's tears. "Your mama will be just fine in a little while." Another scream mocked his words. Soren could tell by the way Papa kept raking his fingers through his hair and clearing his throat that he was worried, too. "Sit on my lap, and I'll tell you a story. Which one do you want to hear?"

Soren scrambled onto his father's lap. "The one about the fire."

"That story?" He laughed. "That one will give you night-mares, boy." But Soren waited, hoping he would tell it anyway. "Let's see now . . . You were only a tiny baby when the fire destroyed this city. The neighborhood next to ours had caught fire the night before, but the firemen put it out, you see, before it reached us. So we figured we'd be fine when the alarm bells started ringing again on Sunday night. But then our rooms started filling with smoke, and we saw a bright yellow glow in the sky like the sun was coming up, and everyone started yelling that we needed to run. The fire was coming right at us, you see. Your mother grabbed you from your bed, but before I had time to think what to pack, we heard flames crackling on the roof—that's how fast it spread. There was a devilish wind blowing that night, you see. So we ran out the door, leaving everything behind—and just in time, too. When I looked back, I saw the roof caving in, right where we'd been sitting a moment ago.

"We kept going, hurrying to get across the river where we figured we'd be safe. The streets were filled with all kinds of people—rich and poor, young and old, all carrying sacks and trying to drag their worldly goods to safety. They chose the strangest things to save—a chair, a clock, even a birdcage with a parrot in it. I didn't have anything to carry, you see, so when people got tired and started leaving things behind, I stopped to look through some of the bundles. 'Get across the river,' I told your mother, 'and I'll meet you at the Great Central Depot by the lake.' I knew this was a golden opportunity for me to get ahead in life, you see. The flames were as high as the sky and racing toward all those grand homes near the lake, and those rich folks were running for their lives, too. Now was my chance to take whatever they left behind. They didn't want it, and it was all going to burn up anyway, so why not? Besides, there were a lot of other fellows who had the same idea as me and were doing the same thing, right?"

Soren nodded, hoping Papa would continue. He told the story a little differently each time, with one or two new details added. But Soren loved the delicious fear he felt as he listened to him describe the danger and the race to outrun the soaring flames.

"I got two nice suits of clothes that night. I put them on right overtop my own while standing in some gentleman's bedroom. One suit over the other until I looked as plump as a rich man. That way I wouldn't have to carry them, you see. But I mostly took small things, valuable things like gold jewelry and silverware and such, and I stuffed them inside some pillowcases I found. The rich people had jumped clear out of their beds without bothering to look back. I could've gotten rich that night, taking whatever I pleased from those homes, but there was no safe place to stash the goods, you see. The fire was going to eat up the whole city.

"I managed to stay just ahead of the flames as they roared across Chicago, helping myself to whatever I could find. It was like the fires of hell itself were chasing me, raining down on me like brimstone."

Soren didn't know what brimstone was, but he pressed closer against Papa's chest as he imagined Mama fleeing from it with him in her arms. If only he could help her now as she cried out in pain from the other side of the door.

"I reached the train depot, but you and your mother weren't there," Papa continued. He was well into his story now, and Soren could tell he enjoyed retelling the tale. "It was the dead of night, but the sky was almost as light as day. The heat was like standing beside an oven, and I was sweating like a dockworker with all those clothes on. The fire was spreading toward the depot, and with the flames behind me and the lake in front of me, the only way to run was north. Your brave mother fled for many miles that night with you in her arms while the firestorm chased her all the way to Lincoln Park. I found her in the cemetery the next morning with thousands of other people, leaning against a tombstone. Both of you were sound asleep. She nearly jumped out of her skin when I shook her awake. She didn't know it was me, all dressed up in my new clothes, my face and hair black with soot. She thought I had burned up." Papa laughed, but Soren didn't understand why.

"When it was all over and we could go home again, there was nothing left. We had no place to live. But neither did an awful lot of other people."

He paused, and Soren was about to ask him what happened next, when suddenly he heard a different kind of cry from behind the closed door. It was a baby's cry, like the dozens he heard every day in his tenement. "Sounds like your mama just gave us a new baby," Papa said. He looked relieved. He lifted Soren off his lap and set him down on the step before standing. "I'll go inside and see what's going on. Stay here until I come back."

Time passed slowly, and Papa didn't return. Soren kicked his feet against the steps, causing an army of black ants and several shiny roaches to scurry out of the cracks. He wished Papa would hurry up. At last their neighbor, Mrs. Donovan, opened the door behind him. "You can come inside now, Soren, and meet your new baby sister."

Mrs. Donovan led him through the first room, where Papa sat at the table with a bottle in one hand and a glass in the other, and into the second room where Mama was sitting up in bed, smiling. She was beautiful, his mama was, with golden hair and eyes as blue as the sky. "Come meet your new sister," she said. "Her name is Hilde." She let Soren climb onto the bed beside her so he could see Hilde's round, red face and tiny, clenched hands. "You'll be a good big brother and help me take care of her, won't you?" Mama asked. He nodded and took his sister's tiny hand in his. He would protect Hilde with his life the way Mama had protected him from the flames.

Soren was sleeping later that night when Hilde's cries woke him up. His father was already awake and dressed in his dark clothes. Papa lifted the baby from the wooden crate beside the bed where she'd been sleeping and kissed Hilde's forehead before placing her in Mama's arms, holding her as if she might break. "Please don't go, Erik," Mama said, clutching his sleeve. "If anything happens to you—"

"Nothing's going to happen. I have three of you to support now, don't I? I need to make a living, don't you see?"

"Then find a different job, a real job. You could work in the stockyards or down at the docks like the other men do."

He pulled free and stepped away. "I'm no good at taking orders, you know that. Putting up with some arrogant boss all day, and for what? They expect a man to break his back for a few lousy dollars. I can take in that much money and more on a good night."

"Yes, on a good night. But what about all the nights when you come home with nothing? At least the stockyards or the docks would be steady work. How will the children and I live if the police catch you and—"

"They won't catch me. I work with a good gang of lads. We know what we're doing."

"No trees grow to the sky, Erik." Soren heard the quaver of fear or maybe anger in her voice. "Some night your luck might run out."

Papa moved toward the door. "I'll be leaving now. I'll bring home something nice for you and the baby."

"Make sure you don't drink it all away!" She was clearly angry this time.

"A man has to do something to wind down after a long night's work." He closed the outside door behind him. Soren wondered why Papa's feet didn't rumble down the wooden steps like all of the other men's did. He always moved as silently as the stray cats that roamed the alley behind the apartment. After Papa was gone, Soren thought he heard his mother crying.

≫ ≪

When Soren was six and Hilde was old enough to toddle around, Mama went to work as a seamstress in a shirtwaist factory. "I need you to take care of Hilde while I'm gone," she told Soren. "Can you do that for me?"

"Why can't Hilde and I come with you?" he asked. "I want to be with you."

She smoothed the hair from his eyes, then rested her hand on his cheek for a moment. "They don't let babies like Hilde in the factory. And if I don't go to work, we may not have any food to eat or a place to live."

Tears filled Soren's eyes as he watched her go. Then Hilde started crying, too. He knew it was his job to keep her quiet while Papa slept, so he carried her down the wooden steps and outside to the front stoop. He made up games to play with her and sang all the songs that Mama had sung to him as they waited for her to return home at the end of the day. He missed his mama and wished he and Hilde didn't have to be alone all day. But no trees grow to the sky, Mama assured him as she kissed him good-bye every morning. And she was right. A second sister, Greta, was born a year after Hilde, and Mama worked at home while Papa slept, sewing buttons onto piles of thick, woolen coats that a delivery boy brought to their apartment. Now Soren had two sisters to take outside for walks and soothe when they grew hungry and rock in his arms when they were fussy. He loved Hilde and Greta with all his heart and practiced carrying both of them at the same time—one on his back and one in his arms—in case he ever needed to save them from a fire.

Then Papa struck it rich. He arrived home one morning just as the sun was rising, laughing and bragging that he'd found a gold mine like the ones in California. "Erik, you'll wake up all the neighbors," Mama said, shushing him.

He shouted all the louder. "Who cares? I got us enough loot to move out of this rathole!" He collapsed onto the bed without even taking off his shoes and was soon snoring loudly.

They didn't move after all, but for the next few months, Mama no longer had to take in piecework. Every day, she took Soren and his sisters around to the street vendors to buy potatoes and apples and sometimes a fresh chicken. It was Soren's job to carry everything home so Mama could carry baby Greta in one arm and hold Hilde's hand with the other. But then Papa's gold mine ran out, and Mama went back to work in the factory. Greta was just learning to walk by then, and once again it was Soren's job to guard his sisters while Papa slept. He didn't mind. He loved them, and they loved him.

One afternoon while Mama was still at work and the girls were napping, Papa woke up earlier than usual. "Would you like to learn a new game?" he asked Soren, "and help your mother and sisters out?"

"Yes, Papa."

"If you learn to play the game well, your mother won't have to go to work anymore."

"What game is it?" Soren asked. The only ones he knew were the games the neighborhood children played in the streets using sticks and metal hoops and other items they'd picked from the garbage.

"I'll show you in a minute, but first you need to promise me that it'll be our little secret. Just between you and me and nobody else. That way we can surprise your mother, you see?"

"Can Hilde and Greta play, too?" Soren asked.

"Sure, when they get a little older. They're not grown up yet, like you are. Let me show you what to do." To play the game, Papa would hide things like coins or maybe a leather wallet in one of his pockets. Then he would close his eyes, and Soren would have to take the coins out again without Papa knowing he had done it. They practiced every day while his sisters slept and before Mama got home, until one day Papa said Soren was ready to play the game out on the street, in a crowd of strangers.

"How will we know if the strangers want to play with us?" Soren asked.

Papa laughed out loud. "We won't, son. That's the game, you see? We're playing a trick on them, and they don't even know it. The money you get for winning the game will buy nice things for your mother and sisters. You'd like to buy them nice things, wouldn't you?"

"Hilde loves peaches," Soren replied. "So does Mama."

"That's my boy! Let's go see if we can make enough to buy them some peaches."

Soren was very good at the game. He was slender and quick, and could slip in and out of a crowd of people in the marketplace or as they waited for the streetcar, lifting coins from their pockets and items from their shopping bags without them knowing. All the while, Papa used pretty little Hilde and Greta to distract the people so they wouldn't realize what Soren was doing. They bought lots of nice things with the money from their game.

Then one morning Soren couldn't get out of bed. His head ached and his body felt as if it were on fire. He struggled to get up, panicked that the heat was from another fire. He had to save his sisters from the flames, but he couldn't seem to move. "Lie still, Soren," Mama said as she laid a cool cloth on his forehead. "It's the fever that's making you feel hot, not a real fire." He was sick for a long time, sometimes burning like a log inside the stove, and sometimes shivering with cold as if he slept outside on the back stairway as the wind blew off the lake. His insides turned to water, and he couldn't stop them from pouring out, nor could he make it all the way downstairs to the privy on fever-weakened legs. Mama took care of him, bathing his forehead and changing his clothes and whispering songs to him and Hilde, who lay curled on the bed beside him, her body as warm as a kettle of water.

When Soren finally woke up, the fever was gone—and so were Hilde and Greta. Tears welled in Mama's eyes when she told him that the angels had taken them to heaven. The sickness had been in the water—the same water that Soren carried upstairs from the spigot for his sisters to drink. "I'm sorry, Mama. I'm sorry," he wept. She told him it wasn't his fault, but he blamed himself. He was supposed to take care of Hilde and Greta and protect them. But he hadn't.

One morning a few months later, Papa didn't come home from work. He didn't come home the next morning, either. Or the next. When two weeks passed and he still hadn't returned, the landlord told Mama they had to move out. Soren helped her pack everything they owned and move it to a room in the basement of a run-down building near the railroad tracks. The only window in the room had a chip out of it that Mama stuffed with a rag to keep out the cold. The water spigot, which was a long way from the building, was always crowded with people waiting in line. The reeking outhouse overflowed whenever it rained, and the contents ran across the barren ground and into their apartment building. Soren missed his home. It held the only memories he had of Hilde and Greta. He worried that he would soon forget all of the things they'd done together, like going for walks and singing songs as they'd sat together on the front stoop.

"Where's Papa?" Soren asked. "Will he be able to find us here?"

"Your father is going to be away from us for a while," she explained. "The police caught up with him and his Swede Gang.

But don't worry. We still have each other, Soren. And remember, no trees grow to the sky. "

Soren saw his papa one last time when he went with Mama to visit him in jail. "I'll be home before long," he assured them. "They have nothing on me. Take good care of your mama for me, Soren. Promise?"

"I promise."

But they sentenced Papa to ten years in prison for robbery. Before he finished serving his first year, he died in a prison fight. Soren had just turned ten, and now it was up to him to take care of his mama.

CHAPTER 25

S oren's mama was worried. He saw it in her eyes as she slid her bowl of porridge across the table to him after he'd eaten all of his. "Here, baby, you can have mine. I'm not very hungry, and you're a growing boy." She rose from the table and walked back and forth in front of the door as if there was something terrible outside that might try to come in. He noticed as she paced that her clothes didn't fit her right, hanging on her slender body as if a person twice her size had given them to her. His stomach still rumbled, but he got up from the wobbly table, leaving the porridge for her. He had promised Papa that he would take care of her.

"I'll go get some coal for the fire," he said, pulling on his shoes. The laces had rotted away and the shoes were so tight they made his toes hurt, but they were the only shoes he had. They didn't have money for new ones now that the factory where he and Mama worked had laid them off. They'd feared the layoffs for weeks, and it had finally happened.

"There's no work to be found anywhere," one of the men

had said as Soren stood in line to be paid for the last time. "It's happening all over the city and the country, too. The rich people are losing their shirts." Soren wondered if the shirts had simply disappeared while the rich people were wearing them, and if their pants and other clothes were getting lost, too. If so, maybe he could find them. But what he really needed to find was a new pair of shoes.

Soren finished cramming his feet into his shoes and grabbed the burlap bag he used to carry coal and other items he found at the dump. "I'll be back soon," he told his mama. She surprised him by pulling him into her arms and hugging him tightly. He was as tall as she was now.

"I'll find a way to take care of us, baby, don't worry," she said. "We're going to be fine."

"I know," he said. "No trees grow to the sky." He walked for several miles along the railroad tracks, picking up pieces of coal that had fallen from the railcars. Dozens of other boys were doing the same thing, so Soren could find only pebble-sized pieces. Still, they would keep him and Mama warm. Next he picked through the debris at the dump, searching for scraps of metal to sell to the peddler and anything else of use that the rich people had discarded. He'd found the two bowls they used for their porridge that way. One was a little chipped and the other had a small crack in it, but they were better than nothing. Sometimes he'd find cooking pots that were only slightly dented, and he'd sell them at the pawn shop on the corner. What he hoped to find today were shoes that fit him. Even if he found only one shoe, which sometimes happened, at least one of his feet would be comfortable.

After a long morning of searching, Soren limped home with just the coal. He removed his shoes and carried them for the last mile, preferring cold feet over squashed ones. He wished he still could pick pockets as he had as a boy, but he was too tall and raggedy to slip through a crowd without drawing attention to himself. Besides, he smelled like the dump. People moved away from him when he got too close.

As Soren walked down the basement steps to his apartment, he heard voices inside. The door was open, and he saw Mama pleading with Mr. Fulton, their landlord, who lived on the first floor. "One more day. I promise I'll pay you tomorrow. We have no other place to go."

"Fine. One more day. Then I'll have to rent this place to someone else."

"I'm sorry I didn't find anything today," Soren said when Mr. Fulton had gone. "Maybe if I leave earlier tomorrow—"

"No, baby. I know where I can find work. I'll get money for us." She went out that night after dark, leaving him alone in the apartment. And she must have found work, because they were able to stay in their apartment for the next several months. They had enough to eat, and Mama even gave Soren a quarter to buy a pair of shoes from the ragman.

Then one night Mama fell sick. She sent Soren upstairs to ask Mrs. Fulton for help, and a few hours later, little Gunnar was born. Soren was a grown boy of twelve and much too old to cry, but he couldn't help himself as he held his baby brother for the first time. Gunnar reminded him of Hilde and Greta, and it was almost like having them back again. This time Soren vowed to take care of the new baby no matter what. A woman had come around to all the tenements warning everyone to boil their water on the stove before drinking it, and Soren made sure he never gave baby Gunnar a single drop of water that he hadn't boiled first. It was up to him to earn the rent money until Mama was back on her feet, and he managed to find work as a runner at a garment factory that recently reopened, delivering piecework to the tenements and carrying the finished goods back to the factory every day. Mama was one of his customers.

She worked long into the night earning a few pennies for each hem she stitched. Soren's little family managed to get by until Mama was able to go back to work, this time as a laundress in the Palmer House Hotel. "Take good care of Gunnar while I'm at work," she told Soren.

He scrounged through several dumps until he found enough wood and four discarded wheels to build a little wagon so he could take Gunnar with him when he made his deliveries or scavenged for coal. He dug through garbage bins behind restaurants and grocery stores and bakeries for whatever scraps of food he could find to help feed his family. Soren sang songs to Gunnar when he cried and stole clothes for him from the neighbors' clotheslines when he outgrew his. He taught Gunnar to walk and talk and slept beside him to keep him warm at night. "You're a good big brother," Mama told him. "Someday soon we'll find a better place to live than this rathole. No trees grow to the sky."

But someday never came. In the spring when Gunnar turned four years old, Mama got sick and couldn't stop vomiting. She grew so thin and weak that she couldn't go to work in the laundry. Soren asked Mrs. Fulton to come downstairs to help her. "I don't know what to tell you," she said, pinching her nose shut. "I don't suppose you have money for a doctor?" Soren shook his head. Mrs. Fulton bent down a few feet from Mama's bed and shook her awake. "Mrs. Petersen . . . ? Mrs. Petersen, is there a relative you'd like me to contact to come and help you and the boys?"

"There's no one," she said, her voice as soft as a whisper.

"You must have a family somewhere. . . ."

"Just my two boys."

Mrs. Fulton took pity on them and returned a while later with some chicken soup. "Try to get her to drink the broth, Soren. You and Gunnar can have the rest." The soup was the best Soren had ever tasted. Gunnar cried for more when it was gone. But Mama couldn't swallow a drop.

The next morning when Soren tried to wake her up, Mama didn't move. He ran upstairs to the landlord's apartment where they were eating eggs for breakfast. Soren couldn't recall the last time he'd eaten an egg. "Please help me," he begged. "Something's wrong with my mama."

Mr. Fulton came downstairs with his wife this time. He bent down beside Mama's bed to shake her awake, then quickly stood again. "Take the boys upstairs to our apartment," he told his wife. Mrs. Fulton tried to herd Soren and Gunnar toward the door, but Soren held back.

"I don't want to leave Mama here all alone. I need to help her."

Mr. Fulton shook his head. "There's nothing you can do, son, I'm sorry. She's gone."

Soren didn't have to ask where Mama had gone. The angels had taken her just like they'd taken Hilde and Greta. He crouched down and hugged Gunnar tightly. Soren was sixteen and too old to cry, but he did. Gunnar wept with him.

Eventually, Mrs. Fulton convinced Soren to come upstairs with her while her husband notified the authorities. She made eggs for them to eat and sliced thick pieces of bread. Sick as he was with grief and sorrow, Soren wolfed down the eggs and bread and watched Gunnar do the same. "Do you have any money at all to bury your mother?" Mr. Fulton asked when he came upstairs again.

Soren shook his head. He knew where Mama hid the tea tin with her money in it, but he didn't trust the man. Besides, he and Gunnar would need that money to live on. In the end, Mama was buried in a pauper's grave. Soren had no idea where.

A week later Mr. Fulton knocked on their basement door. "I don't suppose you have money for the rent, do you?" Soren showed him everything he had. He couldn't count very well and didn't know how to add up all the pennies and dimes he had earned that week. Soren was old enough for a factory job and had heard they were hiring again, but who would take care of his brother all day? Gunnar was skittish and shy and frightened of strangers. It terrified him when people yelled, and he would cling to Soren, who was the only one able to comfort him. "It's not enough," Fulton said after counting the change. "Sorry, but I have to rent this room to someone who can pay for it."

Soren tried not to reveal his panic. "I'll find a job and pay you as soon as I can."

"You're already a week behind, and I can't afford to wait. I got plenty of people wanting to move in here. Don't you have any relatives who'll take you in? Aunts and uncles?" Soren didn't know what Mr. Fulton was talking about. The only ants he knew of were the insects.

"Everyone has a family somewhere," Fulton said. Soren didn't reply. He had never heard Mama or Papa talk about a family. "I'll give you another day to think about where you can go, but I need you out of here after that."

Soren gathered up all their bedding the next evening, along with the few pots and pans they owned, and loaded everything into his wagon. He found a place in the alley behind the neighborhood bakery where the heat from the ovens came through a grate, and he built a little shelter there. He let Gunnar curl up in the wagon away from the stray rats that roamed the street and tucked the blanket around him against the cold night. "Are we going to live here from now on?" Gunnar asked.

"Just for a little while until I find a job. No trees grow to the sky, remember?"

A week later, Soren awoke just after dawn and left Gunnar sleeping while he walked down the alley to rummage through the garbage bins. He hadn't been able to find a job yet, but today he would walk across town to the stockyards and look for one there. Once he found work, he would look for a safe place nearby where his brother could hide all day.

Soren was deep in thought and worrying about finding work when he heard Gunnar scream. He dropped the rotting potatoes he'd found and raced up the alley as fast as he could. Three men stood over Gunnar and were trying to pull him out of the wagon while he screamed in terror. One was a stranger, one a policeman, and the third one, who was tugging on Gunnar's arm, was Mr. Fulton. "Let him go!" Soren shouted. Fulton quickly released Gunnar, and Soren scooped him up. "What do you think you're doing? Get out of here!"

"You boys can't live like this," Fulton said, shaking his head. "It isn't right. You'll freeze to death come winter."

"He's right," the officer said. "We can't have you sleeping in the street."

"You can't arrest us," Soren said. "We aren't doing anything wrong!" He wanted to run but knew they would easily catch him if he was carrying Gunnar. And Gunnar couldn't run fast enough to get away.

"Now, now . . . calm down," the officer said. "We're here to help you, not arrest you. Mr. Miller and I want to take you to the orphans' home where he works. You can sleep in a real bed and get plenty of food to eat."

"What are orphans?" Soren asked.

The three men looked at each other. "They're children who don't have a mother or father to take care of them," Mr. Miller, said. "We help them find new parents and a home to live in. You want a good life for your brother, don't you?" Soren didn't know what he meant by "a good life." This was the only life he knew. "Come on, you'll be safe with me, I promise."

"What about our things?" Soren asked. He still held Gunnar, who wasn't going to let go of him for any reason.

"Leave it all. This stuff is no good," Fulton said.

"Maybe not, but it's ours. It's all we have."

"Gather up what you want, then," Mr. Miller said. "But you can leave the dishes and clothes. We'll cook all your meals for you and give you new clothes at the orphanage."

Soren took the tattered blanket out of his wagon and wrapped it around Gunnar. It had always been on Mama's bed, and he remembered Papa sleeping beneath it during the day while Soren took care of Hilde and Greta. "I made the cart for Gunnar," he said. "We might need it."

"You won't need it, son," Mr. Miller said. He had a kind face and a warm smile that made it easier to do what he asked. "If you leave it here, maybe someone else can use it." Soren decided he was right. He carried Gunnar to the waiting horse and wagon. Mr. Miller patted the driver's seat and invited Soren and Gunnar to climb up beside him.

"Their mother was a good woman," Mr. Fulton said as Mr. Miller prepared to leave. "She tried hard to take good care of them. Her sons were everything to her. Make sure you find a good home for those boys, okay?"

They drove a very long way, crossing two bridges before coming to a halt in front of a large two-story building made of bricks. It had a big sign outside that Soren couldn't read. He heard children's voices, and when Mr. Miller escorted them around to the back, he saw the children playing in the yard. A kind-looking woman with gray hair and a flowered dress came out to greet them. "Welcome. I'm Mrs. Miller, the matron. We've been waiting for you. What are your names?"

"Soren Petersen. My brother is Gunnar."

"Well, this will be your new home for a little while. Come inside, and I promise we'll take good care of you."

Soren was still clutching Mama's blanket as he followed her inside with Gunnar clinging to his leg. "How old are you boys?"

Mrs. Miller asked as she led them into a huge, warm kitchen where several women were chopping vegetables and kneading bread and stirring a huge pot on the stove. The aroma of spices and baking bread made Soren's stomach rumble.

"I'm sixteen and Gunnar is four," he said. He knew their ages because Mama always kept track of their birthdays and told them whenever they turned a year older.

"Have you eaten breakfast yet?" Mrs. Miller asked. "I'm guessing you haven't since it's still early in the day. Sit here at the table and I'll fetch you each a bowl of porridge. Do you like porridge?" Soren nodded. It had been a long time since he'd had any warm food, let alone porridge. The bowlful she set in front of him was unlike any he'd ever tasted—thick and sweet and made with milk. After he and Gunnar gulped down their food, Gunnar lifted the bowl to lick it. "Would you like some more?" the matron asked. Soren was too stunned to reply. Mrs. Miller chuckled and refilled their bowls. "Eat as much as you like. You'll always have plenty of food here. When you finish, I'll fix you a warm bath and bring you some clean clothes to wear." Neither Soren nor Gunnar had ever had a bath. He couldn't get used to the feeling of being clean, as if he had exchanged his old skin for new. Afterward, Mrs. Miller led them into a large room with rows of beds. "This will be your bed, Gunnar."

"Where's Soren's bed?" he asked.

"I'll show him in a minute. You'll sleep in this room with the other boys your age, and Soren will sleep in the dormitory upstairs with boys his age."

Gunnar wrapped his arms around Soren's leg like a vine. "No! I want to stay with Soren!"

"I'm sorry, but that's not possible. We have rules—"

"I don't want to stay here! Take me home, Soren!"

"Let me talk to him," Soren said. He waited for the matron to back away, then crouched down beside Gunnar. "We need to stay here so we'll have food to eat. You don't want to be hungry anymore, do you? And wouldn't you rather sleep here than outside where the rats run around? Remember how scared you were of them?"

"I want to sleep by you."

Soren cupped his hand around his brother's ear, whispering so only Gunnar could hear him. "I'll sneak into your room and sleep right beside you as soon as everyone falls asleep, okay?" Gunnar answered with a hug.

Soren saw Miss Flora for the first time at an Easter party. She was beautiful with hair like gold, and when she walked into the dining room it was as if warm sunshine and light entered with her. She reminded him of Mama, except Miss Flora's eyes were the color of wood, and Mama's had been as blue as clear water. And Mama had been much thinner than Miss Flora, especially in the end before she died. Soren had worried that he and Gunnar would forget what Mama looked like, so he pulled his brother onto his lap and whispered, "That's what our mama looked like, remember? She had hair that color and the same beautiful smile. When we see Miss Flora, she'll help us remember her."

Miss Flora was loving and kind, too. Soren was less fearful of what would happen to them after he overheard her saying that family members could never be separated. Then Mrs. Miller told him he didn't have to sneak downstairs to sleep beside Gunnar anymore because Miss Flora was letting them bend the rules. The only time they were apart was when Soren went to school. At first Gunnar screamed and cried every morning, begging him not to go. "Why can't he come with me?" Soren asked. "I promised Mama I would take care of him."

"We'll take good care of him," Mrs. Miller said.

Soren hated school. He was so worried about his brother he couldn't concentrate. Besides, he'd never attended school and had to go to a class with kids not much older than Gunnar. He barely fit in his desk. "I missed you," Gunnar said every day when Soren got home. "Why do you have to go away all day?"

"I don't want to, but they say I have to."

❧ ❦

One bright Saturday morning the matron told everyone to wash their faces and comb their hair and put on their best clothes. Soren didn't understand why. "What's going on?" he asked a boy his age named Dan.

"Some families are coming who might want to adopt us."

"They'll look us over and choose one of us," another boy named Ronald added. "Whoever gets chosen will live in a real house with a mother and father."

"I don't believe it," Dan said.

Soren had no idea what it meant to live in a "real" house. He remembered sharing a two-room apartment with Mama and Papa and Hilde and Greta, but the angels had carried them all to heaven, and no one could ever take their places.

"They always want little kids, like your brother," Dan said. "You watch. They'll pick someone his age. Nobody ever wants us."

"You have to smile a lot," Ronald said, "and then maybe they'll choose you."

Dan shook his head. "Nah, who knows where you really end up after they take you away. We're better off here." Soren decided that living here with Gunnar was good enough for him, too. As soon as he was old enough, he would find a job and take care of Gunnar himself.

Mrs. Miller led Soren and Gunnar downstairs to the director's office when it was their turn. Soren gripped Gunnar's hand tightly so the people would know they belonged together. The woman crouched down in front of Gunnar and smiled as she asked, "How old are you, honey?"

356

"He's my brother," Soren said. "He's four, and I'm sixteen."

The woman stood again and turned to the man behind her. He shook his head, and the matron led Soren and Gunnar out of the room again. Soren wasn't sure if Gunnar understood what had just happened, but he did. And as he led his brother upstairs again to change into play clothes, he squeezed his hand tightly and said, "I promise we'll always be together, Gunnar. I'll always take care of you."

CHAPTER 26

The sky outside the window was still gray one morning when the matron came into Soren's dormitory room. "Wake up, boys," she said, shaking some of them awake. "You need to get dressed and come downstairs. Quickly, now. The new director wants everyone to line up outside in the play yard."

Gunnar lay curled in the bed alongside Soren, still asleep. Soren hated to disturb him, but he shook him gently. "Come on, Gunnar. There must be some people coming to look us over." He put on his own clothes, then helped his sleepy brother get dressed.

"I'm hungry," Gunnar said, rubbing his eyes.

"I know. We'll probably eat in a minute." He held Gunnar's hand as they walked outside to the yard and joined the rows of waiting children. They were told to stand three feet apart, but Gunnar refused to let go of Soren's hand. A few minutes later a short, dark-haired man came outside to face them, his back as stiff as an iron pole.

"I'm Mr. Wingate, the new director of this orphanage," he

358

said. "The rules are much too lax around here. From now on, order and discipline will be strictly enforced." Gunnar clung to Soren's leg as Mr. Wingate detailed his new rules and the punishments they would all face for disobeying them. He had a mean face and a snarling voice. Suddenly the director stopped and glared at Gunnar. "You there! I said to stand three feet apart. That's this far." He held up his hands to demonstrate. "Move away from each other." Soren felt his brother trembling with fear as Wingate waved the little whip he carried.

"Do what he says. Move away," Soren said, nudging Gunnar. His brother clutched his leg tighter still. Mr. Wingate took a step toward them and ordered him to move for a second time, but Gunnar was frozen in place. "What's your name?" Mr. Wingate asked as Soren tried to pry Gunnar's hands loose.

"Soren Petersen and—"

"What? Speak up!"

"I'm Soren Petersen, and this is my brother, Gunnar. He doesn't like it when people yell at him or try to separate us."

Wingate grabbed Gunnar and yanked him away, then made him stand apart from Soren. Gunnar wept in terror, but he stayed put. "As the former headmaster of a boys' school in Ohio, I've learned that everyone is happier when there's order in an institution." He went on and on about the new rules and all the chores they would have to do from now on, with new standards of cleanliness, too. He finished by saying, "My job is to find good homes and families for everyone in this school. You'd like that, wouldn't you?" Soren felt a shiver of fear. Wingate was looking at Gunnar when he asked the question.

In the weeks that followed, more people than ever came to look the children over. The new director insisted that Gunnar sleep in his own dormitory again, and he beat Soren with his little whip when he caught him sneaking downstairs at night. "Do it again, and you'll both be whipped," Wingate warned.

Soren tried to be patient and wait for Miss Flora to come back, certain she would tell the new director to keep them together. But the matron said Miss Flora was away on a trip. The entire summer passed, and she still hadn't returned. Soon the new school year began. "Please don't cry and fuss when I leave for school," he begged Gunnar, who still wasn't old enough to go. "Wingate will punish both of us if you do."

Soren hated school. The students who weren't from the orphanage mocked and taunted the orphans. But if they fought back or tried to skip school, they felt the director's whip. The moment school was dismissed each day, Soren would push his way past the others and race to the orphanage as fast as he could, where he would find Gunnar waiting for him in the play yard. "What have you been doing all day?" he would ask. "Did you have fun playing with the other kids?"

Then on a warm, sunny day in September, Gunnar wasn't waiting in his usual place when Soren arrived home from school. "Where's my brother?" he asked the playground monitor. "Have you seen Gunnar?"

The woman looked away, not at Soren. "You need to go inside and see Mr. Wingate." Soren was already breathless from running, and now the rising panic he felt made him dizzy. He couldn't make his feet move fast enough as he stumbled into the building and barged into the director's office. Wingate looked up in surprise from where he sat behind his desk.

"Where's my brother? They said you know where he is."

"First of all, you can't barge in here without knocking—"

"Tell me where he is!" Soren shouted.

Wingate stood and snatched up his little whip. "He's someplace happy and safe, with a new family to—"

"*NO!*" Soren skirted the desk with a savage cry and pushed Wingate backward against the wall. "You can't do that!" he cried, shaking him by his lapels, banging his head against the wall. "Tell me where he is! Bring him back! I want my brother!" The commotion brought Mr. Miller and some of the other workers at a run. They pried Soren away and held him back, but he continued to scream, "Give me back my brother!" Rage and grief turned him into a madman. Wingate beat Soren with his whip to make him stop struggling, but he barely felt the blows. The terrible pain in his heart was the worst he'd ever known.

"Drag him down to the basement and lock him in the coal cellar until he calms down," Wingate ordered.

"You can't separate us!" Soren screamed on the way down, thrashing and struggling to free himself. "We're brothers!"

"No, you're not," Wingate said before slamming the door shut. "Your mother was a prostitute, and your brother was a bastard. You're probably one, too!"

Soren wept and screamed for hours at the huge injustice and at his own helplessness. He beat and kicked at the door until his fists and feet were sore and his throat ached, but it did no good. On top of it all, he was sick with fear for his brother. Gunnar would be terrified. He had never been separated from Soren in his life and was afraid of strangers. He would think Soren had broken his promise and abandoned him.

When Soren finally gave up trying to batter down the door, he sat in the dark cellar planning revenge. He would torture the director until he told him where Gunnar was, then murder him with his bare hands.

Soren was in and out of his basement jail several times over the next month. He would calm down enough to be released so he could ask Mrs. Miller and her husband and anyone else who worked there if they knew where Gunnar was. Then he would see Director Wingate and be unable to control his anger. "The next time you attack me, I'll have you sent to jail," Wingate threatened before locking him in the cellar yet again. That night Wingate beat two boys from Soren's dormitory, Ron Darby and Dan Nobel, and locked them in the cellar along with him.

"We don't have to take this treatment from him," Ron said. "As soon as I get out of here, I'm running away."

"Me too," Dan said. "In fact, let's go right now. I bet we could squeeze through that chute up there." The tiny opening high on the wall was the only source of light besides the crack beneath the locked door.

"How would we climb that high?" Ron asked.

"I think I know how," Soren said. He had been considering the idea all month but couldn't manage to escape on his own. "I want to go with you."

"You're too soft," Dan sneered. "What do you know about living on the streets?"

Soren stood and inched toward them. The boys had witnessed his fury at the director, and they backed up a step. "Gunnar and I lived on the street before they brought us here. My father is a famous thief. Ever hear of the Swede Gang? He was their leader. He taught me how to steal. I'm good at it, too."

"Makes no difference to me, if you come with us," Dan said. "What's your plan for getting out of here?"

"First you have to swear that you'll help me find my brother and get even with Wingate."

"Sure. We hate him, too."

"Good. . . . We'll need to pile all the coal beneath the chute so we can climb up it. There's a shovel we can use over by the door. Then we'll lift each other up and out." They piled the shifting coal as high as they could, then Ron boosted Soren and Dan up so they could climb out. Soren leaned back inside for Ron. They were free.

Soren lived on the street with his friends for months. He tried a few times to get a regular job but couldn't control his anger whenever he was bullied or treated unfairly by the boss. He and his friends survived by breaking into houses or robbing people who made the mistake of being out on the streets after dark. Sometimes his partners became violent, beating anyone who didn't hand over his valuables quickly enough. "You don't have to hurt them," Soren said, but the other two boys seemed to enjoy it. They spent a great deal of their money getting drunk, while Soren spent his share on streetcar tickets. Each week, he rode to a different part of Chicago and walked through the parks and neighborhoods, searching for his brother. He planned to run away with Gunnar to a place where no one would ever find them. But despair overwhelmed him when his searches proved futile. He feared he would never see his brother again.

"I'm tired of listening to your excuses," Soren told his partners after nearly a year had passed. They had splurged on a cheap hotel for one night and were sitting around the dingy room, drinking. "You swore you'd help me find my brother and get even with Wingate."

"How are we supposed to do that?" Dan asked.

Soren had been pondering that question for some time. "He keeps records in his office of all the adoptions. Help me break in so I can look in his files."

"What's in it for us?" Ron asked.

"He keeps cash in his desk drawer. I was in his office one day and saw him take out a roll of bills to pay a deliveryman. Besides, I thought you wanted to get even with him, too."

Two nights later on a moonless night, Soren broke a pane of glass in the office window, reached around to unlock it, then opened the window to climb inside. Dan and Ron rifled through the desk for money while Soren went straight to the files where the records were kept. He opened a few drawers, crammed with papers, but the moonless night made it difficult to see. Besides, he couldn't read well enough to recognize Gunnar's name. He searched for *Petersen*, which he'd learned to spell in his few brief months of school, then noticed numbers on some of the drawers. Maybe they were years. He found one marked 1887 and had just begun sifting through it when he heard a shout.

"Hey! What do you think you're doing?" Wingate stood in the doorway with his cursed whip.

A year's worth of fury and frustration boiled up inside Soren and he rushed at the man, knocking him down, pummeling him with his fists. "Where's my brother? Tell me where he is or I'll kill you!" He was dimly aware of Ron calling to him, telling him to run. Mr. Miller was outside on the street, shouting for the police. Soren didn't care. He was desperate to beat the truth out of Wingate. He might have, too, if the police hadn't pried him away and thrown him in jail.

That long, hopeless night, sitting alone in a prison cell, was the lowest point of Soren's life. Would he spend the rest of his life there, dying in jail as his father had? He considered ending his life, ending the pain and grief that burned inside him, but if he did, Gunnar would never know the truth. He would think Soren didn't love him anymore. Soren longed to bury his face in his hands and weep for all the loved ones he'd lost, but he feared the violent men who shared his cell.

The next morning guards fastened a pair of heavy shackles on Soren's wrists and took him to another building across the street. He had no idea what was happening. Then he saw Miss Flora and nearly wept. She told the judge that she wanted him, and after sitting in his jail cell for a few more hours, Soren was set free. He was afraid Miss Flora would take him back to the orphanage, but instead, she took him home. A few weeks later, she and Miss Rebecca somehow made things right with Mr. Wingate and saved Soren from going to prison for attempted murder. The moment they told him the news, he silently vowed to take care of the sisters and protect them for as long as he was able.

For the first time in his life, Soren lived in a house—even though he was only a servant and slept on the third floor. It was a peaceful place, with laughter and food and music filling the downstairs rooms. Miss Flora and the others were kind and patient with him, and although their gentle treatment should have calmed his rage, it seemed to enflame it. The sisters were inseparable—as he and Gunnar should have been.

Soren would never give up searching for his brother. He saved the money the sisters paid him to buy train tickets so he and Gunnar could disappear. The sisters expected him to attend church with them every Sunday, but Soren spent the rest of the day exploring different sections of Chicago, walking up and down neighborhood streets, following the sounds of children playing, searching for him.

"Tell me what work you would like to do," Miss Flora said when he first arrived. "Is there a particular job you'd like to try?"

"I want to drive the carriage," he replied, even though he knew nothing about horses and was afraid of them. If he was out of the house and driving the sisters or Mr. Edmund around, maybe he would see Gunnar.

"Well, let's give it a try," Miss Flora replied. Soren was terrible at driving. The horses seemed wary of him; the regular driver, Andrew, grew impatient. But Soren wouldn't give up.

Then it happened. As Soren was driving the sisters home one day, he saw Gunnar walking down the opposite side of the street, holding a woman's hand. He wasn't wearing a hat, and his fair hair shone in the summer sunlight. Soren yanked on the reins and the brake, causing the horse to rear back and bringing the carriage to a screeching halt. The sisters cried out as they were jolted out of their seats. The driver in the carriage behind his, which also came to an abrupt halt, began yelling obscenities. Soren didn't care. He leaped down from the driver's seat and ran toward his brother, zigzagging through traffic as he crossed the avenue, shouting, "Gunnar! Gunnar, wait! It's me! Soren!"

The boy wasn't Gunnar.

Shock and disappointment struck him like blows. Tears blurred his vision as he returned to the carriage and tried to calm the horse and the angry driver. Then he checked on his passengers. Thankfully, both sisters were fine. "I'm sorry. . . . I'm so sorry. . . . I thought . . ." He couldn't finish.

"Soren, what's going on?" Miss Flora asked.

"I thought I saw my brother," he said, wiping his tears on his sleeve. "I've been trying to find him for so long. . . . We didn't have a chance to say good-bye. . . ."

Miss Flora took his hand. "That was very wrong of Mr. Wingate to separate you."

"Gunnar won't understand why I'm not with him. I promised I would always take care of him, and he will think I broke my promise."

"He's in a good home, you can be certain of that. The orphanage selects their adoptive families very carefully."

"I need to see for myself how he is."

"Soren, I'm so sorry. But that just isn't possible."

He nodded as if he understood, but he didn't. He climbed onto the driver's seat and drove the rest of the way home, unable to control his tears or his trembling hands.

Andrew banished him from the carriage house when he saw his bruised horse and learned what happened. "Go back inside and work as a footman, if they'll still have you. But you're not coming near my horses again." Soren slunk into the house by the back door and was passing through the hallway near the pantry when he heard the sisters talking in the kitchen.

"We should help him find his brother," Miss Rebecca was saying. Soren's heart began to race. "We could at least give him a chance to see that his brother is well cared for, and to say good-bye."

"Becky, the adoption records are sealed to everyone but the director, including me."

"That's ridiculous. You not only founded that orphanage, but you contribute great sums of your time and money to it. Why on earth can't you see the records?"

"They're kept in Mr. Wingate's office under lock and key."

"Listen, God commands us to pursue justice and to love mercy, and Soren's situation clearly falls into those categories. What was done to those brothers was a grave injustice, and we need to extend mercy to them."

"How?" Miss Flora asked.

Miss Rebecca was silent for a long moment. Soren was about to tiptoe away when she suddenly said, "We haven't gone on an adventure in a long time, Flora."

"I suppose that's true. . . . What do you have in mind?"

"Something a little unethical—and perhaps slightly illegal—but it's the right thing to do in this case. Don't you want to help right this terrible wrong?"

"Of course I do. But Gunnar has a new family now. We can't disrupt his life."

"I'm not suggesting we kidnap the child. I simply want to give Petersen a chance to visit him for a few minutes."

"I would like that, too, but Mr. Wingate isn't going to let us waltz into his office and look at his records."

"Then I suppose we'll have to break in. We'll wear masks and dress all in black and smash a window in the dead of night. This could be fun!"

Soren wondered if Miss Becky was serious. She was unlike any woman he'd ever met, and he didn't doubt for a moment that she was capable of doing it. But when Miss Flora laughed, he realized she'd been joking.

"We'll do nothing of the sort, Becky. But if you can think of a way to distract the director for a few minutes, perhaps I could sneak in and look through his files—"

"Nothing doing, Flora. I would much rather play the part of the burglar. I don't have as much to lose as you do if I get caught and sent to prison. You're a much-loved member of Chicago society. I would hate to see your reputation soiled. Or Edmund's, either, for that matter. You need to think of him."

"You just want to have all the fun, don't you?"

"Of course I do. How soon can we go on this caper?"

"Let me think. . . . Our annual Easter party is coming up in a few weeks. If Mr. Wingate is at the party with all the children, we might have a chance to sneak into his office."

"Perfect. It'll be your job to keep him occupied, Flora."

"That will be a challenge, since there's no love lost between Mr. Wingate and me."

Soren's heart had begun to beat so loudly in his ears that he didn't hear the cook come in through the back door until it was too late. "Hey, there!" she shouted. "What do you think you're doing?"

"I . . . I was just . . ."

"You were eavesdropping, weren't you?"

Miss Rebecca came to the door a moment later. "What's going on?"

"I caught Petersen eavesdropping," the cook said.

"But you were talking about me and Gunnar. I want to be there to help you, Miss Rebecca. Let me drive the carriage—"

"Absolutely not! You must promise that you'll stay right here at home and not go anywhere near the orphanage. If Mr. Wingate sees you, it will ruin everything. He'll figure out what we're up to."

Soren wanted to punch the wall in frustration. Miss Flora came to the doorway, too. "Do you trust us, Soren?" she asked. Experience had taught him to trust no one, but he had no choice. He nodded.

Soren felt as though he couldn't breathe as he watched the carriage leave on the day of the Easter party. The housekeeper put him to work polishing the silver while he waited, and it was the longest afternoon he could ever remember. The moment he heard the carriage returning, he dropped his polishing cloth and raced outside. "Did you find out where Gunnar is?"

Miss Flora smiled. "Everything went smoothly," she said. "We have his address. Let's go inside so we can talk about what comes next."

"Please, tell me where he lives," Soren begged as they went indoors. "I need to see him!"

"Rebecca and I will visit his new home first and——"

"No! I want to go with you! I want to see Gunnar! Please!" He hated to beg, but it was the only way he could see his brother. The ladies removed their hats and wraps and handed them to him to put on the hall tree, but he wasn't leaving them without an answer.

"We can't let you disrupt Gunnar's life," Flora said. "We learned that he lives in a very nice neighborhood, and his adopted father owns his own business and makes a good living. Gunnar has been with them for more than a year——"

"I need to know if they're treating him right."

"You can trust Becky and me to investigate and tell you the truth. If it isn't a good home, I promise we'll get the proper officials involved and have him taken away from his adoptive parents."

The tears that burned in Soren's eyes made him furious, but he pressed on. "I promise I won't disrupt anything. Please let me see him. Let me talk to him. I never even had a chance to say good-bye."

The sisters looked at each other, silently communicating. "Do you promise you won't try to run off with him?" Miss Becky asked.

"How can I promise that until I see how he's doing and how they're treating him?"

"If there's any abuse or mistreatment, you have my word that we'll report it to the authorities," Miss Flora said. "But we'll only give you a chance to see each other if you promise not to interfere with his new life."

"And you'll have to promise not to make a scene," Miss Rebecca added. "Can we trust you?"

Hope made Soren's heart pound painfully. "Yes. I promise."

Miss Flora turned to her sister. "Are you ready for another adventure, Becky?"

"Do I get to wear a mask this time?"

"No. But you'll probably get to tell a pack of lies, God help us all. Will that do?"

"I suppose it will have to."

Miss Flora laid her hand on his arm. "Now, I need you to understand, Soren, that it's wrong to tell lies—"

"Except to save a life," Miss Rebecca quickly added. "Or to correct an injustice when there's no other way to do it. Remember how Rahab lied to save the Hebrew spies? And didn't King David's wife, Michal, lie to save her husband from King Saul?"

Soren had no idea what they were talking about. "When do I get to see Gunnar?" he asked.

"As soon as Becky and I come up with a plan."

Soren heard them whispering and plotting all week, but they were always careful to keep him from overhearing their plans. He struggled to be patient. Even Mr. Edmund noticed how jittery and anxious Soren was while he waited. "They're going to help you, Petersen," he assured him. "You can trust them."

Finally, more than a week after the sisters learned Gunnar's address, they called him into Miss Rebecca's study after breakfast. "Here's what we've planned," she began. "We'll visit your brother's new home on the pretense that we're making a follow-up call for the orphanage."

"Now remember, lying is a terrible thing to do," Miss Flora interrupted, "and I'm sorry that we're forced to do it. We just can't see any other way to pursue justice and show God's mercy to you and your brother, so this is the way it has to be."

Miss Rebecca smiled as she rolled her eyes. "Hopefully, the Good Lord will forgive us just this once, as long as we don't get into the habit of lying or make it a way of life. Now, Flora will stay inside and talk to Gunnar's new parents about any problems they may have encountered, and ask them if they have any suggestions to make future adoptions go smoothly. Meanwhile, I'll ask Gunnar to walk outside with me—where you'll be waiting. You'll have a very small window of time to talk with him, Soren. Then we'll have to leave. Understand?" He nodded.

"No, you need to give me your word," Miss Flora said. "The same way you did after we paid all that money to bail you out of jail. You'll get us into terrible trouble if you don't keep your word."

Soren didn't want to make that promise. He had searched for Gunnar for more than a year, and now he longed to run away with him. But if he didn't do exactly as the sisters said, he might not have a chance to see him at all. He swallowed hard and said, "You have my word."

Waiting was the hardest part. The sisters didn't tell Soren when they were going until the morning arrived. Miss Flora insisted that Andrew drive the carriage, and Soren rode inside with the window shades pulled down. "So no one sees that you're with us," she said. But Soren knew it was so he wouldn't see where Gunnar lived. His stomach burned as if it were on fire.

When they first started out, he tried to pay attention and count the turns but there were too many. Besides, Andrew might be driving on a winding route on purpose. It was a gray day without any sunshine, so Soren couldn't even use the sun to keep track of which direction they were going. He listened to the sound of the road beneath the carriage wheels, and for other clues such as streetcars rumbling past and train whistles in the distance. A fishy smell in the air told him they might be near Lake Michigan or maybe the Chicago River. Then they halted, and he recognized the creaking, groaning sound of the swing bridge opening to let ships pass. Miss Flora talked to Soren all the way there, asking him questions about his brother and what their life was like before they moved to the orphanage as she tried to distract him. In the end, after traveling for more than an hour, Soren had no idea where he was.

But he would see Gunnar again. Tears sprang to his eyes just thinking about it—and he was much too old to cry. Could he really keep his promise not to snatch his brother and run? Soren decided that the answer would depend on Gunnar. If he was happy there, and if living with his new family was truly a better life than the one Soren could offer, then he would let him be. Soren had failed all of the other people he had promised to care for—Hilde, Greta, his mama—and he feared that he would fail once again with Gunnar if they ran away together.

At last the carriage halted. "We're here," Miss Rebecca said. "It's the house on the right." Soren lifted the shade and peered out. A row of trees shaded the street, and he heard birds singing. The two-story brick house had big windows and green grass in front. It was the kind of house he would never dare to dream of living in when he was Gunnar's age. Before they got out, the sisters joined hands with him so Miss Flora could pray. Soren's heart thumped so loudly in his ears he barely heard a word until she said "Amen."

"Remember, wait here in the carriage until Flora and I are both inside," Miss Rebecca told him. Soren nodded. His hands trembled as he lifted the window shade again to watch them walk up the steps and stand on the porch. A woman came to the door. He held his breath as the sisters talked with her for a moment. Was she a servant or Gunnar's new mother? What if Gunnar wasn't home? Then the woman opened the door a little wider, and Miss Flora and Miss Rebecca disappeared inside. Soren thought his heart would burst as he stepped out of the carriage.

"Good luck, Petersen," Andrew said from his perch on the driver's seat.

Soren looked up and nodded. Then he hurried around to the backyard as the sisters had instructed him to do. It was a small, grassy space with a big tree in the middle and flowers all around. He found a place to wait, half-hidden behind a bush, and watched the back door. After what seemed like an eternity, Miss Rebecca came outside, holding Gunnar's hand. Soren's vision blurred with tears as he stepped from the bushes, careful not to startle his brother. "Hey, Gunnar. Remember me?"

"Soren!" His brother gave a cry of joy and raced into his arms. His little body felt different to Soren after more than a year—stronger, more filled out—yet achingly familiar. They belonged together, he was convinced of that.

"Hey, let's have a look at you," Soren said as he pulled away, wiping his eyes. "You look great, Gunnar. I see you got some new clothes. Those look like pretty nice shoes, too."

"They told me you didn't want to be my brother anymore," Gunnar wailed. The look of desolation on his face ripped Soren's heart in two. He pulled him into his arms again.

"That's a lie, Gunnar! The man at the orphanage tricked both of us. You'll always be my brother, forever and ever. Nothing will ever change that. That's why I came here today. I've been trying to find you ever since they stole you away from the orphan's home. I've been searching and searching, taking streetcars to every neighborhood in Chicago. Miss Flora and Miss Rebecca helped me find you."

"Can I go home with you now?"

Soren closed his eyes. How he longed to take him home! He chose his words carefully, aware that Miss Rebecca was listening. "Do they treat you pretty good here?"

"Yes. . . . I have a new mama and papa now," Gunnar said, managing a weak smile. He wasn't thin anymore, and his cheeks looked as bright and healthy as two red apples. He must be eating well and playing in the fresh air and sleeping in a soft bed at night, with a mother to kiss him and sing to him the way their mama used to do. Soren knew he couldn't give his brother any of those things. He brushed his fingers through Gunnar's silky hair.

"That's great, Gunnar. Do you have fun with your new family?"

"Papa carries me on his shoulders when we go to the park, way up high in the air. And Mama reads me stories at night. . . ." Soren looked away, swallowing tears.

"That's good, then. They must love you, right? And you love them?"

"Yes . . . but I miss you, Soren. I want to be with you."

He remembered how he'd failed to take care of Hilde and Greta and knew he couldn't take care of Gunnar, either. Miss Flora was right—this was where Gunnar belonged. Soren loved him more than anyone in the world. He had to do the right thing. "You have a pretty nice home, here," he said, gesturing to it. "I can't give you a house like this or nice clothes to wear or food to eat. I would love to do all those things for you . . . but I can't." The truth was like a knife in his heart.

"Why don't you come here and live with us? I'll ask Papa if—"

Soren pulled him into his arms again and held him tightly.

"No, don't do that. Don't say anything to your new papa. He doesn't know that I came to see you today. He might get mad at Miss Flora if he finds out, and I don't want to get her into trouble."

"But I don't want you to go away again."

"And I don't want to go, believe me. But it's just for now. Remember what Mama always said?"

"No trees grow to the sky," Gunnar said softly.

"That's right. We have to live apart for now. But I promise I'll come back, Gunnar. Miss Flora and Miss Rebecca will help us figure out a way that we can see each other once in a while." He looked up at Miss Rebecca from where he was kneeling in the grass and saw her nod as she dabbed her eyes with her handkerchief. "I'm a grown man, Gunnar, too old to have parents taking care of me. But I'm glad that you have a mama and papa who love you."

"Do you still live in the orphan home?"

"No, I work for Miss Flora and Miss Rebecca. I live in a nice house, too."

"I'm sorry, but it's time to go," Miss Rebecca said, glancing at the back door.

Soren hugged his brother again. "I have to say good-bye. It may take a while, but I'll be back to see you again."

"Promise?"

"I promise." He squeezed him tightly one last time. "Now dry your eyes and go inside with Miss Rebecca, and don't let anyone see that you've been crying. This has to be our special secret for now." Gunnar hugged him in return. How Soren missed the warmth of him, the comfort he felt by having him near. "See you soon," Soren whispered, then released him.

Miss Rebecca reached for Gunnar's hand. Soren watched them go up the back stairs and into the house. He turned and sprinted back to the carriage and ducked inside. Then his tears came. He covered his face with his hands and sobbed for all the people he had loved and lost—for Mama and Papa, Hilde and Greta, and most of all, for Gunnar. He considered leaping out of the carriage again and hiding in the bushes where the sisters couldn't find him. Maybe he could live on the streets and watch his brother from afar and talk to him once in a while. But Soren didn't run. Gunnar was happy here. Besides, the sisters trusted him to keep his word.

They came out of the house a few minutes later and climbed in beside him. "Thank you, Lord," Miss Flora said with a huge sigh. "Everything went well." Miss Rebecca closed the curtains again as Andrew whistled to the team and the carriage rolled forward.

Soren wanted to say something to them, to thank them for helping him find his brother and giving them a chance to see each other. But he couldn't speak past the knot that choked his throat. Saying good-bye to Gunnar was the hardest thing he had ever done.

CHAPTER 27

CHICAGO
1889
ONE YEAR AGO

S oren took each step carefully, trying to keep the tray of food
steady and not spill anything as he climbed the stairs to
Mr. Edmund's bedroom. What had begun as a bad cough
had left Mr. Edmund bedridden, and Soren had been taking
care of him for several weeks, helping him use the bathroom,
fetching things for him, carrying food upstairs when he felt well
enough to eat—and ushering in the steady stream of doctors
who came with medicines and poultices and remedies to ease
Mr. Edmund's cough and fever. Nothing helped, and his cough
was so bad at times he couldn't catch his breath. Soren had to
pound his back until he could breathe again.

He reached the bedroom without spilling anything and set the
tray on a small table. "Thank you, Petersen," Mr. Edmund said.
"Will you help me sit up?" Soren gently gripped him beneath his
arms, propping pillows behind him to make him comfortable.
He felt so much thinner than before he got sick.

"Cook sent up a cup of tea and some toast for you, too,

Miss Flora," Soren told her. "Would you like them there by your chair?"

"Yes, please. That would be wonderful." Miss Flora was still in her dressing gown, her golden hair in a long braid. She had spent the past few nights sleeping in a chair near her husband while Soren slept on a cot in Mr. Edmund's dressing room so he would be nearby if they needed him. He brought Miss Flora the tea and toast, then set the breakfast tray on Mr. Edmund's lap. His hands were so shaky, Soren had to help him eat.

Miss Flora read books aloud to her husband when he was awake, which meant Soren also got to hear them—tales of danger and exploits in faraway places like Troy and Greece. The stories made Soren wonder what the world was like beyond Chicago, and what it would be like to travel there. Miss Flora spent the long hours when Mr. Edmund was asleep teaching Soren to read and write. "You're doing so well," she'd told him last week. "Soon you'll be able to read books to Mr. Edmund yourself." They were also learning numbers and how to add, subtract, multiply, and divide them.

Soren lifted the cup of tea to Mr. Edmund's lips so he could take a swallow. "I hate it that my illness is spoiling everyone's plans." Edmund spoke in a near-whisper to avoid starting a coughing fit.

"I don't have any plans, Edmund, dear, except to help you get well."

"But summer is nearly here, and I won't be able to travel to the Sinai as we'd planned. You and Rebecca must go without me."

"Nonsense. We can forego a summer of traveling while you recover."

"But Rebecca has been working so hard to learn photography for our trip, and I know how eager she is to find more manuscripts so she can convince Timothy—" He began to cough and couldn't finish. Miss Flora set down her cup and went to sit beside him on the bed.

"Don't fuss about it, Edmund. There's always next year. The monastery and its manuscripts aren't going anywhere."

"What about your Sunday schools?" he asked after Soren helped him swallow some water. "You haven't gone to work there since I became ill."

"I'm certain they're surviving without me."

"But I don't want you to stop doing your charity work. Please, hire a nurse to stay with me so you and Rebecca can go next Sunday." Miss Flora started to protest, but he put his pale fingers over her lips. "Petersen will go with you, won't you?" he asked, turning to him. "The church is in a rather rough part of town. Andrew will be driving, but I would feel better if you were there as well."

"Yes, sir. I'll be glad to go."

"Then it's settled. Don't argue with me, Flora, or I may start coughing again." He smiled at her, then lifted a piece of toast in his shaky hand and took a tiny bite.

Soren rode with Miss Flora and Miss Rebecca to one of their Sunday schools the following week. Memories of his childhood and of his mama and papa came flooding back to him when he saw the crowds of raggedy children streaming into the church. He had grown up with children like these, scavenged for coal with them along the railroad tracks, fought over the same garbage cans for something to eat. Back then, Soren never could have imagined living in a mansion. He listened to the sisters teaching the Bible lesson and thought about how much they had done for him. And he thought of Gunnar. His brother wouldn't grow up in a tenement or play on a dirty street like these children. He wouldn't die from drinking bad water like Hilde and Greta had. Soren knew he should be happy for Gunnar, but the ache in his chest whenever he thought of him refused to go away.

Nearly an hour had passed when Soren saw a girl slip in through the back door, then halt to look around. Miss Rebecca had finished the Bible story and the children had divided up into groups to study reading and writing. The girl looked nervous, as if ready to run if she didn't like what she saw. Bright red hair peeked out from beneath her bowler hat, and she was dressed funny, wearing what looked like a man's shirt and nothing more over her petticoat and bloomers. Soren guessed her to be in her late teens—older than most of the other children. Miss Flora saw her, too, and hurried over to greet her.

"Hello, are you new here? I'm Miss Flora. What's your name?"

"Kate." She continued looking around, as if searching for all the exits. Soren had acted the same way when he'd lived on the streets with Ronald and Dan.

"I'm afraid you're too late for the Bible story," Miss Flora said, "but would you like to learn to read or to write your name?" She reached out to touch Kate's arm, but the girl flinched and backed away.

"I'll just watch."

"That's fine. But if you change your mind, please join us." Miss Flora returned to her students. Soren watched the girl for a while as she inched further into the room as if she might join in after all, but he eventually lost interest in her and began to daydream. He was worried about Mr. Edmund and his worsening cough. The doctors continued to come and go, and Miss Flora and Miss Rebecca continued to pray, but neither the prayers nor the medicines seemed to do any good.

Suddenly an abrupt movement caught Soren's attention. The red-haired girl sprinted past him in a flash, racing toward the door with Miss Flora's purse in her hand! Soren chased after her, but Kate was far enough ahead to slam the heavy door in his face. By the time he jerked it open to follow her outside, she had disappeared. He spent the next twenty minutes searching behind garbage cans and down narrow alleyways, but she had vanished. Soren kicked an empty bin in frustration, furious with the girl and with himself. Mr. Edmund had asked him to look after Miss Flora, and he had failed. Her purse was gone.

"Never mind," Miss Flora said when Soren returned inside in defeat. "The Lord must know that poor child needs the money more than I do."

How could Miss Flora feel pity for her? She was nothing but a dirty thief—just like him. Soren couldn't meet Miss Flora's gaze as he remembered all the people he'd robbed, the street vendors he'd stolen from. He and his friends had once robbed a drunken man, then beaten him and left him lying in the street. Soren felt deep remorse for what he'd done in the past, and worse still for not staying alert today. Kate deserved to go to jail for robbing the sisters. They did so much to help the poor—and him.

Soren stood guard the following Sunday, watching to see if the red-haired thief would be bold enough to return and steal from them again. He scanned the streets all the way there and back, searching for the girl in the bowler hat, but there was no sign of her.

≫ ≪

The following Saturday morning, Professor Dyk arrived at the sisters' home for a visit. He'd become a regular guest, and he greeted Soren with a huge grin and a clap on the back when he answered the front door. "How are you today, Petersen?"

"Fine, sir. Thank you."

"Good. Glad to hear it." He chatted with Petersen, telling him about the streetcars he'd taken to get there and how busy the traffic had been. Soren liked Professor Dyk almost as much as he liked Mr. Edmund. He had a funny, bumbling way about him and always took time to talk with Soren and the other servants. Soren was waiting for a chance to ask if he could take the professor's hat when Miss Rebecca came out of her study and beckoned to them.

"Stop talking that poor boy's ear off, Timothy, and come inside. . . . You, too, Petersen, there's something we want to tell you." He followed her and the professor inside, surprised to see Miss Rebecca's camera equipment packed in carrying cases near the door.

Miss Rebecca smiled as she turned to Soren. "We didn't want to mention it until we were certain, Petersen, but we've made arrangements for you to visit with Gunnar. There will be no sneaking around this time, either. His new parents were very upset to learn that you and he had been separated, and—"

"When?" he interrupted.

"Today."

Soren opened his mouth to speak, but nothing came out. His heart raced so fast he feared it would burst.

"Flora and I went back to speak with them, and although they were sympathetic, they expressed concern that seeing you again would disrupt Gunnar's new life. He's still a very sensitive child. So they asked if we could start with a short trial meeting today, to see how Gunnar reacts. And since they didn't wish us to come to their home, we've arranged to meet beside the bear cage at the Lincoln Park Zoological Garden."

"I—I don't know what to say. . . ."

"You don't need to say anything, Petersen. Now, if you wouldn't mind helping me with my camera things, we can be on our way. I'm going to ask Gunnar's parents if I can take a photograph of you and him together, so you'll each have a picture to look at while you're apart."

Soren quickly bent to gather up the cases and tripod, hoping Miss Rebecca wouldn't see his tears. Andrew had the carriage waiting outside. Within minutes they'd loaded the camera equipment and were on their way. Miss Rebecca had been learning to take photographs for several months now, and copies of her work were in frames all over the house. She'd had carpenters build a darkroom in the basement, and she'd invited Soren to come downstairs and help her develop the pictures. He loved watching the faded images emerge from the pan of pungent liquid and hanging them up on the little line to dry.

Soren's stomach churned with excitement as he sat on the seat beside Andrew. He was glad they hadn't told him about this visit sooner, or he would have been too distracted to do anything else. Even now, everything was happening so fast he wasn't entirely sure that he was awake and not dreaming. It was a beautiful fall day and Professor Dyk and Miss Rebecca rode with the carriage top open on the way to the park. He could hear them talking and laughing as they headed toward the city.

"Isn't this a gorgeous day?" Miss Rebecca asked.

"Spectacular! If you would just give in and marry me, every day would be as beautiful as this one."

"You know I'd marry you this afternoon if you were a believer. What will it take, Timothy? Why can't you just let go and make that leap of faith?"

"I can't answer that. . . . I honestly don't know."

"What obstacle is your too-logical mind stumbling over today?"

"Rebecca, my love, I did as you asked and read the Gospel of Matthew, and I don't understand how a brilliant woman like you can honestly believe that Jesus performed all those miracles. Walking on water? How can a rational person be expected to believe anything that contradicts science? This is the problem I have with all religions. From the very beginning of history, primitive people have invented gods to explain things in nature. As science continues to progress, no one will believe in supernatural miracles anymore."

"Miracles are absurd only if you don't believe in an all-powerful God. You shouldn't look at just that isolated story in Scripture but at the totality of the Bible. It provides a picture of who God is and what He's like. Once you know Him, Timothy, once you've felt the enormity of His love, you'll know He's capable of miracles. Isn't life itself a miracle? The love of a man and a woman? A child growing in its mother's womb? A caterpillar becoming a butterfly? The only reason we don't recognize them as miracles is because we're used to them. As for walking on water, the New Testament was written when eyewitnesses to these events still lived."

"How do you know the stories weren't changed and embellished by later copyists?"

"Here we go again," Miss Rebecca said. "We've had this argument before, and I don't care to rehash it. Besides, there's Lincoln Park up ahead. Let's not spoil this lovely day. We'll finish this discussion later."

Soren had been to Lincoln Park before. During the year that he'd lived on the street, it was one of the places he visited to search for Gunnar. Today he would really see him. He lifted Miss Rebecca's camera equipment out of the carriage and carried it down the walkway toward the bear cage. He hoped he wouldn't have to wait long. He'd never endure the suspense. What if Gunnar's family changed their minds and decided not come after all . . .

Then Soren saw him! Gunnar stood beside the cage, looking at the crowd, not the bear. When he saw Soren, he let go of the well-dressed man's hand and raced toward him. Soren set down the camera cases and pulled his brother into his arms, holding him tightly. He was determined not to cry or do anything else to upset Gunnar. This must go well so they could see each other more often.

While Miss Rebecca and the professor talked with Gunnar's parents, Soren sat down on the grass and pulled Gunnar onto his lap. "You're so big now, Gunnar. Tell me how you've been. Do you go to school now?"

Gunnar told him all about his life, and Soren had never seen his brother so happy and talkative. He was most excited about the new puppy his parents had bought for him. "I wanted to bring him to meet you," Gunnar said, "but Papa said maybe next time. You're going to come and see me again, aren't you?"

"I would love to. But it's going to depend on you, Gunnar. You have to be a big boy and not cry when our time is up today because your mama and papa don't want you to be upset. If you fuss, they won't let us see each other. Can you be brave and trust me when I say that I'll come back again?"

"Why can't you live with us?"

"Because I have a job now. And you have to go to school."

"Then why can't I live with you?"

Soren longed to bring his brother home so they could be together every day. The pain of their unjust separation welled within him. But he knew that he needed to control himself or he would lose Gunnar forever. "Your new mama and papa would miss you very much if you lived with me. And wouldn't you miss them, too? And your new puppy? This is what's best for all of us. I'm still your brother, and I still love you very, very much. And from now on, we'll see each other as often as we can."

They talked for nearly an hour, until Soren noticed Gunnar's parents moving closer. His mother looked anxious. "Miss Hawes would like to take your picture now, Gunnar," she said. "And then it will be time for us to go." Miss Rebecca had the camera and tripod all set up by a park bench and was waiting for them to sit for their photograph.

"Remember . . . no crying," Soren whispered as they looked up at the camera. They shared one last hug, and their time together was over.

Soren felt a mixture of joy and pain on the ride home. He wanted to ask Miss Rebecca if they could go down to the basement and develop the pictures right away. But before Soren could swivel around on the seat to ask her, she and the professor started debating again.

"The world is so complex, Timothy. You saw those zoo animals today—how can you possibly believe that a bison or a bear evolved from a simpler species?"

"How can you believe that they all fit into a giant boat?"

Miss Rebecca huffed in irritation. "Even if I were willing to accept that they did evolve, where did that first specie of animal come from? Where did the minerals and other components of life come from?"

"I trust science will discover the answers to your questions in the future."

"Just for once, Timothy, use your heart instead of your mind. You've made reason and logic your god—which is exactly why ancient cultures made idols of wood and stone. They only believed in gods they could see and touch. You're doing the same thing!"

She had raised her voice, and the professor gently shushed her. "Let's not argue, my dear. Petersen has just had a wonderful visit with his brother. Let's enjoy the afternoon."

Much to Soren's disappointment, Miss Rebecca didn't have a chance to develop her photographs that day. He would have to wait. He was taking care of Mr. Edmund a few days later when the professor came upstairs to visit him. Mr. Edmund was so weak after a night of terrible coughing that he couldn't sit up or even feed himself without help. Soren feared he was dying, and he didn't want to lose him, too.

"Should I come back at a better time?" Professor Dyk asked.

"No, come in and keep me company," Mr. Edmund said, opening his eyes. Soren was sitting at a little table, doing the page of arithmetic problems Miss Flora had given him. He rose to leave, but Mr. Edmund said, "You may stay and finish your work, son. You won't bother us."

Soren concentrated on his work, not really listening to the men until the professor's voice grew louder. "Believe me, Edmund. I've thought about how easy it would be to say that I believe what you and Rebecca and Flora do. I would be able to spend the rest of my life with her. But it would be a lie, and I can't bring myself to lie to the woman I love."

Mr. Edmund managed a weak smile. "But if there's no God, no standard of right and wrong, then what makes you believe that telling a lie is morally wrong?"

The professor laughed. "I suppose you have a point. But Rebecca believes that it's wrong to misrepresent one's faith, and I don't want to debase myself in her eyes. It's bad enough that she thinks less of me for not being a Christian. The least I can do is adopt her standards of right and wrong."

"She loves you very much."

"I know she does . . . I know. And I love her."

"You're not drawn just to Rebecca's mind, you know, but to her soul—and that's the Holy Spirit living in her. Let me ask you something, Timothy. Where do you suppose love originates? Is it purely biological? Something that has evolved in our hearts and minds as we've evolved from the lower species as Mr. Darwin believes?"

"That's an interesting question. . . . I suppose it must have."

"Or could there be another explanation? Perhaps we love because we are made in the image of a God who loves. How would it change your thinking if you knew that what you felt for Rebecca is just a tiny taste of what the God who created the universe feels for you?"

Soren looked up. Was it possible that God loved him as much as Soren loved Gunnar? That was a lot! He would die for his brother. And according to the minister at church, that was exactly what Jesus had done.

"I've seen too much suffering," the professor said, "including what you're currently enduring, to ever believe in a loving God."

"We've talked about the issue of suffering before. I've explained how the evil in this world was man's choice, not God's. How His Son suffered and died to set us free from that evil."

"Then why aren't we free? Why does the darkness continue?"

"I won't pretend to know all the answers, but I believe that one of the reasons God delays in judging evil is because He's waiting for everyone the world over to have a chance to know Him. Every tribe and nation and tongue and language. As for my suffering, the Bible says 'the sufferings of this present time are not worthy to be compared with the glory which shall be revealed in us.' What you see isn't all there is."

"You believe in heaven, then? Without any scientific proof?"

"Yes. I find it quite easy to believe in heaven because I've seen little glimpses of it here on earth. Holding my wife in my arms, laughing together—that's a tiny piece of heaven. Looking at the beautiful world God created just for us, the millions of stars in the universe, the variety of flowers and animals. God created earth as our home, and it was the perfect place for us to live until evil was introduced."

"You believe in a devil with horns and a pitchfork?"

"You fought in the War Between the States, Timothy. You saw firsthand what man is capable of doing to his fellowman and the inhumane way the slaves were treated. That's evil. You can't deny it exists."

"We don't seem to have learned too many lessons from history, have we?"

"Jesus died to redeem us from evil. He rose again from the dead, and so I know that I will, too. We'll live forever on a brand-new earth. In the meantime, God gives each of us a task to do to help reclaim His kingdom, one life at a time. "

Professor Dyk didn't reply. Was he convinced by what Mr. Edmund had said? Was Soren? As he waited for the men to speak again, it occurred to him that Mr. Edmund had been speaking a lot without pausing to cough.

"You always give me much to think about, Edmund," the professor finally said. "I didn't mean to stay this long and tire you out. I'll stop in again another day."

"How's your arithmetic coming along?" Mr. Edmund asked after Professor Dyk was gone. Soren handed him the completed page of problems. Mr. Edmund looked it over, then smiled. "You're a very smart young man, Petersen. Keep studying."

Soren looked at the untouched glass of water on his nightstand, the tray of uneaten food, then back at Mr. Edmund, whose skin looked as pale as the piece of paper in his hand. "Is there anything you need?" he asked. "Can I get something for you?"

"No, please sit down, Petersen. I want to ask you something." Soren perched on the edge of the chair where the professor had just sat, ready to spring up at a moment's notice. "I may be going to heaven before too much longer," Mr. Edmund said, "and I want to ask you to do something for me. . . . Will you help take good care of my wife and her sister for me? They are very special ladies, and they're both very fond of you. If I don't get well, I need you to watch out for them after I die. They have each other and their faith, so they'll keep going. But it might take a little while until they're back on their feet again."

Soren wanted to refuse. He needed to tell Mr. Edmund that he was no good at taking care of people. He had promised to take care of Hilde and Greta, and they'd died. He'd promised Papa that he would take care of Mama, and she'd died. He'd promised Gunnar that he would always take care of him, and he'd failed. Now his job was to take care of Mr. Edmund, and he was dying, too. Soren cleared his throat. He had to say something. Mr. Edmund was waiting.

"I promise," he said at last.

"Good. That's good. Thank you, Soren. I know I can trust you." He reached out and took Soren's hand, holding it between his own.

⇒ ⇐

Miss Flora and Miss Rebecca were praying so hard for Mr. Edmund to get well, and so many doctors were coming and going with their medicines, that Soren didn't want to ask when he'd be able to see Gunnar again. For now, he had the photograph Miss Rebecca had taken of the two of them, and she had sent one to Gunnar, too, so his brother wouldn't forget him. In the meantime, Soren took his task of looking after the sisters very seriously. Whenever they volunteered at the Sunday school, Soren went with them. He was standing in the back of the room listening to Miss Rebecca tell how Jesus raised Lazarus from the dead and wishing that Jesus would heal Mr. Edmund, too, when he saw her—the thieving little redheaded girl named Kate. She wore a straw hat this time to cover up her hair, but he recognized her just the same. He watched as she edged into the room, and he positioned himself near the door as he waited to catch her in the act. Miss Flora approached her and spoke with her, but the girl shook her head. Had Miss Flora recognized her? Probably not, because she returned to the other children.

Soren never took his eyes off Kate as she drifted closer to Miss Flora's purse. The moment she put her hands on it, Soren sprang across the room and grabbed her. "Stop! Thief!" he shouted as he wrenched the purse from her hands. He had his other arm around Kate's waist, gripping her tightly as she squirmed to free herself.

390

"Let me go!" she yelled, punching and kicking Soren. He was taller and much stronger and didn't mind the blows.

"This is the same girl who stole from you before," he said, yanking off her hat. "I'll hold on to her while you send for the police."

The children had abandoned their schoolwork to gather around and stare wide-eyed at the drama. But instead of calling for the police, Miss Flora said, "Let's go into the church sanctuary while we deal with this so the children can continue their studies." Soren dragged the girl through the doorway and into the church with Miss Flora and Miss Rebecca following. Once Kate was inside, the hushed stillness seemed to calm her. She stopped struggling and gazed up at the stained-glass windows, sparkling like jewels, and at the wooden cross hanging in the front of the sanctuary.

"What's your name, dear?" Miss Flora asked.

"Kate Rafferty."

"I would hate to see a lovely young lady like you go to jail. Why don't you tell me what you need money for?"

"To live," she said with a defiant look. She didn't seem the least bit remorseful or ashamed that she'd been caught.

"Are you having trouble finding a job?"

"I had a job in a factory, but I hated it."

"Becky and I understand," Miss Flora said. "We tried working in a garment factory, and the conditions were so horrendous we only lasted one day." Kate relaxed in Soren's arms, but he knew it was a trick. The moment he eased his grip, she would take off. She kept glancing over her shoulder at the door, as if looking for someone. Soren wondered if she had an accomplice. He gripped her tighter.

"Do you live nearby? Do you have a family?" Miss Rebecca asked.

"That's none of your business."

"Well, in a way it is our business," Miss Rebecca said, "for two reasons. One is that you chose to rob us—twice, if I'm not mistaken—so we're connected by your crime. And second, your welfare is our business because the Bible says we must help the poor and the homeless who come our way. I'm asking for information because I'm trying to determine the best way to help you."

"I don't live anywhere," Kate said. "I need money to eat."

"How old are you?" Miss Flora asked. "Perhaps you can live at the orphan's home that we—"

"I'm not an orphan. I'm eighteen and old enough to take care of myself."

"Stealing from people is hardly a proper means of taking care of yourself," Miss Rebecca said. "Listen, I don't suppose you can repay the money you already stole from us, can you?"

"'Course not. I came back for more, didn't I?"

"Here's the thing," she continued. "The Bible says that if a thief can't pay for what she's stolen, she must work to pay off the debt, plus an additional fine. Have you ever worked as a servant, Kate?"

"Ha! Who would have me?" she asked gesturing to her ragged clothing. She was no longer wearing only a man's shirt over her petticoat, but her well-worn blouse and skirt looked as though they belonged to a much larger woman.

"We'd be willing to take you to our home in Evanston," Miss Flora said, "and give you food and a warm place to live. But in return, you would have to work to repay the money you stole."

"Unless you'd rather go to jail," Miss Rebecca added. "They'll give you a bed and a hot meal there, too."

"But if you work hard, Kate, it could become a paying job for you in the future."

Soren couldn't believe what he was hearing. The sisters didn't need another servant. How could they even trust a thief like Kate in their home? Then he recalled how they had trusted him and brought him into their home. And he'd done much worse things than simply steal.

"What do you say?" Miss Flora asked.

Kate glanced toward the door again. "I got nothing to lose. I'll do it." Soren thought the sisters had plenty to lose if Kate betrayed their trust.

"Do you need to tell your parents or anyone else where you're going or that you'll be staying with us?" Miss Flora asked. "We could stop and pick up your belongings—"

"I got nothing and nobody. And you can let go of me, now," she told Soren. "You're hurting my arms."

"How do I know you won't run if I let go?"

"'Cause I said I won't."

Miss Flora nodded, and Soren released her. But he was braced to grab her again if she bolted. Kate rubbed her skinny arms. "Now what?"

"Give us a few minutes to finish up here at the church, and we'll be on our way," Miss Rebecca said.

Soren stuck close to Kate's side once they arrived home, watching her survey the beautiful house and its furnishings with the greedy eyes of a thief. It seemed suspicious to him that Kate would be so eager to begin a completely new life, especially since it meant taking orders and learning manners. He'd had his own reasons for doing it—to find his brother, in the beginning, and later because the sisters had promised to help him visit Gunnar. As time passed, he'd wanted to help the sisters because they'd been good to him. But what were Kate's motives? He wished he knew. He wouldn't be able to watch her continually, and it worried him.

The housekeeper led Kate away to be fed and bathed and dressed in a simple maid's uniform. Soren turned to the sisters and asked, "How do you know she won't steal from you again and take off with something?"

"She might," Miss Rebecca replied. "But that's a risk I believe God would have us take."

"We need to show her grace, Soren," Miss Flora added. "Jesus said, 'Freely ye have received, freely give.' We must pray for her, too—not that she'll change into what we want her to be, but that she'll become all that God intends her to be."

"Do you suppose He intends her to be a thief?" Miss Rebecca asked.

Miss Flora laughed. "You're outrageous, Becky!"

⇛ ⇚

Soren thought Kate looked ridiculous in a gray maid's uniform and white apron—like a stubborn mule wearing a bonnet. Kate always looked disheveled and smudged, and when the sisters tried teaching her to serve at the table, she kept dropping things. The cook refused to allow Kate in the kitchen. "I keep knives in here," she said, "and that girl can't control her temper." The housekeeper lost patience with Kate after she knocked over the scrub bucket three times in one day and tried to start a fire in the parlor fireplace without opening the flue. Miss Flora decided to teach Kate to be a lady's maid, which Soren guessed meant taking care of Miss Flora the way he took care of Mr. Edmund—laying out her clothes, making sure they were clean and pressed, hanging them up again, freshening Miss Flora's bonnets and gloves. With Kate's newest job, Soren bumped into her all the time because Miss Flora and Mr. Edmund shared the same bedroom. Mr. Edmund had his closet and dressing area on one side of it, and Miss Flora had hers on the other.

Miss Flora was endlessly patient with Kate, even though in Soren's eyes, she was useless. "I know Kate is a bit of a challenge," he overheard Miss Flora telling Miss Rebecca, "but it would be cruel to send her back into the streets. And she's too wild to work for anyone else." Soren thought she was like a banked fire. All it took was a breath of wind—usually from him—for Kate to erupt into flames.

Soren hardly noticed it at first, but Mr. Edmund's health slowly began to improve. He stopped coughing. His color improved. He regained the weight he'd lost. His doctors called it a miracle. By the time winter ended, he was strong enough to get dressed and take his meals downstairs. By spring he was able to attend church, and he talked about returning to work.

"You would think Timothy could see how our prayers for you have been answered," Miss Rebecca said one day on the way to church. "But he gives all the credit to the doctors."

"Then we must make sure Timothy hears the truth from them," Mr. Edmund said. "Dr. Owens says he can't account for my recovery."

"I'm getting nowhere with Timothy," Miss Rebecca said with a sigh.

"You'll never be able to convince him, Rebecca," Mr. Edmund said. "Only the Holy Spirit can do that."

"I know, I know. But the other day he went on and on about not believing in the accuracy of the Scriptures, and it got me thinking. Remember how we talked about going to the Sinai to search for ancient manuscripts? What if we planned a trip this coming summer?"

"I don't know," Miss Flora said. "I'm afraid a trip like that would be too rigorous for Edmund so soon after his illness. Perhaps we should wait—"

"Nothing doing!" Mr. Edmund interrupted. "I won't have you postponing your trip again on my account. I know you ladies are perfectly capable of going without me."

Soren knew it was wrong to eavesdrop, but he couldn't help himself. Something began stirring inside him as they talked about traveling, and he wondered what it would be like to see a different city, a different country. The books Miss Flora had read aloud had given him a taste of a much bigger world filled with new and interesting things. The farthest he'd ever traveled from Chicago had been here to Evanston, twelve miles away. He turned from where he sat beside the driver and said, "I'll be glad to go along and take care of them for you, Mr. Edmund."

Miss Flora's brow creased with worry. "The Sinai Desert is halfway around the world, Petersen. It's nothing at all like Chicago. There would be a long voyage across the ocean, first, and then you'd need to ride on a camel and—"

"Let him come if he wants to," Miss Rebecca said. "I think it would be wonderful for him to see a bit of the world."

"Would you really be willing to go in my place?" Mr. Edmund asked.

Soren felt a funny feeling in the pit of his stomach as he considered it. He'd visited with Gunnar two more times since Mr. Edmund had been better, and he would miss seeing his brother if he went on a long voyage. But he may never have a chance to take a trip like this again. "Yes, sir," he finally replied. "I would."

"Then it's settled," Miss Rebecca said.

"What about me?" Kate asked. She sat on the driver's seat, as well, on the other side of Andrew. Miss Flora and Miss Rebecca insisted that she attend church with them every week, even though Kate showed no interest at all and barely paid attention to the service most of the time. At least she hadn't stolen anything—yet.

"Would you really like to come with us, Kate?" Miss Flora asked. "I never realized you were interested in traveling."

"I'm interested in getting out of this stupid city."

Soren closed his eyes, hoping the sisters wouldn't give in and bring the ornery girl along. He was weary of dealing with her every day and would enjoy getting away from her for a few months.

"Well," Miss Flora said, "it would give you a chance to travel a different road for a while than the one you've been on."

Kate looked over her shoulder the way she always did, as if expecting to see someone following her. She folded her arms across her chest and said, "I want to go."

"Very well, then," Miss Rebecca said. "You may both come along."

PART IV

Kate

CHAPTER 28

"Look! There it is!" Miss Rebecca said as they reached the top of a low hill. "That must be the monastery up ahead." Kate squinted into the distance where Miss Rebecca was pointing and saw square, man-made walls tucked into a rocky cleft on the desert floor. The walls were the same dull, tan color of the surrounding rocks and blended so well into the endless terrain that only their shape gave them away. "You're joking," Kate said with a huff. "That's the place? We rode on stinking camels for days and days through miles of empty desert to get *here*? It looks like something a child built in the sand." She felt like spitting.

It took another half hour to reach the monastery, and the place didn't look any better to Kate up close. She had hoped it would provide a safe place to hide, far away from the sheikh and his men, but the walls that surrounded the cluster of ancient buildings looked as though they might crumble at the slightest touch. And she was still stuck in the middle of nowhere. She hadn't expected a city, of course, but this wasn't even a village!

"Who would want to live way out here?" she asked. "And how will we ever get home again?"

"I've been told that the monks here at Saint Catherine's are very hospitable to pilgrims," Miss Rebecca said. "As for getting home again, we'll have a few weeks to figure that out and plenty of work to do in the meantime."

They reached the large wooden gate that led inside the enclosure, and Kate was relieved to see patches of green plants and a sprinkling of skinny evergreens springing up from the desert. There must be water here, somewhere. They dismounted outside the walls, and Miss Rebecca and Miss Flora spoke with a bearded man who had come to the gate as they'd approached. He was dressed all in black and wore a strange black hat on his head—like a short stovepipe hat without the brim. After talking for a few minutes, Miss Flora turned to them. "He's going to take us to see the monastery's prior. You should come with us, Soren. You too, Kate."

Kate followed them inside the compound and through the narrow streets, past a stone church with a square, stone steeple on top. All of the men inside the monastery looked tall and very thin to Kate, and wore long, black robes, scraggly beards, and hats just like the man at the gate. They looked so much alike, she wondered how anyone could tell them apart. Their guide stopped at a small wooden door in a stone and plaster building. He went inside and after a moment, beckoned to the sisters to come in.

"If you don't mind, he wants you two to wait out here for now," Miss Flora said. The door closed behind them and Kate was left outside with Petersen.

"I can't believe we traveled all this way just to get *here*," she said. "What could they possibly have way out here that we couldn't get in Chicago?"

"Ancient manuscripts, for one thing." Petersen sounded

grumpy and impatient as usual. "Miss Rebecca warned you what this trip would be like, Kate. I was there. I heard her. You shouldn't have come if you weren't willing to visit strange places or try new things."

"Don't nag me. You're not my boss."

"Yes, I am. You—"

"I'm going to look around. You can stay here and boss yourself." She started down the narrow street toward the old church, but Petersen grabbed her arm, jerking her back. "Ow! Let go of me!"

"You can't wander around here on your own," he said in a low voice. "This is a private monastery, where monks live. It would be like . . . like snooping through someone's house, uninvited. Besides, Miss Flora told us to wait out here, and she is your boss."

"Fine! I'll stay here. Let go of me."

"No. I don't trust you. You've caused enough trouble for everyone already."

"I didn't do a single thing wrong. It's not my fault the stupid sheikh wants to marry me. I certainly never encouraged him. And if you don't let me go this minute, I'll scream as loud as I can." He dropped her arm.

With nothing else to do, Kate sank down in the shade beside the door to wait. In the distance beyond the walls, towering stone mountains surrounded the monastery, making her feel very small. A long time passed, but she figured things were going well inside because she heard laughter from time to time. Petersen stood over her as if he were made of stone, too—and he wasn't laughing. In fact, she couldn't remember ever hearing him laugh in all the time she'd lived and traveled with the sisters. He was so tall, pale, and cold. He reminded her of an icicle.

After what seemed like a very long time, the door opened again and the sisters and two bearded monks came out. Kate scrambled to her feet and dusted off her skirt. "Sorry you had to wait," Miss Flora said. "The prior is going to show us around now and introduce Becky to Father Galakteon, the librarian. They've agreed to let us stay here and set up camp outside the gates in the monastery garden, so that's good news."

"Why can't we stay inside the walls, away from the sheikh and his men?" Kate asked as they started walking toward the church.

"Because this is a monastery," Miss Flora replied, lowering her voice. "It's a religious place. Only men live here."

"Did you tell the monks how the sheikh left us all alone in the desert and—"

"Shh . . . hush, Katie dear," Miss Flora said. "One tiny step at a time."

They peeked inside the church, and Kate never could have guessed from the outside how beautiful and mysterious it looked on the inside. She'd thought it would be dark and dreary, but the desert sun poured through windows high above the ornate pillars and lit up the gold that covered the front of the church as if it was on fire. A huge chandelier hung from the lofty ceiling, along with dozens of smaller dangling things. The entire place was very hushed and still and smelled like strong perfume.

"This church is more than one thousand years old," Miss Flora whispered to Kate and Petersen. "Can you even imagine that?" Kate couldn't. She couldn't count that high. Living on the streets, she'd had no way to keep track of the months and years except by the changing weather.

She shaded her eyes as they came back outside into the blinding sunlight, and they walked around the church to look at a scraggly tree that seemed to be growing out of the side of a building. The sisters seemed very impressed and reverent, nodding solemnly as the monks gestured to it and went on and on in their mumbling voices. "They're explaining that this is the burning bush that Moses saw in the desert. Its roots are beneath this chapel."

"The same Moses from the Bible story?" Kate asked in disbelief. "Wasn't that a long time ago?"

"Yes, thousands and thousands of years," Miss Flora said.

"I don't believe it," Kate said. "That bush would be a lot bigger if it was thousands of years old."

"I'm skeptical, too, Kate," Miss Rebecca said. She looked as though she was trying not to laugh. "But we need to act as if we're very impressed. Otherwise, we'll be back out in the desert with the Bedouin." Kate did her best not to roll her eyes.

The last stop was what they called a library, even though it looked like a dusty storage room to Kate with shelves full of old papers. The librarian, Father Galakteon, looked exactly like the prior and all of the other monks except that he was much more enthusiastic as he greeted them, chattering away with the sisters as if he hadn't had anyone to talk to in a thousand years. Maybe he hadn't. They talked and laughed for such a long time that Kate started looking around for a place to sit down. No sooner did she find one than it was time to leave.

"Wonderful news!" Miss Flora whispered on the way back to where the camels were waiting. "The librarian remembers my Edmund from years ago. He has agreed to let Becky and me work in the library with him. We can start tomorrow morning."

"That's good news," Petersen said with his customary frown.

Kate simply shrugged. At least they hadn't come all this way for nothing. "Is he going to help us get rid of the sheikh and get home again?" she asked.

"Never mind the sheikh for now," Miss Flora said. "I'll ask around and find out what we can do about him. We came all this way to work in the library, and now that we have permission, we need to concentrate on that."

"You can work in the library with me, Kate," Miss Rebecca

said. "Maybe if you're out of sight for a while, the sheikh will lose interest."

Mr. Farouk and the Bedouin drivers had set up both camps by the time they were led back outside to the garden. Kate was distressed to see that the camps were within sight of each other, as if the sheikh was determined to keep his eye on them. The cook had uncrated the chickens and turkeys, and the birds were running around the enclosure squawking and pecking as if savoring their freedom. Little did they know how temporary their freedom would be! Her own situation was the same as theirs, Kate realized. She had hoped to be safe at the monastery and rid of the sheikh and his men for good, but she still felt a cleaver hanging over her head—or in the sheikh's case, his rusty, old rifle.

"We're no better off here than we were in the desert," Kate said as she plopped down on a camp stool. "Those skinny, old monks couldn't defend themselves, let alone us."

"The Lord knows when the hour of our end will be," Miss Flora said.

Kate wanted to scream every time Miss Flora repeated those words. All they did was remind her that she was going to die, and she didn't want to. "Call me when supper is ready," she said and went off to hide inside her tent.

Early the next morning, Kate awoke to what sounded like fire alarm bells. She leaped right off her cot, ready to run, her heart racing. "Don't worry," Miss Flora said with a yawn. "The bells are calling the monks to prayer."

"I thought only the Bedouin prayed this early in the morning. The sun is barely up."

"I know. But as long as we're awake," Miss Rebecca said, "we may as well have a quick breakfast and get to work."

Petersen came with them to the monastery's library, lugging the heavy camera equipment. While he unpacked, Kate turned in a small circle in the room, surveying the dusty shelves. "What is all this stuff? It doesn't look like the library at your house."

"That's because these 'books' are very old," Miss Rebecca said, "from a time when things were written on scrolls that rolled up instead of in leather-bound volumes. I'm hoping that some of these date from the time of Jesus. Can you imagine? Our job will be to look over each one and help Father Galakteon catalogue them."

"What does that mean?"

"We'll make a list of everything that's here and put things in order so the monks will know what they have and where to find it again. Then scholars who want to come here and study will know what's here, too. I also plan to photograph some of the scrolls so biblical experts who can't travel to the monastery can begin studying the pictures right away."

"Why can't the monks do it themselves?" It still wasn't clear to Kate why they'd traveled all this way in the first place.

"Well, because many of these scrolls and codices are written in Syriac," Miss Rebecca said, "and in other languages that the monks don't understand. I've been studying ancient languages for just this purpose."

"And because we hope to find an ancient copy of the Bible," Miss Flora added, "so that the professor will see that the words of Scripture haven't been altered over the centuries."

They began working in one corner of the room, close to the door, with plans to make their way around the perimeter of the room first, then tackle the shelves in the middle. Miss Rebecca made Kate wear silk gloves and gave her the task of carefully removing the scrolls and documents from the shelves, one by one, and unrolling the delicate parchment and vellum leaves so Miss Rebecca could examine the writing with her magnifying glass and decide what it said. Miss Flora wrote everything down in a huge ledger for the monastery to keep, and made a second copy for the scholars back home. Miss Flora's other job was to talk to Father Galakteon, the librarian, and keep him occupied and out of Miss Rebecca's way, so she could work faster. It helped that he kept jumping up and running off to pray a bunch of times a day.

Kate and Miss Rebecca worked at a little table that looked so old Kate wondered if Moses had built it himself. They went through each manuscript, one by one, and Kate had to be very careful or the pages would crumble in her hands. Her nose tickled from all the dust, and every now and then she had to turn away and sneeze. She'd never had a job like this before where she needed to be so patient and still. And except for Miss Flora and the monk chattering away in Greek, it was very quiet in here, much different from the noisy garment factory where she'd once worked. "You're very good at this," Miss Rebecca said after Kate had opened a particularly delicate scroll. "You have a very gentle touch."

"I learned that by picking pockets."

Miss Rebecca laughed out loud, making Miss Flora and Father Galakteon stop talking and peer over at them. "Sorry . . . sorry . . ." Miss Rebecca said before saying something else in the monk's language. The pair resumed their discussion, and Miss Rebecca turned to Kate again. "I admire your honesty, Kate. It's very refreshing in someone who's . . . well, basically dishonest. You're a curious contradiction. I like that. It's so much better than being boring."

Kate wasn't sure if Miss Rebecca had just praised her or not, but she thought so. Even after all this time, she still didn't know what to think of the sisters. But they had been very kind to her. And generous. And Kate had never met anyone else in her life who'd been kind without wanting something in return.

"What do you most wish for, Kate?" Miss Rebecca suddenly asked her. She had stopped working and laid down her little magnifying glass.

"What do you mean?"

"Is there something you long to do or see? Something you dream of doing with your life?"

"I can't think of anything," Kate said with a shrug. "I just take one day at a time. . . . Find something to eat, a place to sleep, watch out for—" She'd almost said *Joe and his men or the police* but she caught herself in time.

"Watch out for what, dear?"

"You know . . . for trouble . . . and for bad people. Where I come from, there's always someone trying to get the better of you. I learned to look out for myself because nobody else will."

"This situation with the sheikh must be very hard for you. You're obviously used to taking care of yourself. You know your way around the streets, so being way out here where you're no longer in control must be difficult."

Kate felt tears spring to her eyes and quickly looked away. She'd never felt so out of control in her life. "I didn't know it would be like this," she said when she trusted herself to speak. "I never imagined anything like this place."

"I'm so sorry. It's my fault for not making certain you were better prepared before you made the decision to come. But I was surprised and very glad when you did because it showed that you have a sense of adventure. You've got fortitude and courage, Kate Rafferty, and I admire you for that. Yet it remains to be seen what will come of this journey you've undertaken."

"What do you mean?"

"Well, whenever Flora and I have gone on one of our trips, we've always discovered another piece of the puzzle of our lives, and we've returned home with a renewed sense of purpose. I was glad when you came on this trip because I've been hoping that you would also learn about yourself and what God wants for you. You have so many admirable qualities that He could use."

"Ha! Like being a thief?"

"He's using your light-fingered touch right now. All of our experiences make us who we are. And if we're willing to ask, God will show us how He wants to use those experiences."

Kate bent over the scroll again, concentrating on her work. She was growing very uncomfortable with this conversation. If God really knew everything about her, like Miss Rebecca said, then He wouldn't want anything to do with her.

"Let me ask you again, Kate—what would you like your future to be when you get home?"

"You mean *if* we get home," she said, desperate to change the subject.

"Oh, we'll be fine," Miss Rebecca said with a wave of her hand. "I don't think God is ready to take any of us to heaven just yet. Surely there's something you'd like to do besides work for Flora and me. What do you most enjoy doing?"

"I never had a chance to think about it."

"Would you like to go to school? Fall in love and get married?"

Kate felt her temper flare at all the nosy questions and fought to keep it under control. "I've never loved anybody or been loved by anybody."

Miss Rebecca didn't reply, and when Kate looked up at her, she saw that she had tears in her eyes. She rested her gloved hand over Kate's. "I want you to know that you can take a chance and dare to dream, Kate. God created you for a purpose. Can't you see how He has directed your life so far? It wasn't an accident that He led you to us." Kate didn't reply, hoping Miss Rebecca would take the hint and stop prying if she kept quiet. Did she dare to imagine a future that didn't require running from Joe or from the police? What would she like to do if she had a choice?

"Give it some thought, Kate," Miss Rebecca said, patting her hand, "and we'll talk about it again."

A week passed, and Kate enjoyed working with Miss Rebecca so much that she could almost forget about their problems with the sheikh. Miss Rebecca was teaching her how to operate the camera, and although Kate wouldn't be able to see her finished photographs until they returned home, the process fascinated her. Working together, they had made their way around the perimeter of the library, cataloging each item. They were ready to start on the shelves in the center of the room next.

"We've found some interesting texts," Miss Rebecca was telling her sister as they sat around the camp table after dinner, "but I'm sorry to say that we haven't unearthed anything I can use to change Timothy's mind. But there are still a lot of documents to go through, so I'm hoping that—"

Suddenly the quiet desert evening exploded with gunfire, followed by what sounded like a war cry from the Bedouin camp. Kate leaped up, searching for a place to run and hide. The sisters had jumped up from their camp stools, too, nearly upsetting the folding table.

"What in the world is going on?" Miss Flora said. "Do you know, Mr. Farouk? I hope the Bedouin are simply having a celebration."

Mr. Farouk ducked his head, as if he feared one of the sisters might strike him. "The sheikh is angry. . . . He asks to speak about the girl, but I told him he must wait."

"So now he's shooting at us to get our attention?" Miss Flora asked.

"Why would you say such a foolish thing?" Miss Rebecca asked him. She looked ready to shake some sense into the little man. "You should have told us right away! Isn't that how you got us all into trouble in the first place?"

"I did not wish to disturb you—"

"Disturb us!" she shouted. "He's firing his rifle to get our attention! You and I need to get over there right now and calm them down."

"Too late," Miss Flora said. "Here they come."

Kate could see Mr. Farouk trembling as he and Petersen stepped forward to meet them. The sheikh was carrying his rifle, and the Bedouin men surrounding him were all yelling and acting crazy. "Get in the tent, Kate," Miss Rebecca said. Kate backed up a few steps as if she was going to obey, but she stayed close enough to hear what was going on as Mr. Farouk and Miss Rebecca translated.

"The sheikh is accusing Petersen of going back on his word," Miss Rebecca said as the man ranted. "He says he brought us to the monastery, and now he wants to know what Petersen has decided."

"What should I tell him?" Petersen asked calmly. The man was an icicle. Nothing ever got through to him, even gunfire.

"Did you have a chance to talk to the monks?" Miss Rebecca asked her sister. "Can they help us?"

"I tried. They aren't interested in this drama. The prior said the reason they live out here is to get away from the world and to commune with God. And since the problem has to do with worldly lusts and they've taken a vow of celibacy, they're staying out of it."

"Did you explain that we have no way of getting home except by the sheikh's caravan?" Miss Rebecca asked.

"The prior said we're welcome to wait here until another group of pilgrims pays a visit. He says they do get visitors every now and then. But he can't guarantee that any of them would be willing to take us with them or that they'd have enough camels for all of us."

"Our food is going to run out before too long," Miss Rebecca said. "If we make the sheikh angry, he might ride away and leave us."

"He waits for your answer," Mr. Farouk said. "What do I tell to him?"

Petersen drew a deep breath, as if steeling himself. "Tell him that I've decided to marry the girl myself. The sheikh has helped me see how desirable she is, and now I'm eager to marry her. I would also like to have a son."

Miss Flora laid her hand on his arm. "Soren, wait. Are you sure you want to do this? You don't have to, you know. We could try to find another way."

"Yes, I'm certain. Tell him, Mr. Farouk."

The little man translated Petersen's words, and before he even had a chance to finish, the sheikh went into another tirade, waving his gun and shouting.

"He's asking, 'When? When?'" Miss Rebecca said. "He doesn't believe Soren. He says if he truly wanted the girl, he would take her into his tent right now. He says the fact that he doesn't proves that we're lying to him." When the sheikh finally finished shouting, he stood with his rifle pointing to the sky as he glared at Petersen.

Kate could no longer keep quiet. "What are we going to do?"

"You're supposed to be in the tent!" Miss Flora said in an angry whisper. "You need to stay out of sight!"

"No! This has to do with me, so I have a right to hear what's going on."

Miss Rebecca turned to her. "Well, if we want to make it out of here alive, it looks as though you may have to marry Petersen."

"I'd sooner die!"

"That's one option, I suppose," Miss Rebecca replied, as if trying not to smile. "Your other choices are to marry the sheikh or to live in the monastery with the monks for the rest of your life. Or to hope someone comes along someday who will take you home."

"And what if I refuse? What if I don't want to marry either one of them? Are you going to force me to?"

"No, of course not," Miss Flora said. "But if you choose to marry Petersen, the marriage will be in name only. No real marriage union would take place. I can't promise the same with the sheikh."

"And you'll be Petersen's only wife," Miss Rebecca added. "I understand that the sheikh has several. Oh, and he expects you to produce a son. It's hard to say what will happen if you give him a daughter like all his other wives have."

Kate growled in frustration. "Who came up with this stupid idea, anyway?"

"I'm no happier about it than you are," Petersen said. "But I'll do anything to keep Miss Flora and Miss Rebecca safe— even marry you!"

"So, if I go through with this fake marriage," Kate said, "then what happens?"

"Well, we're hoping it will convince the sheikh that he can't have you," Miss Flora said, "and he'll give up the idea of marrying you."

"And hopefully, it won't make him so angry that he'll take his camels and his caravan drivers and leave us stranded here," Miss Rebecca added.

"He will not do that," Mr. Farouk said. "His camels make much money for him. He wants your money, too."

"I hope you're right, Mr. Farouk," Miss Rebecca said. "You've gotten everything else wrong so far."

"Will I still have to be married to Petersen when we get home?" Kate asked.

"There won't be a marriage license, dear," Miss Flora replied, "so it won't be legal. And you won't be saying any real vows since we're the only ones who understand English. It will be as though you're acting in a play."

"Are you willing to give it a try, Kate?" Miss Rebecca asked. "For all our sakes?"

The sheikh had them backed into a corner. This seemed like the only way out. "I guess so," Kate replied.

Petersen gave a huge sigh, which Kate interpreted as relief. He took over. "Tell the sheikh that I'll marry the girl right away. We'll hold the wedding in two days so we'll have time to prepare. He and his people are invited to the celebration."

"Won't that be throwing this in his face?" Miss Flora asked.

"Maybe. But he needs to believe it's real."

After Mr. Farouk translated, the sheikh stared at Petersen for what seemed like a very long time. The icicle-man never flinched. "Two days," the sheikh finally said. "I will be here to witness." He turned and strode off with his men following close behind.

"Do we have enough supplies left to stage a wedding celebration?" Miss Flora asked.

"I don't know," Miss Rebecca replied. "Maybe the sheikh will sell us a goat or two to roast. Listen," she said, turning to Kate, "if this plan stands any chance of working, you're going to have to act nicer to Petersen in the days leading up to the wedding. The reason the sheikh is attracted to you is because he thinks you're fiery. If you act subdued, maybe he won't want you."

"I don't know what *subdued* means," Kate said.

Miss Rebecca laughed and surprised Kate by putting her arm around her shoulders for a quick hug. "Your words are truer than you intended, my dear. I like you, Kate! . . . Now, you know once you're 'married,' you and Petersen will have to pretend to live together."

The thought of it made Kate shudder. "I don't know if I can do that. I need to think about this." She stalked off to her tent to be alone, wondering how she ever got into this mess. Was this pretend wedding really the only way out? She lay down on her cot and stared up at the canvas ceiling. It seemed like people were always using her.

How did she end up here anyway?

CHAPTER 29

Kate Rafferty sat on the floor of the jail cell, trying not to gag as one of her cellmates heaved into a bucket. Kate had been in some pretty low places, but this was the lowest. All those times when she'd thought her life couldn't get any worse—like when her father got drunk and beat her and when the factory foreman cornered her and tried to grab her—they'd been nothing compared to being locked behind bars in a freezing cold cell with four other women and only a metal bucket to do her business in—right in front of the guards and everyone else, no less.

Before tonight Kate had lived day-to-day for almost a year, ever since her father threw her out for quitting her factory job. He hadn't cared that the foreman wanted Kate to do a lot more than stitch seams. "If you can't keep a job and pay your own way," her father had shouted, "then you can't live under my roof. This isn't a blasted hotel." He'd started swinging his fists, and Kate had run out the door with only the clothes on her back. She'd been stealing in order to live ever since, and doing pretty

417

well at it, too, until she'd gotten overconfident and tried to snatch a woman's purse outside a theater and some do-gooder on the street managed to catch her. "You're in a lot of trouble," the policeman told Kate as he'd slammed the cell door shut.

The night seemed endless, and since there were only two beds in the cell and the other women were larger and meaner than she was, Kate sat down in the corner—as far from the stinking bucket as possible—and tried to sleep. It proved impossible, worried as she was about what would happen to her and if she would ever get out of jail. When daylight started creeping through the cell's only window, the jailors brought watery oatmeal and stale bread.

Afterward, Kate had no choice but to use the bucket. She felt like crying but refused to give anyone the satisfaction of seeing her beaten down. When the jailor returned for the breakfast dishes, he brought a bucket of water, a bar of soap, and a threadbare towel. "Clean yourselves up, girls," he said. "You've got a court appearance this morning."

Kate waited until last to wash, aware that at barely eighteen she was the youngest and smallest of the women. They all acted as though this stint in jail was routine. "What's going to happen to us?" she asked as the last woman to wash handed the towel and soap to her.

"You never been here before?" the woman asked. Kate shook her head. "You want me to ask Joe if he'll help you out when he comes for me?"

"Sure," Kate said with a shrug. She pretended to be indifferent, but any help, even from a stranger, was better than none. A few minutes later a handsome, well-dressed man in his forties with shiny black hair and shoes strode down the corridor to their cell. He was followed by a short, portly man with wire-rimmed glasses and a leather satchel. The woman Kate had spoken to leaped up from the cot when she saw him.

"Joe! You come to get me out of here?"

"I'm going to try, Sugar. Hey, who's that little beauty?" he asked when he spotted Kate.

"I'm Kate Rafferty," she said, hurrying over to stand by the bars. "Can you get me out of here, too?"

"Well, I don't know. You didn't murder anybody, did you?" He smiled, and some of his teeth were coated with gold, giving him a handsome, glittery grin.

"I tried to snatch some big-mouthed lady's purse," Kate replied. "She squealed like a stuck pig, and I got caught. If you can tell me how to get out of here, I'd be obliged."

"This your first offense, Kate?"

"What do you mean?" It wasn't the first time she'd snatched a purse, but should she tell him that?

Joe gave a little laugh. "I mean, have you ever been caught and sent to jail before?"

"No."

"Hmm. Let me see what I can do. I'll meet both of you ladies in court."

A short time later the jailors herded Kate and the other four women into a courtroom to stand before the judge. Kate had no idea what was going on, but true to his word, the golden-toothed man told the man with the briefcase to stand beside her and help her talk to the judge when her turn came. A few hours later, Kate and the woman Joe called Sugar were released from jail. Joe was waiting for them with his carriage. "Climb in and I'll take you home, Sugar. You too, Kate."

She hesitated. Should she trust this stranger? What did he expect in return for helping her? "Come on, hop in," Sugar said. "Joe's a nice guy."

Kate decided to take a chance, figuring she could jump out and run if she needed to. "Why did you help me today?" she asked as the carriage started to move.

"You want to hear my story?" he asked. He leaned back in his seat and crossed his long legs, getting comfortable. "I grew up in the streets, just like you girls. I know what it's like to end up in jail and have no one to help you out. The judge doesn't care one bit that you don't understand what's going on or how to defend yourself. He just wants to see people like us locked away for good so he can clean up the streets of Chicago. So after I figured out how to make it off the streets, and I had a good job and lots of money in my pocket, I made up my mind to come down to the Cook County Jail with my lawyer now and then and help other people get out of trouble."

His story seemed believable to Kate. He talked and acted like he came from the rough side of town, yet he was well-dressed and riding in a fancy carriage, so he must have made it big. The driver seemed to know where Sugar lived, and he dropped her off first. "Where to next, Mr. Joseph?" the driver asked.

Joe turned to Kate. "Listen, I know we're strangers, and I can understand why you'd be unwilling to trust me. But you look as though you've been down on your luck. And—no offense—you could use a bath. If you're willing, I'd be happy to take you to my house and let my housekeeper take care of you. I'm off to work, so I won't even be home. But if you'd rather not do that, tell me where you'd like to go, and my driver will take you there."

The offer seemed too good to refuse. Kate was tired and hungry and filthy, like Joe said. She decided to take a chance. "I guess I'll take you up on your offer. But I can't pay you back for all your help or—"

"Don't worry about it," he said with a little laugh. "I enjoy helping beautiful young girls like you." Something about the way he said it made Kate wary. But she was too exhausted and too worried about going back to jail to question it. True to his word, Joe took her to his house in a very nice part of town and introduced her to his housekeeper, Mrs. Stevens. Then he left again. Mrs. Stevens looked too small and plump to win a wrestling match against Kate and take her captive, so after checking three or four ways to escape, Kate submitted to a warm bath and a hot meal. Her hair hadn't felt so clean and shiny in a long time, and she left it unpinned, falling around her shoulders.

"Mr. Joseph won't be home for several hours," Mrs. Stevens said afterward. "You look as though you could use a nap." Kate was exhausted after barely sleeping all night, so she curled up on the sofa in the parlor, close to the front door in case she needed to run. The house was on a side street, far from the noise of traffic. The only sound was the clock ticking on the mantel. Kate felt safe and warm, and it was such a new feeling to her, she closed her eyes and fell sound asleep.

She awoke to the sound of a key turning in the front door lock. Kate scrambled to her feet, ready to run. Mr. Joe stood in the foyer with an armful of parcels. "I'm sorry, Kate. I didn't mean to startle you. Here, these are for you," he said, holding them out to her. "It looked as though you could use some new clothes, so I had one of my employees run out and buy you some. I hope you aren't offended."

"Thanks," she said as she took the parcels from him. Her heart still felt like it was beating in her throat.

"Show her where she can change, Mrs. Stevens." Kate followed her to the tiled room where she had taken her bath and quickly changed into the skirt and shirtwaist Mr. Joe had bought her. He had even included a pretty little chemise, a petticoat, and frilly bloomers. And shoes. Kate had never owned such fine clothes in her life. She looked at herself in the mirror and didn't recognize the girl she saw. The change frightened her. This was all too much. She needed to get out of here. Now. She hurried out of the room and back down the hallway to the front door.

Mr. Joe was sitting in the parlor reading a newspaper, and he rose to his feet when he saw her.

"Stunning!" he breathed. "Do you have any idea how beautiful you are?"

Something about the way he looked at her made Kate's heart beat so fast she feared it might burst. She reached for the front door handle and turned the knob. It opened. "Thanks for the clothes and for all your help, Mr. Joe. I-I'll be glad to try and pay you back when I can, but I need to go now."

"I understand. I would be frightened, too, if I were you and a stranger was doing all these nice things for me. But you don't need to be afraid, Kate. You're free to leave, if you'd like, and I'll even drive you any place you'd like to go. Just tell me where you live." Kate didn't know what to say. She looked down at her feet and the brand-new leather shoes Joe had given her. "Oh, Kate," he said with a sigh. "I have a feeling that you don't have a place to live—am I right? I've been where you are. Listen, I have a lady friend you can stay with for a few days until you're on your feet again. May I drive you to her house? If it doesn't suit you, you can always leave again."

"I guess so," Kate said with a shrug. It was getting dark and cold outside, and she certainly couldn't stay here with Joe.

"Good. Let's go." He led her out front where his carriage was still parked. Kate shivered in the cold. Mrs. Stevens had taken her jacket away with her other clothes. "You're cold," Joe said. "I should have thought to buy you a shawl. Maybe my friend has one you can borrow." They drove through the central part of Chicago on Lakeshore Drive to a very nice neighborhood a few blocks from the lake. "You know where you are, right?" Joe asked. "See? I'm not taking you anyplace strange." They halted in front of a stately, three-story brick house. Lights glowed softly from behind the curtains. A burly man in a uniform stood near the door, like the men who guarded the doors outside fancy downtown hotels. He opened the door for them and tipped his hat.

"Evening, Mr. Joseph."

Inside, the house was gloomy and spooky-looking, with dark, swirly wallpaper and dim lights. A grand staircase led to the second floor, and on either side of the entry was a sitting room with more dark wallpaper, velvet drapes on the windows, and plenty of plush sofas and chairs scattered around. Joe led her into one of the parlors where three well-dressed men sat with drinks in their hands. The way they looked her over from head to toe sent a chill down her spine. She needed to run.

"I-I don't like it here, Mr. Joe. I'll be leaving now." She retraced her steps to the foyer and found the guard from outside blocking the front door. "Get out of my way," she said. She tried to push past him, but he grabbed her and clapped his hand over her mouth. Kate kicked and fought with all her strength, but he was much too strong for her. He carried her up the stairs to another dimly lit parlor on the second floor. This one was filled with women wearing nothing but their undergarments.

"You may as well stop struggling, Kate," Joe said as she fought for her life. "You'll only hurt yourself if you do." She knew it was true. She already felt bruised from the man's brawny hands, yet he shrugged off her kicks and blows as if they were nothing. "This is where you'll be living from now on. You're a beautiful girl, Kate. You're going to make a lot of money for me."

Joe nodded to her captor, and he dropped her to the floor. Kate knew he would grab her again if she tried to run, and besides, she was trembling so violently she didn't think her legs would work right. She glanced around at the other women who were watching her with mild interest. None of them showed any pity for her. Why had she trusted Joe? How could she have been so stupid? Being in jail would have been better than this.

"You can't keep me captive here," Kate said in a shaking voice.

"I got you out of jail and made the theft charges go away, didn't I? You're mine now. You're going to work for me to pay me back for all my trouble. Take off your skirt and blouse, Kate. And your shoes." When she hesitated, Joe said, "Either you do it, or my friend, here, will help you." Kate did what he said, her fingers trembling so badly she could barely manage the buttons. Joe took the clothes and shoes from her and turned to leave. "And don't even think about running away. I own the streets. I'll find you. Tell her what will happen when I do, ladies." He left with the guard, closing the door behind him. Kate heard a key turn in the lock. She couldn't breathe.

"Why don't you sit down, sweetie?" a blond-haired lady said. "You won't be going anywhere tonight. And like Joe said, if you do try to run, he and his men will find you and beat you half to death."

"We had a gal here named Honey who ran away a second time," a buxom little brunette added. "Joe beat her so badly she died."

"He has men working for him all over the city," the blonde continued. "They'll find you. There aren't very many redheads like you around. Joe has police on his payroll, too. And judges and lawyers. They like coming here to visit us."

"How do you think Joe got you out of jail?" the brunette asked with a little laugh.

"I'd rather be in jail," Kate said. "Or dead!"

The blonde rose to her feet and tried to put her arm around Kate's shoulders and lead her to one of the sofas, but Kate pushed her away. "Suit yourself!" she said with a shrug. "But you'll find it's not so bad here. Joe has nice customers, rich men who smell good and give you nice presents. He won't allow bad people to visit us no matter how much money they offer him. You'll have a good life here."

"A good life? Selling myself? Never!"

"You think you're better than we are?" a third woman asked. She was stretched out on a chaise lounge, smoking a cigarette. She blew a puff of smoke at Kate.

"The only reason I ended up here is because Joe tricked me," Kate replied.

The women laughed at her. "Are you that stupid?" the brunette asked. "Did you really think you could get something for nothing? But Eva is right, Joe does take good care of us. We're better off than we ever would be on the street. Where would you be living right now if Joe hadn't come along? Still in jail, I'll bet."

"This is how women like us survive," the woman with the cigarette said. "There's no other way. Do you think a girl like you could ever find a nice husband, especially now that you've been in jail? Face it, in the neighborhoods where we come from, the only future we have is to work in a factory or a hotel laundry until we marry a dockworker or a roughneck from the stockyards—and those men all want the same thing the men here do. Only you would live in a pigsty like the ones we grew up in, with no running water, a houseful of babies you can't feed, and a husband who drinks away his paycheck leaving you and your children to starve."

"That's the way you grew up, isn't it?" the blonde asked.

The smoker took another drag on her cigarette. "At least we're warm and well-fed and taken care of here," she said, releasing the smoke. "The men who visit us have wives who are as cold as ice and never show them any love. Believe me, you'll be well-appreciated—maybe even loved if the right John comes along and takes a fancy to you."

"You ever been with a man?" the brunette asked. When Kate didn't reply, the other women exchanged glances. "Joe has a very rich client who pays extra for young, inexperienced girls like you. I'm guessing he'll save you until he comes in."

A door in the back of the room opened, and an older woman in a low-cut silk dress and glittering necklace entered. She wore her hair elaborately pinned and might have passed for one of the society women Kate had seen outside the theater last night—was it only last night? How had she ended up in this nightmare in such a short time?

"Hello, I'm Madame Augusta," the woman said. Kate folded her arms across her chest as the woman looked her up and down. "Joe wasn't kidding when he said you were a beauty. But you could still do with a little grooming. Come with me, Kate." She gestured to the door behind her, then rested her icy hand on Kate's shoulder to guide her through it. For now, Kate had no choice but to obey. She decided in that moment to play along and make them think she was giving in while she figured out a way to escape and run for her life. It would be hard to get very far without clothes or shoes, but she would rather die than do what they wanted her to do.

Kate heard the sound of men's laughter from downstairs as Madame Augusta led her down a long hallway to a bedroom with a frilly brass bed. A single gas lamp lit the room and a warm fire burned in the gas fireplace. Beside the fire was a table with a tray of food—roast beef and potatoes and green beans, a basket of dinner rolls and butter. Kate's stomach rumbled with hunger. "You can relax and have something to eat," Madame Augusta said. "Joe told me to give you a few days to adjust to your new home before you entertain guests." Kate squeezed her hands into fists as she fought back her rage. She had to play along. She had to escape. She shivered as she sat down at the table and picked up one of the rolls.

"Good girl," Madame Augusta said. She turned and left, locking the door.

With each day that passed, Kate pretended to relax a little more. Madame and her servants gave her warm, perfumed baths and beauty treatments, trimming her nails and her hair. She was allowed to walk down the hallway to the upstairs lounge where Joe had first brought her so she could visit with the other women. Kate did her best to laugh with them and not let on that she was terrified. The food was plentiful and delicious, the room warm, the bed soft and luxurious, yet Kate knew she was running out of time. The only way out, she decided, was through the window in her bedroom. It was a long way down to the alley two stories below, but she figured she might make it without breaking both of her legs if she tied her bedsheets together and fastened one end to the bedpost. She was looking down from the window one evening after supper when she heard her door open. She whirled around in terror. Joe was standing there.

"Hello, little beauty." He slowly walked toward her, looking her over. "I see Augusta did a good job with you. Turn around for me." Kate did as she was told. "Good. Good," he said when she faced him again. "Now, remember to smile, and try not to look so frightened." He left again. Her time was up.

Kate tore the sheets off her bed with shaking hands and knotted them together as fast as she could. Would her makeshift rope be long enough? She dragged the bed closer to the window, then fastened one end of the sheets to the post. A gust of icy air blew in as she opened the window. She couldn't go out half-dressed, but where could she find clothes? Kate could tell by the sounds coming from the room next door that her neighbor was entertaining a gentleman. She decided to take a chance. Kate slipped from her room and opened the neighboring door as quietly as she could. A bowler hat lay on a chair just inside.

She could use it to cover up her hair. A man's striped shirt lay on the floor a few feet away. Kate dropped to her hands and knees and crawled inside to snatch the shirt and hat, then raced back to her own room.

Don't look down, she told herself as she swung her legs over the windowsill. The rough bricks scraped her skin all the way down but she didn't have time to worry about it. Her makeshift rope ended a good ten feet from the bottom, so she had no choice but to let go and drop, hoping she wouldn't break any bones. Her landing sent a jolt of pain through her body, but she picked up the bowler hat, which had fallen from her head, staggered to her feet, and ran.

Kate needed to get as far away as she could as fast as she could, so she ignored the bruising pain in her feet from the cold, stony pavement and the stitch in her side that felt like a knife blade. She ran down the dark alleyway until her lungs gave out and her heart felt like it would burst, then collapsed to the ground and crawled behind a garbage bin until she could gather enough strength to run some more. This was a wealthy part of town, and Kate knew she would arouse suspicion if anyone saw her running around at night in her undergarments. She waited until she could breathe again, then stood and kept going, on and on throughout the long, cold night. The most dangerous part would be crossing the river. Surely Joe's men would be watching for her there. She chose to cross at one of the swing bridges, waiting in the shadows until it opened and a line of vehicles gathered to cross. Kate crawled into the traffic jam on her hands and knees, then clung to the back of a covered carriage until she reached the other side. She made it to the Southside by dawn, battered and exhausted—but safe. She crept into an unlocked stable behind a grocery store, curled into a ball in the hay, and slept.

The sound of church bells awakened her the next morning.

She remembered seeing a church the night before and wondered if someone there would help her. Kate peered out of the stable window to watch the front of the sanctuary and saw that even the poor people in this neighborhood dressed in their Sunday best to attend church. She would surely stand out wearing nothing but her undergarments and a man's shirt. These Christian people would be appalled by her and by where she had been living. She stood at the window for a long time, until the service ended an hour later and people started coming out again. A man in a long black robe and clerical collar stood on the steps shaking everyone's hand. Then a curious thing began to happen. Dozens of children began streaming toward the church, going in through a door on the side. Most of them were dressed in rags, and many of them had bare feet, just like her. She decided to take a chance and follow them, knowing it was only a matter of time before someone came to the stable to tend the horses. She tucked her hair inside her hat and went outside.

The scariest part was racing across the street in the open. But she made it without attracting attention and slipped in through the back door where she'd seen the children go. Kate stood in the little vestibule for a while, peering inside at the activity. Two middle-aged women were telling stories to the children, and just beyond them on a chair was a woman's purse. It was leather and expensive-looking and probably held a lot of money. Kate was trying to figure out how to get past all the children so she could steal it when they suddenly stood and went to another part of the big room to sit down at the tables. Kate summoned her courage and inched her way into the room. She hadn't made it very far when one of the middle-aged ladies hurried over and asked Kate if she would like to join them. Thankfully, the woman went away again after Kate told her "No, thanks."

Kate continued her slow journey across the room, keeping one eye on the purse and the other on a tall, skinny man with blond hair who stood around doing nothing. The moment she had the purse-handle in her hand, Kate raced from the room, slamming the door in the blond man's face. She knew she would be easy to spot, running down the street, so she circled around to the front of the church and crawled into the dense thicket of bushes that flanked the front door. Relief flooded through Kate when she opened the purse and saw how much money was inside. There was enough to buy clothes and shoes and food, enough to stay hidden for a while until Joe got tired of looking for her, enough so she wouldn't have to steal and get caught by the police again. Joe had said he had policemen working for him. Kate thought about buying a train ticket and getting out of Chicago for good, but she didn't know how she would manage it since she couldn't read. Besides, Joe's men might be watching the station.

In the end, the money from the purse didn't last nearly as long as Kate had hoped, even though she bought clothes and shoes and a straw hat from the secondhand man. Before long, she found herself back at the church on a Sunday morning, hoping she could get away with stealing from the middle-aged women a second time. Everything was just as it had been before—the ladies, the dozens of children, the skinny man with the blond hair. And the purse, sitting right where it had been the last time. But this time the blond man caught her before she had a chance to get away. "Stop! Thief!" he shouted as he wrenched the purse from her hands. He had his other arm around Kate's waist, gripping her tightly as she punched and kicked to free herself.

"Let me go!" she yelled.

"This is the same girl who stole from you before," the man said, yanking off her hat to reveal her bright red hair. He was taller and stronger than she was and didn't mind her blows. "I'll hold on to her while you send for the police," he said. Kate was wild with terror, certain she would end up in jail where Joe would find her.

But the ladies didn't call for the police. "Let's go into the church while we deal with this," one of them said. The man dragged Kate into the sanctuary, and there was something about the quiet peace and grandeur of the place that calmed her down a little. Even so, she couldn't understand why these ridiculous rich women were offering to take her home and let her work for them. She'd been fooled once before by Joe, who'd seemed so nice until he'd taken her captive. Yet if she didn't agree, Kate would end up back in jail, where Joe would surely find her. She was trying to decide what to do when one of the ladies mentioned that they lived in Evanston. Joe would never think to look for her there.

"What do you say?" the fair-haired lady asked her.

Kate glanced toward the door again, half-expecting to see Joe or the police. In the end, she feared him and his thugs more than she feared these women. "I got nothing to lose," she said. "I'll go."

CHAPTER 30

THE SINAI DESERT
1890

The sheikh brought his rifle to Kate's phony wedding ceremony. She happened to peer through the tent flap and saw him arrive with his band of men. "He makes me nervous," she told Miss Flora and Miss Rebecca. "He acts like he's some sort of prison guard."

"He's probably more of a danger to himself with that silly gun than to any of us," Miss Rebecca said. "But just in case he understands a word or two of English and hasn't told us, we'll need to make this wedding look as authentic as possible. In fact, if you don't need me, I think I'll hover around outside and eavesdrop on his conversation to see if our preparations are convincing him." She untied the flap and disappeared outside.

"Hold still, dear," Miss Flora said, "so I can finish pinning your veil." Miss Flora had taken some greenery from one of the trees in the monk's garden and twisted it into a crown to attach to Kate's veil. The sisters had scrounged through all their clothing, and after a bit of sewing, Kate was now dressed in a lacy blouse and long, cotton skirt that Miss Rebecca said made her look very pretty. The wedding was set to take place outside the monastery in the garden, which was a lot nicer than the rest of the desert surrounding them. The monks, who wouldn't be attending, had agreed to let Miss Flora's cook use the monastery's kitchens to prepare the feast, something that would have been impossible to do on his tiny camp stove. Kate had already decided she wasn't going to eat any of it—first, because she was too nervous to eat, and second, because Miss Rebecca had sent Mr. Farouk over to the Bedouin camp to buy a goat to roast, and Kate certainly wasn't going to eat any of that!

"Time to go, dear," Miss Flora said when the last pin was in place. "You look beautiful."

Kate drew a shaky breath and ducked beneath the tent flap. Miss Flora linked her arm through hers to walk Kate down the aisle between the garden beds. Miss Rebecca, who would perform the ceremony, stood beside Petersen at the end of the stony path. A trickle of sweat ran down Petersen's thin face. He looked as if he were melting.

"Dearly beloved," Miss Rebecca began. "We are gathered here today to partake in a terrible deception, with the hope that our lives will be spared and we won't have to live out our years in this monastery. . . . Smile, everyone," she added. "This is a joyful occasion." Petersen pasted on a quick smile—the first one Kate had ever seen—but she didn't bother, since no one could see her beneath the veil.

They went through the motions of the simulated wedding, joining hands at one point after Miss Rebecca asked, "Do you wish to get out of the Sinai Desert and back home to Chicago again? If so, smile and repeat, 'I do.'"

"I do!" Kate said.

"The ring, please," Miss Rebecca said. Petersen pulled out the ring Miss Flora had let him borrow and slipped it onto

Kate's hand. "Do you promise to return this ring to its rightful owner when this phony marriage is dissolved?" Miss Rebecca asked with a bright smile.

"I do," Kate and Petersen said at the same time. Then came the moment Kate had dreaded the most. Petersen had to lift the veil and give Kate a convincing kiss. He held her carefully—the way you might hold a dog you weren't too sure about—and his lips touched hers for a moment. Kate looked up at him afterward and pretended she had liked it. Better him than the sheikh, she thought with a shudder.

There were congratulations all around, and Mr. Farouk helped carry the food and one of the refectory tables out to the garden. Petersen held Kate's hand in his large, sweaty one as the sheik and his men came forward to greet them. Miss Rebecca and Mr. Farouk stood nearby to translate. "Please tell the sheikh that I'm sorry things didn't work out for him, and that I know he must be disappointed," Petersen said.

"And tell him that we'll pray to our God for him, and ask that He gives him the son he wishes for," Miss Flora added.

"That was a nice touch," Miss Rebecca whispered as Mr. Farouk translated. Kate hoped this would be the last of the sheikh but he began talking loudly and waving his rifle all around. "Uh-oh," Miss Rebecca said. "It seems he wants us to come and pray for his wife right now."

"Well, I don't mind doing that," Miss Flora said. "Kate, you should come with Becky and me to show the sheikh that you don't hold any ill will toward him."

"I don't like this," Kate mumbled as she followed the sheikh and his entourage out of the garden to the Bedouin camp. The sheikh halted in front of a tent and gestured for the three women to go inside. They all bent down and crawled forward into the darkness with Miss Flora leading the way.

"Oh dear, oh dear, oh dear," Miss Flora said after she halted in front of the sheikh's wife. Kate saw why when her eyes adjusted to the dim light. The woman reclined on a rug in the middle of the tent, propped on a pile of pillows while four other women fanned her to keep her cool. Judging by the enormous bulge in the front of her black robe, the woman was very, very pregnant. "Oh, dear," Miss Flora repeated. "I thought we would be praying for a son to be born in the distant future when we would all be back home in Chicago—not for a child who might be born any minute!"

"Now what?" Kate whispered.

"See where all this lying gets us?" Miss Flora said, turning to her sister. "This all began with one tiny, white lie and now our situation is getting worse and worse. Let that be a lesson to all of us."

"You're right," Miss Rebecca said, "but I'm not sure we could have done anything differently under the circumstances. We've been at the sheikh's mercy—and God's mercy—ever since we landed in the Sinai."

"If we pack up and leave for home right away," Kate asked, "do you think we can get out of here before she gives birth to another girl?"

"Possibly," Miss Rebecca said, "but I can't leave yet. I haven't finished what I came here to do in the library."

"Then let's start praying," Miss Flora said. "Down on our knees, everyone."

"How can God answer our prayer?" Miss Rebecca asked as she sank down to pray. "The child could be born any day, and it's already whatever sex it's going to be."

"I believe in a God of miracles," Miss Flora said. "If He can give Abraham and Sarah a child in their old age, He can certainly give the sheikh a son. Besides, I'm not just going to pray for our own sakes, so we get out of this mess, but because I want the sheikh and his family to see that our God is a personal

God, who cares about us and answers our prayers. I want this to bring glory to Him."

Kate thought both sisters were crazy, but she followed their example as they knelt and closed their eyes and laid their hands on the pregnant woman's shoulders. Miss Flora begged God to forgive them for lying when they should have trusted Him to protect them. She asked Him to have mercy on them and miraculously answer their prayer for a son for the sheikh—or at least keep his wife from going into labor until they were safely back in Cairo. She went on and on for several minutes, ending with what Kate recognized from church as The Lord's Prayer. Kate joined in with the sisters, afraid that if she didn't ask God for help, she would end up dressed all in black and living in this stifling tent with these wild-eyed women and their gun-waving husband for the rest of her life. It was bad enough that she had to live with her pretend-husband for the next few weeks.

They all returned to the monastery garden afterward, and the sheikh and his men seemed to enjoy the wedding feast. But they showed no signs of leaving, even after all the food was gone. Kate was tired of sitting beside Petersen on a camp stool, and was about to get up and do something else when Miss Rebecca came over to speak to them. "I have some upsetting news for you," she said. "I've been listening to the Bedouin conversation and it seems that it's their tradition to stay until the bride and groom go inside their marriage tent. They want to serenade you with songs while you . . . you know . . ."

Kate longed for for a place to run and hide, but of course there wasn't one. "You said we didn't have to . . . you know."

"You don't. Just hold Petersen's hand and go inside the tent. Soren can stick his head out and wave in an hour or so."

Kate was angry enough to start punching somebody, but it wouldn't do any good. She let Petersen take her hand and lead her into the tent while the Bedouin shouted and cheered.

The tent still held the heat from the afternoon sun, and sweat beaded on Kate's face as she found a place to sit as far away from Petersen as possible. "I have a knife," she told him. "I stole it from the cook. You try anything, and I'll stick it between your scrawny ribs."

"Not a chance!" he said, holding up both hands. "I'd sooner live with a nest of sand vipers than with you." They glared at each other in the growing twilight while the noise outside continued.

"Why'd you agree to do this?" Kate asked him.

"I already told you—for Miss Flora and Miss Rebecca's sakes. They've been good to me. I promised Mr. Edmund I'd take care of them, and if that means sharing a tent with you in order to keep my promise, then I'll do it."

"Ha! You want out of this desert as much as I do. You're doing it to save your own skin."

"Of course I want to go home. I have promises to keep and people who are counting on me to come back. But if anything happens to the sisters, well, I suppose I'd fight to the death for them because they fought for me." He paused for a moment, then said, "They've been good to you, too."

Kate looked away so he wouldn't see the tears glistening in her eyes. They had been good to her, and kinder than anyone in her entire life had been. She was growing fond of them and knew in her heart that she was doing this for their sakes, as well. She still wasn't exactly sure what Miss Rebecca hoped to find in the library but Kate was determined to help her find it so she could marry the funny professor she loved so much.

Kate got tired of sitting after a while, and when the tent grew so dark she could barely see Petersen, she wrapped up in one of the blankets and lay down on the camp cot. "The noise outside is giving me a headache," she mumbled. Petersen crawled across the floor to lift the flap and poke his head out. An enormous cheer went up and the sheikh's rifle boomed. Kate wished she could see if Petersen's face was turning red. She let out a sigh when he came back inside and the noise died away. "Maybe we can get some sleep now."

She heard shuffling sounds on the other side of the tent as Petersen lay down and got comfortable. She was still staring up at the canvas ceiling when she heard him whisper, "Good night, Kate."

The Bedouin camp remained quiet for the next week, and Kate dared to hope that the sheikh had believed their ruse. She spent her days in the library with Miss Rebecca, and as they began working on the very last shelf of manuscripts, Kate could see her growing disappointment. "We've found some exciting documents," she told Kate, "and I know the scholars will be pleased, but still no Bible."

"Maybe the monks have more stuff stored away, somewhere. Want me to look in these closets?" Kate asked. Miss Rebecca looked doubtful. The two tiny doors Kate pointed to, tucked beneath the eaves, looked more like trap doors to a miniature dungeon than real closets. Everything in the monastery was so ancient and creepy that Kate found herself hoping Miss Rebecca would say *no*. The monks had taken the sisters on a tour beneath the sanctuary, where they saw skulls from the hundreds of monks who had lived here over the years. Kate would faint dead away if she opened one of the little doors and a skeleton fell out.

"Well, maybe we could just peek inside and see what's there," Miss Rebecca finally said. Kate got down on her hands and knees, steeling herself as she prepared to open the little door. It was stuck at first, and she pulled so hard on it that when it did open with a loud *creak* it sent her flying backward onto her bottom. She wiped the dust from her eyes and saw a wooden crate that looked a million years old. She slid it out of the closet and into the light.

"That looks like a treasure chest, doesn't it?" Miss Rebecca asked. She hurried over and sat down on the floor beside Kate to open it. The wooden lid was on hinges and swung open with another rusty *creak*. "Oh my," Miss Rebecca said as she peered inside.

"What are those things?" Kate asked. The box held six moldy-looking, book-sized blocks of pages. Kate could see writing on them.

"They're codices, I think—ancient books that were hand-written and bound between two covers. Take them out carefully, Katie dear. I'm so excited my hands are shaking."

Kate rose to her knees and lifted them out one by one, gently laying them on the floor. They were filthy and looked as though they had been in the closet since Jesus was a boy. Miss Rebecca grabbed her spectacles and magnifying glass to peer at the decrepit writing on each one. "I don't think any of them is a Bible," she said, sounding disappointed. "Would you mind carefully opening this one so I can look at the first pages?" Kate inserted the thin-bladed knife she had learned to use these past weeks and gingerly turned the page, aware that it might easily crumble into dust. Miss Rebecca studied it for several minutes before straightening up again. "It's a volume about the life of a woman saint. No wonder the monks stashed it away."

Kate used the knife to carefully turn the second page. She peered at the strange writing and grimy vellum and said, "I don't know how you can even read this. It looks like somebody scribbled all over the pages."

"Let me see." This time Miss Rebecca studied the page for several minutes, and when she finally looked up at Kate she appeared shaken, as if they'd found a skeleton behind the little door after all. "Katie! This is a *palimpsest*!"

"A what?"

"I've never seen one before, but I've been told that in earlier times, the monks reused old vellum pages to create a new book by scraping off the ink and writing on top of it."

"Well, they didn't do a very good job of scraping because I can still see the old writing."

"I know. Isn't that wonderful? Open another page for me, Katie, then go find Flora and tell her to come right away." Kate did as she was told, running through the monastery grounds and out to the garden where she found Miss Flora and Petersen taking stock of their dwindling food supplies while the cook and Mr. Farouk tried to capture one of their few remaining chickens. The birds had obviously figured out what their fate soon would be and were on the run.

"Miss Rebecca wants you to come right away," Kate said, gasping for breath. "I think she might have found something important." Petersen came, too, as they hurried back to the library.

"Flora, I found a palimpsest," Miss Rebecca said as the new-comers arrived and took turns sneezing. "Or rather, Kate found it for me. The writing on top tells about the life of a woman saint, but see the faint writing beneath it? The page heading on this one says *of Matthew*, and this next page, which was reused upside-down, says *of Luke*. It's a Bible, Flora! We found pages from an ancient Bible!" The sisters hugged each other as they did a little dance, then Miss Flora hugged Petersen, while Miss Rebecca surprised Kate by hugging her tightly. Kate couldn't recall the last time she had been embraced this way and the warmth of Miss Rebecca's arms along with her contagious joy brought tears to Kate's eyes. "We did it! We did it!" Miss Rebecca said. "I'm so proud of you, Kate, for discovering this!"

"This is wonderful news!" Miss Flora said before letting loose another hearty sneeze.

"Here's the best part," Miss Rebecca said. "I already figured out how old this Bible is! While Kate was fetching you,

I found the date and signature of the scribe who copied the book on top. See? It says '1009 years Alexander,' meaning Alexander the Great. That makes it somewhere around AD 700 by our modern calendar. And that's just the date of the book on top!"

Oh my!" Miss Flora breathed. "So the pages from the Bible must be even older?"

"Yes! I figure it has to be at least 200 years older for it to be over-written this way. If I'm right, we're looking at around 500 AD—making it one of the earliest known Syriac Gospels that has ever been found!"

Miss Flora sat down, as if her legs wouldn't hold her any longer. "Oh my! Oh my! I wish we had some champagne so we could celebrate."

"We don't have time to celebrate," Miss Rebecca said. "We need to show this to the prior and to Father Galakteon right away. We have a lot of work to do if we hope to photograph the entire codex before our time here at the monastery is up. The world needs to see this!"

The sisters hurried off to see the prior and soon returned with him and Father Galakteon and a dozen other curious monks. Kate could tell they were excited about this gummed-up block of pages even if she couldn't understand what they were saying. The librarian and several of the others offered to stay and help, and they set to work right away. Kate had the most difficult job of all, carefully separating the pages that the centuries had stuck together. The vellum was as dry and brittle as fall leaves, and it crumbled and flaked into bits if she wasn't careful. She passed each page to Miss Flora and the monks, who gently scraped away the top layer of ink so the underwriting would become visible. Petersen had set up the tripod and camera, and he took photographs of the pages, then removed the used negatives and carefully stored them away before replacing them with fresh ones. Miss Rebecca sat with a pen and paper and her magnifying glass, working to decipher the words of the text.

Kate keenly felt the importance of her work. She and Miss Rebecca weren't just recovering this ancient Bible for the professor's sake, but so the entire world could see it. How had it happened, Kate wondered, that she had gone from living on the streets and in a brothel, to making a discovery of such importance? She bent to loosen another leaf, scarcely daring to breathe.

"I'm so proud of you," Miss Rebecca had told her. It was the first time in her life that Kate Rafferty had ever heard those words.

CHAPTER 31

I can't believe we actually finished on time," Kate said as she gazed around the library for the last time. She was ready to return home. Petersen had photographed the last page of the codex, and after Miss Rebecca had gathered the loose pages into a book again, Miss Flora had placed it inside a silk pouch she had sewn from one of her scarves. The monastery's prior now kept the ancient codex in a place of honor in his office. Kate and Miss Rebecca had searched both of the library's tiny closets but hadn't found anything as important as the palimpsest.

"Are you ready to get on a camel again tomorrow, Kate, and head back across the desert?" Miss Rebecca asked as they walked through the monastery grounds to their camp in the garden.

"I can't say I'll enjoy the camel ride, but it'll be nice to see maple trees and green grass again—and even snow," she replied. She saw Miss Flora talking to Petersen in front of the so-called "bridal tent," and they both turned as Kate and Miss Rebecca approached.

"We have a problem," Miss Flora said. "Mr. Farouk informed

the sheikh that we're ready to leave tomorrow morning and told him to get his caravan ready, but he refuses to budge. He said we must all wait here until his son is born." Panic twisted through Kate's stomach at the news. She felt trapped, just as she'd been when Joe had locked her inside the brothel. This time, there was no window she could climb out of.

"What if the baby is a girl?" Kate asked.

"The sheikh is under the impression that we promised him a boy," Miss Flora replied. "Who knows what will happen if it isn't."

Miss Rebecca removed her hat and wiped the sweat from her brow with her sleeve. "Does he know we barely have enough food left to make it back to the gulf? Or that we have steamship tickets to America waiting for us?"

"He doesn't seem to care. He's going to hold us hostage until his wife has a son."

"I'll go tell the cook not to make any dinner for me," Miss Rebecca said. "I just lost my appetite."

Kate didn't have much of an appetite, either, nervous as she was about the sheikh's newest demand. Their food was running out. The dates that she'd grown to love were nearly gone, and the cook was down to his very last chicken, whose life had been spared so it could provide them with fresh eggs. Before going to bed that night, Miss Flora asked Kate and Petersen to hold hands with her and Miss Rebecca so they could all pray together. The sisters did all the praying while Kate looked up at the brilliant full moon and numberless stars and wondered who she was more afraid of: Joe and his men or the sheikh and his. They all haunted her nightmares. After they finished praying, she spotted one of the white-robed camel drivers standing by the garden gate as he did every night to make certain that she and Petersen really slept in the same tent. She quickly went inside to undress and climb beneath the covers.

444

Petersen came inside a few minutes later and pulled off the long, white robe Mr. Farouk had given him when they'd started on this trip. True to his word, he had stayed on his side of the tent these past weeks, and Kate had finally returned the kitchen knife to the cook. She glanced over at him in the moonlight, stretched out on his back with his hands folded behind his head. He was too tall for the cot and his feet hung over the end by several inches.

"Hey, Petersen," Kate said. "Do you believe that it really works?"

He turned to face her. "Do I believe what works?"

"You know . . . praying the way the sisters do. Are you a Christian like they are?"

He was quiet for a moment, then asked, "Are you?"

"No fair. I asked you first."

Petersen huffed and turned to look up at the canvas ceiling again. "Miss Rebecca asked me what I thought about prayer the morning after the sandstorm. I guess I still don't know how to answer that question. Sometimes it seems like God is listening and that He's answering people's prayers—like when Mr. Edmund got better. And yet . . . I don't know . . ." His voice trailed away, and he was quiet for a moment. "As for being a Christian . . . I'm not a good person like the sisters. I don't know if they told you, but I was arrested and sent to jail in the past."

Kate swallowed. "Me too," she said softly. She remembered where she had ended up after getting out of jail and closed her eyes in shame. No, she wasn't a very good person, either. "Miss Rebecca asked me what I wanted to do with my life, and I didn't know how to answer her. Do you know what you're going to do when we get back to Chicago?"

"I would like to keep working for the sisters and Mr. Edmund, if they'll let me."

"You're a better servant than I am. . . . I suppose I could

try harder if I do decide to stay." She waited, wondering what
Petersen would say. He was her worst critic, always yelling at
her for getting everything wrong. She had no idea why she
was talking to him this way, but after working so hard on the
palimpsest these past few weeks and then having her hopes
dashed of finally going home tomorrow, Kate just didn't have
any fight left in her. If the sisters' prayers didn't work, there
was nothing much any of them could do.

"I hope you don't go back to being a thief," Petersen finally
said. "You're a really smart girl, Kate. You probably could do
anything you wanted to once we're home."

"Thanks." Kate wanted to say more but couldn't speak. A
lump had risen in her throat at the mention of *home*. Unless
she worked for the sisters, she had no home to return to. She
swallowed and said, "Good night, Soren."

Three days passed. Kate waited inside the tent every morning
while the sisters and Petersen went to the Bedouin camp with
Mr. Farouk to talk to the sheik. He refused to budge.

With little else to do, Miss Rebecca asked Kate if she'd like
to learn how to read and write. "I guess so . . ." she said with
a shrug. If she could read, she'd be able to buy a train ticket to
get out of Chicago. They sat in the shade of the monks' acacia
tree every day, filling up the blank pages in the back of Miss
Rebecca's diary with letters and words. Each night before bed,
all four of them held hands and prayed.

On the fourth night, the sound of gunfire jolted Kate straight
out of bed. Petersen ducked out the door while Kate crashed
around inside the tent, bashing her shins and stubbing her toes
as she searched in the dark for a place to hide. She was too
panicked and too groggy with sleep to think straight. Then
Miss Rebecca came inside, and a moment later Kate felt her
arms surrounding her and heard her voice soothing her. "You're
safe, Kate. You don't need to be afraid. It's just the sheikh

shooting off his rifle." Miss Rebecca held her until she calmed down again, then said, "Stay here while I go outside and see what's going on."

Kate could hear the Bedouin shouting in the distance by the garden gate, and she dropped to her knees and closed her eyes. "Please let the sheikh have a baby boy," she prayed. "Please, Lord. I-I promise I won't steal anymore if you just get us all out of here!"

Miss Rebecca stuck her head through the tent door a few minutes later. "The sheikh wants us to come to his tent and pray. His wife is about to give birth."

"Doesn't that stupid man know it's too late to change whatever kind of baby he's about to have?" Kate asked as she searched for her clothes and shoes.

"Apparently not." Miss Rebecca went outside again.

Kate clung to Miss Rebecca as they crossed the stony ground in the dark to the sheikh's camp. They could hear his wife's moans and cries of pain from a distance. Kate didn't want to watch his wife or anyone else giving birth, and neither did the sisters, but they had no choice. Miss Flora led the way inside the tent, and they sat in a circle near the woman's mat, holding hands as they prayed. Kate never could have imagined a night as strange as this one. She was on the other side of the world, sitting in a goat-hair tent in the middle of the night, waiting to learn if this Bedouin woman would give birth to a boy and set them free, or to a girl and doom them all.

"This night seems endless, doesn't it?" Miss Rebecca whispered between her prayers and the woman's groans.

"Yes—and probably even more so for that poor mother," Miss Flora whispered back. "Imagine how she's going to feel if her baby is another girl."

"I'm so sorry I got us into this," Miss Rebecca said.

"Nonsense," her sister replied. "A boring life is hardly worth living. This is where we belong, isn't it? On the path that leads to serving God? Isn't that the essence of faith—walking forward, trusting what you can't see?"

Kate was certain that even if God didn't answer their prayers tonight, the sisters would continue to believe in Him. She had never met anyone like them, and in that moment, her own deepest prayer was to be able to live with them and work for them when they got home. And learn from them.

Kate had just nodded off when a baby's frail cry awakened her. The sky outside the tent was growing light. "Is it a boy?" she whispered, afraid to ask.

"I'll go see." Miss Flora stood, stretching her back and arms. She peered over at the circle of women surrounding the new mother. "God be praised!" she said lifting her hands. "The sheikh has a son!"

"That's wonderful news," Miss Rebecca said. "Thank God, thank God!" She pulled Kate into her arms, holding her tightly as the sheik's rifle boomed.

Joy washed over Kate, bringing tears to her eyes. God had answered their prayers. She could leave this place and go home— wherever that was. She would worry about that when the time came, but for now she no longer needed to worry about the sheikh.

Miss Rebecca held Kate tightly in her arms, and for the first time that she could ever recall, Kate hugged someone in return.

PART V

Rebecca

CHAPTER 32

The Atlantic Ocean
1890

Rebecca looked up from the book she was reading and gazed out at the vast expanse of gray-green ocean filling the horizon. The rhythmic *thump* of the ship's boilers beneath her feet was comforting. She and Flora sat outside on deck chairs, their legs covered with plaid blankets as they read. "Thank heaven the voyage home has been smooth so far," Rebecca said.

"Please don't speak too soon, Becky," Flora said. "You'll jinx us! Remember that terrible storm on the Mediterranean years ago?"

"I thought for certain we'd be shipwrecked like the Apostle Paul. But I'm especially glad this voyage has been uneventful for their sakes," Rebecca said, gesturing to Kate and Petersen, who were striding around the promenade deck in opposite directions, getting some exercise.

"They've had more than their fair share of adventure on this trip, haven't they," Flora said with a laugh.

"That's for sure! And I think marriage has suited them, don't you? Even if it was a phony, temporary one. It appears they've signed a peace treaty of sorts."

Flora closed the book she'd been reading and folded her hands on top of it. "I've been doing a lot of thinking about Soren and Kate, and all that they've endured for our sake. I've been praying about their future, Becky, and I've decided—"

"Wait," Rebecca said, stopping her. "Before you say another word I want to tell you what I've decided, first."

"Oh, dear. This sounds very serious."

"It is serious." Rebecca paused to draw a fortifying breath. "You know how hard I've been praying for Timothy to become a believer. I love him so much, Flora, that I get an ache in my soul whenever I think about being separated from him for all of eternity. It hurts so much!" Even now, the pain was so real Rebecca wanted to double over from it.

Flora reached for her hand. "God gave us a miracle with the sheik's son, so maybe—"

"I know He did. I know. And I know that God can hit Timothy like a bolt of lightning and change him instantly the way He changed Saul on the road to Damascus. I also know that God respects Timothy's free will, and that ultimately the choice to believe or not to believe will be his. But that's not what I wanted to tell you. I'm not going about this the right way, Flora. Let me start all over." She paused again. Once she spoke the words, they would become real, and she would start down the path of her next adventure. Was she certain she wanted to do this? She drew another breath. "Whether or not I ever have a future with Timothy, I don't want to spend the rest of my life alone. And so I've decided to adopt Kate Rafferty as my daughter."

"What?" Flora asked in quiet disbelief. "You mean, legally adopt her?"

"Yes. I want to take her into our home and raise her as my daughter, not as a silly lady's maid—a job at which she's quite terrible, by the way. Kate and I have shared a lot of experiences as we've worked together, and I've come to the conclusion that she doesn't need a job or new clothes or to learn good manners or even how to read and write, although we've been working on that. What she needs is love. She told me that no one has ever loved her, and that she has never loved anyone."

"Oh, that poor girl."

"I've tried to convince her that God loves her, but she has no way of comprehending that basic truth because she doesn't understand what love is. She has never experienced it. I want to show her that I love her, Flora, rough edges and all, so she can begin to believe that God loves her, too."

"Oh, Becky." Tears filled Flora's eyes. She leaned over to give her a hug. "That's a wonderful, beautiful idea!"

"I know it won't be easy, but being a parent rarely is easy. She's a lot like me, you know, stubborn and pigheaded. She says what she thinks, and I like that—most of the time. I haven't had much practice in truly loving others the way Jesus wants me to, but God knows I need to try."

"You'll have my full support, Becky. And Edmund's, too, I'm sure."

"Good. Thank you. Now, you were about to tell me your thoughts concerning Soren and Kate before I interrupted."

"We think alike, Becky. We always have. I was going to tell you that I plan to ask Edmund if we can legally adopt Soren. I want him to be our son. I'm certain Edmund will agree because he loves Soren, too, but I was worried about how my decision would affect Kate, and what it would do to our household. You've now resolved that problem for me."

"Imagine us becoming parents at our age!" Rebecca said as Flora hugged her again.

"I know that making such monumental changes in our lives won't be easy for any of us but—"

"Bah! Who cares about 'easy'?" Rebecca replied. "Easy is boring. We could use a good challenge to shake things up."

"How do you suppose we should tell them the news? After all, they're both over eighteen years old. For all we know, they might refuse to be adopted."

"I don't think they'll refuse, Flora. We've been through a lot together, and we're a family now." No sooner had Rebecca spoken than Kate and Soren came into sight again as they rounded the deck from opposite directions. Soren gave a little wave when he noticed her and Flora staring at him. Rebecca laughed as another thought occurred to her. "How are we going to explain to them how wealthy they're going to be? Petersen knows how to add and subtract, but Kate can barely count past one hundred."

"We'll figure something out. I know you'll enjoy raising Kate as your daughter and teaching her things," Flora said as the young people disappeared from sight again. "But what about Timothy? How will he fit into this new family picture?"

Rebecca felt the familiar ache in her stomach at the mention of his name. How could love bring such overflowing joy and such deep heartache at the same time? "I don't know whether or not Timothy will be convinced by the discovery we made in Sinai. In fact I doubt it, especially since it's going to take scholars a long time to make a complete transcription of the pages." She paused, determined not to cry. "I think I'm going to have to let Timothy go. We'll always be friends, nothing can change that. But I need to stop courting him and accept the fact that I may never be able to marry him. It's just too painful."

"Oh, Becky . . ."

"Please don't feel sorry for me, Flora. You know how I hate pity. At least I won't have to spend my life alone if I adopt Kate. And God has given me a lifetime of work to do for Him—along with enough joy and excitement to fill two lifetimes. I would be selfish to ask for anything more."

Timothy was waiting at the train station in Chicago with Edmund when Rebecca and Flora arrived home. One look at the darling man with his rumpled hair made Rebecca's resolve evaporate. She loved him. It felt wonderful to be held in his arms again after all these months, and she wanted to be with him forever. How could she let him go? Yet she knew she had to.

Timothy had hired a carriage so the two of them could be alone to talk, while the others rode home with Andrew. After the porters finished loading the luggage into the two vehicles, the carriages drove off for home. "Timothy, I found what I was looking for!" Rebecca said the moment they began to move. "I think my discovery may turn out to be a complete set of the Gospels! The pages were all out of sequence, so I won't know for certain until we make a complete transcription, but I was able to date it to around AD 500! Can you imagine? That would make it one of the earliest copies ever found! Oh, how I wish you had been there with me to see it! Kate found it in a tiny, dusty closet with a half-dozen other codices, and the pages were all stuck together—and it was a palimpsest, Timothy. I didn't realize what it was, at first. I thought it was a useless volume about the lives of saints, but then Kate noticed the underwriting, and I deciphered one of the headings—of Luke—and I nearly fainted! I grabbed my magnifying glass and . . . Why are you looking at me like that?"

"Because I want to kiss you so badly, and you won't stop talking." He pulled her close and kissed her until the carriage hit a bump, and they were bounced apart. He sighed with satisfaction. "I love you so much, dear girl! Only my Rebecca would be this excited about an ancient codex. And I don't know any other woman in Chicago who would even know what a palimpsest is." He kissed her again, then said, "You may continue now, my dear. You were telling me about this magnificent find of yours."

"It is magnificent, Timothy, because it proves that what I've been trying to tell you is true. The Gospels haven't been altered and edited over the years. They're the same as they were more than a thousand years ago. *A thousand years!* I know it's going to take time to make a complete translation of the pages and compare them in detail with our modern Gospels, but I already determined that the pages from the Gospel of Luke that I worked on are the same. The story of the Virgin Mary, Jesus' birth in Bethlehem, the angels appearing to the shepherds—they're all there in a copy of the Gospels that's centuries old!" Rebecca looked into his eyes, willing him to say that he was convinced, that he now believed, but she knew it was too much to hope for. She'd witnessed at least one miracle this summer when the midwife had held up the sheikh's squalling son, and she scarcely dared hope for a second miracle. "Say something, Timothy. I promise I'll stop talking for a minute."

"I was miserable without you, Rebecca," he said as he stroked her cheek with his fingers. "I don't ever want to be apart again."

Rebecca had to look away. She prayed for strength to do what she needed to do. "I can't be with you this way anymore, Timothy. I'm sorry, but it's just too difficult. I love you more than you'll ever know, but there's no future for us except as friends." He leaned back against the seat and closed his eyes. "The Bible tells me to love God with all my heart and soul and mind and strength," she continued as her tears fell. "How can we be joined together as one when loving God is the very goal of my life, and He is absent from yours? I'm sorry, Timothy. . . . I'm so, so sorry."

He gave her his handkerchief to dry her tears, then held her against his chest as he tried to soothe her. "I'm sorry, too, dear girl. . . . I spent time with Edmund while you were away, and he warned me this might happen. He also told me that logical arguments had never wooed anyone into the kingdom of God. He said I needed to lay aside my need for reason and logic and simply ask God to speak to me. Then wait for His reply."

"And have you done that?" she asked, afraid to hope.

"Yes, Rebecca. I've been trying very hard to shut down the debate in my mind and simply listen. I don't want to lose you."

"But . . . ? I can hear your hesitation, Timothy."

He sighed. "I'm afraid I have no experience in hearing the voice of God. It's sad to say, but if He has been trying to communicate with me through a burning bush or an angelic messenger, I've missed it completely."

"I won't give up hope. Jesus said that if we seek Him we'll find Him, if we search for Him with all our heart. In the meantime, my discovery should put at least one of your arguments to rest."

"Yes, well, it does sound promising. And speaking from a strictly historical perspective, you've made an incredible find. I'm proud of you."

The first thing Rebecca wanted to unpack when they arrived home was the crate of artifacts and manuscript fragments that she and Flora had purchased in Cairo. She sent Andrew to find a pry bar after he'd dragged the box into the foyer. "I can't wait to show you and Edmund what we bought," she told Timothy. "We met the same little dealer at the rug shop, and he had several wonderful things to show us. I'm certain we paid too much for them, but at least they'll be accessible to scholars now."

After Andrew returned and opened the crate, Rebecca dug through it, pulling out each prize and scattering packing material all over the floor. While Edmund and Timothy admired the treasures, Rebecca pulled her sister aside.

"Can we tell Soren and Kate our decision tonight? I don't want to wait another day. I want to start treating them as children right away and not as servants."

"I don't want to wait, either. I'll talk to Edmund. We'll invite

Kate and Soren to join us for dinner this evening, and we'll tell them the news."

It took a great deal of coaxing on Flora's part to convince Soren and Kate to sit down at the table and eat with them rather than serve them as butler and maid. "What's going on, Rebecca?" Timothy leaned over to whisper. "Why are your butler and maid sitting with us?"

"You'll see." Their servants' uneasiness was so apparent that Flora decided not to wait until the end of the meal to tell them the news. Rebecca felt excited yet so nervous she could scarcely sit still. She had asked Flora to go first so she'd have time to gather her thoughts.

"Edmund and I have something we want to tell you, Soren," Flora began. "The reason you're eating dinner with us tonight is because we no longer want you to be our servant. We want you to be our son." Soren's face went pale as he sank back in his chair. Rebecca thought she could hear his heart pounding from across the table, and the look of wonder and hope and disbelief on his face brought tears to Rebecca's eyes. She had witnessed the "adoption parades" at the orphan home when the children would file past prospective parents for inspection, always wondering if this would be the day they'd find a new home. She could only imagine the thoughts that were whirling through Soren's mind right now at finally being chosen. He seemed unable to speak.

"I should have adopted you and Gunnar when you first came to the orphanage," Flora continued, "but my own stubbornness prevented me from seeing what God intended. Edmund loves you as much as I do. Will you agree to be our son?"

Soren folded his arms on the table atop his empty plate and hid his face in them. His shoulders shook as he wept. Flora and Edmund both rose to go to him, hugging his shoulders and patting his back. "What do you say?" Edmund asked. "Please say you'll agree." Soren looked up, his face wet with tears, and nodded.

"There's more," Rebecca said, unwilling to wait a moment longer. She turned to Kate, who looked stunned and confused by what had just happened. "Kate, you remind me of myself, full of contradictions," she began. "You aren't a very good lady's maid, but you're an excellent assistant and friend. I would like to adopt you as my daughter. I believe we could have a very interesting life together."

Kate's eyes went wide with fear as she shook her head. "No. . . . No, you can't do that. You know I'm a thief—"

"You *were* a thief," Rebecca interrupted. "Your past doesn't matter anymore. We all forgive you, and God will, too, if you ask."

"But you don't know all the other things I did," she said, still shaking her head.

"I don't need to know, although you're welcome to tell me if it will make you feel better."

"No, I can't! And I can't be your daughter. . . . I'm not good enough!" She stood, nearly upsetting her chair, and ran from the room.

"Excuse me." Rebecca also rose. "Please, go ahead and eat." She followed Kate all the way up to her room on the third floor and was breathless by the time she reached it. The irony wasn't lost on Rebecca that both of the people she loved—Kate and Timothy—were refusing to accept grace and a brand-new life. Kate's door was open, and she was lying facedown on her bed, sobbing. Rebecca sat on the edge beside her and stroked her beautiful red hair for a few moments before speaking. "I don't need to know your past, Kate. It won't change my mind about wanting you for my daughter. You can tell everything to God and ask Him to forgive you, and He will. That's why Jesus died for you."

Kate's sobs gradually died away. At last she rolled over and sat up to face Rebecca, wiping her tears as they continued to fall. "You need to know the truth about me. The reason I came here to Evanston to work for you was so I could hide out. There's a man named Joe who got me out of jail after I got caught trying to steal a purse, and now he's looking for me. He said he owns me, and he tried to make me work in his brothel, but I ran away. He says he has policemen and even judges who work for him, and if they find me I'll be in a lot of trouble. That's why I wanted to go on the trip to the desert with you. I needed to get as far away from Joe as possible."

The load of fear and guilt that Kate had been carrying stunned Rebecca. She could have cheerfully murdered this "Joe" with her bare hands for putting an eighteen-year-old girl through such an ordeal. "You should have told me sooner, Kate. Flora and I have lawyers who can take care of problems like this."

"How? If Joe finds me he'll beat me and take me back to his brothel!"

"There must be a record of your arrest. My lawyers can find out the name of the person who bailed you out and paid your fine. Once we have Joe's full name, we can go after him. It's against the law for policemen and judges to take bribes, not to mention against the law for Joe to operate a brothel. He's the one who will be on the run, not you. I assure you, Kate, you don't need to live in fear a single day longer."

Kate stared at her as if afraid to believe that what she was saying was true. "Why would you do all this for me?"

"Because I've grown to love you, and I want you to become all that God created you to be. I believe you'd make a wonderful daughter." Rebecca took a chance and pulled Kate into her arms. Tears of joy filled her eyes when Kate hugged her in return.

At last they pulled apart, and Rebecca handed Kate her lace handkerchief. "When we come to Christ, our past is forgiven, and we get a brand-new start. That's the way it will be for you, too. From now on, your name will be Kate Hawes. All of this is yours," she said gesturing to the room. "You no longer have to sleep on the third floor. You may choose any bedroom you'd like. Tomorrow you can help me develop the photographs, and we'll see how they came out. You were so good at handling ancient manuscripts that I know you could continue doing that kind of work, if you'd like. Professor Dyk and I have talked about starting an institute for ancient Near Eastern studies once the University of Chicago is up and running. John D. Rockefeller is interested in supporting it, and I would like to as well. . . . But I'm getting way ahead of myself, aren't I?" she said with a laugh. "The question is, will you allow me to adopt you, Kate? Will you be my daughter?"

Kate nodded and fell into her arms again, crying as if she might never stop. Rebecca thought of all the wonderful moments in her life—traveling the world, seeing the pyramids, falling in love with Timothy, finding the ancient codex with the Gospels—and knew that this moment was one of the very sweetest.

"It's official," she said when she and Kate had dried their tears and splashed water on their faces and rejoined the others in the dining room. "We're a family now." Her smile faded when she noticed that Timothy's place at the table was empty, his chair pushed away. "Where's Timothy?" she asked.

Edmund's expression looked pained. "He asked us to convey his apologies. He said he needed to leave."

"Did he say why?" Rebecca asked. Edmund shook his head. She reached for Kate's hand and squeezed it as her heart seemed to break in two.

CHAPTER 33

Rebecca huddled in the basement darkroom with Soren and Kate, developing the pictures they'd taken in the Sinai. "Look how perfect this one is," she said, holding up the finished photograph. "I'm thrilled that they came out so well. And the academic community will be pleased, too." So far, all of the photographs they had developed looked perfect, the underwriting visible enough to translate. "Let's quit for today," she said, switching off the light. They could only work in the darkroom for a short time before the odor of the pungent chemicals drove them upstairs again. It was going to take a long time to process the hundreds of pictures of the codex, but there was no reason to hurry. More than a week had passed since Timothy walked away, and Rebecca had heard nothing from him. Even so, the newfound Gospels would prove invaluable to scholars and other skeptics, if not to Timothy.

Rebecca had kept busy with plenty of other work besides developing the photographs. She'd spent time searching for the right venue to publish the catalogue of works in the monastery library. She'd begun an outline of the book she planned to write about the palimpsest she'd found, along with her own conclusions. She'd gone downtown to Flora's office to speak with their lawyers about hiring a Pinkerton investigator to locate "Joe" and make certain he was sent to jail where he belonged. And most important, she and Flora and Edmund had gone to the Cook County Circuit Court with Soren and Kate to begin the adoption process.

"I think we should all travel to Cambridge next year," Rebecca said as they climbed up from the basement darkroom. "There's a specialist there who can help me confirm the date of our Gospels."

"Do they have camels in Cambridge?" Kate asked. "And sheikhs? Because if so, I think I'll stay home."

"No," Rebecca laughed. "Cambridge is in England, where Edmund is from. It's a very civilized place, I assure you." They had just reached the top of the stairs when the pounding of the front door knocker echoed through the foyer.

"I'll see who it is," Soren said. He still hadn't broken his habit of attending to visitors who came to their door. They hadn't hired a new butler yet, but knowing Flora, she would be bringing a candidate home from the orphanage any day now. Rebecca let Soren answer it while she went into the kitchen in the rear of the house to ask the cook for a cup of tea.

"I'll bring it to you in your study when it's ready, Miss Rebecca," the cook said. Rebecca pushed through the swinging door from the kitchen to the hallway, then froze when she heard a familiar voice coming from the foyer.

Timothy.

Her heart began to thump painfully. She didn't think she could bear to see him face-to-face yet. She needed more time to heal. She had tried a dozen times to write him a letter and say all of the things that were on her heart, but each attempt had ended up wadded into a ball and tossed into her wastebasket. She held her breath, praying that Soren wouldn't tell him she was home or invite him in. She inched closer so she could hear what Timothy and Soren were saying, and was surprised to hear a third voice joining the conversation—Kate's.

"You listen to me, Professor," Kate said. "Miss Rebecca . . . I mean my mother . . . went to the ends of the earth for you! We know exactly what she lived through because we lived through it, too! We rode on two trains and three different ships just to get to the Sinai Desert. Then we had to ride on camels. Did you ever ride on a camel, Professor? Because if you had, believe me, you'd know how much Miss Rebecca loves you! So you'd better not tell me that the Bible she found doesn't convince you to believe."

Rebecca smiled as she closed her eyes and leaned against the wall, out of sight. She could easily picture Kate standing with her hands on her hips as she fearlessly confronted Timothy. Poor man. No wonder he seemed to be speechless. Then soft-spoken Soren joined in the argument, surprising Rebecca.

"Professor Dyk, I want you to know that I became a believer out there in the Sinai, and it wasn't because of the book we found. I've been going to church with the sisters ever since I came to work for them, but the stories they told there and in Sunday school seemed like fairy tales to me. Then we got stranded out in the desert with a crazy sheikh who liked to fire off his rifle and scare everybody half to death, and I no longer saw a religion, I saw faith—just like in the Bible. We were completely helpless out there, but God protected us."

"It's true," Kate said. "There were times when I was scared out of my mind, but the sisters weren't. You'd never see any other fine ladies like them traveling all alone to the middle of nowhere like that, but the reason they're fearless is because they trust God. They would make us join hands and pray whenever we got into trouble, and you know what? I didn't think God could possibly come through for us, but He did. He even gave the sheikh a baby boy because Miss Flora and Miss Rebecca prayed."

"God answered their prayers for Mr. Edmund, too," Soren continued. "He got better when the doctors thought for sure he would die. But it wasn't just the fact that he didn't die that convinced me to believe. It was because Mr. Edmund wasn't afraid to die. It's like the sisters always say, 'God knows when the hour of our end will be.' And Mr. Edmund told me that whether he lived or died, he still believed that God loves him."

"I'll tell you something else," Kate said the moment Soren paused. "They could have left me out there with the sheikh in order to save their own lives, but they didn't. I've seen a lot of bad people in my life, greedy people who wanted to hand me over to men like the sheikh because they only cared about themselves. But I've never seen people like Miss Flora and Miss Rebecca. I want to be just like them. They'll tell you that they're the way they are because they know Jesus. Then I guess I want to know Him, too."

Rebecca covered her mouth to hold back a sob. She wished her sister could hear what Soren and Kate were saying. Flora was going to dance for joy when Rebecca told her.

"Most rich ladies don't have time for people like Kate and me," Soren said, "or those poor, raggedy children in Sunday school and at the orphanage. Most people turn away and walk in the other direction when they see us coming. But Miss Flora and Miss Rebecca look us right in the eye and tell us that God loves us—and then they show us that it's true by loving us themselves."

"You know, a smart man like you should stop and think," Kate said. Once again, Rebecca could picture her with her hands on her hips and her chin jutting forward in that cocky stance of hers. "The sisters have everything in the world. They could sit here in their mansion like queens and let people wait on them all day. But they don't. Miss Flora goes to the orphanage and over to the rotten parts of town, and then she spends the rest of her time in her office figuring out how to give her money away to people who no one else cares about, because that's what Jesus would do if He were as rich as she is. And Miss Rebecca—my mother—travels to dangerous places to study, then spends hours and hours writing books so she can convince smart people like you that there really is a God who loves you."

"Kate's right, that's the point of everything they do. They want everyone to know that God exists and that He loves us. I've been hearing in church how Jesus came and died for us so that all the bad things we've done could be forgiven and we could become God's children. But it never made sense to me until the sisters did the same things for us. Kate and I both spent time in jail, yet they rescued us. We had nothing to offer but a pile of troubles—" Soren's voice broke, and he had to pause for a moment. "And yet they adopted us as their son and daughter. Everything they own is now ours. Can't you see that it's not a fairy tale? That it's the gospel story?"

"If you don't believe that the Bible is true, Professor, then you may be a smart man but you're a fool. And you're going to miss out on a whole lot more than just marrying my mother."

No one spoke for a long moment. Rebecca longed to know what Timothy was thinking. She waited, holding her breath until he finally broke the silence.

"I-I don't know what to say." No one else seemed to know, either, and there was another long pause. "I-I came to speak with Rebecca . . . if she'll see me. Do you think she—?"

"I'm right here, Timothy," she said stepping from the shadows.

Timothy's eyes shone with tears. He looked as though he had just survived a windstorm and needed to sit down. He looked from Kate to Soren and back to Kate again, as if expecting them to say something more. Then he turned to Rebecca. "My dear," he said in a hushed voice. "I believe I've just encountered my burning bush."

Rebecca went to him and took him into her arms, silently praising God.

EPILOGUE

S oren sat in Gunnar's parlor, watching his brother play on the floor with the toy train he had bought him for Christmas. Soren had just finished telling him about his adventures in the Sinai Desert—how he'd seen the ancient pyramids of Egypt, ridden on a camel, and eaten dinner with a Bedouin sheikh.

"That was quite a trip you took, young man," Gunnar's father said from his chair near the fireplace. He puffed on his cigar, blowing fragrant smoke throughout the room.

"Tell it again!" Gunnar begged.

Soren laughed and ruffled Gunnar's hair. "I think once is enough for today. Next summer I'll be going on a trip to England, so I'll have lots of new stories to tell you when I get back. We're all going this time, even my new father, Mr. Edmund. And the professor is going, too, now that he and Miss Rebecca are married." He was supposed to call them Aunt Becky and Uncle Timothy, but Soren still wasn't used to the new names. "I have a cousin named Kate who's coming on the trip, too."

467

"Is she a girl?" Gunnar asked. "I have three cousins and one of them is a girl. She gets real mad when we tease her."

"My cousin has a temper, too. But Kate and I are learning to get along. She spends most of her time studying with Aunt Becky and Uncle Timothy because she never went to school, and she's trying to catch up." Kate had calmed down a lot now that she didn't have to worry about Joe anymore. He was in jail where he belonged, and he would never know that Kate was the one who had put him there.

"Can you come here and live with me now?" Gunnar asked, climbing up to sit on Soren's lap.

"I live in my own house, Gunnar, with my new mother and father. But your mama said that I can come here and visit you anytime I want, and you can visit me at my house, too. Maybe you can even stay overnight sometime." Gunnar seemed to accept that arrangement. He smiled and settled back in Soren's lap. "I have a new job," Soren said, "and you'll never guess where—the orphanage!"

Gunnar looked up at him, frowning. "I don't like that place."

"I know. I didn't, either. But Mr. Wingate is gone, and they hired a new director. I'm his assistant."

"Why?"

"Because you and I know what it feels like to live there, don't we? We understand how scared and lost those kids feel. I have lots of ideas about how to make the orphan home better. For instance, they're going to have a classroom for the older kids who can't read and write so they won't have to go to the public school with all the little kids. But the main reason I wanted to work there is because I enjoy taking care of people." It was what Soren had been doing for most of his life, and now he would have the resources to care for children like Hilde and Greta and Gunnar properly. His new mother and father had assured him that he could be anything he wanted to be, but for now he'd chosen to look after the children who needed him the most.

"It's almost time for dinner," Gunnar's mother said, coming into the living room in her apron. "Are you boys hungry?"

"Yes!" Gunnar said, scrambling down. "I could eat a . . . a camel!"

Gunnar's parents laughed, and Soren saw the love in his mother's eyes as she looked at him. It was the same way their mama had looked at him and Gunnar. Soren silently thanked God that they would never be hungry or homeless again. It was what Mama would have wanted.

The doorbell rang, and Gunnar's aunt and uncle and cousins piled into the room, including the little girl cousin who was dusting snowflakes from her coat. Soren would stay for dinner, but he'd promised to return home in time for the midnight Christmas Eve service at church. "You have to be there," Kate had told him in her irritating, outspoken way. "This is the first time the professor will hear the Christmas story as a believer, and we have to celebrate with him."

"It's the first time for us, too," Soren had pointed out.

"I know," she'd said with a huff. "That's why you'd better be there."

Soren sat beside his brother as they gathered around the table for the meal. Everyone bowed their heads while Gunnar's father said the blessing. There was so much food that Soren couldn't fit it all on his plate. Tomorrow he and his parents would eat Christmas dinner at the orphan home. Kate and Miss Rebecca and the professor would be there, too. Soren had decided to use his pay to buy a present for every child in the orphanage, and Kate had gone with him to pick out items for all the girls. "I hope my mother buys the professor—I mean, my father—a new suit for Christmas," Kate had told him. "He sure could use one."

Soren leaned back in his chair, smiling at Gunnar's family and thinking of his own. The joy that welled up inside him brought tears to his eyes. This was why God had given His Son to the world at Christmas: to bring new life and joy. Joy to the world.

Author's Note

The inspiration for this novel came from the true story of remarkable twin sisters, Agnes and Margaret Smith, born in Scotland in 1843. The account of how these brilliant, self-educated women discovered a copy of the Gospels dating from AD 500 at the monastery on Mount Sinai is told in the fascinating book *The Sisters of Sinai: How Two Lady Adventurers Discovered the Hidden Gospels* by author Janet Soskice. While I borrowed some of the details of their lives, I moved my fictional sisters to Chicago, a city I'm more familiar with.

Agnes and Margaret Smith discovered the "hidden Gospels" in a palimpsest—a book that has been overwritten by a newer book, probably to conserve writing materials. Once the sisters scraped off the top layer, the biblical manuscript could be photographed, transcribed, and studied by scholars. The Smith sisters were also key figures in the discovery of the Cairo Genizah, a collection of some 300,000 ancient manuscript fragments found in a synagogue storeroom in Egypt. Proficient in several modern and ancient languages, Agnes and Margaret were well-respected scholars in an era when advanced degrees weren't available to women. Because the sisters were women of deep faith, they fearlessly traveled the Sinai on a Bedouin camel caravan, hauling crates of chickens and turkeys (but without the amorous sheikh of my novel). I also borrowed the sisters' favorite motto: *"God knows when the end of our days will be. We have nothing to fear."* Their trust in God led them to accomplish extraordinary things and live a rich, adventurous life for God's glory.

For readers who are interested in learning more about early archaeological discoveries in the Middle East, I recommend the book *Gods, Graves, and Scholars* by C.W. Ceram. To learn more about the rational arguments for Christianity that my character Rebecca used to persuade Timothy, I recommend books by Lee Strobel, such as *The Case for Christ* or *The Case for Faith*.

I would also like to thank the winners of a fund-raising event for our local symphony orchestra for "loaning" me their names. I'll let my readers guess which two characters in *Where We Belong* are named after the highest bidders, who won the prize of having a character named after them in my novel.

Bestselling author **Lynn Austin** has sold more than one million copies of her books worldwide. She is an eight-time Christy Award winner for her historical novels, as well as a popular speaker at retreats and conventions. Lynn and her husband have raised three children and live in Michigan. Learn more at www.lynnaustin.org.

Sign Up for Lynn Austin's Newsletter!

Keep up to date with Lynn's news on book releases and events by signing up for her email list at lynnaustin.org.

More from Lynn

In 1897 Michigan, Dutch immigrant Geesje de Jonge recalls the events of her past while writing a memoir and twenty-three-year-old Anna Nicholson mourns a broken engagement. Over the course of one summer, the lives of both women will change forever.

Waves of Mercy

You May Also Like . . .

This powerful series captures the incredible faith of Ezra, Nehemiah, and their families as they returned to God after the Babylonian exile. These stories of faith, doubt, and love encompass the Jews' return to Jerusalem and their efforts to rebuild God's temple amid constant threat.

THE RESTORATION CHRONICLES: *Return to Me, Keepers of the Covenant, On This Foundation* by Lynn Austin
lynnaustin.org

After a terrible mine accident in 1954, Judd Markley abandons his Appalachian town for Myrtle Beach. There he meets the privileged Larkin Heyward. Drawn together amid a hurricane, they wonder what tomorrow will bring—and realize that it may take a miracle for them to be together.

The Sound of Rain by Sarah Loudin Thomas
sarahloudinthomas.com

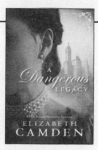

Telegraph operator Lucy Drake is a master of Morse Code, but the presence of Sir Colin Beckwith at a rival news agency puts her livelihood at risk. When Colin's reputation is jeopardized, Lucy agrees to help in exchange for his assistance in recovering her family's stolen fortune. However, the web of treachery they're diving into is more dangerous than they know.

A Dangerous Legacy by Elizabeth Camden
elizabethcamden.com

⬥BETHANYHOUSE

More Historical Fiction

Egyptian slave Kiya leads a miserable life. When terrifying plagues strike Egypt, she chooses to flee with the Hebrews. Soon she finds herself reliant on a strange God and falling for a man who despises her people. Will she turn back toward Egypt or find a new place to belong?

Counted With the Stars by Connilyn Cossette, OUT FROM EGYPT #1
connilyncossette.com

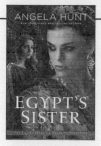

Chava, the Jewish daughter of a royal tutor, vowed to be true to her friend Cleopatra always. But after they argue, she is ripped from her privileged life and sold into slavery. Now, alone in Rome, she must choose between love and honor, between her own desires and God's will.

Egypt's Sister by Angela Hunt, THE SILENT YEARS
angelahuntbooks.com

After being unjustly imprisoned, Julianne Chevalier trades her life sentence for marriage and exile to the French colony of Louisiana in 1720. But soon she must find her own way in this dangerous new land while bearing the brand of a criminal.

The Mark of the King by Jocelyn Green
jocelyngreen.com

The lifeblood of the village of Ivy Hill is its coaching inn, The Bell. When the innkeeper dies suddenly, his genteel wife, Jane, becomes the reluctant owner. With a large loan due, can Jane and her mother-in-law find a way to save the inn—and discover fresh hope for their hearts?

The Innkeeper of Ivy Hill by Julie Klassen, TALES FROM IVY HILL #1
julieklassen.com